THE OATH SAGA

VOLUME FOUR

LIGHTNING'S FURY

WRITTEN BY:

KARIN REEVE

& JOLIE MARVIN

A.K.A. KARLIE MAVRE

Acknowledgements

We would like to thank everyone who has supported us while we brought this story to life. You have all been incredible and we love you.

Contents

CHAPTER ONE

Standing on the sidewalk in front of the first home they had ever shared in Rockford, Illinois, Taryn and Keiryn Knight exchanged glances.

The white paint on the tall two-story structure's exterior had all but peeled away. A broken porch swing creaked in the slight breeze and the layer of grime covering the windows swallowed the sun's rays.

Keiryn's heart raced as numerous memories of his lost childhood flickered about inside his head. Swallowing hard, he reached over and laced his fingers with his sister Taryn's.

Sensing her brother's apprehension, Taryn gave his hand a gentle squeeze. "We don't have to do this, Keiryn. We have our family now. It's the only thing that matters."

With pursed lips, he nodded. "I know." Taking a deep breath, he pushed the gate on the worn out picket fence, causing the rusty hinges to creak in protest as it swung open. The siblings stepped through, still holding hands.

Taryn glanced back toward the others, focusing on her parents Gracyn and Theron, and flashing them a soft smile. "Give us a few, okay?"

Theron nodded, sliding his arm around his wife's waist.

With a contented sigh, Taryn looked back to the house and moved forward with Keiryn.

The warped stairs wobbled beneath their feet as they made their way to the front door. Reaching out, she pulled on the tarnished copper handle, opening the screen door. Keiryn secured it as she took hold of the inside door's antique glass knob. Pausing, she glanced down at the sparkling knob. A smirk formed on her face as she recognized that it was not glass at all, but rather a massive diamond that had been cut to have rounded edges. Giving the priceless gem a twist, Taryn pushed the door open and entered the building.

Holding his breath, Keiryn followed behind her.

With a slight wave of her hand, the lights turned on inside their abandoned home. A thick layer of dust coated every visible surface hiding the once vibrant colored décor.

Keiryn's hands balled into fists and the vein in his forehead bulged as the last memory he had from their home replayed over in his thoughts.

"The telephone rang and dad answered it…" he started.

Taryn nodded. "It was Uncle Julius calling to warn him that someone was coming."

"Dad was frantic. He grabbed me and the car keys and ran to the garage. After securing me in the front passenger seat, he rushed back inside and grabbed Ralph. I screamed that I didn't want to go but he said we had to. He said we had to take Ralph with us or they would use him to find you and mom," Keiryn shared.

Reaching up, Taryn placed her hand on his shoulder. "What they did to our family was wrong. But it doesn't matter now, we are together, Keiryn, you, me, mom and dad. No one will ever come between us again, I promise you." Taryn paused, glancing toward the staircase. "If you're okay...."

He nodded. "Yeah, go ahead. I'm good."

Taryn turned away and stepped toward the staircase. Placing her foot squarely on the bottom step, she grabbed hold of the dusty railing and began moving upward. With each step, visions of the past surrounded her. A much younger version of herself and Keiryn stood at the top of the stairs plotting the best way to procure the desired vanilla ice cream that awaited them in the freezer. Soon they were sitting on their bottoms sliding from one step to the next until they made it downstairs. A few moments later she could hear her mother and father having a spirited debate about why they should or should not have ice cream before bedtime.

Making it to the second floor, Taryn stared down the short hallway to her left. Nails protruded from the walls where family photos had once been prominently displayed. Few still remained on the wall, covered with a thick layer of dust. Many more frames lay shattered on the hallway floor. The small table that had always held a vase of the fresh flowers her mother preferred still set at the end of the hall, the buds in the vase long dead and brittle. Taking a few steps, she peered through the open doorway of the room she and Keiryn had once shared.

Just like downstairs, everything in the room was covered with a thick layer of dust. Against one wall was a twin bed with a royal blue comforter. Adjacent to it was another bed of equal size, adorned with a pale pink cover. Taryn ran her fingertips down the side of a toy fire truck. The button to sound the sirens no longer worked. She could only assume the batteries had corroded.

Memories from their last night together in the house surged from within the deepest part of her mind. Though her two-and-a-half-year-old self could not understand the gravity of the events that had unfolded, her now seventeen-year-old self did.

Suddenly, the sound of her mother weeping uncontrollably caught her attention. She turned and walked to the opposite end of the hall.

Standing outside of her parent's bedroom, she pressed her hand against the door and pushed it open. There she saw the room as it had been all those years ago. Her mother was sobbing in her father's arms as they sat on the floor.

After several seconds, she heard her mother speak.

"How?" Gracyn whispered.

"I don't know, Baby. She's too young. Maybe the fish wasn't dead," Theron suggested hopefully as Taryn looked on.

"We both saw it. It was dead until her finger touched it. I don't know if I can do this." Her mother's voice broke with fresh tears. "Why, why does it have to be our little girl?"

"Shhh," Theron soothed her as he ran a hand down her hair. "We don't have a choice. It's the only way to keep them safe."

Gracyn reached up and kissed Theron.

Taryn felt the shattering of her mother's heart at the thought of leaving her husband and son behind. The pain pierced her deeply.

Unable to watch anymore, Taryn headed toward the stairs. Bumping into Keiryn at the top step, she feigned a smile before rushing past him and her parents on her way to the front door.

"She's upset. I should go after her," Gracyn stated.

Theron shook his head. "I think we should let her be, Gracie. Larkin's outside waiting if she needs anything."

"Don't forget about the soul-sucker. He's out there, too," Keiryn added with a growl.

His mother shot him a stern look. "Lazryn is one of your sister's dearest friends and she would not take kindly to you speaking of him in such a way."

"Yeah, maybe not, but he's still a soul-sucker," Keiryn insisted.

∾◌◌◌◌∾

The screen door swung open and Taryn stepped onto the porch. Her eyes locked on Lazryn as she jumped over the steps and landed on the sidewalk.

"You and I need to talk later," she stated sternly.

He nodded and stepped aside as she passed by.

Joining her, Larkin reached out and wrapped his arm around her shoulders. "I take it this homecoming was everything you thought it would be…"

Taryn pursed her lips and shortened her stride. "Just like you, your dad, Uncle Julius and Jonesy…my parents and Keiryn needed to see the home they'd left behind." She paused. "Will you stay with Lazryn?"

Larkin kissed the top of her head. "If that's what you need…"

"Thanks," Taryn replied and then disappeared.

ഇൽഗ്രെഇൽഗ്ര

Beneath a large white oak tree on the edge of the park, Taryn stood, watching as children and their parents played beneath the clear blue sky.

Her eyes drew toward the large sandbox off to the left where several children sat playing with shovels and pails. Their laughter lessened the knot that had formed in her stomach from earlier.

"Hello, Taryn," a familiar voice stated.

"Farren," she replied coolly.

The well-dressed man moved closer. "Still, after all these months you remain angry with me, why?"

"Sorry, Deadman, I'm on my first official spring break, and I don't have any effort to spare," she answered, scanning the large park.

Farren reached out to place his hand on her shoulder, but withdrew before touching her. Disappearing, he reappeared directly in front of her. "You are unhappy?"

"Unhappy, no," she replied shaking her head.

"Perhaps, burdened?" he suggested.

"I suppose so." Taryn shrugged. "It feels like so many people are focusing on the insignificant issues from last fall. I don't think they understand that we've been given an opportunity to have a fresh start. We can really make a difference, not just in the lives of our kind, but the regular people, the animals and all of the worlds. We could use our gifts for something more than power and prestige."

Staring into her weighted eyes, Farren pressed an issue that no one had dared to address after the Trials. "Then why, during Nelmaryc's trial, did you not use your Influence? You could have banished the ill-will lingering within the hearts of so many and brought peace to your kind."

Rolling her eyes, Taryn growled as she brushed past him. "Why am I not surprised that you would think taking away everyone's free-will would be an option to solve our issues."

"Would it not be the better option in comparison to the instability and fear that has ignited in the wake of your unveiling?" Farren questioned.

Taryn's nostrils flared. "Everything that's happened up until the moment I knew the truth about who I am and where I came from, that's not on me, it's on you."

The swirling blue within his eyes intensified. "You have always been strong willed, Taryn, but even you must recognize our options were significantly limited when it came to keeping you hidden. The others could not see what I saw inside of you. They believed you to be another Gaias-born blight."

"Thanks for confirming my suspicions, Deadman. And as far as what others think of me, I don't care. Tell Thantos and your other brother to believe what they want, but to leave me alone. Your kind has meddled enough in my life," Taryn replied.

"Why must you continue to be so angry with me, and why have you not put a stop to the instability of your kind?" Death pressed.

Taryn paused, glancing around the park once more. "I revived a dead fish, and from that moment on everyone I knew had their entire lives turned upside-down. My mother and I went on the run, while my father and his best friend became strangers overnight. You forced Julius to be the keeper of all our secrets and tore his son away from him." Taryn turned with her jaw drawn up tightly. "Free will isn't free if restrictions are placed upon it. I will never do to another living soul what has been done to me and my family."

"But it was your Influence that unbound those who suffered from the Affliction from the Elder Council," he commented.

Shaking her head, Taryn's face softened. "You're wrong, Farren. it was my bond with Larkin that secured their freedom. My connection to him made it possible to undo Elanya's will."

"Several of the Afflicted have chosen to back Nodryck and what is left of the Council. What do you say to this?"

"It's their right." Taryn paused again, this time eyeing a little girl in the swings being pushed by her father. "People make choices every day, and I choose to believe they are capable of making the best decisions for themselves. What is right for one isn't necessarily right for all."

Farren's neutral face grew tense. "Do you believe it possible to ever trust me again?"

A faint smile formed on Taryn's face. "We're still friends, Deadman. You just happen to be the one friend that I'm less than happy with at the moment."

The calm restored within his swirling irises. "You are not enjoying this family outing?"

"No. Not particularly," Taryn replied.

"When one comes face-to-face with their lost memories it can evoke an unpleasant response," he offered.

Taking a seat on a nearby bench, Taryn ran her hands through her hair and sighed. "It's not the memories as much as recognizing how different I was, even back then."

Farren nodded. "You are truly exceptional, Taryn Knight. Even amongst those held in the highest regard of your kind, you eclipse the totality of their greatness and continue to ascend beyond."

"There's no need to lay it on so thick, Deadman. I have already told you that I'll forgive you someday," Taryn stated with an ornery smirk.

Farren stared at the teen curiously. The twinkle in her eyes raised his suspicions. "What are you up to, young Taryn?"

The teen deliberately glanced to the father still pushing his daughter in the swing before turning her gaze back to Death. "It's unfair that such a sweet little girl will grow up without her father, wouldn't you agree?"

"As you are painfully aware, life is often unfair." Farren replied.

Taryn gently shook her head. "If only there was someone who could heal his damaged heart before it kills him."

Suddenly Farren's swirling eyes widened and the blue color churned franticly. "You must not interfere, Taryn."

Rising from her seat, the teen shrugged. "Sorry, Deadman, it looks like your services won't be needed here after all."

"You mustn't interfere again," Death scolded as he faded away.

₧℃₧℃

On the curb across the street, Larkin and Lazryn sat quietly discussing Taryn's ongoing suspicions about the Mortari's impending return.

"She's not wrong about much." Larkin paused. "Are you positive that you didn't find some hidden code or veiled threat in Chrystian's letter?"

"You read the letter same as I, young wolf. Chrystian sent me as a peace offering in hopes of preventing Taryn from returning to Mors. They fear her bringing about the decimation of the Mortari." Lazryn paused, glancing up at the second story windows. "I know you believe us all to be monsters, but regardless, he does care deeply for her."

Larkin shuddered. "You don't have to remind me. It's not like I could ever forget seeing him trying to kiss her."

"Taryn stirs something within Chrystian. When he speaks of her, I see a glimpse of my lost friend," Lazryn replied.

Appearing suddenly between them, Taryn leaned over and kissed Larkin. Pulling back, she smiled. "Hey."

"Hey, yourself." Larkin ran the tips of his fingers gently down her cheek. "Better?"

Glancing toward the house, she gave a slight nod. "I take it the others are still taking a stroll down memory lane."

"Yeah, I think they've all migrated to the backyard now," Larkin replied.

"Good. We have a bit of reminiscing of our own to do," she stated, her eyes panning to Lazryn.

ಬಂಛಬಂಛ

Standing in the bedroom she once shared with Keiryn, Taryn noted the tension in Lazryn's stance. "You know why we're here, right?" she asked.

Lazryn sighed heavily. "Yes."

Glancing between the two, Larkin remained silent in the doorway.

Running her hand over Keiryn's old pillow, Taryn took a deep breath and stared distantly at the wall. "You came here. Why?" she finally asked.

Lazryn's eyes darkened with the heavy shame weighing on him. "Coyan presented me with vague orders to scout out a potential threat. Upon my arrival, I spied a man with a small boy who appeared as equally confused as he was paranoid. I watched him for the better part of three days."

"What happened when you reported back to Coyan?" Taryn questioned.

"He had me return with a small army. It was his desire for the father and son to be captured alive. He wanted them to be taken to Mors for a more thorough observation," Lazryn explained.

Taryn's brow arched. "Coyan thought my father was sick?"

Nodding, Lazryn continued. "Upon our return we discovered the man and child were gone. We tried searching for them and even watched the home for several weeks, but Coyan finally called for our return."

A smile curled on Taryn's face. "You lost Theron's scent only a few blocks from here."

"That is correct," Lazryn stated with a puzzled look settling on his face. "It was the most peculiar event. His scent was strong and laden with something highly unusual, and then it abruptly disappeared at the stop sign, two streets over."

Taking a seat on her old bed, Taryn shook her head and smirked. "It was Farren. He prevented you from tracking them." She paused, her breath catching in her throat.

A second later, Taryn found herself standing alone in absolute darkness. There was a chill in the air that collided against the warmth of her skin. Instead of casting it away she embraced it, letting it sink deep inside.

"Why have you brought me here?" she asked.

After several long moments without a reply, Taryn chuckled. "You're wise to remain hidden." She paused, holding her hand out and creating a small glowing orb that resembled the earth's moon. "It's been a very long week, and my patience is running thin. I suggest you return me to my friends before things get heated in here."

From the silence rose dozens of quiet whispers. The different tones covered one another creating a low buzz that Taryn could not decipher.

Unable to tolerate anymore, Taryn growled. "You can't say I didn't warn you."

Instantly, the white glow of her orb turned a fiery shade of red. Flames shot out the top of the sphere and began circling the teen. With each loop the flame's intensity grew as it spread outward, further into the darkness.

"There's only one way to make the flames disappear. Send me back," Taryn called out.

An instant later, Taryn found herself sitting on her old bed. She quickly glanced around the room. Lazryn stood in the doorway while Larkin knelt in front of her.

"You okay, Tare-Bear?" he asked.

She nodded. "What did you see?"

Sweeping a few stray hairs behind her ear, he flashed a caring smile. "You were talking about Farren and then you stiffened like a statue. Your eyes widened and your skin was so cold."

Taryn's brows furrowed.

"Where did you go this time, Taryn? What did the place look like?" Lazryn inquired.

She shrugged. "I don't know. It was dark like the other times. I couldn't see anything and..."

"And what?" Larkin pressed.

Rolling her eyes, she released a hefty sigh. "There were others there. I couldn't understand what they were saying, but I didn't get the feeling that they wanted to harm me."

Staring out the dirty pane of glass, Lazryn stepped forward. "Are you certain about that?"

Moving from the bed, she rushed to the window. Ominous dark clouds were forming over the city, swallowing every bit of daylight as far as the eye could see.

Without a word, Taryn rushed from the room into the backyard.

Keiryn stared at his sister as she exited the backdoor. "It isn't me, I swear."

"I know," she replied, walking past him with her eyes fixated on the darkening sky.

Theron followed his daughter. "What is it?" When she didn't answer, he nudged her. "Taryn..."

A deafening boom of thunder sounded overhead. The noise was so immense that he and the others ducked, covering their heads, while Taryn remained unaffected.

Holding the door open, Larkin shouted, "Everyone, get inside now!"

Lazryn pointed to Taryn. "Go to her, Larkin. I will see to it that the others are safe."

Nodding, Larkin ran to her.

"We've got to get inside, Taryn," he shouted, panning his eyes upward.

Magnificent waves of blue electricity pulsed menacingly overhead.

"Come on, we need to go now!" he warned, grabbing her by the hand. Feeling the stiffness in her muscles, he looked into Taryn's eyes. Within each, he witnessed a strange swirling that was utterly mesmerizing. It was like looking into a sea of churning emeralds, each glimmering as if the light from a thousand moons was shining from within, trying to break free.

From the back steps, Theron and Lazryn watched the pair standing out in the open, exposed to this unknown threat.

Taking a step down, Theron growled. "What is he doing? Why aren't they coming inside?"

"Larkin will not allow any harm to come to her. This you know to be the truth." Lazryn paused, placing a hand on Theron's shoulder. "However, should I permit you to take another step into harm's way Taryn will most certainly claim a pound of flesh from me for allowing you to be hurt."

Glaring up at the former Mortari, Theron shoved the man's hand from his shoulder. "She is my daughter, and if he isn't going to protect her, I will."

Lazryn moved swiftly to block the man from taking another step. "The young wolf is her protector in ways we will never begin to comprehend. You will allow him to fulfill his duty as such, and there will be no further discussion on the matter."

Theron opened his mouth to object, but found himself distracted by the prickling sensation creeping over his body. The hairs on his arms and neck were standing straight on end.

Feeling the same sensation, Lazryn turned toward the teens with wide eyes. Before he could utter a single syllable, the sky opened up and an immense bolt of blue lightning raced toward the pair.

Captivated by the beauty swirling within Taryn's eyes, Larkin instinctively glanced up and saw the threat raining down over them. Pulling her against his strong frame, he knelt on the ground, covering her protectively.

The tip of the bolt was mere inches away when it suddenly split apart, striking the ground in a circular pattern around the pair before disappearing.

Theron maneuvered around Lazryn and ran to the teens. Nearing, he noticed the hollow expression on his daughter's face. "Taryn?" he questioned.

With her eyes no longer swirling, they darted to him. "I'm fine, Dad. Nothing to worry about," she replied, glancing toward the dark sky with a weighted sigh.

Larkin helped Taryn to her feet. "I think we should go inside until whatever this is blows over."

Nodding in agreement, she followed the others to the door. Looking over her shoulder, she paused. In the opposing backyard, Farren stood watching them with an eerie smile. Scanning the area for whatever passing soul made him visible to her, Taryn found herself at a loss. She could not feel a single person facing an impending death.

Larkin took Taryn's hand into his own, grabbing her attention.

"Come on. We can wait the storm out inside with the others," he smiled.

Taryn glanced back to Farren. There he stood, still smiling. Tilting his head toward the storm clouds overhead and then to Taryn, he gave a slight bow and dissipated into the breeze.

Stepping onto the grass, Larkin looked up at the diminishing clouds. "Now this is new."

"It is certainly something," Taryn replied.

CHAPTER TWO

Clutching an old photo and frame against her chest that she had taken from their old home, Gracyn Knight stared distantly out the car window.

Theron reached over, squeezing her knee. "You know, Gracie, the things we left behind today we can go back and get another time."

A pained smile formed on her face. "Thank you," she replied, placing her hand over his.

Seeing the hurt so clearly etched on his wife's beautiful face, Theron struggled to keep his own subdued. "Keiryn seems to be enjoying the trip, don't you think?" he asked.

She sighed. "Yes, our son certainly enjoys life to the fullest with Nalani by his side."

A moment of silence lingered.

"But our daughter is another story," Theron stated.

"Taryn is amazing. She is considerate, and more tolerant than anyone is deserving of." Gracyn paused, swiping at a rogue tear. "She's been miserable on this entire trip, but she grins and bears it to make us happy."

Nodding, Theron pursed his lips. "It doesn't seem fair…we finally have our family back and our daughter must carry the weight of all the planes on her shoulders."

A warm smile curled on Gracyn's face. "At least she isn't alone."

Theron gave a grumbling chuckle. "Every time I look at that boy, I am in constant conflict, Gracie."

"Now, Theron, be fair to Larkin. He makes our daughter smile in the midst of so much madness. He also protects her without hesitation, just like he did earlier. Larkin could have run back to the house, but he stayed, forcing the lightning away," she countered.

"I know, and I'm glad that she has someone to be there for her. But as her father, it destroys me to know that I was robbed of being that person for her. A father should protect his daughter, not the other way around," he replied.

Gracyn squeezed his hand and pulled the old picture frame from her chest. "Do you remember the day we took this photo?"

Theron nodded.

"Do you recall how protective Larkin was of her, even then?" she smiled.

He chuckled. "Taryn was only a few weeks old when Keiryn and Larkin would crawl over one another to get closer to her."

"I remember how they would sit and watch her for long periods of time without making a sound. It was so odd, them barely being toddlers themselves. They both loved her so much, even back then," Gracyn stated with a sigh.

Rolling his eyes, Theron took a deep breath. "That certainly hasn't changed any."

Still gripping the picture frame, Gracyn leaned toward the driver's seat, planting a tender kiss on her husband's cheek. "You know you wouldn't want it any other way."

"I don't know. You weren't around for that first year or so between Larkin and Keiryn after Taryn moved to town, it was painstakingly intense, to put it lightly," Theron replied and then suddenly gasped. "Gracie, I'm so sorry. That was a stupid, insensitive thing for me to say considering what you must have experienced living on Hypatia."

The warmth in her eyes quickly disappeared, replaced by a distant stare as she placed the picture frame over her heart.

⊰⊱⊰⊱

Passing beneath the metal gateway into Williams, Arizona, Taryn released a hefty sigh. She glanced around the small town as they drove through. It was buzzing with vacationing families taking advantage of the near perfect temperature and ample sunshine.

Suddenly she shouted, "Stop the Jeep!"

Larkin slammed on the brakes, but before the vehicle could come to a complete stop, Taryn jumped out. She ran toward the crowded sidewalk, disappearing amongst the sea of people.

Horns honked, filling the air. Not wanting to draw any additional attention, Larkin quickly found a spot and parked his Jeep.

Leaning forward from the backseat, Lazryn grabbed Larkin by the shoulder. "Let me go collect her this time?"

"It's the third time this week that she's thought she saw him." Pausing, Larkin sighed. "You've told me over and over how much he cares for her. If he truly does, then why won't he stay away and leave her alone?"

Shaking his head, Lazryn shrugged while reaching for the door handle.

Suddenly, Taryn appeared, opening the Jeep door. She slid into the front passenger seat. Her jaw drew up tightly. "Let's go."

"Everything okay?" Larkin questioned.

Taryn gave a slight shrug. "Yeah, we're good."

Starting the Jeep, Larkin backed out and headed toward the stoplight. While waiting for the light to turn green, Taryn focused her gaze onto the side rearview mirror. With watchful eyes, she scanned the many faces gathered on a nearby corner. When the light turned green, disappointment settled in. She gave a brief, final scan before they disappeared from view.

ಬಂಧಬಂಧ

Freshly showered, Taryn exited her bathroom and headed to the bedroom window. Below in the backyard, her friends lounged about next to the pool while Andyn, Kellan and Gerrick tossed around the football. Sounds of their laughter filled the air, providing her a glimmer of peace.

Sensing an impending knock at her bedroom door, Taryn used her gift of Imperium to turn the knob and pull it open.

"Come in, Ilya," she stated, her eyes still focused on the happy smiles of her friends.

"Do you have a moment?" Ilya inquired.

Taryn turned to face the woman, giving her a warm smile. "I'll always have time for you."

The beautiful woman smiled back fondly. "I just wanted to tell you, it's okay that we didn't stop by Galatia on our way back." She paused. "I understand how seeing some of our old neighbors and that tiny bungalow might have brought up some unpleasant memories for you."

A lump formed in Taryn's throat. "Ilya, you don't always have to be so gracious about things. I know you were looking forward to visiting our old home, and I'm sorry that it didn't happen…but it will, I promise."

Ilya moved closer to the window and glanced down at the teens. "Hava said once they knew you were back, they couldn't wait to come over and hang out. I think they're all getting a little anxious."

Taryn sighed. "Unfortunately, they're going to have to wait a bit longer. Blayne called and apparently some of the communities on Relles are having a meeting, and they have requested my presence for whatever reason."

Reaching across, Ilya squeezed Taryn's hand. "It's not fair of them to ask so much of you after you handed them their freedom."

"And you're one to talk." Taryn paused, smirking playfully. "I burned down my father's home, and you give my family yours while you move with Maxym to his place."

Ilya swallowed hard, fighting to keep her tears at bay. "Teigan, I mean, Theron, and your mother needed a place to live while you worked to rebuild your family. Plus, you needed space for everyone to come over and visit. Besides, Taryn, you truly love this place. And to be honest, I find that Maxym's home suits me quite nicely."

"My mother returning doesn't change anything between us, Ilya." Taryn paused. "You raised me. Protected me. You cared for me when I had no one else. You sacrificed so much. Above all, you showed me the love that only a mother can show their child."

Swiping away her tears, Ilya smiled. "Don't ever lose that beautiful heart of yours, Taryn. It is what separates you from everyone else."

ᏳᎾᏓᏳᎾᏓ

Waiting to step thru the Adora Gateway, Taryn glanced up at Larkin. "Stay and go fishing with your dad and the others. Blayne and I will be fine."

Larkin wrapped his arm around her waist, pulling her close. "Andyn's with my dad keeping him company." He paused, kissing her softly. "As for me, I'm exactly where I'm meant to be...at your side."

Clearing his throat, Blayne grabbed the couple's attention. "Are we ready?" he asked.

Taryn shrugged. "Relles or bust, right?"

He nodded in response. "My insider tells me the communities are in rare form as of late."

ᏳᎾᏓᏳᎾᏓ

Exiting the gateway, Taryn and the others found themselves standing toward the rear of a very vocal crowd of people who had gathered around the Stone of Relles. The stone was the central location for the different communities to come together to voice concerns, and she had seen a lot of it in recent months.

"Effective immediately, all women shall be required to wear dresses no shorter than two inches above the ankle bone. Formal collars will be required, and all sleeves must reach the wrist bone," an older man announced.

Unhappy grumbles filled the air.

"That's not fair!" one young woman shouted.

Another yelled, "You're taking us back to the dark ages."

The older gentleman shot them both a silencing glare before continuing. "Furthermore, all unions must be sanctioned by this new combined community council."

The grumbles turned into a roar of disapproval.

"You cannot do this. It's not right," a young man voiced.

"This is no different than having the Elder Council in control," a man shouted.

Another man stepped forward, joining the speaker front and center. "This is for the good of Relles. If we wish to compete and secure our place amongst the planes of the Gaias Elite, we must implement an order of selection. Never has there been a call more urgent and necessary than to control the stock of our gifts."

"Order of selection?" Taryn thundered, drawing the attention of all in attendance. The crowd parted as she headed toward the men.

Upon her approach, the two vocal men suddenly fell speechless.

"Did I hear you correctly? Did you really just say order of selection?" she questioned sternly.

"Taryn Malone, you are not from this plane. This is an internal community matter, and it does not concern you," a dark haired man stated, stepping forward.

"The last name is Knight. And for the record, your communities requested my presence, so that makes it my concern." She paused, eyeing those present. "Imposing an order of selection is not only despicable, but it is also quite dangerous. Or should we invite a few members of the Mortari here to educate you on the issues?"

The dark haired man stepped closer to Taryn, garnering a growl of warning from Larkin.

"Your pet needs to learn his place," the man stated with a snarl. Raising his hand, a bolt of golden colored lightning streamed from the sky toward Larkin.

Taryn immediately raised her hand creating her own bright white lightning that swallowed the man's creation before disappearing into the sky.

Turning to address the crowd, Taryn's face remained neutral, as if unaffected by the man's attempt to harm Larkin. "Many of you here today wear a mark on your wrist that promises you freedom. Know that this freedom extends beyond the rule of the Elder Council or the Mortari. You remain free to make your own decisions as long as I draw breath, this is my word."

"So much for your promises meaning anything," the dark haired man admonished. "You assured each plane that we could govern ourselves, and yet here you are attempting to dictate what we can and cannot do."

Taryn's eyes focused firmly upon him. "Tell me, were you elected by your communities, or did you simply elect yourselves based on age and strength of gifts and nothing more?"

"I'm more than three hundred years old," he barked.

"And somehow because of this, you feel entitled to dictate how everyone else should live." She paused, glancing to a young couple standing near the front of the crowd. "You are nothing more than a bunch of Elder Council wannabes, and I will not permit you to force your fears upon these people. If you want to be in charge of Relles, you need to obtain the vote of the majority who reside here without the assistance of an Influential."

"But we deserve respect," the first man stated.

Taryn shook her head. "You act as though you are owed something in this life, when none of us are owed a damned thing. What benefit is there in forcing women to hide beneath layers of clothing, but still keeping the expectation that they will work the fields like you? What does this save? Who does this protect? And then there's your order of selection…it is nothing more than a polite way to segregate the Gaias population according to gifts."

"You removed the Elder Council from power without so much as a thought to what would happen to the rest of us. The power vacuum is real and it will happen. If we do not act decisively in this very moment, our communities will be an easy target in the next generation," the man replied.

"He's right, we must build a stronger, more efficient army to defend Relles' future," a woman agreed from the crowd.

Glancing over her shoulder, Taryn sighed. "Fear mongering at its best...you're sad little men with fragile egos and equally fragile spines." She paused, addressing the group. "Those of you who wear my mark are free to live your lives as you see fit, regardless of their rules."

"What happens when one of them attacks us without cause? Will you continue to protect them even then?" the dark haired man pressed.

Taryn chuckled. "Assuring a person's freedom is not the same as assuring a person freedom from consequences of their actions and choices." She paused, her face turning void of expression. "Speaking of consequences for one's actions...you intended to harm Larkin earlier. You really shouldn't have done that."

The man licked his lips nervously as beads of sweat formed across his forehead. "I believe your pet meant to harm me first," he retorted.

"First, his name is Larkin and he is not my pet. Second, you and everyone else were warned about messing with my family. Third, you are not exempt from consequences for your actions," Taryn stated clearly.

"What are you going to do to me?" the man questioned, his voice cracking with worry.

Stepping toward the man, Taryn placed her hand on his shoulder as she passed by. "I think I'll let it be a surprise. I do promise it's something you won't ever forget."

Taryn looked to Blayne, and he quickly opened the gateway to Williams.

"To the rest of you, I again remind you that you are free. However, your actions are never free of consequence. This is something I want you to think about for the next month." She paused, turning her focus back to the first two men who addressed the crowd. "You both should think long and hard before you utter another word. I left my friends and family to come here and listen to you spew this nonsense at these good people. Refocus your efforts by including them in the conversation, and do not give me reason to return here."

ଈୠଔଈୠଔ

Exiting the gateway, Blayne looked to Taryn. "I'm curious. What consequence did you bestow upon that man?" he asked.

Also curious, Larkin listened for her response on the matter.

"He was so anxious to implement those ridiculous rules, so I thought I'd give him a little taste," she replied with a smirk.

Blayne's eyes widened. "Tell me you didn't..."

"Oh, I most certainly did." Taryn paused looking to Larkin. "He will be wearing that ridiculous and outdated dress code for the next thirty days. He also will only find his voice to speak when in the presence of others who share his specific gift profile."

Shaking his head, Blayne opened a new gateway. "Remind me to stay on her good side," he stated, while giving Larkin a nod. Flashing a final wide grin, he stepped into the awaiting gateway and disappeared.

Taryn's eyes fell heavy upon Larkin's face. "You're absolutely beautiful," she exhaled.

"You think I'm beautiful?" he questioned with a smile.

~ 23 ~

Giving a slight nod, Taryn moved in a blur to stand toe-to-toe with him. She smiled wildly. "Did I say beautiful? I meant absolutely breathtaking."

Larkin ran his hand down the length of her hair. "I could say the same about you and your mesmerizing emerald eyes." He paused, leaning down and kissing her lips tenderly. Pulling back slightly, he placed a kiss on her forehead and sighed. "This isn't fair..."

Reaching up, Taryn ran her fingers along his tense jawline. "You know I wish things could be different."

He took her hand, pressing it against his cheek. "If not for Blayne returning us a few miles away from your home, we wouldn't even have these few minutes alone." He paused, taking a settling breath. "It's not fair that we have to steal moments away from the worlds. You're not responsible for everyone else, Taryn."

Her eyes softened as she inhaled deeply. "But I am responsible, Larkin. Right or wrong, my actions removed the Elder Council from power, creating a vacuum." She turned and walked to a nearby pine tree. Looking out across the sandy terrain, Taryn released a slight sigh, creating a gentle rain across the desert. "The moment we released the werewolves and the first wrist was tattooed with my promise of protection, I became responsible."

Appearing in a blur behind her, Larkin wrapped his arms around her waist and pulled her in tight. "Maybe so, but I don't think that includes you running to listen every time two groups have a simple disagreement."

"They're lost, trying to navigate this new found freedom. For each person who wants to live free, it seems there are three more wanting to become a smaller version of the Elder Council." She paused, resting the back of her head against his chest. "If I don't continue to show, what will happen to the weak or the young?"

For several moments, the pair stood silently as the rain moved closer.

"Taryn." Larkin repositioned himself in front of her. "I love you with every ounce of my being, and I worry about you. During the Trials, you destroyed pieces of yourself to protect everyone else." He paused, cupping her cheeks between his hands. "At what point do you stop punishing yourself for something that never happened?"

Closing her eyes, she bit her bottom lip and sighed. The memories from that day came rushing back vivid, as if they were currently taking place. The smell in the air permeated her sinuses. Fear's treacherous laughter echoed in her ears.

"Don't do it, Taryn. Don't you dare go back there," Larkin warned, nudging her.

"Ripping Fear to pieces was the best decision I have ever made. Those particular demons are dead and gone. I burned them to ash, and I don't regret my actions one bit. If my Rage would have survived, nothing else could. It was the same with my Fear. All the planes, including the Earth, would have either burned in fire or fallen into an endless ice age," she stated.

Larkin kissed her temple and whispered in her ear. "But neither of those things happened, Taryn. You willingly destroyed pieces of yourself to save all of the planes."

She wrapped her arms around his neck, hugging him fiercely. "I guess it's a good thing I have you to fill the void left in their absence."

„‥„‥

Following Taryn to the back of the Jeep, Lazryn studied the grey skies overhead. "Young Andyn appears to be in good spirits after your one-on-one time with him earlier."

"Did you expect him to be otherwise?" Taryn replied with an arched brow, not realizing how much attention the former Mortari paid to her comings and goings.

"Of course not. I was only stating the obvious." Lazryn paused, stepping to the side as she opened the hatch. "Was your visit last evening to Relles uneventful?"

With a heavy sigh, Taryn grabbed one of the sleeping bags from the back and handed it to her friend. "I know Larkin told you everything. So why don't you just ask me whatever's on your mind?"

His eyes softened. "I think it is unwise of you to go with your friends tonight."

Setting a few more sleeping bags on the ground, Taryn turned, leaning against the Jeep. "They need this. I need this." She paused. "Every day that I put it off causes more stress and confusion. And that's not fair to anyone."

Straightening himself, he inquired, "So you have made a decision?"

She nodded. "I think it's something I've always known. Gerrick, Thorne, Kellan, Bency and the others…they are fierce, loyal, brave and so much more. They are going to make an incredible true pack."

"Then congratulations are in order. This news will be of great relief to their parents as well as your friends," he stated, giving her a strong one-armed hug.

Feigning a smile, Taryn rested her head on his shoulder.

CHAPTER THREE

At the bottom of one of the Grand Canyon's most isolated areas, Taryn and her friends set up their camp.

A small stream flowed along the base of the adjacent canyon wall, adding to the peaceful aura of the location. Blue skies and the bright sun shone overhead, highlighting the myriad of red hues that made up the canyon walls.

"Wow. To think we've flown over this area a few dozen times and never thought twice about it," Kellan stated, taking in the site's serene beauty.

"My sis really knows how to pick a setting, doesn't she," Andyn replied, glancing in her direction.

"Hell yeah she does. Bentley Hadley haven't complained once since we arrived," Eben stated, referring to the twins and their disdain for the outdoors.

Gerrick wrapped an arm around Eben and Thorne's shoulders as he gave a look to the others. "I have a good feeling about this, boys. I think tonight is finally the night we become part of a true pack," he grinned.

Andyn gave a faint smile before heading over to where Keiryn and Nalani were laying out their sleeping bags.

"That was strange, don't you think?" Dalen asked, referring to Andyn's demeanor.

Kellan shook his head. "Cut the kid some slack. If Gerrick's right, Taryn's made up her mind, and their pack of two won't be the same after tonight."

℡ℂℛ™

After hiking a few miles from camp, the group found themselves at a dead-end in the canyon.

"I guess we go up from here," Kellan stated with a smile.

Looking to Jonesy, Gerrick grinned. "What about it, Blake, do you think you can beat me to the top?"

Jonesy glanced over to Bency. When she nodded, he stepped to the sheer rock wall. "I'll do you a solid and give you a head start."

"That's what I'm talking about, brother," Gerrick replied, rubbing his hands together.

The rest of the group made themselves comfortable while the two prepared to race.

When it was time, Andyn counted down from three and Gerrick began ascending the wall in a near blur. When he was a little more than half way up, Jonesy started following behind him. At first, he climbed slowly. He had barely made it midway when Gerrick reached for the ledge, but in a blink Jonesy made up the lost ground, catching Gerrick with ease.

A few moments later, Jonesy jumped from the rock wall doing a spectacular backflip. His feet landed firmly atop the bare soil as he motioned for Gerrick to do the same.

Never being one to back down from a challenge, Gerrick accepted, howling as he flipped from the wall. His landing was nowhere near as graceful as Jonesy's, but it, too, solicited approval from his very vocal friends.

After most of the boys and Bency had their turn racing to the top and jumping off, Taryn rose to her feet.

"You want a turn?" Kellan asked.

She shook her head. "I had something else in mind."

"What is it?" Keiryn inquired.

A wide smile formed on her face as an Adora Gateway opened. When Lazryn appeared from within, he was greeted with a large number of scowls.

"What's the monster doing here?" Keiryn growled.

Taryn shot her older brother a frosty glare. "He's here at my request, doing us a favor."

"Oh, no," Keiryn argued. "He might as well go back, because there is no way that I'm going to be in his debt."

Taryn stepped to him, standing toe-to-toe. "You don't have to like him, but you're not going to disrespect him. Understood, big brother?"

"He's Mortari, Taryn," Keiryn challenged.

Taryn shrugged. "Yes. Thankfully, he was Mortari, because if he hadn't been, you most likely would never have seen me again." Pushing up on her toes, she kissed Keiryn's cheek. "And I would have never known the truth about who we were to one another." Dropping back on her heels, she turned, walking to Lazryn and Larkin.

The older man smiled as she approached. "As always, you are far better to me than I deserve."

Placing his hand on Lazryn's shoulder, Larkin nodded. "She's right, you know. You returned her to us, and for that you will always have my gratitude."

Taryn looked around the many faces. "Does anyone else have an opinion they'd like to share on Lazryn's presence?"

While her tone was pleasant, her eyes held a quiet warning. After a few moments of silence, she looked to Lazryn and smiled softly.

Taking his cue from her, he raised his hand in the direction of the dead end wall, forming an Adora Gateway.

"What are you playing at here, Taryn?" Keiryn asked.

She shrugged. "If you don't want to come with us, that's fine. For anyone curious about what lies within this particular gateway, follow me."

Moving to stand beside his big sister, Andyn arched a brow. "Dang sis, you know I'll follow you anywhere." Leaning toward Lazryn, the young boy held out his fist.

Obliging, Lazryn bumped his knuckles against Andyn's.

Kellan stepped forward. "Count me in."

"Me too," Gerrick added.

"Us too," the twins agreed.

Soon, everyone was on board with the exception of Keiryn and Nalani.

Wrapping his arm around her waist, Larkin kissed Taryn's temple. "You should go ahead and take the others. I'll talk to him and Nals."

Flashing him a grateful smile, Taryn nodded, before leading the others through the gateway.

"Hey, Lazryn, if you wouldn't mind, we could use a few minutes," Larkin stated while nodding him on.

With the portal still open and Lazryn no longer in sight, Keiryn released a heavy sigh. "I know what you're going to say, Brother, but I can't pretend that I'm okay with that monster lurking around."

"Your reservations are duly noted, but you know it won't change Taryn's mind on the issue. She cares deeply for him, and has promised him her protection," Larkin replied.

Keiryn began to pace about. "Out of everyone here, how can you be okay with him? His kind killed your mother."

Angered by his friend's words, Larkin stepped in front of Keiryn, blocking his way.

"He didn't mean it like that, Larkin," Nalani insisted while trying to step between the pair.

"Stay out of it, Nals," Larkin warned, gripping Keiryn's shirt collar. "I was there. I saw her lifeless body as those two heartless soul suckers stood over her, laughing, amused by what they had done. My father and I were devastated by my mother's death. Not a day goes by that I don't think of her." He paused, releasing his grip. "When I first met Lazryn, I hated him with every ounce of my being. After all, he was Mortari and I was Afflicted, and then there's that thing with me being bound to your sister."

Keiryn bared his teeth with flared nostrils. "He's the one who stole her away from us. I will never forgive him for that."

Larkin ran his hands through his hair and exhaled loudly. "The Brothers C could have sent any one of their faithful to collect her, but they sent him. Taryn took a gamble, and we were fortunate it was Lazryn. He showed restraint in sparing everyone that night. If it would have been any other Mortari or one of the Lessor's, do you think they would have done the same?"

"If he is so good, then why didn't he bring her back sooner?" Keiryn shouted.

A few moments later, Taryn exited the open gateway.

"Larkin, Nalani, would you please give us a few minutes?" she asked.

Nalani started to object, but Keiryn motioned for her to go on. She and Larkin disappeared into the portal.

Taryn circled her brother, taking in his heaving chest and tense brow.

"You're searching for the easy answer. I am here to tell you there isn't one." She paused, brushing her fingertips through his hair. "You look so much like dad...so handsome."

Stiffening the set of his jaw, Keiryn struggled to contain his emotions. "He's a monster who doesn't deserve your love."

Her eyes softened. "Many people think I'm a monster after witnessing the Trials. Would you agree with them?"

He shook his head. "Don't be ridiculous, Taryn. You are all that is right in this life. We're fortunate to have you."

"What makes you so certain that I'm not what they say I am?" she asked.

Rolling his eyes, Keiryn released a loud sigh. "It's because I know you, and I know your heart."

"That's exactly my point. I know Lazryn, and I know his heart," she replied.

"Don't try to confuse the two situations. He's killed people to steal their gifts," Keiryn countered.

"You're absolutely right, Keiryn. We are talking about two different situations. Lazryn's killed a few thousand beings after watching his wife and child die because he put his trust in the wrong people. And then there's me...the girl who intended to destroy all life because she was full of hate, rage and fear." She paused. "I was so close to letting them win."

He shook his head defiantly. "No. I'll never believe that."

"I know it's difficult to accept, but it is the truth. If it hadn't been for Larkin, I would have stayed lost in my own head, and I would have ruined everything and everyone." She paused, intertwining her arm with his and beginning to walk. "Do you remember how the slightest change in your emotions would cause your hidden gifts to escape?"

He nodded.

"Do you recall the burn in the pit of your stomach during those times? You know, the one that would spread like wild fire if left unchecked for even a moment?" she asked.

He shivered, recalling those times. "Of course I do. That sensation is permanently seared into my mind. The only thing that could make it go away was you and your Influence."

Releasing his arm, Taryn moved to stand directly in front of him. Her eyes were soft, yet laden with pain. Raising her hand, she caressed his cheek before placing two fingers against his temple. "Please, forgive me," she whispered.

Keiryn started to push away but it was too late. She had already started filling his mind with someone else's memories.

The first images he saw were of a young boy and girl playing in a meadow. They appeared to live in a different time. They were content, happy and full of love. Soon those childhood memories faded, shifting to their teenaged years. Here, he began to see life through the boy's eyes. Happiness and love still reigned during this time, but it would not last through the next transition. Now a grown man, Lazryn's memories of falling in love and becoming a father filled the teen's heart with unabated joy. He felt the same euphoria Lazryn had on the day he held his daughter in his arms for the first time. Tears of joy streaked Keiryn's handsome face.

Taking a deep breath, Taryn allowed the worst night of Lazryn's life to play out freely in her brother's mind.

The euphoria he felt quickly faded, replaced by a moment of brief confusion. He watched as a man he understood to be a dear friend to Lazryn and his family, betrayed them all, causing a firestorm of emotion within the teen. The more he witnessed, the more he, too, became unhinged by blind rage. Veins bulged in his neck as his nostrils flared. A distinct growl rose from deep within him.

Watching her brother teeter on a dangerous edge, Taryn pulled her hand away.

"I will kill them all!" Keiryn roared with a heaving chest.

Taryn wrapped her arms around him. Her touch slowly diminished the rage, bringing him back to the here and now.

Pulling away, Keiryn stared at his sister. "Why would you do that to me?"

"Because you needed to see that Lazryn wasn't born a monster, but he was coerced into becoming one," she answered.

Keiryn frowned while rolling his eyes. "This doesn't change anything, Taryn. The things he has done…I know he was the one who brought you back, and I am thankful for that, but I won't forgive him for taking you in the first place."

"I'm not asking you to forgive him, Keiryn. I'm just simply hoping that you can understand where I'm coming from," she replied.

He shrugged. "You are the most compassionate person I know, so I get it, but your little stunt here changes nothing."

Taryn bit her lip and gently shook her head. "I adore Lazryn, so I am asking you, Brother, be civil and bury your hate." She paused. "Our family has a big night ahead of them, and I will not allow it to be sullied by anyone, especially you. I trust you to do right by them, and to put your issues with Lazryn aside. If you cannot find it within yourself to do this one thing, then it changes everything."

"What's that supposed to mean?" he asked.

Taryn gave him a stern look before silently walking to the gateway.

₧₧₧₧

On the other side of the portal, the teens from Williams splashed about in the glowing blue waters. Embedded crystals lining the walls reflected the light of the water, giving an ethereal look and feel to the enclosed space.

Taryn smiled, watching as each one appeared to be thoroughly enjoying their time in the secret cavern.

Jonesy and Bency jumped from the tallest ledge into the pool below, garnering howls from the others.

With water dripping from his shaggy hair, Andyn ran to his sister. "Okay, now that you're back, are you going to tell us where we are?"

The others quickly gathered around to hear the answer.

"This is going to come as a bit of a surprise, but this is part of the Grand Canyon," she stated.

Gerrick shook his head. "We've flown over the Canyon a hundred times and I've never seen this."

Taryn smiled. "You were looking above ground. We are beneath it."

"But how did you know it was here?" Kellan questioned.

Sensing her older brother's presence entering the portal, Taryn paused, flashing a warm smile. "It was actually Lazryn who told me about it."

Turning his head in the man's direction, Kellan waved him over. "Lazryn, come tell us how you knew about this place."

With Keiryn now in the cave, the man allowed the gateway to close and approached the group. "When I was a young boy, I had a gift for locating voids beneath the ground's surface. It was extremely helpful in finding underground water sources when there were no Elementals in the group."

Jonesy shook his head. "But this isn't just any underground water source."

Lazryn looked around the stunning cave and nodded. "You are correct. The placement of the crystals on the walls, the particular type of flora growing in the water, and the bubbling side pools, this was an intentional design."

"Are you saying this was created by one of our own?" Dagney asked.

"Can you think of a better explanation?" he replied.

While Lazryn shared his thoughts on the origin of the secret cave with the others, Taryn joined Keiryn off to the side.

Admiring the space, he exhaled. "Wow…this is something else."

"It most certainly is," Taryn replied with a smile.

Standing side by side, the pair watched as their friends remained captivated, listening to Lazryn share his knowledge.

Keiryn gave Taryn a gentle nudge. "Hey, I'm sorry about earlier. I know you care for him, but it's too much sometimes. You know, thinking about all the time we lost, and knowing it was him who took you away that night."

"Believe it or not, I do understand. We did miss out on creating so many memories, but I promise those times are in the past. I won't let anyone do that to us again," she replied.

"Promise?" he asked, holding up his pinky.

Taryn wrapped her finger with his and flashed a beaming smile. "You never disappoint me, big brother."

Leaning down, he kissed the top of her head. "It would break my heart if I ever did."

The pair shared a quiet moment before heading to the tallest ledge in the cavern. Once in place, the two dove into the luminescent water below.

໐Ცჱౖ৩Ცౖ

After spending several hours in the secret cave, the group of teens returned to their campground. Andyn used his dragon, Iggy, to start the fire, while Lazryn made a brief return with trays of prepared sandwiches, chips, drinks and several bags of graham crackers, chocolate bars and marshmallows.

"Lazryn's not such a bad guy," Gerrick stated with a mouth full of food.

Eben laughed. "You're only saying that because he's filling that bottomless pit you call a stomach."

"I'm a man who requires sustenance," he countered.

Howls of laughter filled the night air, followed immediately by a bombardment of marshmallows in Gerrick's direction.

Sitting on a log with her head against Larkin's shoulder, Taryn sighed.

"Is it time?" he asked.

Sitting up straight, she nodded.

Caressing her cheek, Larkin kissed her softly on the lips. "You have my full support."

"Thanks," she replied, kissing him again. Rising to her feet, she moved to one side of the fire and motioned for the others to gather round.

"It's about time," Gerrick whispered to Kellan.

"Cut her some slack. She's been crazy busy since the Trials," he replied.

Looking at each of their faces, Taryn could see the anticipation building. Not wanting to prolong their wait, she addressed the group. "We have an elephant amongst us, and it's been with us for several months now." Pausing, she took a deep breath. "There's been a lot of discussion about forming a legitimate pack, and I understand your desire to do so."

"We'll follow you anywhere, Kansas. Just say the word," Gerrick vocalized, rousing the group.

"Hell yeah we will," Kellan agreed.

With a heavy heart, Taryn shook her head. "I know what you want, but it's not going to happen."

Suddenly the group quieted. Looks of uncertainty passed between the longtime friends before all eyes settled upon her once again.

"It's not going to happen…what does that even mean?" Dagney asked.

Taryn shrugged while taking a deep breath. "Every day I feel your desire burning against the mark on my shoulder. You want me to be your pack leader. As much as I wish I could be, I simply cannot."

"What the hell, Taryn?" Kellan growled. "We welcomed you into our lives, and now you're saying we're not good enough for you?"

With watery eyes, she shook her head. "I love you all so very much. It's because of my love for you that I cannot be your leader."

Gerrick rubbed his temples. "I don't get it…are you afraid if you're our leader, we'll be targeted?"

"No, this isn't about fear. This is about me being fair to each of you." She paused, glancing to Andyn. "My current performance as a pack leader has been subpar, to say the least."

"But you saved Andyn from the Elder Council," Kellan argued.

"Yes, I was there when he needed me the most…but I haven't given him the proper attention that a true pack leader should. It is the exact same situation with the rest of you. We make plans, and I'm called away. We're in the middle of a family cookout and a dozen unhappy Gaias from some other plane show up unannounced. It would not be fair of me to take on a role that I know I cannot fulfill."

Tears welled in Andyn's eyes as he stepped forward to stand beside her. "Earlier today, I went on a walk with Taryn. When she first told me about her decision to refuse to be pack leader, I wasn't happy." He paused, glancing to her and then back to the others. "Knowing that her choice comes from the best of intentions, and a pure heart…I accept her decision." He paused, glancing to her again. "From this moment forward, I reject you as my leader. I no longer have a pack."

Gasps filled the cool air.

Taryn wrapped her arm around his shoulders and kissed his cheek. "You know I will always have your back, little brother."

He shook his head. "I know."

After everyone took a few minutes to come to terms with the shocking revelation presented to them, Kellan stepped forward on their behalf.

"Okay, so you can't be our pack leader, we get it…but where does that leave us?" He paused. "Do we divide into our previous groups…some of us follow Keiryn and the others Larkin?"

Taryn glanced to Larkin before turning back to Kellan. "Is that what you want? To split up into two different packs?"

Slowly, each one began to shake their heads.

Pleased with their desire to stay together, she replied, "Good, because we're family, and family should never live divided."

"So what are the options?" Gerrick asked.

Taryn's gaze turned to her older brother, and she flashed him a warm smile. "While there are a number of you who are more than qualified to be leader, I believe it's in your best interest to accept Keiryn as your one true leader."

The young man's eyes widened. "You want me to be the pack leader?"

She shook her head. "You have proven yourself to be caring, compassionate, fierce, faithful and so much more. But above all, you have shown your ability to look beyond your personal issues and allow understanding and compromise to reign in difficult situations."

Giving his sister a nod, he stepped forward. "Larkin, are you okay with this?"

"I'm good, Brother," he replied.

Hanging back, Nalani shared a brief glance with Taryn and nodded.

Eben moved to the front of the group. "So what happens now? Do we wait for the mark to appear, or do we need to take a vow or something?"

Placing a hand on her brother's shoulder, Taryn nudged him forward. "Go on now. Claim your pack."

He paused, glancing to the ground then back up at her. "Thank you."

Taryn smiled warmly. "You've earned it, Keiryn."

Turning his attention to the others, Keiryn looked around at their eager faces. "After the Trials, I didn't think my sister could possibly have any more surprises left for us...but here she's done it again." He paused, taking a deep breath. "I know practically every one of you expected a different outcome this evening. I know I certainly did. In this moment, we are left disappointed and heartbroken." He paused again, shaking his head. "But in true Taryn fashion, she has thoroughly evaluated the situation. And like so many times before, she has placed our best interests above her own desire." Pausing, he looked over his shoulder at her. "You are the glimmer of light in the darkest of places. We feel your love around us in everything we do."

Larkin wrapped his arm around Taryn's shoulders and pulled her close. "She is all that's right about our kind." Kissing the top of her head, he gave her a gentle squeeze.

Keiryn turned back to the group. "If you are willing to accept me as your true pack leader, I am here, offering myself to you."

With his declaration cheers erupted, filling the evening air.

After several long moments, the celebrations passed and everyone began to grow quiet.

Kellan looked around at the others with narrowed eyes. "Something's wrong." He paused, moving about the group and checking each of their shoulders. "There's not a mark on any of us…"

With clenched fists, Keiryn took a deep breath and closed his eyes. *Come on, we've kept it together for several months now. We can't lose it now,* he thought to himself.

With a shift in the wind, Keiryn held his breath in a desperate attempt to keep guard of the gateway that kept the storm raging inside him from breaking free. Sweat beaded on his forehead and vibrations coursed through every fiber of his being.

He had barely a second left before he would lose control. Feeling the gust of wind spinning internally, he prepared to accept the inevitable. As his immense power began to seep from within, Keiryn suddenly felt peace take hold.

Opening his eyes, he found Nalani standing in front of him.

"Are you okay?" she asked.

He stared into her crystal blue eyes. "Yeah, I'm good." He paused, glancing around with a grin. "So it seems we can't force Mother Nature to act before she's ready."

"That we cannot," Taryn agreed, giving him a wink as she walked past.

"So that's it? There isn't anything we can do to make it happen?" Gerrick sighed.

Kellan patted his brother on the back. "We've already waited this long, so what's a few more weeks going to hurt?"

Shaking his head, Eben growled. "This isn't fair. We've always done what we were supposed to, and here we are…packless."

Larkin approached him. "I, for one, don't need any mysterious ink to prove to me who my true family is. We are family. All of us." He placed a firm hand on Eben's shoulder and looked him in the eye.

"Open your heart to what you already know to be true, and peace will follow."

Eben nodded. "You're right. Our familial bond was forged the moment Taryn came into our lives. So if she's not worried, then I'm not either."

CHAPTER FOUR

Taryn joined Nalani as she sat on a rock formation a few hundred yards away from camp.

Pulling her knees to her chest, Taryn glanced up at the stars. "It's so peaceful out here. I think I can actually hear my own thoughts, for once."

Nalani shrugged. "Yeah, I know what you mean."

The two sat quietly for several moments before Nalani turned to face Taryn. "Why did you pick Keiryn to be pack leader?"

"Why not? He's the best suited to watch over the pack," Taryn answered.

"Maybe so, but Larkin could have done it," she replied.

"Larkin would have made a terrific leader if that were his destiny, but we both know it isn't," Taryn stated.

Nalani laced her arm with Taryn's. "Sometimes I am so jealous of what you and Larkin have." She sucked in a deep breath. "Don't get me wrong. I'm blissfully in love with your brother, and nothing will ever change that, but you and Larkin...the two of you have something beyond incredible."

Taryn smiled softly at her friend.

Nalani sighed. "You know he's never so much as had eyes for anyone until you showed up. It's like he was waiting, biding his time until your arrival."

Looking over her shoulder, Taryn stole a glance at her great love. He and Keiryn were standing next to the fire while animatedly telling the others a story. A quiet giggle passed her lips. "He may be goofy at times and ridiculously overprotective, but I love him endlessly."

Smiling, Nalani looked up at the stars and exhaled. "Skin-Walkers are so lucky."

"Why is that?" Taryn questioned.

Nalani turned to her with wide eyes. "Imagine this, Taryn. All of us girls go out for a night, and at any given time we can opt to ditch our vehicles and transform into any animal we want." She paused, jumping to her feet. "We could run the mountainside for hours, or swim beneath the water's surface without needing to come up for air. Or even better, we could turn into any bird we wanted and soar above the earth."

The excitement teeming in her friend's eyes inspired Taryn. Without warning, she rose to her feet. Grabbing Nalani's hand, she pulled her back toward their friends.

"Hey, everyone," Taryn shouted as they approached.

Larkin turned, watching as the pair neared the fire. "Is everything alright?" he asked, noting the sparkle in Taryn's eyes.

Stopping at his side, she released Nalani's hand while flashing a glowing smile. "Of course it is. We're here with our family."

With arched brows, Larkin leaned down and whispered to her. "I know we are, but you look like you're up to something. Care to let me in on whatever this is?"

She shook her head. "Nope. You'll have to wait like everyone else."

⊱⊰⊱⊰

Standing atop one of the many ridges within the Grand Canyon, the group of friends stared questioningly at Taryn.

"Okay, Sister, we're all here now, so what's this about?" Keiryn questioned.

On the edge of the cliff, Taryn stood holding her arms out as the brisk air encompassed her. She inhaled deeply, basking in the freeing sensation before turning to address the others. Each of their faces shone with trust, laced with a deep curiosity. Tonight, she intended to put the depth of that trust to the test.

"I know most of you were disappointed earlier. Things didn't go the way you expected them too. Even when posed with an alternative, it too, did not go as hoped." Taryn glanced to Keiryn. "But at the end of the day, it doesn't matter if we wear a shared symbol on our shoulders. We are connected in ways that other groups and communities will never fully understand."

Heads began to nod throughout the group.

"With that said, I want to share something with you that no one else will ever experience."

"Oh yeah, Kansas, and what exactly would that be?" Gerrick questioned.

A smile bloomed on Taryn's face. "Why, we're going to jump the Grand Canyon, of course," she answered.

Suddenly eyes widened and gasps filled the air.

"Is everyone up to the task, or should we just go back to the campsite and roast some more marshmallows?" she asked tauntingly.

Nalani joined her near the ledge. Smiling wildly, she replied, "I'm in."

Leaving Thorne's side, Dagney stepped forward. "Me too."

Being the only male present that did not possess the Skin-Walker ability, Andyn joined the girls. "Hell yeah. Let's do this."

Gerrick and Kellan looked to the twins.

"Are you girls in, or are you afraid of messing up your hair?" Gerrick tormented.

Bentley glanced to Hadley. In true twin fashion, they appeared to be having a silent conversation with one another while the others watched.

"Well…are you two in?" Kellan pressed.

Hadley turned, rolling her eyes at him and Gerrick. "We can't imagine that it will be as fun as shopping," she stated.

"But really, what else is there to do out here?" Hadley finished.

Kellan's eyes widened. "So you're in?" he asked, his voice laden with surprise.

Walking past the two boys, the twins answered in unison, "Duh, of course we're in."

Gerrick and Kellan shared a look of their own. With grins on their faces, the friends followed the sisters to the ledge.

Larkin elbowed Keiryn gently and nodded in the foursome's direction. "Didn't see that love connection ever happening, did you?"

Keiryn motioned for the others to fall in line while shaking his head. "Not in a thousand lifetimes, Brother," he answered.

With everyone in place, Taryn took a step away from the ledge and lifted her hand in the air.

"What are you doing?" Andyn questioned.

"Making sure that no one will see us while we're jumping," she replied.

Thorne looked over the edge and then out into the inky darkness. "What about us? How are we going to see anything while we're out there?" he inquired.

Taryn lifted her other hand and clouds began to form overhead.

Thorne rolled his eyes. "Great, now we don't even have the moonlight."

Dagney frowned at him. "Do you honestly believe she's finished?"

With rosy cheeks, he shrugged.

Flicking her wrist, Taryn created lightning that struck between the clouds, illuminating the canyon.

Nalani stepped back. "Wow, Kansas…the view alone is truly stunning."

Smirking, Taryn shrugged. "Wait until you get a bird's eye view during the flyover."

ഇരുഭരു

Holding hands as they stood in a line roughly twenty feet from the canyon's ledge, Taryn counted down. "Five, four, three, two, run!"

Howls pierced the night air as the group rushed forward.

As they reached the ledge, Taryn shouted, "Now!"

The friends bounded into the air. With lightning overhead illuminating the area surrounding them, each of the friends had an incredible view of the canyon below.

"This is amazing," Dagney gushed while the others erupted into shouts of joy and awe.

The group landed with feathered feet across the canyon on a nearby ridge. The moment their feet were safely on the ground, laughter broke out. They cheered and hollered blissfully while hugging one another.

As Larkin hugged Taryn, he whispered in her ear, "It's nice to find that you've improved your landing skills since the last time we did this."

Pulling back, Taryn rolled her eyes and smirked. "You and Keiryn, that was a test run." She paused, kissing him. "Besides, I didn't know what I was doing back then."

"So you decided to wing it?" he inquired.

She shook her head and chuckled. "I had Farren guiding me…sort of."

"Well you've certainly come a long way," Keiryn commented, having overheard their conversation.

Reaching over, Taryn punched Keiryn in the arm. "So have you, Brother. This time you didn't scream like a little school girl all the way over."

Larkin released a hearty laugh and patted him on the back. "Sorry, but she's right. Your scream was pretty hysterical that night."

Shaking his head, Keiryn draped his arm over Nalani's shoulders. "You know how they are always exaggerating to make the story more entertaining."

Nalani bit her lip in an attempt to stifle her laughter. After a few seconds passed, she regained her composure and replied. "Of course. Taryn and Larkin are just teasing you." She quickly bit her lip again, but this time she couldn't help herself. In her attempt to refrain from laughing, a loud snort pierced the air.

"Oh my gosh, Lani. You snorted in front of your boyfriend," the twins gasped in horror.

Poor Nalani's single snort quickly multiplied into several snorts that were broken by the occasional crack of laughter breaking through. Her face turned bright red and tears filled her eyes.

"On occasion I may scream like a little girl, but you're totally snorting like a pig," Keiryn teased.

After several minutes passed and everyone had done their fair share of laughing, things quieted down.

Taryn looked to Gerrick and Kellan, who each carried one of the twins on their backs. "Where are you going?" she asked.

"We thought we'd get a head start on getting back to camp," Kellan replied.

"Oh, I guess you guys are finished jumping for the night?" Taryn questioned.

With her arms wrapped loosely around Gerrick's neck, Hadley perked up. "You mean we can do that again?" she squealed.

"Of course you can. In fact, you can do it until the sun comes up if you like," Taryn answered.

The twin sisters shared a wild look and quickly dismounted from the boys' backs. Grabbing hold of each other's hands, they quickly started directing everyone to form another human link.

Taryn stood watching while snuggling her back against Larkin's muscular chest. It pleased her to see the shared excitement amongst the group. With their eagerness on full display, she felt she should not keep them waiting a moment longer.

Stepping in front of the line, she looked at each of their faces. Their brilliant smiles warmed her heart. "Do any of you recall the sensation that surrounded you while jumping from the previous ledge?" she asked.

Eben shook his head while looking to the ground. "To be perfectly honest, Taryn, none of us are able to do the things you do. So when you said we were jumping together, I pretty much lost my mind."

Several heads bobbed in agreement.

"Okay then, this time I need for you to pay close attention to what it is you are feeling." She paused, holding her hand palm out in their direction. Exhaling slightly, she forced her gift of Imperium around their bodies from the hips down.

Kellan's eyes widened, as did Gerrick's smile while feeling her gifts encompassing them. Her power flooded their cells on a level unlike anything they had ever felt before.

"Wow, Kansas, is this what you feel like all the time?" Gerrick asked.

She shrugged. "And more."

With one slight press of his left foot into the earth's surface, Kellan launched himself several feet into the air. "This is incredible," he howled while coming back down.

Taryn steadied him as he touched back down on the ground. "I suppose we should do a few jumps together as a group before I let you go off on your own," she chuckled.

"Being Skin-Walkers, we have the ability to jump a significant distance, but nothing like what this will allow us to do. You sharing your gifts with us is so generous, but the sensation is something I cannot mentally grasp," Kellan stated with a strange grin.

"Even if we will never wear a shared symbol, it doesn't change how I feel about any of you. You are my family, and I love and care for you all so very deeply. No ink will ever change that." She paused, looking to Andyn. "Our familial bond is too great for anything or anyone to come between us. Remember that little brother."

ဢႵ

Having made several jumps as a group, Taryn released Andyn's hand halfway to their current destination. With Larkin's hand still secured in her own, she pulled back, creating a field beneath their feet as they watched the others land safely below.

When Keiryn looked to the sky for the pair, Taryn pushed her gift of Influence onto him.

Filled with an unwavering desire to continue jumping the Grand Canyon's numerous valleys and crevices, Keiryn instructed the others to follow.

Wrapping her arms around Larkin's neck, Taryn used her gifts to propel them even higher. The pair soared toward the clouds. The illuminating lightning formed a circle, allowing them to pass thru unscathed.

Miles above the earth, Taryn pressed her lips against Larkin's, sending them into a free fall.

Trusting her with his life, Larkin closed his eyes, kissing her back.

Taryn pulled away from her great love. With a sparkle in her eyes, she released her hold on him, allowing them both to fall independently.

With an elated howl, Larkin flipped backwards several times before steadying himself again and giving Taryn two thumbs up.

Raising her arms above her head, she clasped her hands together. Giving him a wink, she plummeted rapidly downward in a spiral, leaving a sapphire blue trail of energy in her wake.

Not wanting to fall too far behind, Larkin leaned forward and followed headfirst after her. Chasing her blue trail that pierced the inky darkness of the night sky, he saw her resting just above a white cloud. Lost in her beauty and the ethereal glow surrounding her, he did nothing to slow himself as he continued to fall directly toward her.

As Larkin neared, Taryn's smile widened. His body stalled, hovering close to three feet above hers.

Staring down, he took in every inch of her face. Eyes the color of emeralds looked back at him. Her skin was flawless, her lips, the perfect shade of pink. Topping off this vision of perfection was her honey colored tresses, floating weightlessly about her head.

Beyond her external beauty, Larkin could see deep within her eyes. Those softly shimmering emeralds were the doorway to Taryn's soul. Within them, he found the warmth of a thousand suns radiating love, care and compassion for all living things. She was more than special, she was truly a gift to their kind and above all, she was in love with him.

Reaching down, Larkin caressed her cheek. "Why me?" he asked.

Taryn placed her hand over his, pressing it against her flesh. Her lips curled with a warm smile. "Fate knew that I would need somebody who was strong. Not only physically, but also mentally fit to keep me grounded in this life. Someone, who could anchor me in reality and make wherever we were together the place I could call home," she paused, admiring his handsome face. "Destiny may have bound us, Larkin, but it's the love in our hearts that we feel for one another that makes this work. Your beautiful heart is forever intertwined with mine."

Pulling her floating frame to his, Larkin pressed his lips heavily against hers. His heart overflowed with love and peace knowing she would never love another in the same way that she loved him.

CHAPTER FIVE

Early the next morning, Taryn and Larkin headed back to join the others at the campsite. Upon their approach, Larkin noticed that everyone was already awake and they all wore the most ridiculous of grins.

"What's up with them?" he asked.

Taryn smiled. "It's finally happened. They bear the mark of a true pack."

Larkin stopped dead in his tracks. "Seriously?"

Taryn nodded as she headed in Keiryn's direction.

When her brother saw her, he ran to her in a blur, wrapping his arms around her. "Something incredible has happened, Taryn." He paused, releasing her. "While we were out jumping the canyon, the marks started appearing. First Jonesy, then Nalani and then everyone else...it was amazing."

She smiled up at Keiryn. "Are you going to show me your ink, or what?"

Pulling the backside of his light blue t-shirt up, Keiryn turned, exposing the newly placed symbol on his right shoulder. "It feels better than I ever imagined it would," he beamed.

Taryn lifted her hand to the dark ink and began tracing its outline with her index finger. The symbol was a perfect circle containing a merged image that was a mixture of one-half falcon and one-half phoenix. Patches of dragon scales were located at the bottom of the circle, tapering as her eye moved upward until they disappeared behind the mixed bird. Fire rose from its wings to the top of circle. On one side of the bird was a tornado with lightning striking through it and on the other a husky wolf standing atop vines.

Tears welled in her eyes. "It's perfect, Keiryn."

Pulling his shirt back down, Keiryn turned around. "Taryn, if you're having second thoughts…"

Swiping away the tears, she smiled proudly. "Absolutely not. I'm so proud of you…all of you." She looked to her younger brother, then to Larkin who was staring strangely in Kellan's direction, before returning her gaze to Keiryn. "Larkin and I have somewhere we need to be, but you guys should take the day and celebrate."

Keiryn reached out, taking her hand in his. "Taryn…"

Gently pulling away, she smiled softly. "Lazryn will be here shortly with breakfast. Just let him know if there is anything else you need."

⌘⌘⌘⌘

After running for more than two hours, Larkin suddenly stopped and released a lengthy howl.

Circling back around, Taryn joined him.

Silence hung heavy in the air for several long moments before Larkin made eye contact with her. "I guess this is the new normal, huh?"

Moving closer, Taryn flashed a soft smile. "Are you having second thoughts?"

His hazel eyes warmed. "Are you asking if I have any regrets about my decision to let Kellan, Gerrick and the others go with Keiryn?"

She shrugged. "Since you were twelve you planned for them to be part of your pack, and now they're with Keiryn."

Larkin slipped an arm around her waist, pulling her close. His eyes scanned her face before locking on her sparkling emeralds. The fingers on his free hand traced along her cheek down to her neck. Leaning down, he placed the softest kisses upon her lips. "I have you." He kissed her again. "And you are everything I want and need."

Taryn smiled. "I know."

Rolling his eyes, Larkin chuckled, then kissed her forehead and hugged her tightly.

ᛒᛟᚷᛒᛟᚷ

Pacing back and forth on the side of the in ground pool, Blayne mumbled to himself.

"How is your father doing?" Julius inquired while taking a seat in a nearby lounge chair.

"He and my brother are in Brazil visiting some old friends," the young man replied.

Julius nodded to the seat to his right. "You've been out here for the past two hours. Why don't you sit for a moment?"

Shaking his head, Blayne continued pacing.

Leaning forward in his seat, Julius studied the young man. "You do realize that I have known you since you were an infant, and I have never seen you appear more anxious than you do in this very moment."

"I need to speak with Taryn, that is all," he responded blankly.

"Did something happen on one of the planes?" Julius inquired.

Blayne abruptly halted his step. "I no longer answer to the Council or its members, current or past. I am here to speak with Taryn, and that is all you need to know."

"You would do well to remember that I am not your enemy, and that Taryn is my niece," Julius countered sternly while rising to his feet.

"Gentlemen, do we have a problem?" Lazryn interrupted.

"I need to speak with Taryn, that is all," Blayne responded.

Approaching the young man, Lazryn sniffed the air. Noticing a familiar scent lingering on the man's clothing, he paused. "So it would appear you do."

Blayne nodded, before resuming his pacing.

Lazryn approached Julius. "As a favor to Taryn, I am asking that you let him wait alone until he has the opportunity to speak with her."

Julius' lip curled. "As a favor to my dear niece, I will do as you requested." Turning to walk away, he paused. "What exactly is it you plan to do?"

"I'm going to find Taryn," Lazryn answered before disappearing into the woods.

ΒΟ ΘΒΟΘ

Sitting at the kitchen table of Larkin's childhood home, Taryn and Ilya drank tea and chatted while Larkin and Maxym sat on the deck.

"In the end it was Keiryn who became the true pack leader?" Maxym mused.

Larkin nodded.

"To be honest, Son, I'm surprised it wasn't Taryn. All of us parents were certain she would be the one," Maxym stated.

Rising, Larkin stretched before running his fingers through his hair. "Taryn became Andyn's leader out of necessity to save his life. She's always thinking of everyone else. Doing for everyone else. In the end, it was her decision to give Keiryn the pack." He paused, glancing toward the screen door. "I'm glad she did."

Maxym shifted in his seat. "And you're not the slightest bit jealous that she chose her brother to lead the others instead of you?"

Larkin smiled wildly. "Keiryn may get to lead the others, but I get to kiss his sister whenever I want."

His father chuckled. "You really do have it bad for that girl."

"So bad," Larkin admitted, looking once more to the screen door. Behind the tightly woven mesh, he watched Taryn's beautiful face. It was soft and light as she and Ilya talked. Suddenly his eyes turned black as night. Spinning around, he found Lazryn standing there. His jaw was ridged and his brows furrowed.

The screen door creaked opened. "What is it?" Taryn questioned.

"Blayne is waiting at your home and he has a message that may only be shared with you, Taryn," Lazryn answered.

In a blur, she was gone.

"At least we know where she is headed," Ilya stated.

Opening an Adora Gateway, Lazryn hoped to leave with the others and return to Taryn's home ahead of the girl.

Arriving a split second before her, Larkin witnessed Taryn's eyes grow hollow as she exited the tree line and headed toward Blayne. "What is it? What are you sensing, Taryn?"

Moving past Larkin without a glance, she touched Blayne's temple. After a brief moment, her cheeks flushed. "Open the gateway, Blayne."

"How can he still be alive?" Blayne questioned.

Taryn shook her head. "I took away their ability to feed on the blood of others. I knew it would take years, if not decades, for him and his Mortari followers to turn to ash."

Stepping forward, Larkin's brows furrowed. "You're talking about Dagrin?"

Nodding in his direction, Taryn frowned. "He's holding Blayne's father and brother hostage until I meet with him." Pausing, she looked to Lazryn. "You should stay here with the others."

He shook his head. "Dagrin is meticulous in his planning. He is far more cunning than what he or Coyan allowed you to believe the first time you met. You must allow me to accompany you. I can be…"

Taryn interrupted. "Lazryn, he's in the rain forest."

The man's shoulders slumped. "Then I do not need to warn you how deadly he and his followers can be."

Larkin stepped between the pair. "What exactly happened in the rain forest?"

Taryn stared with empty eyes in Lazryn's direction. "Dagrin got even with me for embarrassing him in front of the Brothers C the first time we met," she answered.

"What did he do?" Larkin questioned.

Silence filled the air.

The teen sighed loudly. "So I'm assuming it was pretty horrible, whatever he did…"

Shifting her eyes to his, Taryn nodded. "Dagrin, his followers and the Necro-Walkers decimated an entire tribe while I watched."

"Dearest Taryn, you own no part in their deaths," Lazryn stated, with a weighted gaze.

Taryn moved faster than a flicker to stand before the man. She placed her hand on his cheek and began to caress it softly. "Nor do you, my friend."

Larkin remained silent as he took in their private exchange. It was obvious there was something more to the story, but he knew now was not the time to press for details. He glanced at Blayne, then back to Taryn. "Will Lazryn be joining us?"

With her eyes locked on Lazryn's, Taryn nodded. "Before we leave, we need to see if Ibrym can spare a few of his pack members to watch over our family here at home."

ဆဝ၆၃ဆဝ၆၃

With her family back in Williams protected by their California friends, Taryn inhaled deeply as she walked through the gateway. The scent of death permeated her senses, causing her to recoil, but only slightly. Memories of the first time she had set foot there flooded her mind.

Larkin glanced upward at the canopy of thick tree branches overhead. He could not help but notice how the thick foliage blocked out nearly all of the sunlight in area. Leaning forward, he placed his hand on the small of Taryn's back. "You okay?" he whispered.

Pausing her step, she gave him a nod.

The small group walked only a short distance from where the gateway had been before hearing a dark chuckle. The eeriness of it rumbled through the dimly lit forest, filling the air between them and the canopy of tree branches above.

"Show yourself, Dagrin," Taryn stated.

Silence followed.

After several moments passed in deathly stillness, Taryn motioned for the others to hold their positions. Taking a few steps forward, she glanced up at the one ray of sunlight piercing through the branches above. It was an insignificant amount of light. Still, it called out to her, as if a warning for what was to come next.

"You wanted to see me. Now I'm here and you're hiding..." she taunted. A wicked smile curled on her lips. "If I were you, I'd want to stay hidden away, too."

Dagrin's eerie laughter once more pierced the air.

Raising both arms to shoulder height, Taryn held her palms outward. "Enough of these games," she whispered. Her gifts snaked through the forest, poking into every crack and crevice in a half-mile radius.

Growls quickly filled the air.

"You and your followers...you're different than the last time I saw you," Taryn stated with an arched brow.

Appearing before her suddenly within the darkness, Dagrin smiled wickedly. "I'm truly flattered that you noticed, Taryn." His eyes scanned every inch of the teenaged girl before coming to rest on her face. "You are growing into such a stunning young woman." He paused, swallowing hard. "Your very scent makes my mouth water and my bones ache."

With eyes the color of night, Larkin stepped forward. Fangs protruded from behind his curled lips, while black claws extended from the end of each of his fingertips. "Back off," he growled at the Lessor-being.

Dagrin acknowledged the young man's existence with only a slight glance in the direction of his changing hands. Fixating his eyes once more on Taryn's tiny frame, he gave a seductive growl. "You're being uncharacteristically quiet, Taryn. Does the wolf have your tongue today?"

Sensing he was baiting her, Taryn remained silent. She thoroughly studied the vile man's exterior. When she last saw him, he had flawless dark skin and dark colored irises. Now, standing only feet away, his skin appeared to be even more flawless than before. *How is this possible?* she thought to herself. Her eyes met with his. Still an alluring shade of dark brown, she found flecks of golden shimmers within each.

Unable to pull her gaze away, she watched as the golden shimmers began to move in a clockwise direction. The deep brown color of his eyes gave way to a golden hue, mesmerizing her.

Larkin, Lazryn and Blayne watched curiously as she stepped closer to the devilish man.

She slowly raised her hand to touch his face. The instant her fingertip made contact, the warm golden color of his irises shattered, revealing a completely new color.

Taryn withdrew her touch. Her eyes remained locked on his. "Not brown. Not gold. Emerald…" she whispered inaudibly.

Lazryn moved, pulling her back by the arm. "You mustn't allow him to get inside your head," he whispered in her ear.

Shaking off the strange feeling stirring inside, Taryn glanced to Larkin. Worry marred his eyes, igniting a storm in the pit of her stomach.

"Bring Blayne's brother and father to us now," she demanded.

The man smiled. "There's no need to be hostile, my dear. I will bring your friends momentarily."

"No. You will bring them now," she countered.

Tilting his head from one side to the other and then back again, he paused. "The first time I laid eyes upon your angelic face, I knew there was more to you." He paused again, taking a step back. "Even while you hurled insults at me from behind the protection of Clad and Chrystian, I knew you did not require them to fight your battles."

"Bring my friends, now," she stated again.

Ignoring her, he continued. "Just as you do not need the help of any of these sub-species here with you now. And just as you did not need anyone's help the last time you stood in this very forest."

"Taryn, do not listen to him," Lazryn warned.

Dagrin turned, glaring in the older man's direction. "She will not heed the warnings from the man who forced her to watch while my pets and I made the world run with red?"

Larkin growled. "What's he talking about, Lazryn?"

"It would appear someone is keeping secrets," Dagrin chuckled in the direction of the wolf.

Raising the palm of her hand in the direction of the canopy, Taryn used her gifts to shift the branches. Thick rays of sunlight spilled thru, encircling Dagrin.

"This is your last chance. Either tell your minions to bring my friends now, or I will turn you to ash and still force them too anyway," Taryn warned.

Dagrin lowered his head. "Bring them forward," he called out.

Seconds later, two men appeared, bringing with them Nelmaryc and his son, Blayne's twin.

With a slight nod of his head, Dagrin dismissed the dark duo. "Satisfied?" he asked, locking eyes once more with the girl.

Sensing her friends were only frightened and not harmed, she stepped to the edge of the light surrounding Dagrin. "What did you expect to gain here?" she questioned.

Glancing around the forest, he arched a brow. "So much has changed since we last saw one another. You bestowed a wicked little gift upon my kind and our pets."

Larkin glared at the man. "You deserved far worse for what you have done."

Narrowing his eyes on the girl, Dagrin continued. "As I was saying before being so rudely interrupted...much has changed."

"Yes, things have changed," Taryn echoed.

A devilish smirk formed on Dagrin's face. "Do you fear me, Taryn?"

"No," she answered flatly.

"Are you certain you do not fear me?" he asked again.

Taryn stepped into the light surrounding him. "Positive," she stated, her tone ice cold.

Dagrin glanced to Larkin, then back to Taryn. "What about now?" he asked, reaching into the sunlight and stroking her cheek.

Her eyes locked with his as she absorbed every sensation produced by his touch. Even with all that she felt, it did not escape her that the sunlight was having zero effect on the man.

In werewolf form, Larkin moved in a blur to Taryn's side. Grabbing Dagrin, the young man dug his claws into the Lessor's arm.

With his eyes still fixated on the girl, Dagrin reached over, digging his own nails into the wolf's arm.

"Do you still remain unafraid, dearest Taryn?" he asked. His mouth fell into a soft smile before disappearing into the air, leaving nothing but the hollow sound of his laughter lingering amongst the forest.

A few seconds passed before Taryn turned her attention to Larkin. Grabbing his bleeding arm, she caused him to shift back into human form. "You shouldn't have interfered," she stated plainly, studying the small, but deep gashes.

"What did you expect me to do, Taryn?" he questioned with a frown.

Placing her palm over the wounds, she quickly healed his injuries. "Nothing. You should have done nothing."

Larkin's lower jaw jutted forward and his nostrils flared.

Stepping forward, Lazryn placed a calming hand on both teens. "Do not be upset, Taryn. There was no way for your wolf to know the darkness of Dagrin's intentions."

Taryn glanced blankly at the man's hand. He cautiously withdrew his touch from her shoulder. "Blayne, I need for you to take your father and brother home." She paused, glancing to her old friend and Blayne's twin. "I am truly sorry that Dagrin used you to get to me."

The older man nodded, before creating an Adora gateway. He and both sons quickly disappeared inside.

With the woods to themselves, Larkin turned, shoving Lazryn. "What the hell was that demon talking about?"

Lazryn straightened himself while glancing to Taryn. "You should have told him."

Before she could speak, Larkin charged the man, pinning him by the neck against one of the narrow trees. "Don't you dare put this on her. He was talking about you and what you forced her to do," Larkin growled through bared teeth.

"Enough," Taryn sighed.

Larkin suddenly felt his rage washing from his body. His hand fell limp from the man's throat.

"What happened was not his fault, Larkin." She paused, gazing at the branches overhead. "Lazryn was Influenced to do the things he did that night."

Larkin turned his attention to the man. "You were there while they tore people to shreds?"

Bowing his head in shame, Lazryn exhaled. "The night in question, yes, it was I who forced her to watch."

Heated tears swelled in Larkin's eyes. "There was a village here...a village Dagrin and his Necro-Walkers destroyed." He paused, glancing to Taryn. "This is why you focused your rage on him when you were losing control."

Taryn nodded slightly.

"But you forgive him now?" Larkin questioned.

"What I experienced at the hands of the Mortari, it was never his fault. He became my friend under the worst of circumstances, and I forgave him as he has forgiven me," Taryn replied.

"So that's it…there isn't anything more to be said on the subject?" Larkin pressed.

In a blur, Taryn appeared in front of him. Her hand stroked his cheek softly. "You cannot own this pain or the memories that accompany it, Larkin. I, alone, have come to terms with the events that transpired here. Lazryn has come to terms with the part he played in it. And you should keep in mind that not all Mortari are monsters, just as not all Gaias are good natured."

"What hurts you hurts me, too," he whispered, while pulling her flush against his chest. Stroking the length of her hair, he sighed.

ಬಿ಄ಬಿ಄

Sitting on a bar stool at the kitchen island, Taryn drummed her fingertips across its surface.

"Could it be a mutation?" Ibrym questioned.

Taryn shook her head. "The moment I sensed his presence on Blayne, I knew something was different about him." She paused, glancing across to Larkin's forearm. "The sunlight and Larkin's claws had zero effect on him. His followers have changed too, but it is nowhere near the same level as Dagrin's evolution. Sort of like a work in progress."

Silence lingered briefly in the air.

"If Larkin's claws had no effect on him, then what are we to do should they attack?" Alderyc asked.

"I know Dagrin well," Lazryn commented. "Whatever he was after, he most certainly acquired prior to his departure."

"He wanted Taryn to fear him, but she never did," Larkin countered.

Taryn sat quietly for a moment, glancing occasionally between Larkin and Lazryn. Rising from the bar stool, Taryn's eyes stopped on her love's face. "It was you he was after the entire time."

"What are you talking about?" Larkin questioned.

Taryn rushed over to the opposite side of the island where he stood. "He wanted you to fear for me. You responded by revealing your most dangerous self." She paused, taking time to look him over more closely. "Show me your arms, Larkin."

He quickly lifted both into her view.

"No, your other arms," she insisted.

With a weighted sigh, Larkin allowed everything from his elbows down to take werewolf form.

After a brief look, Taryn's jaw drew up tight. "Not only does he have your blood, but he has a tuft of your fur and broken bits from your claws."

Larkin's eyes widened as he looked down at the bare patch on his wolf arm.

"You could not have known this was his intentions," Lazryn stated.

"What is he going to do with it? Make some sort of voodoo doll?" Alderyc mused.

"Don't be ridiculous. There's no such thing as voodoo," Ibrym countered.

"Well he clearly intended to use me for something," Larkin growled, slamming the palm of his hands against the top of the island.

Having been listening from the hallway with Maxym and Gastyn, Theron moved to stand just inside the kitchen. He watched his daughter who remained silent amongst the growing unrest. Her face was stone cold and her green eyes full of turbulence. "Taryn," he whispered.

Her eyes instantly found him. A soft smile flashed on her face. "Dad," she whispered back.

The moment he blinked, the sweet image of his little girl had disappeared. She was now holding Lazryn's hand with a curious look upon her face.

"Coyan banned Dagrin and the others when he no longer found them to be useful…" she mused, still holding onto his hand.

Lazryn nodded. "Coyan insisted whatever curse you had placed upon Dagrin's army would spread to all Mortari. He banned the Lessors from Mors shortly after the first wave of Necro-Walkers turned to ash."

"And you have no idea where they went?" she questioned.

"I searched for them, but it was as if they had disappeared into nothingness," Lazryn replied.

Releasing his hand, Taryn moved to the living room where she stopped at her favorite spot. In front of the large window, she gazed beyond the tree line.

The others trickled into the room, sharing glances as they took a seat.

Larkin joined her at the window, wrapping an arm around her waist. "Care to share your thoughts?" he whispered.

She smiled. "You're not going to like them."

Leaning down, he kissed the top of her head and sighed. "Of course I won't."

Turning her head, Taryn's eyes met with Larkin's. "I need to go to Mors."

He stepped back, running his fingers through his hair. "You want to talk to him, don't you?"

"You know I do. You also know why," she retorted.

Moving closer, Larkin leaned down. "You say it's because of the warning in the letter he wrote you. The letter that neither Lazryn, nor myself, found to be the slightest bit alarming."

Hearing the unspoken accusation within his tone, Taryn shook her head. "You know I don't want him, right?"

Larkin shrugged. "It's hard not to think that on some level you might. You've spent every day since he sent Lazryn to you looking for him." He paused, taking a deep breath. "Considering the number of times you've jumped out of the Jeep while it was still in motion, it's difficult to come to any other conclusion."

Taryn reached up, caressing his cheek. "I know you think he's evil, and after the thing that happened in the woods…"

"He kissed you, Taryn." Larkin growled, his eyes turning black as night, catching the attention of the others.

Theron moved to join them. "She may be more than capable of handling herself, Larkin, but I recommend you take a step back. I will not permit you to speak to my daughter in such a manner."

Taryn rolled her eyes. "Thanks, Dad, but I have this."

He squared his shoulders with hers. "You're not off the hook either, young lady. Do I even want to know who Larkin was talking about that kissed you?"

Pursing her lips together, she sighed. "Unless you want to be scarred for life, I would say no. You definitely don't want to know."

Theron glanced to Larkin. "Would you care to enlighten the rest of us as to who has you so upset?"

"No. Not particularly," he answered.

"Has this mystery person kissed her since?" Theron inquired.

Taryn pushed past both men. "This conversation ends now."

Maxym looked to his son. "Are you good?"

Larkin shrugged.

"Seriously, this is no one's business." Taryn huffed.

Walking in the French doors, Keiryn grinned. "What's no one's business?" he asked.

"Your sister kissed someone other than Larkin," Alderyc answered.

Lightning crackled across the sky as thunder boomed, rattling the house.

"I did not kiss, Chrystian," she hissed.

Everyone but Lazryn's face wrinkled with some form of disgust.

"And I thought Larkin was a questionable choice," Keiryn chuckled, taking a seat beside his buddy Alderyc.

Another boom of thunder shook the house and the sky lit with intense blue colored lightning.

Larkin rushed to Taryn, wrapping her in his arms. "I'm sorry, Taryn. I shouldn't have said anything."

Stepping between Maxym and Theron, Lazryn attempted to convey the depths of his friend's feelings for the girl. "When Chrystian looks at Taryn, he has come to see his dead wife, Loryn. You see, she was my sister, and Chrystian was madly in love with her." He paused, glancing to Taryn. "He wasn't always a monster."

Taryn gently pushed away from Larkin. "I know you don't like it, but I need to speak with him."

"Lazryn said Coyan banished the Lessors. What could Chrystian possibly know?" Larkin sighed with pleading eyes.

"I think he knows something," Keiryn stated.

Larkin turned, scowling at him. "What makes you so sure?"

Keiryn rose from the couch. "Because there's a man standing in the tree line that looks a lot like his picture from our history books."

Larkin's eyes panned to Taryn. "You knew he was there...didn't you?"

Biting her lip, Taryn shrugged. "He arrived when Lazryn was talking."

With a frosty glare, Larkin looked in the former Mortari's direction. "I suppose you knew he was there, too?"

The man nodded.

His eyes turned back to Taryn. "And you're stopping the Affliction within Ibrym, Alderyc and myself?"

"The very fact that he's here without any contact from us should be an indicator that something's wrong," Taryn reasoned.

Larkin reached up, cupping her cheeks. "Tare-Bear, I don't want to fight."

"Then don't," she responded with a soft smile. Pressing up on her toes, she kissed his cheek, then disappeared in a blur out the French doors.

While Larkin and Lazryn trailed quickly behind her, the others began lining up in front of the large windows. They kept watch as Chrystian stepped from the tree line and approached Taryn.

CHAPTER SIX

Watching as Chrystian stepped closer, Taryn swallowed hard. Even though his face was cold and stony, her heart warmed at the mere sight of him.

Taking a step toward him, she gave a faint smile. "Hello, Chrystian."

With a slight nod, he replied, "Hello, Taryn." His eyes drifted to his old friend. "Lazryn," he stated with another slight nod. Shifting his focus to Larkin, he gave a quiet growl. "Wolf."

"Did you come here to pick a fight with my boyfriend, or is there something else you would like to discuss?" Taryn inquired.

Titling his head to one side, Chrystian gazed upon her face. A slight smile curled from his lips. "Why not both?" he purred.

Larkin rushed forward, only to find himself halted after a few steps by Taryn's Influence. His will to do anything other than stand still left his body.

Taryn's eyes hardened. "It's moments like this that destroy my credibility when I insist that you are not a monster."

"Your insistence is precious, Taryn, but we both know it is more for your benefit than mine." He paused, moving to stand toe-to-toe with her. "For your own sanity you must believe there is good within me. Otherwise, how could you ever live with yourself knowing that you are in love with me?"

The girl began to laugh. "Me, in love with you?" she retorted.

Tilting his head to the other side, Chrystian smiled wildly. "You certainly have made this life far more interesting, my sweet, sweet, girl," he purred.

In a flash, Chrystian moved, grabbing hold of Taryn by the throat and hair.

Lazryn wanted desperately to intervene, but found himself rooted where he stood. Inside her home, her friends and family beat against the doors and windows, trying to break free.

Glancing at his father, Keiryn growled. "It's no use, Taryn's put up a shield to keep us inside the house."

Taryn stared into the man's eyes. They appeared more bronze than before. "Do you feel powerful now?" she questioned, placing her hand on his forearm.

He smiled down on her, jerking her head into an awkward angle. He whispered in the girl's ear, "It is *my right* to love you always, Loryn, no matter the vessel you choose to inhabit." He paused, stroking his thumb along her neck, before whispering again. "Remember, we are always watching."

Moving her head into a neutral position, Chrystian removed his hand from her throat. He pulled her tiny frame flush against his, hugging her tightly. He locked eyes with Larkin. "She should be mine," he taunted.

"Never," the teen growled.

Chrystian glanced to Lazryn and winked before pressing his lips against Taryn's mouth.

The moment his lips touched hers, a flash of white light formed between the pair, sending Chrystian flying thru the air, crashing into a nearby tree.

"Don't ever come back here, Chrystian. You are no longer welcome," Taryn seethed behind clenched teeth.

Rising to his feet, Chrystian dusted himself off. "One day your wolf will die and you will seek me out."

"I am with Larkin. I will always be with Larkin. He is my one and only love," Taryn replied.

"You wield such power, yet remain naive. He is but a mere boy, a rabid wolf...barely a step above those filthy humans whom you choose to breathe the same air as. Mark my words, dearest Taryn, one day, you will choose me," Chrystian spat with venom dripping from each word.

Taryn released Lazryn from her Influence. Her friend rushed toward Chrystian with fire in his eyes. As he neared his old friend, an Adora Gateway opened and from within stepped Clad, Coyan and Tedra.

Coyan instantly subdued the approaching man with his own Influence. Lazryn stood like stone, though he cried out in agony.

Taryn waved her hand, undoing the eldest Mortari's gift. Her eyes narrowed on Coyan. "You are no more welcome here than your deranged, lunatic of a brother," she growled.

Lightning rained down from the sky, striking only inches from Taryn.

A dark gleam formed in Tedra's eyes, watching as the teen did not flinch during the nearly two minute bombardment of deadly power.

Coyan motioned for the woman to cease her attack. She did as directed, never dropping her curious gaze from the girl.

"You either have a death-wish, or your hate for us blinds you to authentic danger," Coyan stated coolly.

Without a word, Taryn lifted her hands, palm up, to waist height. A sparkle formed in her eyes as she forced her gifts out, surrounding the Mortari. One corner of her mouth curled upward. "Do you feel that?" she asked.

Coyan swallowed hard while Clad's eyes widened with desire.

"Yes. I want to taste it so badly," the youngest brother exhaled.

Lazryn stepped back, joining Taryn and a now free Larkin. "This is not who you are, Taryn," Lazryn whispered in her ear.

"Maybe it's not right now, but it very easily could be," she growled, drawing in closer to the brothers and their companion.

"Back off, Taryn," Larkin warned.

"Not before I make myself abundantly clear," she replied, now standing toe-to-toe with Coyan. "If I ever lay eyes upon any of your faces again, it will be the moment before you take your final breath."

"You wouldn't," Coyan dared.

Taryn smiled wildly, baring her teeth. She glanced to his brothers, then to his wife, before focusing back on him. "For you, dearest Coyan, I most certainly would."

Sharing a final glance with Chrystian, Taryn turned her back to the destructive foursome. Withdrawing her gifts, she waited for all traces of their power to disappear behind her.

ജഇജഇ

As Taryn, Larkin and Lazryn walked back to the house, Theron and the others rushed outside.

The frown upon her father and Keiryn's faces spoke volumes to their displeasure. Before either could utter a word, she raised her hand. "Not now," she cautioned.

"You are my daughter, Taryn. Do not ever shut me out like that again," Theron scolded.

She stopped in her tracks. "Is that all?" she asked, glancing behind him to where her mother now stood.

"What happened here?" Gracyn demanded, glancing between her children and their father. "Ilya, Jayma and I have been trapped for the past thirty minutes in Ilya's SUV at the entrance to the driveway."

Taryn sighed. "I'm sorry, but I needed to make sure everyone was safe."

Gracyn stood with her jaw agape while Ilya moved to Taryn. "And who is keeping you safe?" Ilya demanded.

Tilting her head slightly, Taryn smiled, looking over her shoulder at her love. "He is," she answered, before disappearing inside the house.

೮ಬಅಉಇಬ

Standing at her bedroom window with a piece of parchment in hand, Taryn waited for Larkin to join her.

Several long moments passed before he entered the bedroom and closed the door behind him. Walking over, he took a seat on the edge of bed. His cheeks were bright red and sweat beaded across his forehead.

"You're mad about earlier," Taryn stated.

With a heavy sigh, he ran his fingers through his hair. "Seriously, Taryn, mad doesn't even begin to touch on what I'm feeling right now." He paused, clenching his hands into fists. "Everyone just reamed me for not telling them that Chrystian had kissed you. Then when I thought they were about finished, they reamed me for letting him kiss you today. Especially after your proclamation that I am the one who protects you."

"It's fear. It makes people lash out so they feel more like they're in control, regardless of whom it targets," she replied.

Sighing, he rose to his feet. "You live without fear. Yet, you understand it better than anyone else I know."

Taryn furrowed her brows. "My fear wanted to feast upon every living thing. It hungered for absolute destruction. When it combined with my rage, it was meant to be unstoppable."

Wrapping his arms around her waist, he pulled her in close. "But you did stop them. No matter the risk to yourself, you silenced them both. You kept them from harming a single soul."

"But they did cause harm," Taryn sighed, pushing back.

Larkin held onto her tightly, shaking his head. "We need to talk about what happened earlier." He paused, exhaling deeply. "You could have stopped Chrystian at any time, but for whatever reason, you chose to let him kiss you, again."

Taryn opened her mouth to speak, but Larkin was not finished.

"I don't want you to tell me that you don't have feelings for him, Taryn. I mean, seriously…your eyes light up every time you see him," Larkin stated.

"Are you finished?" she questioned.

Releasing his hold on her, Larkin shrugged, taking a seat once more on her bed.

Taryn turned, looking out the window to the woods. "I know when you look at Chrystian all you see is a monster." She paused, turning and leaning her back against the window frame. "Through Loryn's eyes, I have seen the beauty of his love. I have felt the warmth of his care and the depth of his compassion. There isn't anything he wouldn't do for those he loves." She paused again, stepping closer to Larkin. "I have also felt the wrath brought on by the pain and suffering he has endured for more than a millennium due to the loss of his wife and the betrayal by his friend."

Larkin leaned back, propping himself up on his elbows. "But you're not Loryn," he growled. "You didn't have anything to do with his friend betraying him either."

Tilting her head to the side, she smiled. "You're right, on both accounts. I am not his dead wife, and I am not the one who deceived him."

"Then why are you smiling?" Larkin asked, rolling his eyes.

Taryn crawled up on the bed, straddling her love. "I know you don't like to hear this, but regardless of the things Chrystian says or does, he is my friend."

"You do realize that your friend tried sticking his tongue down your throat only an hour ago, right?" Larkin grumbled.

Leaning down, Taryn bestowed a passionate kiss upon Larkin's lips. When she pulled away, she held up the piece of parchment.

With an arched brow, he cocked his head. "What's that?" he asked.

Taryn smiled again. "This is the reason Chrystian kissed me."

Larkin snatched the paper from her hand and began reading it aloud. "My Dearest Taryn. You have been looking pale in recent weeks. I suggest basking in the sun poolside, or perhaps a walk through the garden. How I miss the rosy glow upon your cheeks when you smile. My blackened heart aches in the absence of your angelic radiance." Larkin paused, making a gagging sound, eliciting a roll of the eyes from Taryn. "Signed, lovingly, Chrystian." Larkin paused again, wrinkling his face. "Well, I guess there goes my appetite for the rest of my life."

Rolling off to the side, Taryn shook her head. "You still don't get it, do you?"

Larkin rose to his feet. "Of course I do. My girlfriend is like crack to thousand-year-old soul suckers. None of them seem to be able to live without you," he bit, glancing to the door where Lazryn now stood.

With a loud sigh, Taryn grabbed the paper from his hand, walking it over to her friend. "Would you please read this and tell me what you think Chrystian is trying to tell us?"

Lazryn took the parchment and quickly read over the words. "Chrystian has hidden something of value and he wants Taryn to retrieve it," he answered plainly, handing the paper back to her.

Taryn noted the weight in Lazryn's gaze before focusing her attention back on Larkin. "Chrystian wasn't here trying to cause trouble. He was warning me that they have been watching us. And the only way he could slip me the note without being obvious about it was to pretend that he had come for me."

"He kissed you, Taryn," Larkin growled. "You can't seriously believe that he doesn't want you after everything he's said and done."

Looking to Lazryn, Taryn silently pleaded for him to back her stance.

"I have known Chrystian for more than a thousand years, Taryn, and your Larkin is correct. Though Chrystian still loves my dead sister, that love does not diminish his desire to possess your heart, too." He paused, walking to the window, glancing to Larkin before looking out toward the woods. "While I agree that Taryn should never have allowed Chrystian to kiss her, I believe we have a much larger problem on our hands."

Taryn arched her brow and questioned, "And exactly what would that be?"

"Tedra," he replied.

Shaking her head, Taryn chuckled. "Sorry, but I'm not going to concern myself with Coyan's wife."

The edges of Lazryn's mouth turned downward. "I see the change in you, Taryn, and I am most certain others do as well."

Taryn eyed her dear friend and stepped toward him. "Am I not allowed to transform or progress as I age?"

He shook his head. "Little by little, the cracks in your armor are being exposed. When Tedra unleashed lightning only inches from you, you did not even flinch."

With a flick of her wrist, a deafening boom of thunder sounded overhead, shaking the house.

Larkin rose to his feet, holding his hand out to Taryn.

"Do not touch me," she warned, glancing to him then back to Lazryn. "Because I do not cower in fear when threatened, you think that is a sign of weakness?"

"None of us are safe from the lightning's purest power, Taryn. Not even you. If it strikes you, it will drain your gifts and you will die," Lazryn asserted.

A strange smile curled on Taryn's face. "Fear, rage, greed, jealousy and hate no longer reside within me. I destroyed the cruelest parts of myself, to ensure that you and everyone else could survive." She paused, tilting her head. "You should have more faith in me, Lazryn. I am not blind to the influence Tedra wields over Coyan, nor am I ignorant to the fact that her gifts are truly exceptional." She paused again, this time reaching up and running her fingertips of one hand above his brow, then down his cheek. "Besides, it would appear that you fear her enough for the both of us."

Lazryn reached up, grabbing her wrist. "Do not underestimate the secrets of the unknown, Taryn," he warned.

The pair shared a heated glare until Larkin's growl pierced the air around them. Lazryn released the girl's wrist and took a step back.

Taryn's eyes softened as she glanced to Larkin. "Are you up for a visit to Hypatia?" she asked.

Rolling his eyes, he sighed. "When do we leave?"

৪০৫৪৩৪০৫৪৩

Walking thru the garden on Hypatia, Taryn closed her eyes while running her fingertips over the various plants and flowers. Stopping, she inhaled deeply, gently caressing the silky petals of a soft pink rose.

Taryn opened her eyes. "Rosy cheeks when I smile," she stated, glancing to Larkin. Turning her head, she saw the deep purple colored Bleeding Hearts bush on the opposing walkway. Once again, she gazed upon Larkin. "His blackened heart aches," she smiled.

Rolling his eyes, Larkin shrugged. "Okay, so maybe you were right. Maybe the monster's intentions weren't exactly what I thought they were." He paused, looking around. "But I still don't see whatever he's hidden."

Taryn shook her head, lacing her fingers with his. "If it were easily visible, it wouldn't be hidden, now would it?" she smiled.

He smiled back. "I guess not."

Pressing up on her toes, Taryn placed a tender kiss on her love's lips.

"What was that for?" he asked.

With softened eyes, Taryn gazed heavily upon him. "Because I enjoy kissing you," she replied.

Larkin wrapped his arms around her waist, lifting her lips near his. "I enjoy kissing you, too," he replied, before crushing his lips against hers.

Waiting in the area between the magnificent garden and the woods, Lazryn turned away, giving the young couple a few minutes of privacy.

After several moments passed, Taryn slowly pushed back from Larkin. Sadness and pain radiated within her green irises. "One day we won't have to steal away moments like these. They will be ours for the taking, and it will be something truly beautiful," she whispered, before pressing her lips to his once more.

Seconds later, a shrill voice pierced the air.

"You are trespassing in my private garden," Nodryck shouted from near the castle.

Larkin gently placed Taryn's feet on the ground. "Great. Another one of my favorite people," he sighed.

"Don't worry. He won't be bothering us for long," Taryn smiled, sliding her arm around his waist.

Nodryck and several of his followers marched toward them. The man's dark brows were furrowed, and his mouth turned downward in a deep frown. "You have no right coming here, Taryn Malone," Nodryck seethed.

"It's Knight," she corrected.

"Oh yes, the Knight family reunion," Nodryck jeered. A dark smile curled on his face.

Larkin wrapped his arm around Taryn's shoulders. "He's going to try to bait you," he whispered.

"I know," she replied.

Pressing his opposing fingertips against one another, Nodryck stared at the girl. "Tell me, dearest Taryn, how is your mother doing these days?"

Taryn's faced remained soft with a glowing warmth. "She's doing magnificently," she replied.

Nodryck took a step closer. "And what of your father? I suspect he has accepted her back with open arms."

"My mother and father are both doing quite well, thank you." She paused, glancing behind him. "Too bad you cannot say the same for what remains of your council," she stated.

"The Elder Council is very much alive, Taryn. While you have been busy jumping like a puppet to every beck and call from various groups amongst the different planes, I have continued to offer sanctuary to those who are less than fond of this new order you have forced upon us all," he stated.

She shrugged. "All I did was offer an alternative to the Council's archaic rules. Everyone is free to choose the option best suited to their needs and wants."

Nodryck raised his hand.

His action met an immediate growl from Larkin. "That wouldn't be wise," he warned.

Two of the men standing behind Nodryck that were also werewolves growled in Larkin's direction, but the teen paid them no mind.

Knowing there was no way for him to best the girl, Nodryck lowered his hand and nodded for his followers to stand down.

"It's so nice to see you finally understand the hierarchy, Nodryck, as well as your place within it," Taryn stated.

Tasting the bitterness of the girl's words, the devilish man could not hold his tongue. "Speaking of hierarchy, did your mother share with you where she fell in the order of things during her stay here on Hypatia?"

Taryn's face remained soft, though her emerald eyes began to radiate with intensity. "Be mindful of what you say about my mother," she warned.

Nodryck's brows arched as a mischievous smile curled on his face. "Hypocrisy at its finest," he replied, stepping closer to the girl. "You claim to want freedom for everyone, but only when it aligns with your interests. You wanted freedom for those Afflicted and for those bound to the Council…and here you are, still trying to control everyone and everything."

"You're free to say whatever it is you like, but it does not mean you will be free of consequence," Taryn retorted.

"Who are you to determine the consequences of our actions, Taryn Knight? What makes you so special that you, and you alone, shall decide the fate of all Gaias kind, the Elder Council, and even the fate of the Mortari?" He paused, pacing two steps to his left and then two steps back to the right. "Our worlds may not have been perfect before you came along, but at least everyone knew their place and what was expected of them."

"This started long before you or I ever existed, Nodryck. Your precious council tried to commit genocide against the Healers and their families. All they ended up doing was forcing the Healer's hand to find a new way to survive, and survive is exactly what they did," Taryn replied.

Silence lingered for a long moment as the pair glared at one another.

Soon another smile formed upon Nodryck's face. This one was far darker and more sinister than the previous. "At the foot of my bed," he stated.

Taryn stepped toe-to-toe with the man. "What about the foot of your bed?" she dared.

Nodryck arched a brow and smirked. "It is where your mother slept when she lived here."

Taryn opened the palm of her hand, causing the wind to churn around them.

Witnessing the change in atmosphere, Lazryn rushed to the teens. Glancing between the two, he asked, "What has happened?"

"Nodryck pushed her too far. Taunting her about her mom," Larkin replied.

The man stood beside the girl. "I know he is vile, but do not allow him to provoke you into becoming a monster," Lazryn warned.

Taryn's eyes never left Nodryck's face. "One day my mother will no longer think of you. Her memories from her time here on Hypatia will fail to be even a blip on her mental radar," she stated with a terrifying calm.

"If not for Odyn's betrayal to the council, you, too, would have been sleeping at my feet," Nodryck hissed.

Taryn's emerald colored irises began to churn like a violent sea of illuminated gems. "One cannot imagine the torment you must have suffered in your life to become such a vile individual," she stated, raising her hand and cupping his cheek. "Was it that your mother did not love you enough…or perhaps it was your father who failed you?" She paused, staring into his jet black eyes.

Larkin and Lazryn shared a quick glance as Nodryck's followers began to turn and walk back to the castle without a word.

Larkin placed a hand on her shoulder. "I think it's time for us to go now, Taryn."

As if she were deaf to his words, Taryn pressed upon her toes and placed a kiss on Nodryck's cheek.

Lazryn and Larkin watched as the man's eyes widened and his body began to twitch.

"Taryn, what have you done?" Lazryn demanded. Suddenly he felt his right arm lift and his fingers extend. Lazryn shook his head as he fought against her Influence. "If you send him to Mors they will kill him," he warned.

Taryn turned her head, looking to her friend. "No harm will come to him. He now bares my mark of protection."

"Stop this now, Taryn," Larkin shouted.

She turned her head to look over her other shoulder. "Not until he has suffered for what he has done," she stated plainly.

The man watched in fear as an Adora Gateway opened only a few feet away. "Don't. I beg of you," Nodryck whimpered.

Taryn turned her attention back to the dark haired devil. "You shall walk naked on Mors until you are discovered by the Mortari. At which time, you will fall to your knees and beg for their forgiveness for all the vile acts perpetrated against the original Healers at the hands of your precious Elder Council."

"No," he pleaded.

Taking a step back, Taryn smiled. "You should be thankful that rage no longer makes its home within me." With that, she turned and walked away.

Lazryn remained compelled by her Influence. As hard as he fought, he could not force the gateway closed.

Layer by layer, Nodryck began to remove his clothing. In a matter of minutes, he was completely bare without a thread of fabric covering him. Unable to stop himself, he began walking toward the portal. Tears streamed down his face as he stepped inside and then disappeared.

Once the monster was no longer visible, Lazryn closed the gateway. "Dammit, Taryn," he shouted, turning to search for her.

Before he could disappear in a rush, Larkin grabbed his wrist. "She fought back in the most humane way that she possibly could."

The man's brows furrowed. "I don't care about that vile man, Larkin, I care about Taryn's soul and what this will do to her in the long term. Though he may wear her mark of protection, Coyan has a dozen different ways to make him suffer without violating her rules."

"Then I guess Nodryck bet wrong when he started goading her about her mother," Larkin replied.

৪০৪৪৪০৪৪

At the far west end of the garden near the woods, Taryn sat perfectly still on a white marble bench. Her eyes stared straight ahead, focusing on a small creek not far off in the distance.

"Taryn?" Larkin asked as he and Lazryn approached. She remained silent as he knelt down in front of her. "Tare-Bear, are you okay?"

Continuing to stare ahead, she replied, "This was my mother's favorite place while she was a prisoner here."

Lazryn took a seat beside her. "It is a beautiful view," he stated.

A sad smile formed on her face. "Would you like to know why it was her favorite place?" she asked.

"Of course," Larkin answered, placing his hands over hers.

Taryn exhaled deeply. "It was because every day she came here and sat, thinking about drowning herself in the creek to bring her suffering to an end." She paused as tears streamed from her eyes. "He tried to break her. He so desperately wanted her to love him in the same way he thought she loved Julius, but that was the love of a sibling, not a lover, and he could not fathom it."

Tears filled Lazryn's eyes. "I had no idea she would have been treated in such a way while in the company of the council."

Larkin caressed her cheek. "I'm so sorry, Taryn."

Her hands balled into fists and she began to tremble. "I want to hate him. I want to unleash my rage on everyone who owned a part in her kidnapping and confinement. But each time I try to unleash them, I find myself hollow inside," she bit through clenched teeth.

"You don't need hate or rage to make your point, Taryn. Nodryck received your message loud and clear today," Larkin assured.

Taryn brought her gaze to Larkin's face. "At this moment, I would welcome the feeling of fires raging inside me. I miss the warmth and sting they brought, and the clarity they provided at times like this." She paused. "If I still possessed my rage, Nodryck would not be walking naked on Mors, instead, he would have been leveled into a pile of ash and my mother's suffering would be avenged."

"I know you, Taryn, and I know you don't mean that," Larkin insisted.

Lazryn placed his hand around her shoulders. "He is correct, Taryn, you know you are a force to be reckoned with, even without such dark emotion."

"I have never sought revenge for the wrong done to me. However, when my family is threatened or harmed, a siren blares deep inside of my head and it won't be silenced until the guilty have been punished," Taryn stated grimly.

Suddenly the sky turned dark and the ground beneath their feet began to shake. Bright blue streaks of lightning crossed overhead and booms of thunder sounded, nearly deafening them.

More lightning crackled above them as Larkin peered deep within her eyes. Taken back by the emptiness he found, Larkin asked, "Are you causing this, Taryn?"

Her eyes rolled back inside her head and she slumped forward.

Feeling a familiar sensation creeping over him, Larkin put Taryn over his shoulder and grabbed hold of Lazryn's wrist. The strong teen tossed the man several feet as if he were a rag doll and then ran away from the area as fast as he could.

A second later, a massive bolt of lightning hurled downward, striking the exact spot where Taryn had been sitting. Its violent power obliterated the marble into dust.

Sensing this was just the beginning, Larkin laid Taryn on the ground and shielded her with his body as he had done so many times in the past.

More bolts fell from the sky, raining down around the two teens, forming a perfect circle.

Helpless as he watched, Lazryn fell to his knees. The deluge was so intense that he could not see the pair through the wall of lightning surrounding them.

After nearly a ten-minute assault, a final lightning bolt shot downward from the sky, splitting in two as it neared. The two illuminated bolts struck the nearby castle with immense force. Debris from the building flew thru the air. Several pieces of stone narrowly missed striking Lazryn as they came to rest in and near the garden.

Lazryn rushed to the teens. "Larkin, are you or Taryn injured?"

Rolling off to the side, Larkin laid on his back and shook his head. "I'm good, but Taryn's unconscious and I don't think it has anything to do with the lightning storm."

The older man knelt by the girl, pressing two fingers against her neck. "Her pulse is strong...but something is strange."

Larkin sat up. "What do you mean?"

Lazryn shook his head. "Her gifts are barely detectable." He paused. "It feels as if she is holding them deep within herself."

"That's good. It means on some level she's aware of her unconscious state, but still remains in control of her gifts," Larkin reasoned.

"It is a good theory, and one that I hope is correct," Lazryn replied.

Sitting next to his love, Larkin gently swept the hair from her face. "We need to find the bush with the angel flowers and follow through on why we came here in the first place. Once we find whatever Chrystian's hidden, we'll take Taryn to Williams and then we'll come back here with Keiryn to check on everyone inside the castle."

"We should hurry then," Lazryn stated.

Ⅴ℣Ⅴ℣

Searching the garden, Lazryn found a bush with white flowers that somewhat resembled angels. He reached inside, feeling his hand around for whatever Chrystian had hidden. When he found nothing, he knelt down, looking around the base of the bush. Noticing the loose dirt on one side, he began to scoop away the earth with both hands.

After several moments, he hit what he felt to be a wooden crate. Lifting it from the ground, Lazryn held it up. "I've got it," he shouted.

Ⅴ℣Ⅴ℣

From the couch, Keiryn watched as a new gateway opened in their backyard. When he saw Larkin emerge, carrying Taryn, he rushed out to meet them.

"What happened to her?" he demanded.

"We were attacked by another one of those freak lightning storms and for whatever reason, Taryn's unconscious," Larkin offered.

Keiryn's jaw drew up tight. "It's probably because of that monster kissing her earlier today. I bet he's poisoned her somehow."

~ 84 ~

Lazryn shook his head while carrying the hefty crate. "Chrystian would never hurt Taryn. He truly cares for her well-being."

"So says the other monster," Keiryn hissed.

Making his way through the French doors, Larkin sighed. "As much as I hate to admit it, Lazryn's right. Chrystian didn't do this."

Hearing the commotion, Gracyn and Theron exited the kitchen just in time to see Larkin carrying their daughter's limp body toward the stairs.

Gracyn shrieked at the sight. She and Theron followed quickly after Larkin and their little girl to the teen's bedroom.

Theron held Gracyn back by the waist as Larkin laid Taryn on the bed. The moment he had her comfortably positioned, Theron released his wife.

She ran over, taking Taryn's hand in her own. "What happened to her, Larkin?" she demanded.

"It was another freak lightning storm. It came out of nowhere and for whatever reason, Taryn fell unconscious," he offered.

Gracyn turned to Theron. "Why does such deadly power chase our little girl? It's as if it is purposefully stalking her."

Theron placed a comforting hand on her shoulder. "I don't know Gracie. Ilya said that it's always followed her around, striking at curious times."

Larkin rose to his feet and looked to her parents and Keiryn. "We were on Hypatia when it happened, and this time it was different…more intense. It struck the castle. Lazryn and I are going back to check and see if anyone needs help." He paused, focusing solely on Keiryn. "We were hoping you would come, too."

"Why on earth would she ever go back to that awful place?" Gracyn questioned.

"Who among us ever truly understands why Taryn makes the choices she does. But she is wise, and I do not question her reasons," Lazryn offered.

The woman remained silent glancing between the men and her daughter. "Why go back there? Why help any of those vile people?" she growled.

Keiryn placed his hand on his mother's shoulder. "Because it's what Taryn would do if she were awake."

Tears filled Gracyn's eyes as she began to nod. "You're right. It is exactly what she would do."

Leaning over, Keiryn kissed his mother's cheek. "We'll be back soon."

Before leaving, Lazryn placed the wooden crate in the corner of the teen's bedroom.

"What's that?" Theron questioned.

"Something Taryn was searching for," he answered. "If she wakes before our return, please tell her that we found it."

Theron shot the man a questioning look before finally nodding in agreement.

CHAPTER SEVEN

Taryn's eyelids fluttered as she started to come to. The sun-warmed granules of sand beneath her hugged her petite form. Dozens of voices filled the air, overlapping the sound of the water slapping against the seashore. She outstretched her arms for a moment before sitting up.

"Hello, Taryn," one of the voices greeted her.

Turning her head, Taryn stared into a face identical to her own. Though the girl had dark chocolate hair, everything else was exactly the same.

"Hello," Taryn replied.

The girl smiled at her. "It's been such a long time since we've seen you, Taryn. We were starting to grow concerned."

Taryn rolled her eyes as she rose to her feet. "All you have to do is look around and you will find me everywhere," she retorted.

"That's not exactly true," the girl countered. "I know we mostly resemble you, minus some of the hair and eye color, but we alone are not you. We are simply pieces of you."

Shaking her head, Taryn took a deep breath and closed her eyes.

"You're displeased," the girl commented.

Opening her eyes, Taryn looked out across the water that was scattered with her look-a-likes. "More like frustrated," she replied.

"It is the dark haired man. He makes you long for that which you destroyed," the girl stated.

"Something like that," Taryn shrugged.

Silence lingered between the girls as Taryn started to walk the length of the beach.

After walking several meters, the girl smiled faintly. "We finally left the cave…you know, since you terminated the cruel ones."

"The beach is definitely an upgrade," Taryn stated.

"We're glad you approve," the girl replied.

Taryn paused her step as a girl ran in front of them. Once the girl recognized Taryn for who she was, she began to stumble over herself. "I'm so sorry. I didn't mean to…"

Taryn cut her off. "You're fine. Continue as if I'm not here," she directed.

This new girl followed Taryn's orders and went back to frolicking in the sand and sun.

"So life inside my head is now one big party without Rage, Fear and the others?" she mused.

The girl hesitantly nodded. "Yes. At least until a little while ago when you ran into the dark haired man," she confessed.

"You felt it too when he moved closer?" Taryn questioned.

"I felt you," the girl replied. "When he stood too close, I felt you suppressing me. I felt you searching the depths of your soul for any dark emotion."

Taryn stared at her briefly. "So you must be empathy?"

The girl nodded.

"Empathy plays a large part in keeping me bound to my humanity. I was wrong. I should never have tried to suppress you," Taryn acknowledged.

"I'm sure you had your reasons," the girl replied.

Snapshots of memories flashed in Taryn's mind. Her jaw clenched and her nostrils flared. "They kidnapped my mother and no one helped her. Odyn and the others...they knew she was not willingly his wife, yet they did nothing to stop her suffering." She paused, stepping toward the water's edge. "Nodryck kept her wrists bound with rondoring rope and shackled her to a stone post in a room attached to his private chambers. For the first year, he brought her flowers, pastries and various gems each day. Before he would leave her, he asked if she loved him. Her answer was always a simple no." Taryn paused again, stepping into the tempered water. "Nodryck did not love my mother. He only loved the idea of taking away something from my Uncle Julius. He wanted her to love him as he thought she loved Julius. He did not understand their love was that of siblings, and not secret lovers as he had concluded." Taryn stepped further into the water.

"He is cruel," the girl acknowledged.

Taryn gave a dark chuckle. "You simply state he is cruel and I say he is a monster, even amongst monsters." She paused, taking a seat in the knee high water. "During her second year, Nodryck would whip her each day until she begged for him to stop. Again, he would ask before leaving if she loved him now, and still she would say no." She paused, lifting her eyes to the sun. "Several months passed and her flesh became so inflamed and over-sensitized that even the slightest shift in the air would cause her to cry out in horrific pain. When she could no longer bear the torture, she told him that she loved him."

"No one can blame your mother, Taryn. Your bodies are made of flesh and can only tolerate so much," the girl insisted.

Taryn slipped down, letting the water reach just beneath her chin. "The day her physical pain ended, her mental anguish began. He tormented and tortured the very fabric of her soul," she said, her tone cold and indifferent.

Taking a shallow breath, Taryn laid her head back. Exhaling, she allowed herself to sink completely beneath the water. The current within the waters began pulling her outward.

Empathy stood watch as her governess' body swept out towards the depths of the churning waters.

The further Taryn went, the calmer the waters became. Gravity began to pull at her flesh until she neared the floor of the massive body of water, snuffing out the last bit of light.

Feeling the cold permeating her bones, Taryn smiled faintly into the darkness.

ᏕᏬᏇᏕᏬᏇ

Gracyn sat, holding her daughter's hand. "I understand that you've all witnessed this type of thing from her before, but I haven't," she sighed.

Theron took a seat on the opposite side of the bed. "Gracie, it's not that we don't worry about her, it's just that we've come to understand this is a part of what makes Taryn, well…Taryn. When she needs time to herself, she will disappear for a few hours, or she slips into an unconscious state."

Rising to her feet, Gracyn walked over to the window. "Theron, I can't stand seeing her like this. She's so still."

He joined his wife in the sunlight. "After all of these months, it still seems strange to hear people call me Theron instead of Teigan." He paused, wrapping his hands around her waist. "Because of Taryn's incredible gifts and mighty will, we were all able to remember our true selves and the lives we had been forced to forget."

Gracyn sighed. "I know, Theron, I know. Taryn is far more than what we ever knew any of us could be." She paused, resting her head on his chest. "In a few months she will turn eighteen, and the full strength of her powers will set in."

"And our little girl will handle the influx of power just as she has handled everything else in life, with grace, poise and a heart full of love," Theron replied.

Turning to look at their daughter's still frame, Gracyn gave a weighted sigh. "Speaking of love, the connection between Taryn and Larkin is incredible and simultaneously terrifying. When she moves, his eyes follow her every step. He even seems to be aware of each breath she takes. Then there's the way Taryn looks at him. It's as if they are the only two people in existence. They love one another so much that it eclipses every relationship in both of their lives."

Stroking the length of his wife's hair, Theron gave a slight chuckle. "When Taryn and Ilya first arrived in Williams, I know Maxym felt as though he had lost his son. Larkin slept outside Taryn's bedroom window every night watching over her. He barely slept or ate during those first few weeks. He was obsessed. He had to be near her, to have his eyes on her at all times. The poor kid lost his mind when she came along," Theron explained.

Gracyn moved back to the bed. "Do you remember when they were babies and how drawn he was to her even then?"

Theron nodded.

"Do you think it's possible that they knew even back then what they were to one another?" she asked.

Taking a deep breath, Theron leaned against the window frame. "I have a theory, but I've never shared it with anyone." He paused taking another deep breath. "All of my life I thought everything happened by chance. Most of us inherit our gifts from our parents. Every once in a while, someone would inherit a gift that seemed out of place in their bloodline, an anomaly in their genetics. We called them special. Taryn and Larkin have made me reconsider my position." He paused again, this time walking over and staring down at their daughter. "Do you remember how Larkin was inconsolable as an infant when he and his parents would leave our home?"

"Yes," Gracyn replied.

"Larkin didn't cry when he and his parents left when it was only Keiryn and I there." Theron paused, locking eyes with his wife. "He only cried when he left your presence, Gracie. When he had to leave you, while you carried Taryn in your womb."

"Their destinies were always intertwined," Gracyn stated.

Tears streaked down his cheeks. "No, Gracie, it goes deeper than that. I believe they are not only bound to one another, but they were purposely created to walk side by side in this life."

Gracyn's eyes widened. "It makes sense. A being as powerful as Taryn would require an anchor to keep her grounded. To keep her from losing herself under the immensity of such power," Gracyn stated as her tears began to flow.

"I've seen it, Gracie. Larkin's touch calms her even in the worst of circumstances," Theron replied.

As the couple's eyes remained locked on one another, Taryn began to stir. She mumbled quietly as her head rocked back and forth.

"Your dad and I are here for you, Taryn," Gracyn whispered in her ear.

Taryn mumbled again, more audibly this time. "Within the darkness. Why? Why…darkness? Light? Not hot. Cold. So cold."

Rushing into the room, Larkin maneuvered around Theron and began caressing Taryn's cheek. "You're okay, Tare-Bear. I'm right here with you," he stated.

"Not hot. Cold. So cold," Taryn mumbled again. Her body trembled as she spoke.

Theron stepped back, allowing Larkin complete access to his little girl. He watched as the strapping teen lay down next to her and wrapped her tiny frame in his arms. Almost instantly, the shivering subsided and she looked peaceful once more.

Gracyn looked at her husband with fresh tears welling in her eyes. "Sweetheart, I believe Larkin has the situation under control." She paused, smiling warmly. "Let's go downstairs and we'll continue our conversation."

Theron nodded and joined his wife as she walked towards the open bedroom door. "He is good for her," he whispered.

Wrapping her arm around Theron's waist, Gracyn looked up at him. "No. He's perfect for her," she replied.

શ્જ્ઝશ્જ્ઝ

A few hours later, Taryn woke in Larkin's arms. When she began to move, he pulled her in even closer.

"Did you have a nice nap?" he whispered.

Taryn ran her hands over his protective arms. "You're being polite," she replied.

Larkin nuzzled his nose against the back of her neck. "I thought nap sounded better than a self-imposed time-out."

Turning around, Taryn placed her ear against his chest. She listened to his heart as it beat in perfect unison with her own. After several moments, she looked up at him. Her eyes were full of wonder.

"What is it, Tare-Bear?" he asked.

She smiled softly. "You're not even a little bit upset with me?"

"Should I be?" he questioned.

Taryn shrugged. "I don't know. Maybe?"

Brushing the hair from her face with his index finger, he smiled. "I don't own you. I don't get a say in how you're supposed to feel about Nodryck, or anything for that matter." He paused, caressing her cheek with his thumb. "I can't imagine what it must be like inside your head. Knowing what you know, seeing what only you can see. I don't blame you for wanting revenge, Taryn. I don't blame you for punishing him. Your rage is gone, but that doesn't mean you are no longer a force to be reckoned with, or that you are incapable of inflicting harm."

Pushing away, Taryn sat up and scooted to the edge of her bed. "She's my mother," the teen exhaled.

Larkin moved to her side. "What exactly happened today between you and Nodryck?" he asked.

"It's hard to explain. I mean, I can walk into a room and see past events that took place there. Sometimes the visions are just bits and pieces of broken memories, a picture you might say. Other times my visions are like being a fly on the wall, observing history as it happened..." Taryn paused, running her hands over her face. "Today with Nodryck, it felt like I was standing at the base of a massive waterfall and all of his dark emotions were pouring down onto me. I saw what he did to her through his eyes. I felt his fear and loathing, but more than anything, I felt his joy and satisfaction in causing her so much pain."

Larkin placed his hand on her knee. "Your mom is home now. She's safe because of you. He won't ever touch her again."

Leaning her head against his arm, Taryn sighed. "What if that isn't enough for her?"

"What do you mean?" Larkin questioned.

"My mom, she acts like everything's fine, but it's not, Larkin. What I felt and saw when I sat on that bench..." She paused. "The last time she sat there was exactly two days before the Trials began."

Wrapping her in his arms, Larkin kissed the top of her head. "I don't know what to say." He paused, kissing her again. "She's strong, Taryn. Your mom has your dad and all of us."

Tears flooded her eyes. "No one should have to endure what she went through..."

"I'm sorry. I wish there was something I could do or say to make it all go away," Larkin replied.

Taryn buried her head against his chest and wept.

౪౧౶౪౧౶౪

Four o'clock in the morning, sitting on a barstool in the kitchen, Taryn stared blankly at the large bouquet of mixed flowers to her left. While their sweet and spicy fragrance inundated her sinuses, it did little to pull the teen from her wandering thoughts.

Julius, Oleg, Odyn and the others were right there. They could have intervened at any time. They could have stopped what was happening to her, Taryn thought to herself. She pounded her fist against the island's marble countertop. "Why? Why didn't they help her?" she growled.

Seconds passed before the teen took a deep breath. Slumping as she sat, Taryn used her feet to spin herself around. "He's not even all that powerful," she muttered.

"Who's not powerful?" a strange, but quiet voice inquired.

Drawing her shoulders back, Taryn panned her eyes to the kitchen entryway. Her forehead creased as she looked upon a young boy. His curly, dark brown hair and green eyes instantly drew her in. "What are you doing here?" she asked.

"I couldn't sleep. Then I heard someone moving around up here," he answered shyly.

Taryn rose to her feet. "Why are you here?" she questioned, her tone sharper this time.

The boy took a small step back. "You're Taryn, right?" he asked.

Her face was cold and stony as she continued to stare at the young boy. "Correct."

"Your brother and two others saved me," he replied.

Taryn's face softened, but only slightly. "What do you mean, they saved you?"

"I was residing in the Elder Council's castle when a storm hit yesterday afternoon. Lightning struck and caused a lot of damage. Several people were hurt," he explained.

While walking over to him, Taryn ran her eyes over his blue and white checkered pajama bottoms and white t-shirt. "Lightning struck the castle?"

He nodded.

"You don't appear to be injured," she stated.

The boy buckled under her heated gaze, falling to his knees and lifting his arms protectively over his head. "Please, they said I could stay here."

Feeling his fear washing over her in palpable waves, she took a step back.

Before Taryn could speak, Lazryn rushed to the boy, and knelt beside him. "Dedrick, you are safe here. This, I promise." He paused, glancing briefly at Taryn before turning back to the boy. "Go downstairs and rest a while longer. I need to speak with our friend for a moment."

Dedrick rose to his feet and flashed a faint smile before disappearing into the darkness.

Lazryn listened intently. When he was certain the boy was no longer in earshot, he turned his attention to Taryn. "One can only assume by your behavior that your wolf failed to mention the child."

Taryn shook her head. "No, Larkin did not mention our guest." Pausing, she moved back to the barstool. "The kid said lightning struck the castle…when?"

Sighing heavily, the man walked around to the opposite side of the island from her. He strummed his fingers loudly against the hard surface. "You were sharing with Larkin and I the events that had affected your mother during her stay on Hypatia. The sky grew dark and you fell unconscious. Moments later a barrage of lightning unlike anything we have ever witnessed before rained down around us. As always, Larkin protected you."

Taryn began biting her bottom lip with a furrowed brow. After a few moments, she looked to her friend. "So you're telling me that one of those freak lightning storms that follows me around struck the castle? She paused. "And people were actually hurt this time?"

He nodded. "We brought you and Chrystian's gift back here to your home. Once you were settled in, Keiryn joined Larkin and myself as we went back to check on those who reside within the castle walls."

With a weighted sigh, Taryn rose from her seat. "The storms that follow me, they have never targeted another soul."

"Then it would appear your storms and you were both acting out of character yesterday," Lazryn stated with a stern look.

Taryn's gaze turned frigid. "Do I detect a hint of disdain in your words?" she asked.

Placing both hands against the island's smooth surface, Lazryn's jaw drew up tightly. "You go on and on about free will, yet today you took mine away so that you could have your revenge," he answered.

Several silent moments passed as the teen stared at the man. Suddenly, a burst of laughter escaped her lungs. Once the laughter quieted, Taryn appeared like a ghost at Lazryn's side.

"You dare to judge me?" she growled, pushing up against him.

Lazryn turned to face her directly. "You used me, Taryn. You used my gifts to seek retribution."

Her eyes widened, highlighting a violent storm brewing within their beauty. "I see. Retribution is only deemed appropriate when it is your family who has been harmed." She paused, tilting her head to one side. "The pain and suffering that my mother endured at the hands of that vile demon warranted a sentence far worse than the one I handed down."

"Your mother is here with you now. Why is that not enough? Why must you press this matter?" Lazryn demanded.

Studying the man's face, Taryn finally spoke. "I see now. You're afraid that I'll become like you."

Lazryn swallowed hard. "You are immensely strong and gifted beyond all others...but you are not infallible, Taryn. Look at what nearly happened during the Trials. If not for your bond to Larkin, you would have destroyed us all."

"I see...you're only worried whether I am able to control my emotions. Yet, you weren't worried when I was roasting you from the inside out. In fact, you welcomed death because of the guilt you hold onto." She paused, walking into the living room. "Why don't you do us both a favor, Lazryn, and say what's really on your mind?"

His face softened as he gazed upon her. "I have come to see you as the daughter that I lost all those years ago. You are good and kind, but darkness lives within us all...I simply do not desire to see you struggle the way in which I, and so many like us, have."

Taryn turned, staring out the window. "What you mean to say is you do not wish to see me struggle like Chrystian."

Tears welled in Lazryn's eyes. "The night Loryn died, Chrystian snapped. The light that lived within him up until that moment, it was swallowed whole by one act of darkness."

Looking up at her friend, Taryn smiled faintly. "He's not all bad, you know? He helped you warn the Elder Council of Karvyn's activities, stopping what would have been the single largest slaughter of our kind."

Lazryn leaned over, kissing her atop her head. "You sweet, sweet girl. He only helped me because I was his only remaining link to my sister. But you, you stirred the light within him from the first time he laid eyes upon you."

Taryn shook her head. "No. He hated me. I felt the heat of his emotion rolling off of him."

Giving a slight chuckle, Lazryn smiled warmly. "It is the very fact that you made him feel anything at all that speaks volumes to your effect on him. He truly loves you, Taryn. Not the vision of Loryn residing within you, but you."

"I know how much he cares for me, Lazryn. After all, it was Chrystian who sent you to me," she replied. Wrapping her arms around his neck, Taryn hugged him tightly. "And I am thankful every day that he did."

He hugged her back for a long moment before gently pushing away. "This is exactly why I fear for you, Taryn. You are good. Too good at times. But what you did, forcing me to brandish a gateway to Mors...it is something Chrystian would have done if he had not possessed the gift himself."

Taking a deep breath, Taryn settled her churning emotions. "You're right. I should not have forced you to do something against your will. For that, I am truly sorry," she stated.

Moving to sit on the arm of the couch, Lazryn rubbed his forehead. "Every day is a struggle to take a step further away from the monster I became after the murder of my wife, daughter, and sister." He paused, his jaw drawing up tightly. "All you had to do was ask and I would have willingly opened the gateway. I battle my own demons, Taryn, but I have not grown numb to the injustices surrounding me."

Taryn's eyes narrowed. "But I thought…"

"I worry with each bit of darkness that touches you, that it is leaving a mark upon your soul. I cannot bear to lose you in the same fashion that I lost not only Chrystian, but also myself," Lazryn explained.

Leaning with her back against the windowpane, Taryn closed her eyes, holding her breath. Moments passed before she exhaled. Looking to her dear friend, she smiled. "For each breath that I have cursed him, I take two breaths that say I love him." She paused glancing over her shoulder at the moon's light, shining above the treetops. "Chrystian is proof that even within the darkest of days, light will always be found. Light will always find a way to shine for anyone brave enough to seek it out."

With his jaw agape and a creased forehead, Lazryn stumbled from the arm of the couch to one of its cushions. He stared at the girl and the multiple images visible in the window's reflection with wide eyes. "Taryn, are you here with me?" he stammered.

Her eyes were luminescent as she gazed into the distance.

Swallowing hard, Lazryn fought to find his footing as he rose from the couch. "Taryn…" he whispered.

"Do you ever wonder how?" she questioned.

Hesitantly, the man stepped toward her. "What is it I should wonder, dear one?" he inquired.

"Do you ever wonder how we became to be?" she replied.

He shook his head. "No, because we are of the earth. We only exist because that which we control is also what makes us whole."

Closing her eyes once more, Taryn pressed her cheek against the cool glass. A euphoric smile curled on her face as she began to hum quietly.

Lazryn took another step closer to the girl, this time reaching his hand out. He listened as she hummed. The more engrossed with the strange tune she became, the more he dared to press forward. Once she was within reach, he grabbed her wrist, pulling her into his arms. She struggled against his grip, but he held her firmly. Slowly, the fight began to leave her body, causing her to fall limp.

Cradling the girl in his arms, Lazryn stared at the window, watching as the images of the others faded away.

Stepping up behind him, Larkin questioned, "Who were the people in the reflection, Lazryn?"

"Those, my young friend, are the ghosts of Gaias past," the man replied.

Larkin shared a brief glance with Lazryn before panning his eyes to Taryn. He moved to stand in front of the man holding his love. Lifting his hand, he stroked her cheek. "It's not possible…" he began to speak, then paused.

"What is it, young wolf?" Lazryn questioned.

Taking a deep breath, Larkin stared at the sleeping girl for several seconds before looking up. "After reading Chrystian's letter, she was adamant that *they* were coming. We both assumed she was talking about the Mortari, but what if these ghosts were who she meant all along?"

A grim look washed over Lazryn's face. "Taryn is exceptionally attuned to things that the rest of us cannot understand or see. It is entirely plausible that even she was unaware of the meaning of her words at the time. Perhaps it was Chrystian's letter that opened her subconscious to future events."

Larkin's jaw drew tight and his nostrils flared. "I refuse to lose her to whatever's out there. I won't allow these ghosts to claim her," he growled.

Nodding, Lazryn made a vow. "Then it is agreed. No matter the personal sacrifice to ourselves, no harm shall come to her."

"Whatever it takes, no matter the cost," Larkin echoed.

CHAPTER EIGHT

Sitting upon their jewel-encrusted thrones, Coyan, Chrystian and Clad watched as a nude Nodryck was ushered through the crowd of awaiting Mortari.

The instant Nodryck laid his eyes on Coyan, he threw himself at the man's feet. "Please, please, I beg of you…forgive me and my brothers for the horrific acts of violence and deception we bestowed upon the Healers all those years ago."

Coyan's brown eyes lit with delight. "My, my, how the mighty have fallen." He glanced to his brothers, giving a quiet chuckle. "I do believe our dearest Taryn has sent us a gift."

While rising to his feet, a widening grin curled on Clad's face. "Not only does she send him to us bare from everything that would show his station in life, but she also forces him to grovel at our feet." He paused, glancing to his eldest brother. Laughter escaped his throat, filling the air around them as he clapped his hands together. "Oh, how that magnificent girl stills my beating heart," Clad lauded.

As Clad celebrated, Tedra drew her husband's attention before nodding discreetly in Chrystian's direction.

Rising, Coyan turned to his younger brother. "Does this offering not bring even the slightest of joy to you, Brother?" he asked.

Chrystian's gaze narrowed on the naked man, paying no mind to Coyan.

Irritation began to course through the eldest brother's veins. "Perhaps you did not hear me, dearest Chrystian, but I have asked you a question."

Continuing his silence, Chrystian stared ahead.

Having grown tired of his brother's insolence, Coyan raised his hand in Chrystian's direction. "As the leader of all Mortari, I demand you answer me."

Pulling his gaze from Nodryck, a slight smirk crept across Chrystian's face. "I hear you, Brother, just as I am able to see you," he replied, rising as well.

The crowd of Mortari gasped and began to back away from the thrones.

"Someone fetch this man a robe," Chrystian demanded.

"Yes, Sir," one of the guards replied. He quickly took the cloak from his own shoulders and wrapped it around Nodryck.

Stepping forward, Chrystian gave only a glance to his brother's hand before focusing on the cowering man at his feet. "Rise," he ordered.

In his weakened state, Nodryck struggled to do as directed. Once to his feet, he stared at the floor. "Do your worst," he seethed.

Coyan lowered his hand as he looked on.

A full-fledged smile grew from Chrystian's lips. "How exceedingly brave of you to say, knowing that you bear her mark of protection."

"She has defiled me against my will. I would rather die than wear her mark. I do not need her protection," Nodryck spat.

Leaning down, Chrystian whispered, "Again, so brave, but only when you know we cannot touch you."

Coyan watched eagerly as his brother stared daggers at the man. "What shall we do with this gift, Brother?" he asked.

Chrystian shook his head. "You fools. This man is no gift. He is merely a means to an end should we react instinctively."

Tedra moved like a flash to her husband's side.

Waving his hand, Coyan motioned for her to stand down. "What exactly do you mean?" he questioned.

"If we harm him, she will come," he warned.

"My dear brother, the girl obviously sent him here to suffer. I am most certain in this instance, even she would make an allowance if we were to have a bit of fun with him," Coyan reasoned.

"Any pleasure we may derive from bringing pain upon this demon will have no measure in comparison to what she will rain down upon us. This devil being on Mors and falling at our feet is not by mere coincidence, but by her well-constructed design." Chrystian paused, turning to Nodryck. "You must have done something unforgiveable to someone she holds dear for this to be your punishment."

Nodryck began to laugh deviously. "I took her mother and kept her as my prisoner for a great number of years. Apparently our dearest Taryn did not approve of my methods."

In hearing the man's words and the contempt he held for the girl, Chrystian, without a second thought, swung his arm backward, sending Nodryck crashing into one of the stone pillars. "Be mindful of what you say about her," he growled.

Tedra moved to the injured man, inspecting him. "Take him to my chambers," she ordered.

A guard stepped forward, looking to Coyan before continuing.

"Do as she directed," he stated.

In a flash, the guard picked Nodryck up, placing him over his shoulders and disappearing from the grand room.

Coyan began to clap with mock praise. He shared a brief glance with Clad and Tedra before addressing Chrystian. "Congratulations,

Brother. Your misplaced love for a girl who despises your very existence has placed us all in grave danger."

A hush fell over the crowd as all eyes focused upon Chrystian's tall frame.

"I will go to Taryn and explain that it was I, and I alone, who inflicted harm upon the man," Chrystian offered.

Coyan stepped to his brother, placing his hands on either shoulder. "How very noble of you, dearest Chrystian. However, do you think after you tried kissing her, she will be open to such a discussion?"

Chrystian's face was somber. "To be fair to you, Clad and the others, mustn't I at least try?" He reasoned.

"I fear your fondness for our enemy will be your undoing, Brother." Coyan clasped his fingers behind Chrystian's neck, pulling them face-to-face. "It is time to let go of this ridiculous notion, Brother. Accept the truth. A girl as self-righteous as our dearest Taryn could never love you, knowing all that you have done. She casts her judgment upon you with every encounter."

Staring his brother in the eyes, Chrystian nodded. "You could not be more right. I will go to her and beg for mercy. If she allows me to live, I will come back and wash her name from my lips and burn the memories of her face from eyes."

"I knew you would make the right choice, Brother," Coyan smiled. He leaned in, kissing each of his brother's cheeks before giving him a strong hug.

ℝ℔ℤ℔ℝ℔

Sitting up in her bed, Taryn looked around her room. It was empty and quiet. Tossing the covers back, she swung her legs over the edge of the bed. Before her toes touched the floor, Larkin appeared in the open doorway.

"Crazy night, huh?" he stated.

She shook her head.

Larkin exhaled, his shoulders falling sharply. "Things have to change around here, Taryn. You cannot continue to carry everyone else's burdens."

After sitting quiet for a long moment, Taryn nodded. "You're right, I can't. I can't keep doing the same thing," she admitted.

He arched a brow in her direction. "What, no fight? No argument? No using your Influence?" he asked.

Taryn ran her fingers through her hair and sighed. Opening her mouth numerous times to speak, she found her words would not come easily.

Walking over to her, Larkin knelt on the floor directly in front of her. "You remember them being there next to you, don't you?" he asked.

Tears filled her eyes as she nodded slightly.

"Do you feel them now?" he questioned.

She nodded once more. "Their presence is everywhere, but yet nowhere," she stated.

Moving to the bed, Larkin took her hand within his own, lacing his fingers with hers. "Are they trying to possess you like Loryn when you were with the Mortari?"

Staring at the floor, she took a deep breath. "No. It's more like they were whispering in my ear, but I couldn't make out what it was they were saying." She paused, looking up at him. "Their presence didn't make me feel threatened, but it didn't make me feel safe either."

Larkin lifted her hand to his lips and he placed a tender kiss on her skin. "Did you recognize who they were?" he questioned.

"No. I could only hear voices," she replied.

Larking ran his free hand through his hair.

Picking up on his stress, Taryn pulled her hand away and rose to her feet. "You recognized them, didn't you?"

Reaching his hand out to her, Larkin tried grabbing her wrist.

She jumped out of the way and headed for the door. "Now is not the time to try to handle me, Larkin. If you recognized any of those ghosts, you had better tell me now."

"I'll tell you, Taryn, but you're not going to like it," he stated.

Stopping in the hallway just beyond her bedroom door, Taryn held her left hand out to her side, creating a protective barrier.

"Taryn, stop!" Lazryn shouted, pulling Dedrick behind him.

With Larkin at her side, Taryn withdrew the shield, pulling her hands to her chest. "The boy...I had forgotten he was here," she stated.

Peaking his head around Lazryn, Dedrick gave a timid smile. "I'm sorry, Taryn. I didn't mean to startle you. Lazryn said I could get a deck of playing cards from Andyn's bedroom while the others are at school."

Placing her hands over her mouth, Taryn whimpered. The boy's fear was washing over her in palpable waves, nearly knocking the air from her lungs.

"Dedrick, you should go back downstairs. We'll be there shortly," Lazryn directed.

The young boy nodded before hastily turning to head toward the staircase.

"No, wait," Taryn called, while walking over to him. Bending down to his level, she flashed a warm smile. "Dedrick, I owe you an apology. I wasn't quite myself when we met earlier this morning, and you caught me off guard just a few moments ago. Do you think you could find it in your heart to forgive me for acting so rudely?" she asked.

A grin widened on his face. "Yeah, sure I can," Dedrick replied.

Taryn held out her hand to the boy. He took hold of it, giving hers a proper shake. Her hold lingered slightly, before releasing his hand. "We'll be downstairs in a few," she stated

The boy nodded, before turning on his heel and heading down the stairs.

Once he was out of sight, Taryn turned to Lazryn and Larkin. "What is it?" Larkin asked.

She motioned for them to follow her back into her bedroom. Standing near the window, Taryn sighed. "Did Dedrick mention how he came to be at the castle?"

The two men shared a tense glance before Larkin moved to stand across from her. He pressed his hand against the window frame just above his head and leaned in. "It's not a pleasant story. You definitely won't like it."

Taryn's face turned stony. "Your concern is noted, but I'm not some fragile little girl who can't handle the truth."

Shaking his head, he glanced to Lazryn before looking back at her. "Dedrick hasn't said much, but when we found him, his back was covered in gashes. Some old. Some new," he offered.

Taryn's hands balled into fists. "Nodryck," she hissed.

Larkin nodded. "One of the wolves in the castle finally admitted that the boy had been found during one of their scouting trips. He was the only survivor amongst more than thirty dead."

Taking a seat on the corner of Taryn's bed, Lazryn hung his head. "The wolf also stated that due to the boy being untouched amongst the carnage, some of the other wolves believed him to have played a role in the death of the others. As such, they shared their suspicions with Nodryck..."

Taryn interrupted, finishing Lazryn's savage tale. "And Nodryck believed if he whipped the boy enough, he would confess to his part in the massacre."

Lazryn again nodded.

Looking out the window, Taryn frowned. Her silence filled the room, if not the entire second floor of the house. The air was heavy as she ran the events of the last few days through her mind.

"I can see the wheels turning in your head, Taryn..." Larkin stated.

She glanced in his direction and shrugged. "When I touched Dedrick's hand earlier, I could sense his pain. There weren't any flashes of imagery, no hints as to what he had gone through..." Taryn paused, turning to Lazryn. "Do you think he was forced to swear a Blood Oath? It could be the reason why I cannot see into his head."

"It is plausible," Lazryn replied. "When a Blood Oath is sworn, it is your blood binding your word. The very fabric of your physical self is at odds against your mental self."

Taryn inhaled deeply, closing her eyes. After several quiet moments, she exhaled looking to her friend. "Dedrick stays, but he's in your charge, Lazryn. I know he's just a boy, but we need to keep an eye on him until we know more about him and what happened to his people."

He nodded in agreement.

Tilting her head, she glanced sharply between the men. "So, now that we have that out of the way, which one of you is going to tell me who you saw this morning?"

Larkin turned to their friend. "Go ahead, Lazryn. Those guests are more in your wheelhouse than mine."

Taryn growled. "One of you had better start talking, now."

"Very well," Lazryn sighed. "It would appear that darkness has left its mark upon you, my dearest friend. For those who follow you are the accursed of our kind."

Taryn rolled her eyes. "Just tell me who you saw."

Lazryn looked to Larkin, and the teen moved to stand behind Taryn, placing his hands firmly on her shoulders.

With a wrinkled forehead, Taryn arched a brow. "Is it really necessary to be coddled like a porcelain doll?" she asked.

"It's just a precaution," Larkin replied.

Rolling her eyes, she turned her attention back to Lazryn. "Please, do proceed," she stated flatly.

The man took a deep breath. "Within the reflection of the downstairs window, I saw the images of who I believe to be Colyn

Danbrym, Malayne Douth, Adora James and Elayna Delrayn. There was a second man, but I could not determine his face," Lazryn stated.

Taryn's eyes widened at the knowledge Elayna Delrayn's ghost had been anywhere near her and her loved ones. She tried to push Larkin away, but he instantly tightened his grasp, refusing to let her go. "Get off of me," she shouted.

Tightening his already tense grip around her tiny frame, Larkin buried his head into her neck and wrestled her to the floor. "No. You need to calm down, and then I will let you go."

Standing over the teens, Lazryn watched as Larkin struggled to keep hold of her. Suddenly, Taryn released an earth-shaking scream. The former Mortari found himself stunned into silence, looking on as her emerald eyes turned an intense shade of sapphire blue.

Falling to his knees, he placed a hand on either side of Taryn's head in an attempt to still her. When she finally stopped thrashing about, he locked his gaze with hers. "I know you despise the Oracle, but you must calm down," he insisted.

Beneath Larkin's powerful hold, her chest continued to heave dramatically. "If she wasn't already dead, I'd kill her again," she growled.

With a soft timbre, Larkin whispered in her ear. "Taryn, you know who they are now, so let's be smart about this. I want to let you go, but I won't until I know you're calm."

Taryn's muscles slowly relaxed, and the blue in her eyes gave way to their normal emerald green color. Lazryn watched the transition in terrifying amazement.

"Taryn?" Lazryn questioned.

She gently pushed Larkin's arms off her and sat up. "The whispers from this morning are the same as the ones I heard that day in Rockford while I was sitting on my old bed. The only difference is, I didn't feel threatened before, but this time I didn't feel safe either."

Reaching up, Larkin stroked the length of her hair. "You can't exactly chase ghosts, so what are you going to do?" he asked.

Taryn smiled darkly. "The last time they pulled me away I warned them what would happen if they didn't return me. If it happens again, I will provide no warning."

Larkin pulled into the high school parking lot and glanced in his rear view mirror. "Andyn, do you have your homework done for second hour?" he questioned.

Rolling his eyes, the young teen leaned forward between the two front seats. "Don't take offense, but Ilya isn't marrying you, she's marrying your dad. So if and when I need a father figure, I'll talk to him…not you."

Putting the Jeep into park, Larkin turned around. "You do realize that once they're married, we'll officially be step-brothers, right?"

Andyn looped one of the straps of his backpack over his shoulder and reached for the door handle. "I already have brothers. It's a perk of being part of a true pack," he retorted.

Before Andyn could give the handle a tug, Taryn used her gift of Imperium to lock all of the doors to the vehicle. "Andyn, did you finish your homework for second hour?" she asked, while staring out the windshield.

The boy hung his head. "No," he admitted.

"After school you do not go with your pack until all of your schoolwork is complete. Is that understood?" she stated.

Opening his mouth to object, he paused, noticing Taryn's eyes fixated on him in the rearview mirror. The intensity in which she gazed upon him sent a shiver through his spine.

"Got it, Sis. Homework first, then I can hang with the pack," he replied.

Taryn unlocked the doors and motioned for him to go on. "See you at lunch, little brother."

Andyn quickly exited the vehicle and made his way to the school steps where the others were waiting for him.

"The kid was a bit frosty this morning," Larkin stated, breaking the silence.

Turning her head to the side, Taryn gazed softly at her love. "Andyn's still hurting over the breakup of our little pack of two."

Larkin shook his head slightly. "I know. Whatever he needs to get past this." He paused, giving a quiet chuckle. "That is, whatever he needs with the exception of having Iggy or any type of flaming insects chasing me."

A grin curled from Taryn's mouth. "If it makes you feel any better, he truly felt guilty the moment he said those things to you."

Reaching up, Larkin caressed her cheek. "I can only imagine how he must have felt when you told him you couldn't be his pack leader. I know it isn't the same thing, but he already lost his mother and Andalyn, and now he's lost you as a pack leader…it'd be a lot to deal with for any of us."

Taryn inhaled as a tear rolled down her cheek. "Andyn's heart will be forever touched by the deep sadness brought on by all he experienced. Anger will always be his first response to any type of pain…"

"Sure he's had a few hiccups, but overall the kid's been doing great…" Larkin stated.

Taryn shrunk in her seat.

Turning, Larkin placed his forearm on the top of the steering wheel and sighed heavily. "The hiccups…they're because of you." He paused shaking his head. "You let just enough of his anger out so he seems fine to everyone else, but not too fine. Am I right?"

Taryn nodded.

"Then why did you tell me months ago that you had stopped using your Influence on him?" Larkin questioned.

She opened her mouth to speak, but the words would not come. Eventually, she shook her head and sighed. "I did pull back my Influence…but his pain, his pain was so great that it began drowning out his happiness. There wasn't a moment that passed where he didn't feel the burn of his father's gifts searing against his flesh, or hear his sister's screams."

Larkin hung his head for a moment before looking up at her. "I know you meant well, Taryn, but you can't go messing around inside someone else's head without their permission. Especially with our friends and family."

Drawing her knees up to her chest, Taryn turned her head to look at Larkin. "He knows."

His eyes widened. "Andyn?"

Taryn nodded. "I had only used a small amount of Influence on him...I didn't think he'd notice its absence so quickly."

"But he did..." Larkin stated.

She nodded again. "Andyn came to me the very next day and begged me to put it back in place. He said without it, his heart could never be whole again. He said that Karvyn's Influence had left him with a deep chill, like there was no hope, no future and no possibility of something better."

Reaching out, Larkin took her hand in his. "And what did he say about yours?"

Taryn smiled softly as she shifted, placing her feet on the floorboard. "He said it feels like being hugged by a blanket of sunshine. That no matter his past, he can find peace in knowing his mother and sister are in a better place."

Larkin drew one corner of his mouth upward. "It sounds like Andyn is at peace with having your Influence balancing him out. So why does it seem like you're not okay with it?"

Taryn shrugged. "I convinced myself that using my gifts to help Andyn was the only option. What if I was wrong? What if I had been a better pack leader? What if I had just been there for him? Would he have needed my Influence to bandage his broken heart? Would he have been able to work through the pain and grief he experienced?"

"There's no way to know the answers to those questions, Taryn. You can't beat yourself up about what might have been," Larkin reasoned.

Tears filled her eyes. "Sometimes it feels like I'm losing myself...like I can't tell where my gifts end and I begin."

Larkin reached up, swiping away her tears. "Since the Trials, you've been under so much pressure. You keep the peace and try to make everyone happy, all while keeping an eye on the Mortari and what's left of the Elder Council." He paused to lean over and kiss her temple softly. "Yesterday you acknowledged things needed to change, I think we should sit down tonight and seriously discuss what needs to happen."

"I created this..." she began to argue.

"There are people willing to step up and help, Taryn. You don't have to carry this burden alone," Larkin assured.

She gave a faint nod before turning and watching their friends disappear into the school.

℠ℹ℠ℹ

The first half of the school day had been a welcome distraction for Taryn. In her Senior English class, she read a book. She was thoroughly engrossed in the story when the bell rang. To gain her attention, Larkin slipped the book from her hands.

Smiling as he marked her page, he nodded in the direction of the opened door. "The second bell's already sounded, Taryn."

"Oh, it's lunch time already," she sighed.

"I'm afraid so," he replied.

After gathering their belongings, Taryn and Larkin headed toward the cafeteria to join the others. Taryn headed to the table where their friends had taken their seats, while Larkin grabbed two lunch trays.

"You're late," Jonesy stated as she took a seat.

"So what..." she said with a shrug.

Jonesy locked eyes with her. "Are you okay, Taryn?"

She sighed. "I'm fine, just a bit tired."

Her cousin continued to study her.

Taryn pursed her lips and arched her brow. "Whatever you're thinking in that big brain of yours, Cousin, keep it to yourself," she warned.

Setting the trays on the table, Larkin took a seat next to Taryn. "What did I miss?" he asked, noting a hint of tension.

From across the table, Andyn smiled an ornery grin. "Jonesy's trying to read Taryn, and she's not feeling it."

Taryn leaned over, kissing Larkin's lips. "Ignore our baby brother, everything is fine," she whispered.

"Your definition of fine or mine?" Larkin inquired.

She rolled her eyes before turning her attention to the food on her tray.

ಬಂಗಬಂಗ

Sitting on the couch in Gastyn's office, Taryn stared at the blank wall to her left.

Entering the small room, Gastyn walked around his desk, taking a seat in his chair. Observing Taryn's distant gaze, he cleared his throat in an attempt to gain her attention. When that failed, he lifted a large book from the corner of his desk and let it fall flat on the floor.

Taryn's stare broke at the sound. She looked at the fallen book and then to Gastyn. "Sorry. I guess I was zoning out."

He smiled fondly at her. "You do not seem to be yourself today. Is everything okay?"

"Yeah…of course." She glanced to the wall then back to her teacher. "What happened to the book shelf that used to sit there?"

Gastyn sighed. "With the prospect of you and the others graduating this spring, I thought it was best for me to start packing up some of my belongings."

Scooting forward on her cushion, Taryn's forehead creased. "What about Andyn…he won't graduate for a few more years?"

"Ilya and I have spoken, and we both agree that it is in Andyn's best interest to be home schooled beginning in the fall," he answered.

Taryn shook her head. "So that's it. You're no longer going to teach?"

Leaning back in his chair, Gastyn took a deep breath. "My services as a teacher in this community have not been required for some time now."

Understanding the meaning of his words, Taryn shook her head. "I never meant to…"

Gastyn quickly cut her off. "Nothing is as it once was. Leaders are now followers. Teachers are now students. And in your case, an isolated girl became the master."

Taryn covered her face with her hands and sighed heavily. After a few moments passed, she placed her hands against the couch cushion and slid back. "I'd do almost anything to be just a girl, for Larkin to be just a boy, for you to be just a teacher, and for Gaias to be regular human beings."

The man's eyes narrowed on the girl's face. "You truly mean that, don't you?" he asked.

She nodded while rising to her feet. "Will you tell Larkin that I'm going for a run to clear my head and I'll see him at home?"

"Of course," Gastyn agreed.

In a blur, the girl disappeared from his office.

⇚ℂℂ⇚ℂℂ

Taryn had no more than made it past the parking lot when she sensed something familiar radiating from within the tree line across the street.

"Chrystian," she whispered.

Without a second thought, she ran straight into the woods, searching for him. Nearly a mile in, she came upon a small clearing where she found him standing there, waiting for her.

"Hello, sweet Taryn," he purred.

Keeping a bit of distance between them, Taryn gave a slight nod of her head. "Chrystian," she stated plainly.

Chrystian smiled wildly. "I see your emotional shield is firmly in place. But one may wonder why a shield is necessary if things are perfect between you and your wolf."

Taryn rolled her eyes. "I have no interest in arguing with you today, Chrystian. So if that's all you have for me, I guess I'll be on my way."

He stepped away from the pathway leading out of the clearing. "If it is your desire to leave, I will not stop you," he said.

Taryn stepped past him. "As if you could," she retorted.

"Before you go, I would like to ask one question of you."

Pausing her step, Taryn exhaled dramatically. "What is it you want to know?"

"Minutes ago you made a declaration to your teacher…did you mean what you said?" he asked.

Slowly turning on her heel, Taryn stared at the Mortari. "Now you're lurking in the school and eavesdropping on my private conversations?"

"Most humans would have made an attempt to answer my question instead of asking a question of their own," Chrystian taunted.

Taryn's stare turned frigid. "Do you, of all people, really want to know if I meant what I said?"

The tall man gave a quick nod. "Of course I do, dear one. If I hadn't, I simply would not have posed the question in the first place."

Rolling her wrists so her palms faced upward, Taryn began to release her gift over the elements. The woods began to darken and the slight breeze that had blown through suddenly stilled. The silence was deafening as she stepped closer to the man.

"I imagine in the beginning it was something truly beautiful to be called Gaias. To be of the earth and have the earth share all its greatness and wonder with us. I shudder to think of how the purity of something so new must have felt flowing through our ancestor's veins." She paused, staring into Chrystian's greenish-brown eyes that held a fleck of amber. "Somewhere in our long history, we became

~ 117 ~

broken as a people. First singularly, but then as a totality we allowed ourselves to become corrupt. And with each passing moment, that corruption continues to fester and grow without bounds."

Chrystian's eyes hardened as he gazed upon the teen. "You are correct. Our kind wields an insatiable appetite for absolute power. We are the greedy that walk the planes thinking only of our own well-being. We take without thought to consequence. We murder, lie, cheat and steal until we possess everything, but still we have nothing." Rushing towards her, he cupped her cheeks in the palms of his hands. "But there is one thing you are wrong about, dearest Taryn." He paused again, his eyes softening as they took in every bit of her face before locking his gaze with hers. "You are nothing like us. You are the only one of our kind who could truly ever possess it all, and yet I believed the conviction of your words when you said you just wanted to be a girl. You may be in conflict with yourself, but your soul burns so brightly that we can only gaze upon a glimpse of its true beauty."

Taryn began to speak. "No, Chrystian, you're wrong…"

He swiped his thumb over her cheek before it landed on her lips, silencing her. "I see you, Taryn. I see you for all that you are, and all that you have the potential to become." A soft smile curled on his face as tears welled in his eyes, eyes that radiated nothing but warmth and love. Leaning forward with her cheeks still secure between his palms, he placed a gentle kiss on her head.

Before Taryn could utter a word, Chrystian ran away in a blur. Sensing he had disappeared within a gateway not far away, she pressed her hand over her heart.

"I love you, too, Chrystian," she whispered.

CHAPTER NINE

The next afternoon, Taryn left Gastyn's class early and headed home to spend time with her father. Sitting on one of the barstools at the kitchen island, Taryn watched as Theron prepared her a plateful of his homemade waffles. The man placed a generous dollop of fresh whipping cream atop her waffles before sliding the plate in front of her.

"Waffles in the afternoon...something heavy must be weighing on your mind," he stated, taking a seat next to her.

Taryn shrugged. "Why can't a girl just want some waffles?"

Studying his daughter's side profile, Theron chuckled. "My waffles are pretty great, aren't they?"

She smiled warmly. "They're amazing, Dad."

After a few moments, Theron placed his hand on Taryn's wrist. "You do know you can tell me anything and I won't judge you, right?" he asked.

Swallowing the last bit of food in her mouth, Taryn set her fork down on the edge of her plate. Turning, she stared at her father's handsome face. Several times she began to speak, but the words seemed to stick in her throat.

Theron turned his stool to face her. He took her hands in his own, giving them a gentle squeeze. "It's okay, Taryn. If you're not comfortable talking with me about what's bothering you, you can always talk to your mother or Ilya. We're all here for you. Whatever you need."

She smiled fondly at him and sighed. "Before, you know, when we didn't really know who we were…you would be on the other side of the island making waffles or pancakes and I'd be sitting here and you would turn and I'd see you standing there wearing armor like a knight would. Looking back, I now understand that on some level a part of me always knew who you were."

The handsome man smiled warmly. "You know I feel the same way. Ilya bringing you here must have awakened fate, because from the first day we met, I felt like you were the daughter I'd always wanted but didn't know I already had."

Biting her lip, Taryn took a deep breath while glancing down at the floor. "I want to ask you something, but I need you to promise that you'll be honest and not hold back."

He nodded. "You can ask me anything, Taryn."

Looking up, she locked eyes with her father. "Do you find me to be duplicitous?" she asked.

Theron's eyes narrowed on his daughter and his forehead creased. "Duplicitous?" he questioned.

"You know, double-dealing, two-faced, dishonest…" she replied.

Scooting to the edge of his seat, Theron shook his head. "I know what the word means, Taryn. What I don't know is why you would ever ask such a thing."

"Why wouldn't I?" she retorted. "You know that I'm almost never honest with any of you about what I'm doing or the things I've done. I keep secrets…"

Grabbing her hand, Theron interrupted. "Keeping things from us is not the same as telling a bold faced lie. And while I, and some of the others, wish that you would let us in more often, we understand that you're only trying to protect us." He paused, studying her angelic face. The torment she struggled with shone heavy in her eyes. "You've taken on so much since the Trials, and it's bound to take its toll."

"But I've done, I've thought and I've wished for things…things that I can't take back. Things that I can't..." she paused.

Theron gave her hands a light squeeze. "I think I understand where all this is coming from." He smiled warmly. "You're one person living two lives simultaneously, while trying your best to keep them separate. Those two lives are bound to bleed into one another, Taryn. So it's no wonder why you would think such a thing. When you stand before the Mortari, the Elder Council or in the face of any sort of adversity, you are absolutely fierce, a force to be reckoned with. Then when you're with us here in Williams, you're Taryn Knight, a daughter, a sister, a friend, our family, a student and a teenaged girl."

Taryn's brows instantly furrowed. *Did Gastyn tell you about our private conversation?* She wondered to herself.

"You know, Princess, if you wanted to talk, you didn't have to pretend to stroke my ego by asking for me to make waffles," Theron stated.

She tilted her head and stared blankly at him. "What are you talking about?" she inquired.

"Look, I know you left school early yesterday and you did it again today. Obviously you have a lot on your mind and needed to talk to someone about it," Theron stated softly.

Pulling away from her father, Taryn turned her focus back to her plate. She picked up her fork and began running its prongs through the whipped cream. "Is it so hard to believe that sometimes a girl just wants to eat waffles?"

Seeing how hard she was working to change the conversation, Theron knew better than to keep pressing her. "The boys will be home soon. Do you think they'll want waffles?" he asked.

"Are you kidding me? Keiryn will pout for at least a week if he finds out that you made waffles and he doesn't get any," Taryn replied.

Cocking his head to the side, Theron listened to the sound of engines racing up the driveway. "The boys always seem to have impeccable timing," he chuckled.

"Hey, at least we know they have good taste," Taryn added.

Moments later the muffled sound of screeching tires and slamming car doors filled the air. The front door to the house opened and heavy footsteps rushed towards the kitchen.

Running into the room first, Larkin wrapped his arms around Taryn. When Keiryn, Andyn and Jonesy came into view, he pressed his lips against Taryn's temple. "I win," he shouted.

Taking a seat next to his sister, Keiryn growled. "Whatever, man. You cheated." Leaning over, he kissed Taryn's cheek.

The girl glanced between the pair before slapping each of them on the back of the head.

"Ouch," Keiryn yelped while rubbing his head. "Take it easy, Sis."

Larkin dared not make a sound as he studied the tense set of her jaw.

"You want me to take it easy?" she growled.

"We were just having some fun," Keiryn insisted.

Taryn's nostrils flared. "You were driving recklessly with Andyn in the car."

"Everything's fine. I had the situation under control," he countered.

Moving off the bar stool, Taryn shoved her brother from his. "Everything most certainly is not fine, Brother. You are a true pack leader now, and Andyn is a member of that pack. You put him at risk, for what…some silly race?"

"Taryn, no one was injured. And I think your brother understands that what he did was wrong," Theron interjected.

Glancing at her father, Taryn's emerald irises churned like a wild vortex. "What he did was not only reckless, but stupid. He had Andyn with him, and Larkin and Jonesy were in the other vehicle. What if something would have happened to one of them?"

The room turned dead silent as she refocused her attention on her older brother.

Keiryn shifted his weight from side to side before finally stepping to her. "Let's be honest here, Sister…what you meant to say is, what if something happened to your precious Larkin."

The venom dripping from his words struck a chord inside Taryn, igniting a strange tingling sensation deep within her soul. She moved away, reclaiming her seat at the kitchen island. Picking up her fork, she began eating her waffles.

Larkin glanced to Theron, then to Keiryn before motioning for his friend to leave the kitchen. Keiryn followed Larkin through the living room and out the French doors.

"What the hell was that about?" Larkin demanded the moment they were away from the deck.

Keiryn rubbed his neck. "I don't know…"

Taking a step back, Larkin noticed the distant look in his friend's eyes. "Hey, are you okay?" he asked.

Too dazed to speak, Keiryn stumbled over to one of the lounge chairs next to the pool and slumped onto it.

Larkin helped straighten his friend in the chair while scanning him from head to toe. "Hold on, Brother. I'm going to make her set this right."

He ran back to the French doors, sticking his head just inside. "Taryn, get out here now," he shouted.

Theron, Jonesy and Andyn rushed outside toward the backyard while Taryn finished the last bite of waffle on her plate.

Stepping outside, Theron gasped at seeing his son slumped over in the chair. "What happened to him?" he demanded, rushing to Keiryn's side.

Larkin shook his head frantically. "I don't know. I think maybe Taryn did something to him when they were arguing in the kitchen."

Now standing near the edge of the deck, Taryn heard Larkin's accusation. Just hearing him utter those words caused a sharp stabbing sensation within her chest. The pain felt like a fiery dagger had been plunged into her heart over and over again. Even in her heartache, her eyes panned, focusing on her brother's limp body. "Keiryn..." she gasped. Suddenly, the voices of the ancient dead screamed inside her mind, causing her to fall and strike her head against the ground.

When Taryn came to, she found herself sitting at the island, watching as Maxym worked to prepare a plate full of waffles.

"Did you want whipped topping or syrup?" he asked.

She sat dazed for a moment.

"Earth to, Taryn," Maxym stated while waving a small plate of waffles.

"Wh...what?" she asked.

Maxym arched a brow in her direction. "Whipped topping or syrup?" he asked again.

"Oh. Um...whipped topping please," she stammered.

With a curious look in his eyes, Maxym placed a large dollop of fresh whipped cream on her waffles and slid the plate across the island to her. "Taryn, is everything okay?" he asked.

A feeling of deja vu crept over her, causing a shiver to course down her spine. Shaking her head to hide her discomfort, Taryn took a deep breath. "Why does there have to be anything wrong? Why can't a girl just want to eat some waffles?"

Stepping back, Maxym leaned against the counter. "You're not an easy person to read, Taryn. I'm sorry if my asking if you were okay upset you, but you are dating my son and sometimes we dads worry, so we ask questions."

Taryn's lips pursed and her forehead creased. "Well, I have a question of my own," she announced.

"What exactly would you like to know?" he asked.

Rising from her seat, Taryn glanced around. "Where's my dad and why are you making waffles?"

The man's face wrinkled while his brows turned downward. "Theron's out back with Larkin and Keiryn trying to save Jonesy," he answered.

Taryn's eyes widened. "What do you mean they're trying to save Jonesy?"

Maxym turned, picking up the glass bowl containing the waffle batter. "Don't ask me, Taryn. You're the one killing him."

She shook her head. "I would never hurt Jonesy," she rebutted.

Shrugging his shoulders, Maxym sighed. "We didn't believe you would either. But now he's outside dying because of what you did."

Confused, Taryn rushed to the French doors, but when she opened them, she once more found herself sitting back at the kitchen island, the smell of waffles permeating the air.

Almost afraid to look up, Taryn slowly raised her head. On the other side of the counter she saw Ilya and her mother working furiously to make waffles. "Mom...Ilya..." she stated just above a whisper.

Gracyn immediately turned around. "Taryn, I didn't realize you had come back inside."

Glancing over her shoulder, Ilya called out, "Hey there, Sweetie, is Andyn doing better?"

Running her hands over her face, Taryn sighed heavily. She sensed a recurring theme, but decided it was best to ask the question anyway. "What do you mean, is Andyn doing better?"

The woman turned around, giving Gracyn a strange glance before looking to Taryn. "You can't possibly be serious," she snapped.

"What did I do?" Taryn questioned.

Ilya's hands fisted. "Gracyn, talk to your daughter. I can't deal with any more of her lies." The woman glared at Taryn as she walked toward the doorway.

Gracyn shook her head. "Ilya's right, Taryn. I will not listen to your lies. You poisoned that boy, and now you're sitting here as if you didn't see it coming."

Noticing the inconsistency within her mother's words, Taryn rose from her seat. "What didn't I see coming?" she asked.

Turning her back to Taryn, Gracyn returned to making more waffles.

"Please, Mom…what didn't I see coming?" Taryn pressed.

The woman paused in whipping the batter. "You are my daughter, but you continuously choose to ignore what is right in front of you. That first time in the garden, when you saw me walking between the guards…you knew, but you chose not to act."

She shook her head. "No…you, you're wrong. I didn't know," Taryn argued.

"You could have ended my suffering before it ever began," Gracyn stated.

Taryn hung her head. "That's not fair. I was just a little girl when they took you."

"Dearest Taryn, what are you babbling about now child?" Nodryck growled.

Hearing his voice, Taryn's jaw drew up tight and her nostrils flared. Lifting her head, she startled in seeing Coyan standing beside the dark-haired devil with a wire whisk in hand.

The Mortari man's eyes lit with delight. "I see you did not envision this to be the outcome of your sentencing."

Sharing a glance, the men broke into laughter.

Taryn slammed the palms of her hands against the granite countertop of the island. "Shut up!" she screamed.

The pair shared another glance before pausing in their merriment.

"Could it be that she truly does not know?" Nodryck stated.

Coyan set the whisk and bowl down on the counter before moving closer to the girl. He stopped once he stood beside her. His eyes drank in her side profile. "My brothers may be blinded by your beauty, dearest one, but I see the desolation that hides within." He lifted his hand to her cheek. "I cannot believe that you are here with us while your wolf struggles to take his last breath."

Locking eyes with the man, Taryn grabbed his wrist. "I will end you," she seethed.

“⎈⎈⎈”

Taryn woke with a start and a death grip on her bedroom pillow. The blood in her veins flowed furiously past her eardrums, causing the sound of her beating heart to drown out all other noise.

From the beanbag in the corner of the room, Larkin saw her move and rushed to her side. She thrashed about frantically until he covered her hands with his own, bringing her calm.

"Easy does it, Tare-Bear. I don't believe that pillow has actually committed any crime," he stated.

The sound of his voice soothed her soul, and the sight of his handsome face brought a smile to her own. "It's really you," she whispered.

He flashed a heart-melting grin. "Of course it's really me. Were you expecting someone else?" Larkin asked.

Taryn sat up in the bed, wrapping her arms tightly around his neck and burying her face against his skin.

"What's this all about?" he asked, hugging her back.

After a long moment passed, Taryn released her grip and leaned back. "It was just a bad dream," she answered.

Larkin pressed his hand against her forehead. "You seem more disoriented than usual. Are you feeling okay?"

She shrugged. "I feel fine. But when did you get home from school?"

Running one of his hands through his hair, he released a hefty sigh. "What's the last thing you remember?" he asked.

"I skipped Gastyn's class and came home," she replied. "My dad was fixing me waffles when…"

Larkin sighed again, this time shaking his head. "Taryn, we haven't been at school since spring break."

Her forehead wrinkled. "No, we were there today. Mr. Reyes assigned us a project during second hour, and you were complaining about it." She paused, studying the unwavering look on his face. "Ask Gastyn, we were there yesterday. I spoke with him in his office and he told me he wasn't going to teach after we graduate. I told him to let you know that I was going for a run…"

Larkin shook his head. "I'm sorry, Taryn, but none of that happened."

"No," she shouted. "I left school yesterday and I ran into Chrystian in the woods. We talked for a few minutes and then I came home. You brought Andyn home and your dad and Ilya came over for dinner."

The young man's eyes grew weighted. "It's impossible, Taryn. You've been unconscious since Lazryn and I told you about the ghosts in the reflection."

Her eyes narrowed as she glanced around the room. "Okay, I've been unconscious for a couple of hours. So why are you looking at me like I'm a crazy person, Larkin?"

Taking her hands in his, he gently shook his head. "You have been asleep for more than a week now, Taryn."

She arched a brow in his direction and pulled away. "I've been out for how long?"

"Almost a week and a half," he answered.

Taryn took a deep breath. "So you're telling me that I slept through the remainder of March, and that it's now April?"

Larkin nodded. "I'm afraid so."

Placing her hands on either side of her head, Taryn fell back into her pillow. "Who's been watching over the communities and the planes?" she asked.

"Keiryn, Jonesy, both your parents and Lazryn," he stated.

She stared at the ceiling. "Seriously, my parents?"

The young man lay down on his side next to her, taking in her face. "They've done well, especially your mother." He paused, chuckling for a moment. "You are most definitely her daughter."

Rolling onto her side, Taryn looked at Larkin. "Why did you say it like that?"

He smiled. "The first time they went out it was to a community on Rongor. Lazryn tried explaining that you had decided to delegate some of the responsibility while you and I took some time to ourselves. A few men started mouthing off about you not being there and said it showed you didn't care and didn't mean anything you said during the Trials. In fact, they called themselves the forgotten ones."

"So what'd she do?" Taryn questioned.

"At first she tried reasoning with them. When that didn't work, she walked right up to one of them and punched him square in the nose. The man fell out like a sleeping baby, and she warned the others not to talk about you in such a way. Needless to say, they all shut up and gave Keiryn a chance to fill in during your absence," he explained.

"And how did my big brother do?" she asked.

Larkin smiled. "According to Lazryn, everyone was happy before they left."

Taryn propped herself up on her elbow. "Good. I'm glad it went well for him."

Reaching over, Larkin brushed a few strands of hair from her face. "It's really good to see you awake and talking, and to see your eyes. I've missed seeing their sparkle."

She leaned in, kissing his lips softly. "I've missed doing that," she whispered. Moving in even closer, she snuggled against his strong frame. "So, what have you been doing while I was napping?"

He kissed the tip of her nose then her forehead before wrapping his arms around her. "Well, I've been doing some reading."

Taryn looked up at him with an arched brow. "You, reading...seriously?"

"I know, I know. I can hardly believe it myself…but these books, they're not your typical everyday read," he replied.

"Oh yeah, why is that?" she inquired.

Larkin scrunched his brow and twisted his lips awkwardly. "I opened your gift from Chrystian," he answered sheepishly.

Pushing back slightly, Taryn stared at Larkin. "Chrystian gave me books?" she asked.

He nodded and motioned to the opened crate sitting on the floor next to the beanbag. "Most of the books are really old. In fact, Lazryn referred to them as ancient, if that tells you anything."

Taryn grinned, thinking about how much it bothered Lazryn to be referred to as old. She could only imagine how he responded to being called ancient. "I bet you had a hard time holding back the old man comments," she chuckled.

"Sorry, Tare-Bear, but I couldn't resist. The old man made it too easy," Larkin replied with an ornery smile.

Taryn looked at Larkin with a weighted gaze. "Speaking of old, there's someone I need to speak with," she stated.

Larkin ran his fingertips up the back of Taryn's neck. "Don't you want to at least look at the books first?" he questioned.

She shook her head. "Sorry, Wolfy, this is one conversation that is long overdue."

৩০০৪৪০০৪

Gripping the metal handle on the heavy glass door, Taryn glanced over her shoulder at Larkin as he placed a strong hand over hers.

"Look, I know this isn't ideal, Larkin, but I need to speak with him," she insisted.

The young man sighed heavily. "It's a hospice care facility, Taryn. Don't you find it a bit…well, rude?" Larkin questioned.

"I don't like it either, but I need to talk with Farren, and it can't wait," Taryn stated adamantly.

"What's the hurry? Why is it so important that you talk to him right now?" Larkin inquired.

Rolling her eyes, Taryn flashed a faint smile. "Can you think of anyone better to ask about the ghosts who've been following me than Death himself?"

Knowing there was no one else that could help, Larkin shrugged, pulling the door open. "Ladies first," he sighed.

80C380C3

Walking down a long hallway, Taryn glanced inside several rooms, looking for any sign of Farren. She felt the cold hand of death in the air, but she could not see her friend.

"I know you're here, Deadman," she whispered, as she moved on to the next open doorway, Taryn was surprised to see an old woman sitting up in her bed, almost grinning while her loved ones surrounded her with tears streaming from their eyes.

Taryn stared at the woman's wrinkled face and faded brown irises. Something about the old woman left her feeling unsettled. Taking Larkin's hand, she continued down the hallway.

In the next room, there was a young man, possibly in his mid-thirties sitting up in his bed while staring blankly out the opened door. Noticing he was alone, Taryn looked to Larkin, then led him into the room.

Once inside, she released his hand and moved closer to the man's bed. His frail body was hooked up to a number of machines and monitors meant to ease his pain as the end of his life neared. Taryn glanced at each one and then turned with a furrowed brow in the young man's direction.

"Taryn, what are you looking at?" Larkin asked.

She pointed to the flat line at the top of one of the monitors, then to the double zeros in the upper right hand corner. "This man is dead," she replied.

Moving closer to his love, Larkin placed a gentle hand on her shoulder. "I'm not sure what you're seeing right now, but there isn't anyone else in here, Taryn."

She glanced to Larkin then back to the bed, then looked around the room. Her eyes narrowed as she observed the now empty bed and the equipment lining the walls, all of which were currently unplugged.

When she turned around to face Larkin, he was no longer there. The unsettled feeling she had experienced earlier, returned with a vengeance.

"Larkin, where are you?" she called out.

With no answer, Taryn ran into the hallway searching for him. She caught a glimpse of him turning the corner several yards away and followed after him in a blur. Only a few seconds passed before she stopped running. To the front of her was an incredibly long hallway that looked as though it would never end. She glanced back over her shoulder and found that the hallway behind her looked the same.

She tried running back to where she had come from, but it was no use. The corner she had turned to get to this point was no longer visible.

Taryn closed her eyes and tried pinpointing Larkin's location, but alas, there were no markers, no traces, no hint of his gifts lingering or any other sign of him.

An electric chill coursed up her spine causing her eyelids to open wide. She spun around, watching as the overhead lights at both ends of the infinite hallway began to go out. One light fixture after another turned off, making a distinct clicking sound as the darkness closed in on the teen. Holding her position, Taryn's nostrils flared and a wicked smile curled on her face. With a final click sounding overhead, she stared ahead, ready for whatever awaited her.

₧∓₧∓

Standing in perpetual darkness, Taryn inhaled deeply. Familiar scents swirled around her, though they were nothing she could identify definitively. Lifting her hand palm up, she created a power orb the size of a basketball. The orb hovered a foot above her palm and emitted a soft glow that was blue in color.

Without a word, she began walking, paying close attention to the shadows lurking within the dark. She watched as they shrank away from the orb's light as she passed.

Taryn walked only a few meters before the low rumble of whispers began to break through the silence. The teen forged on, but was surprised when she was able to identify fragments of sentences.

"Let it go and free..." a woman's voice said before breaking off into something inaudible.

"Only when the fallen rise will there be..." another whispered as her voice faded.

Unfortunately, for the teen, everything after that sounded like a combination of white noise and gibberish.

Stopping in her tracks, Taryn increased her orb's glow until it illuminated everything within a twenty-foot radius. She frowned as she looked down, recognizing the barren ground beneath the soles of her shoes. "The Void? You brought me into The Void?" she growled.

The whispers went silent, and everything stilled around her.

Suddenly a woman's voice called out from the darkness. "Taryn, is it truly you?" she asked

Rolling her eyes, Taryn released a low growl. "Don't even think about trying to steal my body again, Loryn," she warned.

The woman stepped into the glow of Taryn's orb, causing the teen's brows to arch slightly.

Sweeping what remained of her hair off to one side of her neck, Loryn gave Taryn more than an eyeful of her severely scarred flesh.

"If you're trying to guilt me about what happened last time we saw one another, it's not going to work," Taryn stated flatly.

The woman gave a slight nod of her head. "I only meant to give you a better look at your handiwork, Taryn. No one here, not even the mighty Thantos himself, believed that someone living could ever reach into his Void."

Taryn drew her jaw up tight. "Given the circumstances at the time, one might say that I was extremely motivated. But just so we are crystal clear on where things stand between us…if you so much as think about possessing my body again, I will erase every image, thought, and memory of you from the minds and hearts of your loved ones. And when I am finished, I will come back into the Void and I will erase you from existence."

The woman shuddered at the girl's threat. "I no longer wish to return to the world of the living, Taryn. This I promise. I only now remain in the Void to assist you."

Unaffected by the woman's words, Taryn stared harshly at her. "Then tell me, Loryn, why exactly am I in the Void?" she demanded.

Lowering her eyes, Loryn swallowed hard. "Please, Taryn, I am truly sorry for the part I have played in causing you pain."

Growing less interested by the second, Taryn stepped toward the woman. "I don't care if you're sorry or not, Loryn. My only concerns are why have I been brought into the Void, and why are there a group of Gaias ghosts haunting me?"

Loryn nodded. "I will tell you what I know, but it may leave you with more questions than answers."

"Just tell me what you know, and I will decide what questions I have, okay?" Taryn stated coolly.

"Fine, but remember you were warned." Loryn paused, looking to Taryn for acknowledgement. When the teen nodded, she continued. "The ghosts that you are speaking of, when they were alive, they were the elite of Gaias-kind. The very sound of any of their names falling from one's lips struck fear in the hearts of those who understood the immensity of power that these special few held, much the same as it is with you now."

The mere thought of being compared to anyone in this specific group made the bile in Taryn's stomach churn. Her eyes narrowed as one side of her mouth curled into a sneer.

Noticing the look of disdain growing on the teen's face, Loryn interjected her own opinion. "You no more approve of the Oracle, Elayna Delrayn, than I do of Colyn Danbrym."

Taryn's frigid glare softened, but only slightly. "Colyn's been here in the Void with you this entire time?" she asked.

Loryn nodded. "He was poisoned shortly after discovering the talents of none other than the Oracle herself, Elayna Delrayn."

The teen stepped closer to her. "Poisoned?"

"I am quite certain that the Elder Council's history books say otherwise, but yes, Colyn was poisoned, and before you ask, it was with the Cardanous Flower," Loryn explained.

Taryn's mind went into overdrive. "You're telling me that the very man who ordered the eradication of all Healers was then murdered after discovering Elayna's special gifts?"

The scarred woman shrugged. "Remember, I warned you about more questions than answers."

Taking a deep breath, Taryn refocused her thoughts. "Duly noted. Now, what else do you know?"

"In death, the Elites appear to be bound to one another. For decades many of us have tried conversing with them. We consider it a good year if we are able to understand two consecutive words when they speak." Loryn paused. "I believe they want to tell you something, Taryn, but I do not think they are able to."

Releasing the orb to float on its own, Taryn walked to the edge of its glow. "I was able to make out two distinct voices earlier, both women. Most of what I heard was white noise and gibberish, but there was a brief moment when I heard their words as plain as I hear you now."

Loryn's eyes widened. "What did they say?"

"Nothing that concerns you currently," Taryn replied.

Stepping closer to Taryn, Loryn inhaled deeply. "I know this isn't the first time that they have brought you here, Taryn. What if they brought you into the Void in an attempt to make themselves heard by you?"

Glancing over her shoulder, Taryn stared at the woman's disfigured face. "Besides Colyn Danbrym, there is another man accompanying the so called Elites. Who is he?" Taryn asked.

"The man with the shifting face?" Loryn questioned.

Taryn shrugged. "I don't know if his face shifts or not. I only know that Lazryn didn't recognize him."

"Lazryn," Loryn gasped. "He was so angry with me for what I did to you."

"Not just me, Loryn, but Chrystian, too. While I understand why you did what you did, it doesn't change the fact that it was cruel and selfish," Taryn stated flatly.

"My brother hates me," Loryn sobbed.

Rolling her eyes, Taryn exhaled forcefully. "Lazryn doesn't hate you. In fact, he was hoping you found peace."

"I was wrong for what I did. I realize that now. Fate placed you in my path, and when I realized it was possible to reunite with Chrystian, the temptation was too great for me to ignore," Loryn explained.

"You're getting off topic, Loryn. The man with the shifting face, tell me who he is," Taryn insisted.

Wiping the tears from her eyes, Loryn sniffled and nodded. "His name is Laertas Dominion."

Taryn turned, walking back to the orb. "Thanks for confirming my suspicions, Loryn, but it's time for me to leave."

The woman looked to the ground and fought the tears welling in her eyes. "I have no right to ask anything of you, Taryn, but I would be eternally grateful if you could somehow leave your orb behind. Even if it fades after you're gone, it feels good to stand in the light after a millennium of darkness."

Taryn gave a soft smile and raised her hands in the air. "I'll do you one better," the teen said.

Loryn watched in awe as over one thousand glowing orbs formed overhead.

Using her gifts, Taryn pushed the orbs out into perfectly spaced rows, illuminating several acres inside the Void. The air filled with the sound of joyous cries.

The teen's face turned soft. "I realize that you're all dead, but I don't see any reason to keep you in the dark. What purpose could it possibly serve?"

Flashing a slight smile, Loryn began trying to hide her scars with what was left of her hair. "We are not meant to linger here, Taryn. Some of us simply cannot move on until our souls find peace."

Watching as the woman continued to struggle with her hair, Taryn walked over to her, placing her hands on either side of her head. The teen forced her gift of Healing into the woman, restoring her physical beauty.

Feeling Taryn's gifts flowing through her, Loryn fell to her knees. "Thank you, Taryn. Thank you," she sobbed.

Taryn removed her hands and slowly backed away. "You're Lazryn's sister, and I care deeply for your brother. It will make him happy to know that you are whole again. Not just physically, but possibly mentally too."

With tears continuing to stream down her cheeks, Loryn nodded. "You are kind and merciful, Taryn, and I will try to find a way to send you back to your Larkin."

A wild smile curled on the teen's face. "Thanks, but I have it covered."

Loryn watched as the teen turned and disappeared in a blur within the darkness of the Void. She stared in the direction that Taryn went and observed a bright red glow forming in the distance. Waves of heat pulsed against her skin and then abruptly, both the glow and heat disappeared, leaving behind only the illumination from the teen's numerous blue orbs.

The woman glanced over her shoulder as Elayna, Laertas and the others stepped out from the shadows. With an arched brow, she smiled devilishly. "I told you Taryn was the one," she stated while caressing her newly healed flesh. "She is most vulnerable when her mind is soft in sleep and dreams chase her. I want each of you there, creating as much chaos and confusion as possible. Understood?"

Each of the Elite nodded in agreement.

ᾒCᾒC

Pacing the full length of the room, Larkin paused, running his fingers through his hair. A heavy sigh escaped his lips as he stared at Taryn. It had been more than half an hour since her eyes had glossed over and her body stilled.

He moved near her and lifted his hand to her cheek, caressing her soft skin with the back of his fingers. "Come on, Tare-Bear. Come back to me, please," he whispered as he kissed her forehead. Stepping back, Larkin observed Taryn's green irises flicker with an intense shade of blue. "Taryn?" he questioned.

Suddenly, her long lashes began to flutter and her eyes returned to their normal shade of emerald green. Glancing around the room, Taryn shook her head. "Larkin?"

A sigh of relief left his chest. Stepping closer, he wrapped his arms around her. "I was so worried…"

Taryn hugged him back. "Haven't you figured it out yet? There is nothing and no one that will ever be able to keep me from returning to you." She smiled sweetly at him.

Though her tone was playful, Larkin knew she meant every word. Pulling back slightly, he could see the ferocity gleaming within her eyes. He reached up and brushed the hair from her shoulders. "Were you able to speak with Farren?" he asked.

She tilted her head and arched her brows. "No. I wasn't with the Deadman."

Larkin's nostrils flared. "Elayna and the others pulled you away again, didn't they?"

Taking a step back, Taryn nodded. "They took me to the Void. I think it's safe to say that's where they have taken me all the times before as well," she stated.

"The Void?" Larkin growled.

Seeing the mixture of fear and anger dancing in his eyes, Taryn mentally kicked herself for staying gone far too long. "I'm sorry I didn't return sooner, but I think they're trying to tell me something."

"What exactly do you believe the dead are trying to say, dear one?" Farren questioned.

Spinning around on her heel, Taryn glared at her friend. As always, he wore a fancy, dark colored suit. His blond hair cut perfect to accent his handsome face. "You were hiding from me. Why?" she demanded.

Death moved like vapor from one spot to the next. Standing beside her, he whispered. "Only when the fallen rise will there be..."

Taryn turned her head and stared into his swirling blue irises. "What happens when the fallen rise?" she asked.

Farren disappeared, only to reappear on the opposite side of her. "Let it go and free..." he whispered.

The teen turned and he disappeared once again. "You're pressing your luck, Deadman," she warned.

Death appeared in the doorway and smiled. "That which you seek lies within the mind's eye. Clarity is to be had by those able to listen with their heart and feel with their head."

Taryn's brows furrowed. "Is this payback for me saving the man in the park that day?"

Continuing to smile, Farren stepped forward until he stood face-to-face with the girl.

She shook her head and sighed. "I know you won't answer me outright, but I need to understand why I am dreaming of harming my family, and what happened to Dagrin and his followers. He walks freely in the sunlight and werewolf toxins no longer have any effect on him." Taryn paused, trying to get a read on her friend. "He took Larkin's blood, a tuft of his fur and the tips of his claws. What's his end game? What is he trying to create?" she pressed.

Farren reached his hand out and touched her cheek with the tips of his fingers. For a moment, the swells within his watery blue irises stilled, displaying an immense beauty within. His smile softened as he began to press his fingertips firmly against the teen's flesh.

Feeling a strange sensation radiating from his touch, Taryn grabbed his wrist and shouted. "Stop, something's wrong," she said, her words catching in her throat.

Suddenly, Death's fingertips disappeared beneath her skin. "I wish there was another way, dear one. I am afraid this is going to be most painful," he replied with the utmost calm in his silky voice.

She released his wrist and whimpered, "Farren."

The teen's eyes widened as Death pressed forcefully into her, until he was no longer visible. She felt his presence residing within the fabric of her own being.

"Truths are lies in the dreams that are real. You must lose yourself in order for the fallen to rise. The mighty have succumbed, the wise have both withered, a betrayer swallowed betrayal, and the oracle fell victim to her own bonds," Farren's voice whispered inside her head as though his words were her own thoughts.

A harsh chill shook her spine. "Farren?" she gasped as its intensity grew. Screaming in agony, Taryn realized the pain she felt was Death leaving her. She glanced over her shoulder just in time to watch her friend disappear for a final time.

With Farren now gone, Taryn found herself staring at Larkin with the mixture of fear and worry still dancing in his hazel eyes. Swallowing down every bit of emotion that fought to rise up, she shook her head. "We need to leave now. We'll talk it out on the drive back to Williams," she stated, grabbing his hand and leading him to the nearest exit.

₧℃₧℃

Driving past the city limits of Flagstaff, Larkin glanced at Taryn. There she sat, with her arms folded across her waist, narrowed eyes staring off into the distance. He reached over, placing his hand on her leg. "I take it you spoke with Farren," he stated.

The very thought of the Deadman caused a massive shiver to course up her spine. She swallowed hard. "Yeah, something like that," she replied.

Feeling the pulse of her gifts radiating from her, Larkin pulled off to the side of the Interstate. "Do you want to talk about it?" he asked.

She shrugged. "I wouldn't know what to say or where to begin…"

Moving his hand up from her thigh to her forearm, he gave a gentle tug and then slid his hand over hers. "We don't have to discuss what happened if you're not ready." He paused, stroking his thumb over the top of her hand. "The way you practically drug me out of that facility tells me everything I need to know for the moment."

Glancing in the side mirror, Taryn exhaled audibly. "Inside my own head I cannot find a moment of peace." She paused, turning in her seat and pulling her knees to her chest. "We came here for answers and I'm taken into the Void where I'm fed bits and pieces of information by the ghosts of Gaias past. Most of whom I don't care for as it is. Then I leave the Void and Farren's hiding from me. Of course when he decides to reveal himself, he speaks in riddles and…" her voice trailed off.

Leaning in, Larkin asked, "And what, Taryn? What happened while you were with Farren?"

She looked at him with wild eyes. "He merged with me."

Larkin's face twisted with a myriad of unpleasant emotions. "Merged with you? What exactly do you mean by that?"

The girl covered her face with her hands. After a few lingering moments passed, she lowered her hands to her lap and leaned her back against the door. "I don't know…he touched my face and before I realized what he was doing, he began merging his cells with mine." She paused, glancing at Larkin before turning and staring out the windshield. "His thoughts were as clear in my head as my own. It was like he was talking to me, but the only difference was he was part of me, and I was part of him."

Reaching out, Larkin grabbed hold of her hand. He took a deep breath, swallowing down his anger and frustration. "What Farren did, it clearly had an effect on you. Whatever you want or need, Taryn, I'm here for you."

She flashed a faint smile as her eyes panned to his handsome face. "Thank you," she said, biting her bottom lip. With a hefty sigh, she glanced again in the side mirror, and then back to her love. "What Farren did back there, he did it for a reason."

Larkin rolled his eyes. "I'm sure he'll find a way to justify what he did, but I'm not okay with it. He's upset you, and he most definitely overstepped..."

"Please stop," Taryn asked.

Pausing, Larkin saw the pain etched beautifully within her eyes. "I don't understand why you think you deserve the things that happen to you, Taryn."

A faint smile curled on her face. "You know I don't feel guilt, Larkin. At least not like you and the others do." She paused, taking in his handsome face and shaggy hair. "My choices, my decisions cause simultaneous elation and fear throughout our kind. They live in a state of constant worry, afraid to allow themselves to truly be free," she explained.

Larkin's eyes softened as he gazed at her. "That's a bit arrogant even for you, don't you think? To believe that one teenaged girl could have such a profound effect on an entire race of gifted beings. It's simply ludicrous," he said with a warm smile.

Taryn shook her head and grinned. "Let's head back to Williams before the others discover they can't possibly continue to function in my absence," she joked.

Leaning over into her seat, Larkin pressed his lips against hers. "I love you," he whispered.

"I love you, too, Wolfy," she whispered back.

CHAPTER TEN

Walking in the front door of their home, Taryn and Larkin were greeted by the sound of laughter. Keiryn, Jonesy, Andyn, Maxym, Theron, Julius, Gastyn and Dedrick had gathered around the coffee table and were playing a card game.

As they drew nearer, Taryn spotted several spoons sitting on the table in front of them.

"Sounds like you guys are having fun," she stated.

Turning around, Keiryn flashed a warm smile before rushing to her. Pulling her into a fierce hug, he lifted Taryn's feet off the ground and kissed her cheek. "It's so good to see your green eyes, baby sister," he whispered as he placed her feet back on the floor and stepped back.

"You weren't worried, were you?" she questioned.

A serious look washed over his face. "Worried, no. Terrified...maybe. You were gone and..."

Taryn grabbed hold of her brother tightly. "And I'm back now, Keiryn. No one is ever going to tear our family apart again. I promise," she whispered.

Keiryn fiercely held onto his sister as tears streamed from his eyes. "It felt different this time," he whispered.

Pushing back gently, Taryn's forehead creased and the air caught in her lungs. Unable to speak, she took several small steps away from him.

Seeing her distress, Larkin stepped up, placing his hand on the small of her back. "You okay, Tare-Bear?"

She licked her lips, took a deep breath and forced a radiant smile to curl on her face. "Never better," she stated while glancing out the windows. Seeing her mother, Ilya, Nalani and Jayma sitting outside next to the pool, Taryn casually nodded in the direction of the French doors. "I'm going to leave you boys to your game and go say hello to the ladies."

"I'll join you," Larkin insisted.

Taryn shook her head. "You should stay here and have some guy time. Besides, I think I could use some alone time with the girls."

He looked at her with soft eyes. "Yeah, okay. But if you need…"

Taryn interrupted with a warm smile. "I know. You'll be right here." She pressed up on her toes to kiss his cheek before heading toward the doors.

As his sister passed by, Keiryn reached for her hand and gave it a gentle squeeze. "We're all here if you need anything, anything at all, Taryn."

She paused, flashing him a vibrant smile. "I know," she replied, before pulling away. "You guys have fun with your cards and spoons."

☙ℭ❧ℭ❧

Inhaling deeply as she stepped off the deck, Taryn glanced to the sky. There was not a visible cloud anywhere, but she could still smell the impending rainstorm nearing.

"What is it?" Gracyn asked.

Moving toward the small group, Taryn nodded in the direction of the sunny skies. "There's a storm brewing in the distance. It should arrive around twelve-thirty-seven tonight."

While Jayma worked to make room for another chair around the small table, she shared a brief glance with the others. "The weather man called for clear skies for the next three days," she said, patting the seat beside her. "But if you say it's going to rain at twelve-thirty-seven, Child, I'm putting my money in your corner. I'd be a fool otherwise."

Arching her brow, Taryn sat down between the woman and her mother.

"Would you like a glass of tea?" Gracyn offered.

Taryn shook her head. "No thanks, I'm good."

"Are you?" Nalani asked, her face absent of all emotion.

Shifting in her chair, Taryn looked at the beautiful girl. "Am I what?" she questioned.

Nalani looked to Ilya.

The woman smiled warmly at Taryn. "She's asking if you are good now. You gave us a bit of a scare this time," Ilya explained.

Taryn stared in her friend's direction for a long moment before looking around the table. "As you can see, I am perfectly fine. I needed time to myself to work a few things out, that is all," she offered.

"Well, I, for one, am relieved to see you up and about," Gracyn stated while lifting her glass from the table. She took a sip before setting it back down and glancing toward one of the floor to ceiling windows. "I see Larkin still isn't ready to let you out of his sight," she grinned.

Ilya waved at the young man and he nodded politely in response. "He has watched over our girl since we moved to Williams."

Taryn gazed into the distance, recalling the numerous times she had visions of Larkin while living in Galatia. Her cheeks turned rosy and an audible sigh escaped her throat.

"Is there something you'd like to share with the rest of us?" Nalani teased.

An electrifying smile lit Taryn's face. "Larkin has always been with me. Even back in Kansas, he was there whenever I needed him." She paused, looking at her great love. "He's the keeper of my heart, and I know he will always keep it safe for me."

Nalani sighed. "It makes perfect sense. Larkin never showed the slightest interest in a girl until you came along."

Rolling her eyes, Taryn leaned back in the chair. "As fascinating a topic as Larkin and I can be, isn't there something…anything else you guys want to talk about?" she asked.

Gracyn's eyes lit. "Well, since you're asking."

"That sounded ominous," Taryn retorted while tilting her head back and staring blankly at the colorful umbrella.

Jayma elbowed Taryn lightly in the ribcage. "Your mothers want to take you prom dress shopping," she announced.

Taryn leaned forward, resting her forehead against the wire tabletop. "Seriously…prom…I don't even have a date," she sighed.

"If you don't want to, Taryn," Gracyn replied.

"Don't let her off the hook that easy," Ilya insisted. "You want the mother-daughter prom experience, Gracyn. It's important to you. I'm sure Taryn understands that," the woman goaded.

With her head still pressed firmly against the table, Taryn turned her neck just enough to glance at both Ilya and her mother. "Okay. Okay. I surrender. I'll go prom dress shopping with you guys." She paused, lifting her head from the table and straightening up in her seat. "But I have one condition that is not up for discussion," the teen warned.

Ilya and Gracyn shared a glance then focused back to Taryn.

"Go on," her mother prompted.

"Red is not a color option. I don't want to see any red dresses, shoes, jewelry, lipstick or whatever. Anything, but red. Understood?"

Gracyn's smile widened. "Got it. No red."

Sitting on the oversized beanbag in the corner of her room, Taryn stared at the half-empty crate of books to her left. Taking a deep breath, she glanced to the bed where Larkin lay fast asleep. He had left a few books scattered about on the floor, but none of them had stood out to her as special or important. Reaching inside the crate, she carefully withdrew another book. She ran her fingertips over it, taking in the soft grey leather cover. There was a small symbol burned into the upper right corner. Though it had faded with time, she could still see the remnants of a clover-like pattern. Cracking open the book, Taryn thumbed through the first few pages. Again, nothing stood out to her.

Placing it next to her on the floor, she reached in, pulling out the last few books. One was covered with a faded green cloth while another possessed a pristine brown leather exterior. She slipped a book out from the bottom of the stack and gazed at its tattered and torn, white cloth cover. The spine had several dark smudges, though none looked like dirt.

With her curiosity piqued, Taryn pulled at the top cover in an attempt to open the book. Her forehead creased when it would not budge. Again, she tugged at the top cover and like before, it would not open for her.

Frowning, she set the other books aside, giving special attention to the curiously difficult book. She ran her fingers along its spine, studying the varying shades of smudges. For a brief moment, the teen could have sworn that she felt a pulse coming from within its locked pages. Resting the book on its spine, Taryn focused her attention on its paper edges. Unlike the cover, they appeared to be in near perfect condition. There were no visible smudges or inconsistencies.

Weird, she thought to herself.

Gripping the front and back covers, Taryn prepared once more to try to open the book. With all of her strength, she pulled in opposite directions. When they still would not open, not even the width of a hair, Taryn tried forcing her Imperium power between the obstinate pages. Her gift simply rolled over its surface. Stumped, the teen set the book aside and then placed the remaining books back in the crate.

For several moments, she stared at Larkin as he continued to lie fast asleep in bed. Taking a deep breath, she grabbed the book and rose to her feet. She made her way to the dresser and placed the curious book inside the top drawer beneath a few articles of clothing. Once it was no longer visible, Taryn closed the drawer and crawled back into bed. Snuggling against Larkin, she placed her head against his chest and fell asleep listening to the sound of his perfectly beating heart.

૪)୦ଃ૪)୦ଃ

As the sun rose outside their home, Taryn slept peacefully, snuggled in Larkin's strong arms. A dark figure stalked into the room and shadows crept over the bed. Still fast asleep, chills coursed through Taryn's spine, though neither teen stirred from their slumber.

"Those who cheat Death must pay for their insolence," a man's voice whispered in Taryn's ear. Caressing her cheek, he leaned in even closer. "He will not stand for it, nor will the others. In the end, you cannot escape your fate. You will be responsible for the screams of thousands perishing by your hand." The dark figure backed away, watching as Taryn began to toss and turn as images of her loved ones surrounded by Death filled her mind. "One-by-one, you will destroy those whom you hold closest to your heart."

Taryn woke suddenly and sat up in bed, holding one palm outward. Lightning crackled overhead and the rumbling of thunder shook the foundation of the house.

Waking almost instantly, Larkin sat up, staring at Taryn's threatening posture. After a few seconds, he placed a hand on her wrist, gently bringing it down on her lap.

"That must have been some dream," he stated. Glancing around the room, he sighed. "There's nothing here, Taryn, except for friends and family. Everyone is safe."

Turning her head, she nodded slightly.

Larkin pulled her into his arms and gently lay back on the bed. "Do you want to talk about it?" he asked.

Staring at the open bedroom door that led to the hallway, Taryn shook her head. Remnants of a man's warning echoed in her mind. *Why would I destroy those I hold closest to my heart?* she wondered to herself.

৪১৫৪৪১৫৪

Strumming his fingertips heavily over the wooden table, Nodryck stared off into the distance while two of the brothers and Tedra ate their meal.

Having observed a series of shared glances between Coyan and Tedra, Clad dropped his fork against his plate and sighed audibly. "Is it not enough that we have done as you asked and feigned smiles in front of our Mortari brothers and sisters regarding your newest pet? Now you and your wife plot in front of us without our inclusion," Clad seethed as he stared darkly at Coyan and Tedra.

Leaning back in his chair, Coyan laced his fingers together and smiled slyly. "Dearest brother, do you know where Chrystian is at this precise moment?"

"He went to throw himself at the feet of our dear Taryn," the youngest brother answered with a flutter of displeasure in his tone.

Tedra rose from her seat, swiftly making her way to stand behind her brother-in-law. Running her fingers along the back of his seat, she purred, "You continue to fancy the teen-queen…no?"

His face twisted darkly as he looked over his shoulder at the woman. "Why would any man not fancy Taryn? She is most lovely and possesses a wicked sense of justice. Just ask your pet." He paused, looking to Nodryck. The dark haired man's gaze darkened, causing Clad to chuckle. "Lest we not forget, Taryn Knight wields power that is unmatched. There is no one alive that could challenge her and win."

~ 149 ~

Armed with a devilish grin, Coyan leaned forward in his seat. "Have you forgotten how we defeated the great Oracle, Elayna Delrayn by choking her with the power of her own bonds?"

"No, Brother," Clad answered. "I recall each detail of her final moments quite vividly. The way she held her arms up, pleading for her life as her golden locks turned crimson from the blood. Such fear shone in her beautiful green eyes as she realized you held her Zoia-Stone in your hand."

"Elayna's deadly mistake was to tie her life-force to an object that could be possessed so easily by another," Coyan chuckled darkly.

Pulling his gaze from the window, Nodryck pursed his lips.

Tedra moved to stand beside him. She caressed his cheek and leaned in close. "It would appear that the members of the Elder Council did not understand how we managed to destroy their precious Oracle."

Coyan waved his hand in Nodryck's direction, releasing him from his Influence and allowing him to speak. "Is there something you would like to add to our conversation?" he inquired.

Rubbing his throat, Nodryck reached for the goblet of water sitting on the table before him. He quickly consumed the cool liquid and slammed the empty cup onto the table. "If the Oracle was foolish enough to tie her life-force to something as fragile as a stone, her execution was most deserved."

Perking up in his seat, Clad stared curiously at the man. "He speaks," he grinned.

With a furrowed brow, their guest glanced between his hosts. "I have made it abundantly clear that I will not disclose your desires. So why must you continue to prevent me from speaking when in the company of others?" he growled.

With a gleam in his eyes, Coyan lunged across the table, grabbing the man's collar. "Because I can, and you can do nothing to stop me," he roared.

"Come now, Coyan, there is no need for such hostility," Tedra insisted.

Slowly, the eldest brother returned to his seat. He leaned back and a strange smile formed on his mouth. "Please forgive me, Wife. At times I find myself longing to rip the former Council member's throat out for the savagery his predecessors unleashed upon our kind," Coyan offered.

Tedra nodded before reclaiming her seat between the two men. She leaned into Coyan, whispering in his ear, catching Clad's attention.

"Earlier, you spoke of what we did to defeat the Oracle all those years ago. You and your precious wife are planning something for Taryn, and I want to know what it is," Clad asserted.

Skillfully eyeing his brother, Coyan was certain the youngest of his siblings would show loyalty to his familial bond, as well as possess a willingness to do whatever it took to secure his own future.

Coyan rose from his seat, and in a blink of an eye he was sitting beside his brother. "I understand you have feelings for Taryn, Brother. However, she is a threat to our very existence. A threat that must be eliminated," he warned.

"I am quite aware that with every moment the lovely Taryn Knight continues to draw breath, it is a step closer to our ultimate destruction," Clad replied.

Drawing his brother in close, Coyan whispered, "This is why we are going to kill her before she makes her move against us."

Clad looked at this brother with wide eyes. After a few seconds passed, a smile lit his face. "Oh do tell, dearest brother. How exactly do you plan on taking out the most powerful Gaias we have ever stood against?" he pressed.

Seeing the doubt plastered on his baby brother's face, Coyan's jaw drew tight. He began to speak, but was cut off.

"With lightning," Nodryck stated.

Clad began to chuckle. His chuckle quickly escalated into tearful laughter. Fighting to catch his breath, the man, slapped his hand against the table.

Nodryck's face soured as he looked to Tedra.

The woman rolled her eyes and watched as her brother-in-law fell deeper into his fit of laughter.

After several uncomfortable moments passed, Coyan placed his hand on his brother's shoulder, Influencing him to calm. Instantly, Clad's laughter ceased and all that remained were rosy cheeks and a few remnant tears of laughter that still streamed from his eyes.

"Dearest brother, your concern is duly noted. However, it does not change our resolve or redirect our intentions toward the girl," Coyan stated flatly.

Fighting the smile that so desperately wanted to form on his face, Clad took a deep breath. "We have observed what she does when attacked with lightning. She simply creates a counter attack and her bolt absorbs the threat."

"That is only partially true, Clad," Tedra replied.

"No. We have all witnessed her response," Clad argued.

Coyan shook his head while placing his hand on Clad's shoulder. "My wife is correct, dearest brother. Taryn only responds when it is her loved ones who are in danger, but not when it comes to herself." He paused. "Do you recall our last visit with the girl?" he asked.

Clad nodded.

"When Tedra rained down lightning all around the teen, she simply stood there. She offered no reaction to the threat," Coyan explained.

"Have you considered that Taryn was not concerned due to the fact that she could have easily ended Tedra's bombardment by using her Influence?" Clad countered.

Nodryck rose from his seat and meandered to the nearest window. Running his hand over the stone frame, he smiled darkly. "The teen does not possess a stomach for outright murder as evidenced by these very stones. If she had truly wanted to, she would have destroyed the Elder Council upon our first introduction, and she surely could have done the same when she was held captive here." The dark haired man paused. "The act of taking a life offends her sensibilities and shakes her at her very core. So much so that as long as she does not believe her friends and family are in harm's way, the girl will not retaliate."

"But what if…" Clad began.

"You are so smitten with the teen queen that you cannot see what is directly in front of you, fool," Tedra hissed. "During the Trials she lost her ability to fear. Yes, she senses danger for her loved ones, but she does not fear for herself."

Clad pursed his lips and shook his head. "You cannot know this for certain, Tedra."

The woman rose to her feet and lifted her palm in the man's direction. Clad was instantly thrown from his seat and sent crashing into the wall behind him.

Rubbing the back of his head, he slowly rose to his feet while Coyan and Nodryck looked on eagerly. "Brother, tell me you will not stand for this," he growled.

Coyan only shrugged, before panning his eyes to his wife. "Please do keep in mind, dearest wife, that in order for our plan to be a success, we will need my baby brother's gifts," he stated.

Withdrawing her hand and placing it to her side, Tedra took a deep breath. She feigned a smile, starring directly at Clad. "My apologies, Brother-in-Law. I do hope you will forgive my momentary lapse in temperament," she purred.

He looked to his brother, who arched a brow in his direction. With his jaw jutting forward and his nostrils still flaring, Clad finally nodded at the woman. "Taryn will destroy anyone who attempts to harm her, let alone those who seek to end her. Once she turns eighteen, there will be no stopping her," he warned.

"Again, your concerns are duly noted, dearest brother. However, this is the exact reason we intend to strike before the girl has the opportunity to celebrate her eighteenth birthday. We will create the perfect snare for the self-righteous teen," Coyan chuckled.

Clad's face softened only slightly as he took a seat and listened to his brother discuss strategy.

ഇൗ౪ഇൗ౪

Looking over her shoulder, Taryn waved to Larkin as he stood talking with Jonesy and the others. Though he flashed a brilliant smile, she could still sense his displeasure with her decision to go running without him.

Taking a deep breath, she crossed the street near the high school and jogged toward the tree line. Once out of sight, she picked up speed. Her feet carried her so swiftly through the woods, not even a blur was left in her wake. She ducked beneath the low hanging tree branches while easily navigating over large rocks, creeks and a few fallen trees.

After running for nearly a half hour, Taryn found herself standing near the edge of a cliff on the California coastline. Exhaling forcefully, she fell to her knees and looked out over the churning ocean. A storm was brewing in the distance, though it would be a few hours before it made landfall. Holding her arms out to her sides, positioning her palms in the direction of the vast ocean, an image formed in her head. With no more than this simple thought, several waterspouts formed over the water, extending high into the sky as lightning crackled overhead.

Taryn stared at the incredible sight before her. After several moments passed, she slowly breathed in, filling her lungs to capacity while one-by-one the water spouts merged into something majestic. Holding her breath, she rose to her feet as the mammoth sized waterspout drew near. Her hair whipped violently in the wind, and for a brief moment she considered what would happen if she entered the watery funnel.

Stepping to the very edge of the cliff, she reached toward the spinning water. As her fingertips began to feel the spray from the monstrous spout, the hair on the back of her neck stood on end.

Out of nowhere, the teen felt an arm wrapping around her waist, pulling against her forcefully. As her feet were lifted off the ground, she looked upward toward the sky and watched as a spectacular bolt of blue lightning struck the waterspout, illuminating her creation.

The mere sight was indescribable, but the scorching heat from the immensity of the lightning's power searing against and ingraining into her flesh is what held her attention.

As Taryn lay on the ground with the weight of another on top of her, she could think of nothing but the power she felt pulsing against her.

After several minutes passed, the face of an angel appeared above her. His features were glorious; his golden eyes were highlighted by the shimmering halo floating above his head.

"Dearest Taryn, please speak to me," the angel pleaded.

Blinking several times, the angelic face disappeared and she was left staring at one familiar to her. "Chrystian?"

Falling onto his back beside her, he released a loud sigh. "What were you thinking, you silly girl?" he admonished, while placing his hand over hers.

Taryn squeezed his fingers, but remained silent.

He turned his head to look at her. "Why would you do something so foolish?"

"I only meant to see if the waterspout was real, and not just some dream or figment of my imagination," she replied.

Chrystian sat up and peered down at her. "Tell me, why would you believe your creations to be a dream?"

She shrugged as she stared back at him. Observing the fear that shone heavy in his eyes, she reached up, caressing his cheek.

He placed his hand over hers, pressing it into his cheek and sighing heavily. "I am not worthy of your affection or care, dearest Taryn."

She pulled her hand away and rose to her feet. "Why would you say that, Chrystian?"

Moving to his feet, he walked over to the edge of the cliff. Several silent moments passed. "You sent a man you despised to Mors after placing your mark of protection upon him."

The teen stepped closer to her friend. "You're talking about Nodryck." She paused. "I wasn't in a good place when I decided to do that. I used my Influence against Lazryn, of all people, and forced him to open the Gateway."

Chrystian's gaze focused on the darkening clouds in the distance. "I placed my hands upon him, Taryn, and in doing so, I broke your rule."

Taryn laced her arm with his. "Whatever happened was my fault, Chrystian. My actions, my choices created the situation, and you simply reacted to a vile and loathsome man. A man whom I suspect could not keep his mouth shut, even when presented with the opportunity."

"To be truthful, I wanted to rip his throat out. I wanted him to suffer for what he has done to you and your mother. And also for what the council did to my beloved Loryn," he admitted.

Resting her head against his arm, Taryn exhaled. "I think a part of me wanted you to end him. And if I'm being honest, I only placed my mark of protection upon him to absolve myself of any wrong doing if he was murdered on Mors."

The Mortari man leaned his head down, placing a kiss on top of her head. "We are quite the pair, are we not?" he whispered.

"We are," she agreed.

Releasing his arm, she took a seat and dangled her legs over the edge. She patted the ground beside her, and Chrystian joined her without hesitation. They sat for several moments watching the approaching storm.

"How did you know where to find me, Chrystian?" she inquired.

Grinning, he gave a slight shrug. "After living as long as I have, you pick up on certain subtleties that would go unnoticed by most. I would also like to believe that I know you." He paused, gazing at her side profile. "I know it is wrong of me to say, but I cannot help myself. I am drawn to wherever you are, dearest Taryn. I find myself longing to be in your presence."

"You know Larkin is the keeper of my heart, Chrystian. No one, regardless of circumstance, could ever take his place."

He nodded. "I believe you misunderstood. When I am near you, Taryn, I not only feel, but I feel more deeply than I have in a millennium. Before you, the last emotions I felt pumping through these veins was an immense hatred and unadulterated rage."

A smile warmed her face. "My heart belongs to Larkin, but that does not mean that I cannot have love in my heart for you, too. I care about you, Chrystian. I despise the fact that you continue to live on Mors when you should be living in Williams with…"

Chrystian interrupted. "What, with you?" he laughed.

Taryn placed her hand over his. "Please, Chrystian. Coyan and Clad may share your bloodline, but in your heart, Lazryn and I are your true family."

Shaking his head, Chrystian rose to his feet. "It is admirable that you wish to see only good in me, dearest Taryn, but the thought is wasted on the likes of me."

Arching a brow, she gently pushed against his thigh. "When I was your guest on Mors, you kept me safe. You went toe-to-toe with your brothers and Dagrin to do so."

"But I also caused you great heartache. I taunted you. I tried everything within my power to break you," he countered.

Taryn jumped to her feet, grabbing his wrists forcefully. "Yes, Chrystian, you have done horrible things to me. You stole me away from my friends and family. You and Loryn tried stealing my body. You allowed Coyan to Influence Lazryn and force him to take me on those hunts. You tried to make me love you by subjecting me to unspeakable horrors. And let's not forget you kissing me when I did not want you to." She paused, looking him in the eye. "When the Elder Council ordered the genocide of all Healers, they started this war. They attacked you and your loved ones. You simply responded with the only thing you had left in that moment, your rage."

He pulled away from the girl. "You spend a great deal of time in the minds of others, Taryn Knight," he stated sharply.

"Tell me that I'm wrong, Chrystian. Tell me that you are not fundamentally good," she replied.

Shaking his head, Chrystian began making his way toward the trail leading to the empty beach below.

"If I'm so far off base, then why did you come here today?" she shouted.

When he did not answer, she ran to catch him. Grabbing his sleeve, she forced him to turn around. "You didn't come here today because you wanted to tell me about what you did to Nodryck. You attacked him as an excuse to come see me."

His nostrils flared. "Do not presume to know me, dearest Taryn. The hole that is my heart holds a level of darkness that the likes of you cannot begin to fathom."

The green in Taryn's eyes faded, giving way to a stunning shade of blue. "I know darkness, Chrystian. I have walked in its shadow and I have drunk from its cup. I have destroyed pieces of myself to return to the light. Now tell me, friend, why did you come here today?"

Chrystian's eyes widened as he marveled at the teen. Trying to find his words, the middle Mortari brother swallowed hard. "I wanted to discuss the letter I passed to you during our last encounter."

"I have the books, if that is what you wanted to know," she stated.

"Nothing else?" he questioned.

"Only books," she replied.

Furrowing his brows, Chrystian grimaced. "There had to be something more."

Taryn watched curiously as her friend's eyes darkened. Heat radiated from him in palpable waves. "What exactly did you think I'd find in that crate, Chrystian?"

His nostrils flared. "It no longer matters. The item in question was not present."

"I want to know what it was you were hoping I would find in the box, Chrystian, and I want to know now," Taryn demanded.

Defiantly, he shook his head. "It is of no consequence to you, Child."

"Now I'm a child?" she bit. "Seriously, Chrystian, you need to get a grip. You're disappointed and angry, but that's not a reason to try to shut me out."

"No, dearest Taryn, you need to let this go," he warned.

The teen's jaw drew up tightly and the intensity in her blue eyes grew. "You know I can force you to tell me," she growled.

"Please, Taryn, you must let this go," he insisted.

Realizing he was not willing to share the information with her, Taryn grabbed his hand and opened both of their minds. Horrific images, some recent, some old, flashed in her head. She continued to peruse his memories until she came upon a private moment between Chrystian, both his brothers and Tedra. A familiar bowl and knife had been laid out in the center of a small table as they gathered around. In his memories, she could see the sun rising thru a small window behind Coyan.

They're swearing a Blood Oath, she thought to herself.

Curious, she pushed deeper into his memories. However, she kept coming across what appeared to be a repeat of the previous. Beginning to notice the slight differences in the position of the rising sun through the window, Taryn realized it was not the same memory, but instead a daily ritual. Weeks and months of daily Blood Oaths had been sworn.

Why? What secret could they be protecting? she thought.

Releasing his hand, Taryn backed away from the man. "You despise them, Chrystian. I know you do, yet, every morning for months you have been swearing a Blood Oath. Why?"

Lacing his fingers together, Chrystian lowered his head. "You know I cannot answer your questions. I have sworn an Oath and sealed it with my blood."

Her eyes softened, restoring them to their normal color. "Why do you continue to bind yourself to them? To align yourself with them? Why?"

"I cannot say, for reasons you already know," he replied.

Her brows arched. "It's Coyan. He's using his Influence, isn't he?" When Chrystian failed to reply, Taryn moved to him. "For all the darkness your heart has known, I know that you are good, Chrystian. As misguided and lustful as your younger brother is, Clad does not possess an evil heart either. He simply longs for love, but feels that he is truly unlovable."

Heated tears welled in Chrystian's eyes. "And what about you, dearest Taryn? You are only too quick to share the pain and burdens that weigh on the hearts of others. What about your perfect heart?"

"I am far from perfect, Chrystian. I have flaws. I make mistakes," she replied.

"Then let us discuss you for a moment," he bit. "Lazryn took you on hunts with the Lessors and you stood by and did nothing as they slaughtered hundreds. In our castle, you sat silently watching as Dagrin murdered surrogates of your loved ones, and still you did nothing." He paused, reaching his fingers to her cheeks. "You brought our castle down around us for a mere verbal threat against your loved ones. Yet, not a single Mortari was injured beyond a few scrapes and bruises. You also went out of your way to see our prison wing remained untouched."

Taryn slapped his hand away. "What's your point, Chrystian?"

An amused smile curled on his face. "While my Mortari brothers and sisters fear your particular gifts, they are not ignorant to the fact that you fear bringing about the death of others."

The teen's face turned instantly frosty. "Is it really so wrong of me to not want the blood of others on my hands?"

"Of course it is not wrong, Child, but we both know your reasoning goes far beyond having a little blood on your hands," he replied. "You see, I know what truly lies within your heart, and I place no judgment upon you."

"You don't have a clue about me," she snapped.

Chrystian cupped her cheeks in his hands and smiled softly. "At any moment during the time you spent with us, you could have forced our hand to return you to your friends and family. Instead, you tolerated us. You even forged friendships while with us. You permitted us to show you the darkest part of ourselves and yet, you did nothing." He paused, staring in the girl's eyes. "Even now, I see it hiding within your gaze. It is not fear that I see. It is not even disgust. What I see so very plainly etched in your heart is the question of are you more like your wolf and loved ones, or are you more like us, the Mortari." Chrystian leaned down, placing a tender kiss on her forehead. "You need me to not be a monster in order to assure yourself that you, too, are not a monster."

Taryn stood silent, staring straight ahead as the storm over the ocean began moving swiftly in her direction. The green in her eyes dissolved and the blue hue returned.

Taking a step back, Chrystian swept a few strands of hair from Taryn's face, tucking them behind her ear while observing the change. "I will never judge you, my sweet, sweet sister."

The teen continued to stand rooted to her spot while her blue irises churned violently. "You should leave now, Chrystian, while you are still able to."

Waving his hand, Chrystian opened a gateway. Looking behind the teen, he watched as a massive wave swelled in the near distance.

Feeling the burn of her gifts searing against his flesh, he understood this was her creation and did not know how destructive her intent was currently. "Know this, dearest Taryn, the sole determiner of one's fate is held within their own heart. Explore that which you are made of, and learn who you truly are."

With the monster wave mere seconds away, he moved toward the open gateway. Giving the teen a final glance, he felt a stabbing pain within his head. A second later, a gust of wind blew him into the gateway.

Holding fast, Taryn exhaled as the weight of the enormous wave crashed down over her.

CHAPTER ELEVEN

Sitting on the edge of her bed, Taryn gazed down at Larkin's handsome face. His dark brown hair lay perfectly around his face as his tanned skin glowed beneath the soft light of the corner lamp. Running her fingers over his temple, she leaned down, kissing his lips softly.

Slowly, he began to stir and kissed her back. With his eyes still closed, his hands found her waist, pulling her on top of him.

They kissed several minutes before Larkin gently pushed her back. His hazel eyes lit with relief as he looked at her. "You have no idea how much I needed this, Tare-Bear."

Flashing a brief smile, Taryn rolled off to the side to lie next to him. Larkin caressed her cheeks with the back of his fingers before running his hand over her honey colored locks. Twisting the ends of her hair around his index finger, he smiled softly.

"I'm not sure if I'm relieved to see you, or if I want to strangle you," he confessed.

Taryn stared into his hazel colored eyes. The mixture of joy and fear shone heavily within. "I didn't mean to worry you," she whispered.

"I know. You needed a release and you couldn't find it if I was there with you," he replied.

His words caused her heart to ache fiercely. "It's not like that, Larkin. I'm just dealing with a few things and needed to clear my head. That's all."

"So you cleared your head along the coastline of Southern California?" he quipped.

Releasing a heavy sigh, Taryn pulled a pillow under her head. "Look, I didn't invite him to come along, he just sort of showed up," she admitted.

Larkin's eyes narrowed as he sat up in bed staring at her. "What are you talking about, Taryn? Who just sort of showed up?"

Rolling onto her side, Taryn pulled herself to the opposite edge, and sat up, hanging her legs off the side of the bed. She took a deep breath and sighed audibly. "It was Chrystian. He tracked me to the coastline and we had a brief conversation before he returned to Mors."

"You can't be serious, Taryn. Chrystian, as in one of the three Brothers C. The very same Chrystian who's kissed you twice has now followed you to California?" Larkin growled.

Taryn rolled her eyes as she rose to her feet. "He didn't do it in order to steal another kiss, Larkin. He needed to talk to me. That's all."

"Needed or wanted?" he bit.

Throwing her hands in the air, Taryn shook her head and headed toward the bedroom door. "I cannot do this with you. Not right now." With that, the girl disappeared out the door.

Moments later, Larkin heard a splash in the outdoor pool. Walking to the window, he watched as Taryn floated on her back before sinking to the bottom of the lit body of water.

You really stuck your foot in it this time, Larkin thought to himself.

After changing into a pair of shorts, Larkin stopped in the bathroom to grab a couple of towels. Tossing them over his shoulder, he headed downstairs to try and make peace with her.

From the bottom of the pool, Taryn stared at the shadow that appeared over her. She waited nearly a full minute before surfacing.

"If you're here to lecture me, Larkin, I'm not in the mood," she warned.

Noting the seriousness in tone, he shrugged. "What can I say? I acted like an idiot boyfriend who didn't trust his girlfriend's judgment."

She arched a brow. "A few words other than idiot come to mind," she frowned.

Removing the towels from his shoulder, Larkin placed them on a nearby chair. He then walked to the edge of the pool and took a seat while dangling his legs in the cool water. "I was wrong, Taryn. No matter how insane that monster makes me, I had no right to direct my frustrations towards you." He paused, taking a deep breath. "You said he needed to speak with you, may I ask what about?"

Taryn pretended to ponder her answer before finally swimming to the edge and pulling herself up. Cool water trickled from her hair and down her arms as she looked up at the brilliant night sky and sighed. "I don't like tension between us, Larkin. Especially when it involves Chrystian."

"I'm sorry, Tare-Bear. I shouldn't have reacted the way I did," he stated softly.

Taryn's gaze shifted to her love. "I'm curious. How exactly did you know that I had been in Southern California earlier?"

A huge smile formed on his lips as he chuckled. "Seriously?"

She shrugged. "You know I've been trying to stay out of your head."

"And I do appreciate your efforts, but this is one memory you have to see for yourself," he grinned.

Her brows furrowed.

"Trust me. You'll see why in just a second," he stated while extending his hand to her.

Taryn intertwined her fingers with his. "Are you sure you want me perusing your mind?" she questioned.

"I have nothing to hide," he replied.

Connecting her mind with his, Taryn viewed the last several hours of Larkin's day. He had been on a run with Keiryn and the others before walking through the French doors. Entering the house, she immediately saw Gastyn, Lazryn, Dedrick, Ilya, Maxym and her mother and father watching the television. It appeared there was a breaking news story interrupting their usual television show. The look on each of their faces indicated they knew she was the cause.

"Did Taryn tell you where she was headed?" Theron questioned.

Larkin shook his head. "Only that she was going for a run."

Pulling away, Taryn stared at Larkin. "I made the news?"

A deep laugh rose from his chest. "You went International, Taryn. Every news station in the world broke in to warn about the impending Tsunami."

She frantically shook her head. "I would never intentionally do something that could hurt so many."

Feeling waves of heat from her gifts washing over him, Larkin watched her curiously. "Of course you wouldn't, Taryn. Everyone here knew you were just blowing off steam."

Sitting silent for several long moments, Taryn bit her bottom lip and sighed. "I triggered the warning buoys off the coast." She paused. "How stupid of me," she mumbled.

Taryn was clearly affected by what happened, but Larkin knew she was not going to elaborate beyond the frustration etched on her face.

"Enough about what happened earlier," he said while sliding into the water. A shiver coursed through his spine. "Oh, this water is freezing," he shouted, piercing the night air.

A slight smile grew on Taryn's face.

"You think this is funny?" he asked.

The girl shrugged. "Well…"

In a flash, Larkin grabbed Taryn's wrists and pulled her into the water. Unaffected by the cool temperature, she wrapped her arms around his neck and looked him in the eyes.

"I wish things were always this easy," she stated.

Larkin held her waist and pressed his lips firmly against hers. The tension in her muscles gave way, even in the frigid water.

Pulling back, Larkin flashed a beaming smile. He opened his mouth to speak, but was cutoff when Taryn lifted her arm and held her hand out in the direction of the deck aggressively. Her nostrils flared and her eyes narrowed. The harsh set of her jaw was unlike anything he had ever witnessed from her before. His eyes panned toward the threat.

"Please don't hurt me," a small voice cried.

Taryn continued to stare at the young boy with her hand raised.

"Dedrick," Larkin said, tightening his hold on Taryn. "What are you doing out here so late? Where's Lazryn?"

Appearing in a blur, Lazryn positioned himself between the boy and the pool. "What is going on here?" he asked, glancing to Larkin.

The young man wrapped his hand around Taryn's wrist, pulling it beneath the water. "We thought everyone was asleep. I guess the boy startled us a bit."

Lazryn stood in his flannel pajama bottoms and a dark blue tank top eyeing the girl. "Taryn, do you agree with Larkin's summary?"

Pulling away from Larkin's grip, Taryn swam to the edge. "Yeah. The kid caught us off guard," she replied, her eyes boring into the young boy.

With a nod, Lazryn placed his hand on the boy's shoulder, directing him toward the open French doors. The man glanced over his shoulder in Taryn's direction before stepping inside the house and disappearing with the boy.

Larkin swam over to Taryn. "What's up with you and Dedrick?" he questioned.

Still staring in the direction of the house, Taryn shrugged. "It's like you said, he startled me."

"Do you really expect me to believe that?" he asked.

"It's your story and I'm simply sticking to it," she replied.

With pursed lips, Larkin rolled his eyes. "There is obviously something about the kid that spooks you, Taryn. Every time he appears, you go on the offensive. Why?"

"Because..." She paused, taking a deep breath. "Because we don't know him, Larkin."

"So says the girl who invited a strange wolf pack into her family home after a brief conversation," he retorted.

The water in the pool began to bubble. Taryn's eyes narrowed "Are you seriously trying to compare the situations between Alderyc and Dedrick?"

"I guess I am," he replied sternly. "You let several strangers in without batting an eye, but you can't find a way to be okay with a single orphan?"

Taryn balled her hands into fists. "Would it make you feel better if I told you there is something dark attached to him? Something that makes the hair on the back of my neck stand on end every time he gets close to me?"

Larkin's brow furrowed. "I don't understand why you're only now telling me this. If you felt so strongly about him, why didn't you say something sooner?"

She shrugged. "Because I'm not perfect. I make mistakes. If I said something and I was wrong, he would have been exiled to Hypatia to continue being tortured for nothing."

"This doesn't make any sense," Larkin stated. "I say tomorrow you, me, Lazryn and Dedrick sit down and talk about whatever questions you may have for the boy. I'm sure there is a reasonable explanation."

"Whatever you think is best," she replied, before slipping beneath the water. She swam to the center of the pool and sank to the bottom.

"We're not done talking, Taryn Knight," Larkin grumbled. Forcing the air from his lungs, he swam to Taryn, joining her beneath the water's surface. Pointing to the night sky, he looked at her pleadingly.

Unwilling to budge, Taryn stared ahead blankly.

After several minutes passed, Larkin felt the need for air. Pushing off the bottom of the concrete pool, he surfaced quickly. Inhaling deeply, filling his lungs several times over before swimming to the edge. He looked to the place where Taryn continued to sit. "What's going on with you?" he questioned, knowing no one would answer.

Beneath the bubbling water, Taryn closed her eyes. For a moment, peace washed over her. Unlike Larkin, she did not feel the need to inhale to breathe. Her body instinctively pulled air into the water, which she then absorbed.

Alone with her thoughts, the girl began to recall her earlier conversation with Chrystian. *Am I so obvious that everyone can see what he sees in me? Is that why so many of our kind continue to fear me no matter what I do? I don't want to hurt anyone. But sometimes, sometimes I do. I can smell their flesh turning into ash and it's haunting. Are my dreams a glimpse of what is yet to come or a preview of what I must fight to stop?* She pondered to herself.

Larkin stood at the water's edge, helplessly looking on as the water in the pool began to churn violently. "I hope you know what you're doing, Tare-Bear," he whispered.

Of course there's darkness in me. We all possess a certain amount. But it's my choice to tap into it or not. To open that door. I can't. I won't allow myself to taste it. To want it. Whatever happens, good or bad, it's not going to be because of something I have done. If it comes down to them or me, I'll destroy myself before I hurt Larkin or the others. Maybe I should let the lightning have me. Maybe I should let it take my gifts...then the planes might stand a chance.

"A chance for what?" a male voice whispered in her ear.

"To survive. To continue to exist," she answered, feeling the touch of the unknown trailing its fingers across her throat.

"Do you believe that Larkin would want to go on living without you?" the voice asked.

She shook her head. "He's strong. Not because I make him that way, but because he is good and pure of heart. Sure, he may be a little short tempered at times, but he is fierce when protecting those he loves."

"He loves you, Taryn," the voice replied.

"And I, him."

"But you would abandon him to save the lives of the others? You would let him suffer through a life without you?" the voice pressed with a hint of joy in his tone.

Taryn opened her eyes wide. Her blue irises radiated with the heat of a thousand suns. "You think you know me, but I promise you do not. Whether you walk with the living or sleep amongst the dead, or if you are something altogether different, I will see you suffer should you threaten my Larkin. Harm him in any way, I will end you."

"Unleash the fury and control its wrath." The man's voice broke, fading beneath a blanket of indecipherable whispers spoken in familiar tones.

"And what is it you want from me?" Taryn asked of the dead.

Several moments passed, filled with unintelligible words until finally one voice broke through.

"Only when the fallen rise will there be…" the voice trailed off.

Taryn immediately recalled Death's words. *Truths are lies in the dreams that are real. You must lose yourself in order for the fallen to rise. The mighty have succumbed, the wise have both withered, a betrayer swallowed betrayal, and the oracle fell victim to her own bonds.*

"You wouldn't care to expand on how one goes about losing oneself, would you?" Her question was met with deafening silence.

Unamused, Taryn blinked several times, restoring her irises to their usual emerald green color as well as calm to the water around her. Pressing her feet against the bottom of the pool, she shoved off. When she broke the water's surface, she roared thunderously. Lifting her hands, she created dozens of Imperium power orbs and hurled them at the monsters surrounding Larkin.

"Taryn, stop! It's me. Stop!" Larkin pleaded, while dodging her powerful blasts.

Blinded by the image in her head, Taryn intensified her assault, landing a hefty blow. Her orb struck Larkin in the back, sending him soaring thru the air.

His pain filled cry pulled her back to reality.

In an instant, she was at his side, cradling his torso in her arms. Her eyes widened, taking in the damage she had inflicted upon him. With tears streaking down her cheeks, Taryn pulled directly from herself to Heal him.

Seconds later, he opened his eyes. Sitting up, he rubbed his hands over his neck and chest. His eyes panned to Taryn's face. "Are you okay?" he asked.

Biting her lip, the girl shook her head. Tears continued to roll from the corners of her eyes. "I…I don't understand," she stammered. "I saw it. You were being attacked by the living dead."

Larkin cupped her cheeks in the palms of his hands, wiping away her tears with the pads of his thumbs. "We were the only two people, alive or otherwise, out here."

She grabbed hold of his wrists. "I did this…"

"Look at me, Taryn. I'm fine. You healed me. No harm. No foul," he said.

Taryn scooted away from him and jumped to her feet. "I nearly killed you. And if I had, I'm not sure that I could have brought you back."

Sighing, Larkin stood. "You didn't, and I'm still very much alive." He paused. "What's going on inside that beautiful head of yours, Taryn? You haven't been the same since you encountered Nodryck that day on Hypatia."

Her brows furrowed as she glanced to the ground. Several silent moments passed before she lifted her eyes to his. "Maybe it's not me that's changed. Maybe it was something we brought back."

"You think it was the books?" Larkin questioned.

"No. I think it was who we brought back." Faster than a blur, Taryn ran inside the house, heading for the boy.

Larkin chased after her, arriving just in time to see Taryn pull Dedrick from his bed.

"Who are you?" she demanded.

Tears quickly filled the boy's eyes. "You know who I am. I am Dedrick."

"Release the boy at once, Taryn," Lazryn shouted from the doorway.

She shook her head defiantly. "Not until this devil tells us who he really is."

"Taryn, we've been over this a dozen times. His entire family was slaughtered," Larkin stated, before Taryn interrupted.

"Yet he still remains. Doesn't that bother either of you?" she questioned.

"This is madness, Taryn. Even for you," Lazryn admonished.

Releasing her grip on the boy's wrists, Taryn backed away. "Something's not right in this house. It hasn't been since you brought him here."

"The boy is innocent. His only crime being that he survived a brutal attack," Lazryn reasoned.

Exhaling forcefully, Taryn eyed the boy. "It's not enough. There is too much at risk. I have to see for myself what happened to him and his people."

Lazryn inched closer to the boy. "Taryn, think about what it is you are saying."

In an instant, Taryn rushed between both Larkin and Lazryn, placing her hands on either side of Dedrick's head. She flooded his young frame with her gifts until she felt a crack in his mind. Finding the fissure, she pressed with all her might until she gained entry. Her eyes turned the color of blue sapphires as she tapped into his memories. First she saw Larkin and herself out by the pool and felt an immense joy radiating from within Dedrick's memory. Next was a series of happy moments with Andyn, Lazryn and the rest of her family. Then came another memory of her outside her bedroom when she created a shield. Confusion churned within the boy's soul. Afterwards, a few more happy memories, followed by the first time she and Dedrick had met. At first, he was exhilarated. Then as they engaged in conversation, he became scared. Terrified, in fact.

Taryn pressed deeper into Dedrick's mind. Horror. Absolute terror. Shock. Dismay. Hope. Searing pain. Hunger. Death. Fear. Confusion. A flood of emotions surged over her. With wide eyes, Taryn's arms fell to her side.

"Taryn?" Larkin stated.

She bit her bottom lip and backed away from the boy. "Before we arrive home from school tomorrow, Lazryn, I want him gone. Talk to Hava and Beldyn Love. I'm certain they will make room."

Lazryn grabbed the boy's hand, pulling him protectively behind him. "Very well. I will ask if they have room for two."

Taryn's eyes locked briefly with her friend's. Witnessing the polarizing shade of blue staring back at him, Lazryn's jaw fell agape.

"Good night," she said, before heading toward the stairway.

Larkin and Lazryn shared an uneasy glance.

"You have the kid?" Larkin asked.

Lazryn looked in the direction of the stairs. "Yes. Now tell me, do you have her?"

"I won't let Taryn out of my sight," the teen promised.

&)CঝB০Cঝ

Rapping gently on the bathroom door, Larkin rested his forehead against the wooden frame. "Please, Taryn, we need to talk."

The sound of the door lock pinging caught his attention. He straightened himself and took a step back. A few seconds later, Taryn emerged smiling.

"Morning." She walked past him and grabbed her oversized bag from the floor. Walking over to the crate, she took a book from the top of the stack and slid it amongst her other belongings.

"What are you doing, Taryn?" Larkin questioned.

"Getting ready for school. Why? What are you doing?" she asked.

Larkin arched a brow. "Just watching you...acting like everything is normal."

Pulling the bag handle over her shoulder, Taryn chuckled. "We need to hurry. I don't want to be late picking Andyn up from your dad's."

As she strode past, Larkin reached out, grabbing her hand. "Are you sure it doesn't have more to do with you not wanting to see, Dedrick?"

"If there's a problem, I'd be happy to walk to school today," she replied flatly.

Larkin released her hand and held his in the air next to his head in surrender. "Nope. No problem here."

"Good," Taryn stated. "Now, let's go."

ℤскℤск

As the day progressed, Larkin watched Taryn with a keen eye. She smiled with their friends and even laughed at Thorne's terrible jokes. When the twins brought up prom, she immediately joined in their conversation. She even went so far as to compliment each of the dresses that the girls had fawned over.

During their regular classes, Taryn raised her hand and answered questions asked by the teachers. She even opted to sit amongst the human teens.

When the bell rang for lunch, she tossed her notebook and pen into her bag and headed for Larkin. Pressing up on her toes, she kissed his cheek while lacing her fingers with his.

"Love you, Wolfy," she whispered.

"I love you, too, Tare-Bear," Larkin replied, watching as the sweetest smile spread across her face. His heart melted inside his chest, but a pain stabbed in his stomach. *Whatever's going on inside your head, it can't be good.*

ༀ☙ᘓༀᘓ

Standing off to one side of Gastyn's classroom, Larkin stared into the distance. He sighed audibly, grabbing the attention of one of the other students.

"You want to talk about it?" Jonesy inquired.

Larkin shook his head.

Jonesy stepped directly in front of him. "Fine. I'll talk and you listen." He paused, making sure that he had his friend's full attention. "Since arriving at school today, I have listened as Taryn has laughed at Thorne's terrible jokes. She's shown a great interest in prom dresses and hairstyles. Teachers are calling on her to answer questions. At lunch, she giggled like a giddy schoolgirl." He paused again, arching a brow. "Taryn hasn't giggled aloud since before the Trials. It's obvious something is going on with her. And by the troubled look in your eye, I can see it's serious."

Exhaling sharply, Larkin reached up, running his fingers through his hair. "You're right, Jonesy, there is something going on with her. But like always, she's bent on keeping it to herself. She's feigning smiles and doing whatever she has to do to make the rest of us happy."

Jonesy nodded. "It's who she is, Larkin." Pausing, he motioned for Larkin to walk with him. "Taryn is as selfless as any one soul could ever be. What's important to us is important to her."

"I know. I know. But we all have our breaking point...even Taryn," he retorted.

"Have you forgotten who you're talking to? I died several times during the Trials. My gift. My curse. Taryn was the only one who could truly see me for what I was before my unusual gift actually set in." He paused in his step, observing as Taryn worked with Andyn and the others. "Can you imagine what it must feel like wielding such power? Through everything, the highs and the lows, she has always carried herself with such grace and poise."

As the two friends strolled forward, Larkin grabbed the top of Jonesy's shoulder. "I'm scared for her, Blake. I mean, I'm really scared for her."

"Because of the tsunami she unleashed yesterday?"

Larkin shook his head. "No. Because when she came back from her run, she shared with me that Chrystian had followed her. And…"

"And what?" Jonesy questioned.

Lowering his head, Larkin took a deep breath. "She nearly killed me last night."

Jonesy's eyes widened as he stumbled a few steps back. "No. That doesn't sound like Taryn."

Raising his eyes to meet his friend's, Larkin nodded slightly. "She was meditating or something beneath the water. When she came up and broke the surface, she immediately started lobbing Imperium orbs at me."

"Did she say why?" Jonesy pressed.

Larkin licked his lips anxiously. "She thought I was being attacked and her orbs were meant for whatever demons she saw."

The concern in Jonesy's eyes grew. "She still suffers with visions?"

"I don't think they ever truly stopped," Larkin admitted.

Staring at his friend, Jonesy's shoulders rose and fell dramatically. "Has Taryn mentioned hearing garbled voices in the past few weeks?"

"Yeah. Why do you ask?" Larkin questioned.

Jonesy transformed his fingertips into talons and ran them over the unique classroom's textured wall, causing sparks to appear. "I've heard them, too, Larkin."

Halting in his steps, Larkin grabbed his friend's forearm, spinning him around. "And why am I just now hearing about this?" he demanded.

Pulling away, Jonesy locked eyes with his friend. "I followed the pack hierarchy and went to Keiryn with my concerns."

With his lower jaw jutting forward and nostrils flared, Larkin inhaled deeply, trying to get a grip on his anger. He knew Jonesy did right by his pack, but it didn't change his frustration over not knowing. "And what exactly did Keiryn have to say on the subject?"

Jonesy glanced at Taryn in the distance, then back to Larkin. "I think that's a conversation for the two of you to have."

Larkin's hazel eyes turned black as night. "Oh, don't you worry, Jonesy. Keiryn and I are going to talk, sooner rather than later." He paused, looking in Taryn's direction. "See that she and Andyn make it home after school."

"Of course," Jonesy agreed.

ഇരുഇരു

Dust trailed behind Larkin's Jeep as he raced up the driveway to the Knight family home. He barely stopped before slamming the Jeep in park. Jumping out the driver's side door, he walked heavy-footed toward the front door. Reaching for the doorknob, he was not surprised in the slightest when the wooden door swung open before he could grasp the handle.

From within the hallway, Keiryn stood, staring at him. "Jonesy says we need to talk," he said.

Larkin walked past his friend, bumping his shoulder against Keiryn's as he maneuvered by. "Dogtown Lake. Now."

ഇരുഇരു

The pair raced to the water's edge of the reservoir in their favorite form. Larkin, a large black wolf and Keiryn, a massive falcon.

~ 177 ~

Arriving first, Larkin shifted back into human form. He stared overhead as Keiryn came into view.

Screeching as he swooped down, Keiryn shifted into his human form. Glancing at Larkin, he sucked in a deep breath. "I don't remember you being so fast the last time we ran together."

Larkin's nostrils flared. "Why didn't you tell me that Jonesy was hearing voices?"

Noting the heated gaze in his friend's eyes, Keiryn took a step back. "Straight to the point. But why am I surprised, after all, we are talking about my sister."

"Taryn handed you the pack without question, and this is how you thank her? You keep important information to yourself without concern of how it may affect her too," Larkin growled.

Keiryn licked his bottom lip and sighed. "I get that you're concerned for her, Larkin, but Taryn is tough."

Grabbing Keiryn's shirt by the collar, Larkin jerked the teen closer. His heated breath warmed the Keiryn's cheeks, while his eyes turned dark as night. A low growl rose from deep within Larkin's chest. "Tell me everything you know about the voices Jonesy says he heard."

While Keiryn had expected Larkin to be unhappy regarding the withheld information, he never imagined his friend would react quite like this. Glancing down, he caught a glimpse of the dark fur forming along Larkin's forearm as he felt the sharp tips of werewolf claws scratching the surface of his soft flesh. "I get it, Larkin. You love Taryn. But before you go any further down the road to full on beast mode, keep in mind that she is also Jonesy's blood cousin and my blood sister."

After a few moments, the hazel color returned to Larkin's eyes. Clenching his jaw, the larger teen shoved his friend away. "Taryn is my world. And blood or no blood, if your secrets hurt her in any way, you will answer for it."

Keiryn took several steps down the water's edge, staring out over the calm body of water. With a heavy sigh, he began. "Jonesy came to me a few weeks ago. He told me that he was hearing things. It began as buzzing in his ears while trying to fall asleep. Over the next few days, he began to notice voices within the sound. By the end of the second week, he could make out a few words." Pausing, he struggled to find his breath. The weight of their secrets, crushing his chest. "If I thought they meant to harm her…"

Growing impatient and sensing something more, Larkin moved closer to Keiryn. "What aren't you telling me," he demanded.

Inhaling deeply, Keiryn shook his head. "You're not going to like this, but I think it's time that you knew everything."

Larkin's brows furrowed as he shot his friend a heated glare. "Start talking."

"When Jonesy came to me and told me about what was happening, I wasn't surprised. I have been hearing them, too," Keiryn confessed.

With his hands balled into fists, Larkin fought to swallow down the anger and frustration swirling violently within him. "Taryn has walked the razor's edge every day since the Trials ended. Time and time again, she makes sacrifices for everyone else…"

"Larkin," Keiryn began.

"No," he interrupted. "You don't get a pass on this, Keiryn. Not when she handed you the pack. And definitely not when she's your sister." Larkin paused, running his fingers through his hair. "After the Trials ended and Lazryn came to live with us, Taryn started having episodes where she'd space out."

Keiryn nodded. "Yeah, I remember. She said she went into a dark space and could hear…"

"That's right. She heard a low hum the first time, and then she began to hear garbled whispers," Larkin stated.

Tilting his head back, Keiryn stared at the sky for moment. Exhaling loudly, he returned his gaze to Larkin. "The voices, they talk about the fallen rising again. Due to his most recent gift, Jonesy and I assumed they were talking about him being a Phoenix.”

“I don’t care what you believed, Keiryn. She may have given you the pack, but we both know she is the unnamed ruler of all Gaias kind,” Larkin bit.

“That’s a title she doesn’t want, and you know it,” Keiryn retorted.

Gently shaking his head, Larkin walked past his friend. “That doesn’t make it any less true.”

Turning his head, Keiryn looked over his shoulder in Larkin’s direction. His friend’s shoulders rose and fell dramatically while taking a deep breath. “You’re always worrying about her, Larkin. As her brother, I appreciate how much you care.” He paused. “Lazryn and Dedrick moved out earlier today. The monster said they were going to stay with the Love family for a while. When I asked him why, he said the house was cramped and thought everyone could use more space. But you see, I don’t believe him. I think Taryn kicked him out, and I think you know why.”

Larkin released a heavy sigh while glancing to his friend. “She didn’t exactly kick Lazryn out, but she did tell him to make sure Dedrick was gone before she returned home today.”

“Why would she want the kid to leave?” Keiryn inquired.

Shrugging his broad shoulders, Larkin shook his head. “Last night she attacked me.”

Keiryn’s eyes widened as his jaw fell slightly agape. “Taryn did what?”

With a brief glance to his friend, Larkin walked over to the water’s edge. The image of Taryn’s face as she broke the surface of the pool was seared in his mind. There was something far fiercer lying within her than he had ever seen before. Her eyes shifted from emerald green to sapphire blue and then back again. Taking another deep breath, he began to explain. “Taryn’s having visions again. She isn’t able to distinguish between what she is seeing and what is real. When she struck me with one of her orbs, she thought I was the enemy.”

Furrowing his brow, Keiryn looked to Larkin. "Okay. I get that she's having visions again. But why do I feel that you're still leaving something out?"

Larkin's body tensed as he locked his fingers together behind his neck. Barely shaking his head, he sighed. "The orb that struck me…it wasn't meant to slow the threat or even derail it."

"What are you saying?" Keiryn questioned.

Throwing his hands into the air, Larkin growled, "She intended to destroy the threat. Her orbs were designed to kill."

Keiryn's eyes narrowed on his friend. After a long moment of silence, he spoke. "No. You're wrong. Taryn would never intentionally try to end another living being."

"That's just it. Taryn thought she was fighting the living dead. If she hadn't come to her senses when she did, I would be dead." Larkin paused. "She even said that she didn't think she could bring me back if I died."

Walking over, Keiryn placed his hand on Larkin's shoulder. "I can't even begin to imagine what that must have been like for either of you. Taryn loves you more than anyone has ever loved another being."

"For me, what happened, it's over and done. But for Taryn…I think last night was just beginning of something far worse than what she dealt with before and during the Trials," Larkin replied.

"Then we need to talk to her," Keiryn suggested.

Larkin smirked. "And if she's not open to the discussion?"

Tilting his head to one side, Keiryn shrugged. "Simple. We keep pushing until she lets us in. If she tries to shut us down, we keep going back until we know what she's dealing with."

Giving a slight nod, Larkin held his hand out to his friend. "Together we can do this."

Firmly grabbing hold of Larkin's hand, Keiryn looked his longtime friend in the eye. "For Taryn."

"For Taryn," Larkin echoed.

At two o'clock in the morning, Taryn found herself lounging about on the living room couch watching television. With her eyes fixated on the oversized screen, she stared as the eighth straight infomercial played.

Joining her, Keiryn slid into a nearby chair. "Have you decided on a new vacuum yet?"

She shrugged.

"Surely you have a preference," he teased, while motioning to the television.

Transitioning her eyes from the screen to her brother, Taryn gave a faint smile. "Why aren't you at the Skye's?" she asked.

"I don't know. I guess I thought it might be nice to sleep in my own bed tonight," he replied.

With her gaze locked on her brother's face, Taryn shifted on the couch. "How is Nalani doing?"

"She's good. And she's been asking about you," he answered.

Taryn placed her arm on the edge of the couch, resting her head on it. "I'm thrilled that the two of you are together, Keiryn, but I can't be her best friend."

Leaning forward in the chair, he arched his brow. "And why exactly is that?"

"She's part of your true pack, and I'm not. Nalani knows she needs to keep her best friend slot for one of the other girls." Taryn paused. "She and Dagney have always been close."

Keiryn moved to sit on the floor beside her. Twisting his neck, he kissed her forehead. "They're still close, but she says she has a special connection with you."

A smirk curled on Taryn's face. "She does...you."

Rolling his eyes, Keiryn leaned his head back. "Girls," he chuckled.

"It's true. She's connected to me because she loves you. I don't get why that would be such a bad thing," Taryn replied.

He sighed. "It's not."

Several silent moments passed between the siblings before Keiryn turned to look directly at his younger sister. "Lazryn and Dedrick moved in with the Love's…do you want to tell me why?"

Sitting up on the couch, Taryn grabbed a pillow, wrapping it in her arms. "It wasn't working out…Dedrick and Lazryn being here."

"Why?" he questioned.

Taryn's expression turned stony. "Because it wasn't."

"That's not an answer, Taryn."

She shrugged. "It's the only one you're going to get."

Keiryn moved to the couch and sat next to her. "I know something happened between you and Dedrick. I also know that it had to be something significant for you to let Lazryn go with him."

Her forehead creased and eyes narrowed. "You don't know anything, Keiryn. Because if you did, you would pack your bags and run toward the Skye's."

"You are my sister. This is our family home, even if only for the time being. So why would you say such a thing, Taryn?"

Moving to her feet, she headed to the oversized window. With her fingertips pressed against the cool glass, she stared out toward the treeline. "Something isn't right here, Keiryn."

Waves of emotion swept over him as he rose from the couch. "Is that why you sent Dedrick away. Because he wasn't right?"

Taryn shrugged.

"I want to understand, Sister. I want to help with whatever is going on here, but you have to let me in," Keiryn replied.

From the bottom of the staircase, Larkin appeared and added, "We want to understand, Taryn. We want to help, if you will let us."

Hearing her wolf's soft timbre filling the air, Taryn closed her eyes extra tight. "You won't understand. Neither of you will."

"You can't possibly know that unless you give us a chance," Larkin reasoned as he moved closer to her.

Taryn opened her eyes, looking at the two boys' reflections in the glass window. A sharp pain ripped through her chest, though she held in her physical response. "I do know, Larkin. You both will want to help, but I'm not sure there is any help to be had."

Reaching up, Larkin gently tucked a few loose strands of hair behind her ear. "Whatever this is, it has to do with Dedrick. If you're not going to talk to us, then maybe he will."

Her eyes locked with Larkin's through the reflection as her stomach began to churn. Fighting back the nausea that she felt in seeing blood leaking from his beautiful hazel eyes, she choked on her words. "Leave the child alone. He's been through enough already," she replied.

Larkin shook his head. "No. You have been troubled ever since his arrival. There is something about him being here that upsets you, and I want to know what it is."

Stepping up to the opposite side of his sister, Keiryn nodded. "We were the ones who brought Dedrick to Williams. We need to know if that was a mistake."

"I know you looked inside his mind, Taryn. And whatever you saw, it upset you so much that you sent him away, and Lazryn with him," Larkin stated.

Closing her eyes tightly, Taryn focused on the warmth emanating from her brother and her love. *As long as there is warmth within them, they are alive,* she thought to herself. Suddenly, Taryn felt a familiar presence in the air. Her eyes opened wide, highlighting their now sapphire blue color. In the reflection, she saw the faces of the Gaias past staring back at her.

"The uprising is approaching. The fallen will make a stand. Reclaiming the kingdom of the living to control the power of the sands. Darkness will rise. Light will fall. Let it go and freedom be to all," the dead said in unison.

With wide eyes, Keiryn looked to Larkin. "They're here. The voices, they're talking to Taryn."

Before either teen could act, Taryn cocked her head slightly to one side and stared blankly at the window. "Why is it the dead always seem to deal in riddles? It could not possibly kill you to try to speak straight forward, as you are already dead." A dark smile formed on her face as she reached her hand inside the glass.

Larkin and Keiryn looked on in confusion as her hand seemed to disappear within the windowpane.

"How is she…" Keiryn spoke.

Shaking his head, Larkin's eyes grew even wider, watching as Taryn leaned in, her arm disappearing all the way to her shoulder. The glass pane began to radiate with an intense orange glow that caused his hair to stand on end. "Taryn, I need for you to pull back now. You've warned them. I need you to let it go and come back to me."

Looking at him from over her shoulder, Taryn was relieved to find that the dying visions of him had passed, if even only for the moment. But the fear that shone in his eyes stabbed like a thousand daggers at her heart. Withdrawing her arm, she stepped back, glancing between him and her brother. Keiryn's eyes were also laden with fear. She walked to the couch and took a seat, placing her head between her hands. "I'm sorry," she whispered.

Larkin and Keiryn both rushed to the couch, taking a seat on opposite sides of her.

"Why are you sorry?" Larkin questioned while placing a hand at the small of her back.

Keiryn shook his head. "I heard what they said, Taryn, and you have nothing to be sorry about."

She leaned back into the couch and shot her brother a curious glance. "You could hear them?"

He nodded.

"Have they spoken to you before?" she questioned.

Keiryn bit his bottom lip and nodded once more. "For the past few weeks, they've been reaching out to both Jonesy and myself. Neither of us has been able to make out much of what they were trying to say, but I understood every word they spoke here tonight. It sounded like a threat, Taryn. Like they were planning on attacking you."

Rising to her feet, she turned halfway around, taking a seat on the edge of the coffee table. She took a deep breath, settling the emotions she felt rising, and looked at the two young men sitting across from her. "It wasn't a threat. It was a warning," she stated.

Larkin's brows furrowed. "What was the warning?"

Taking another deep breath, Taryn repeated what the ghosts had said. "The uprising is approaching. The fallen will make a stand. Reclaiming the kingdom of the living to control the power of the sands. Darkness will rise. Light will fall. Let it go and freedom be to all."

"What does that even mean?" he questioned.

She shrugged. "I honestly don't know. They always talk in riddles, and it can take a while to decipher."

"If they weren't threatening you, then why the theatrics? Why light the other side of wherever your hand went on fire?" Keiryn asked.

Taryn looked down and stared blankly at the tops of her feet for a long moment. "I feel a ridiculous amount of annoyance when they're around." She paused, glancing up at both young men. "Before the dead interrupted, you asked me if bringing Dedrick here was a mistake." She paused again, this time biting her bottom lip while taking a deep breath. "When I woke after delivering Nodryck to Mors, I felt a dark veil draping this house. Every time I left and each time I returned, I felt the weight growing, seeping into my dreams and daily thoughts. Even as I sit here now, heinous images fill my mind."

"What sort of images, Taryn?" Keiryn asked.

Stepping toward her, Larkin's eyes narrowed as his jaw fell agape, realizing he already knew. "It's our deaths. You're seeing us die."

Keiryn's eyes grew wide. "No. You're wrong. Tell him he's wrong, Taryn."

Kneeling down in front of her, Larkin placed his hands over hers. "The night that you had visions of everyone dying except Jonesy and the Afflicted, your eyes were lit with a hollow gleam. Maybe I didn't want to see it, or maybe it's because your eyes keep changing from green to blue and back again so it didn't register until just now...but it is the same gleam, isn't it?"

Taryn locked eyes with Larkin before glancing briefly up at her brother. "Yes. I have seen your deaths."

Keiryn took a seat on the arm of the chair and stared at the floor. "I don't understand," he mumbled.

Moving from the couch to the window, Taryn gazed into the tree line while Larkin rose to his feet. "What I've seen and the things I have felt, I needed them to be because of Dedrick. I want so badly for the darkness surrounding us to be his doing."

Larkin took a deep breath, trying to stave off the flood of emotions he felt rising inside his chest. He glanced to Keiryn then back to the reflection of Taryn in the glass window. Exhaling, he held his shoulders firm and forced a stiff upper lip. "Why, Taryn? Why do you want Dedrick to be responsible?" he asked.

"You already know why," she whispered.

"I need to hear you say it, Taryn," Larkin stated solemnly.

Taryn leaned her forehead onto the cool glass as a single tear streaked down her cheek. "Because...if it was him, then it couldn't be me. And all the death I see surrounding you, Keiryn and the others...it would mean that it is to be by another's hand, and I could still stop it."

Keiryn turned his head, looking at his sister with a furrowed brow. But before he or Larkin could counter her admission, Taryn disappeared out the French doors and into the night.

"Why are you just standing there? We have to go after her," Keiryn growled as he jumped to his feet.

Larkin shook his head, his eyes laden with heartbreak. "She's gone and she won't be found."

"So that's it? You're just going to let her drop a bomb like that and then walk away?" Keiryn shouted.

Balling his hands into fists, Larkin took a deep breath. "All we can do right now is wait for her to come back to us."

"No! She needs to know that she's wrong and that we're on her side," Keiryn countered, his voice cracking with emotion.

"She knows we're with her, Keiryn. It's the reason she ran. Right now she believes that darkness is consuming her, and she doesn't want to be told otherwise," Larkin replied.

Keiryn walked to the window, placing his hand where Taryn had rested her forehead. "Taryn's full of goodness. Her heart is pure."

"Darkness lives within all of us. Even Taryn," Larkin countered.

"What are you saying, Larkin?" Keiryn demanded.

Taking a seat on the edge of the couch, Larkin stared at the empty fireplace. "Taryn's been conflicted for a long time about taking the life of another. The very thought causes her hell-like torment. When the werewolf died on Hypatia after biting her, it left a mark upon her heart so deep. Even the Mortari who drained your power, she grieved for him. She keeps the pain hidden so far down that when it begins to seep out, it devastates her at a level we will never understand." He paused, running his hands over his hair. "That day on Hypatia when Nodryck confronted us in the garden, I knew we should have left then and there, but she wasn't going to leave without that stupid box Chrystian had left for her. Nodryck began spewing all sorts of venom about what he had done to your mother during her time with him. Taryn wanted to hurt him. But more than that, she wanted him dead, and she wanted it to be by her hand."

Keiryn's jaw dropped open. "Wanting to kill the man who harmed her mother doesn't make her a devil."

"I know that, but Taryn doesn't," Larkin replied, locking eyes with his friend. "I just hope she comes to that realization soon, before she loses too much of herself."

CHAPTER TWELVE

Taryn ran for hours until she found herself standing in the Love's backyard. She looked at the two-story home, her heart laden with conflict.

Without a word being spoken, Lazryn appeared in a blur by her side. "This is not a social call, is it?" he asked.

She shook her head and spoke softly, "There's a place I need to visit, and I cannot get there on my own. Will you please take me?"

"Of course," he replied.

೮‍ಚ‍೮‍ಚ

Taryn stepped through the gateway holding her breath. Looking around at the lush environment, full of vibrant flowers and dark green grass, a feeling of calm washed over her.

"How did you know this plane existed?" Lazryn questioned.

Exhaling, she shrugged. "This isn't another plane. It's part of the Earth. I believe we're somewhere in Russia. One of the books from the crate, I was skimming through it and one of the pages had a map. I guess it sort of stuck in my head or something."

"This land feels different from the other regions of the Earth," Lazryn stated while studying the teen curiously. "What is it you hope to find here, Taryn?"

"The book said there was a cemetery of sorts somewhere near here. I want to find it," she answered.

"A cemetery?" he questioned. "If you are looking for the remains of the dead who haunt you, I do not believe you will find them here. During the time of their reign, our kind did not bury the dead. They were cremated, and their ashes released across the planes."

Taryn began striding forward and glanced back over her shoulder. "In all fairness, I did say it was a cemetery of sorts."

"If you do not know what exactly it is you are seeking, how will you know when you have found it?" Lazryn questioned.

Pausing her step, she shrugged. "I'm not sure, but I have a feeling I'll know when we do."

ഇൻൽഇൻൽ

The pair ran for hours in search of whatever it was that Taryn hoped to find. Without even a hint of success, Taryn stopped at the edge of a modest creek that flowed amongst the rolling hills of the surrounding valley. She dropped to her knees, scooping up a handful of the cool water and drinking it down.

Following closely behind, Lazryn did the same. After drinking his fill of water, he lay back on the soft grass and stared up at the blue sky. "We have been running for hours. How much longer do you purpose we continue doing so?" he asked.

An ornery smirk curled from one corner of the teen's mouth. "This will teach me to bring along antiques when I go for a run," she taunted.

"I am not that old," Lazryn argued.

Taryn chuckled. "Well you're not exactly a spring chicken either,

Turning his head in her direction, he smiled. "You and your wolf could only hope to live half as long as I have. Though, neither of you will ever look as good as I do at this age."

The teen's face turned solemn.

Lazryn immediately sat up and scooted toward the girl. "My words were in poor taste, and I should never jest about my immortality as it was achieved by perpetrating heinous acts upon our kind."

Taryn jumped to her feet and held up her hand, interrupting her friend. "Can you hear that?" she inquired.

He shook his head. "Hear what?"

She moved from one place to another in hopes of identifying which direction the sound was coming from. "It's like the strings of an instrument being lightly strummed. Can't you hear it?"

"I am sorry. I only hear the babbling from the creek," he replied.

Taryn stilled, focusing on the faint sound. After a long moment passed, she locked eyes with Lazryn. "It's coming from the water."

The man rolled onto his stomach and scurried to the creek's edge, dipping his head beneath the flowing water. Less than a minute later, he pushed up, jumping to his feet. His eyes were wide with wonder. "You are correct, young Taryn. I, too, now hear the melodic sound."

The teen quickly began searching along the creek bank for the instrument. She had no more than began when she spotted a thick tuft of long grass. It was located on the other side of the water, only a few hundred yards upstream.

Using her Elemental gift, she created a gentle gust of wind that carried both she and Lazryn across the water. As Taryn approached, she noticed several long blades of grass fallen over into the creek. They swayed peacefully below the water's surface, their movement timed curiously with that of the strumming.

Taryn dropped to her stomach on the bank, plunging her arms shoulder deep into the water. Her fingers traced over the numerous blades of grass and smooth stones beneath the surface until she felt a thin wire against the pad of her right thumb. Feeling her fingers up the length of the thin string, Taryn came across something more solid. It was smooth in texture, but unlike the rocks, it seemed to have a specific pattern cut into it. With her free hand, she pushed back the thick blades of grass, while gently tugging against the solid portion of the object. After a few moments, she freed the string instrument, slinging water and mud into the air.

Lazryn formed a small shield with his gift of Imperium, avoiding the splattering from the debris. Once the air cleared, his gaze narrowed on Taryn's find.

"I think it's a harp," Taryn stated while examining the numerous gold strings and wooden frame. English Ivy vines were intricately carved in the wood. "The detailing is extraordinary."

Taking a step closer, he shook his head. "It is indeed a harp."

Hearing the weight in his words, she looked to her friend, taking in his stiff shoulders and creased forehead. "What is it, Lazryn?"

He walked over and ran his fingers just above the strings. Staring at the design cut into the instrument, he touched it and immediately gasped. "This harp, it is a relic, even when compared to me."

"I'm not following, Laz. You look like you're about to freak out or something," Taryn stated.

Taking a step back, he shook his head. "The instrument you hold within your hands is at least five thousand years old. And it should not exist."

The teen's brow furrowed. "I'm still not following. Are you trying to say the elements should have worn it down, or is it something else?"

"When I was a young boy, my father shared a story with Loryn and I about a harp that strongly resembles the very one you hold now. As I recall, the instrument was gifted to a young woman whose beauty captivated all who saw her. She possessed long blond hair that flowed down the middle of her back, electric green eyes, porcelain skin and rose colored lips. Her mother became jealous of the attention her daughter received, so she betrothed her to a wealthy king in exchange for never having to set eyes on the girl again. Being that mother and daughter were both Gaias, the mother enlisted another of our kind to

Influence the young woman into marrying the king, and to obey his every command. Sadly for the young woman, the king was equally as wicked as he was hideous. As his own appearance was beyond ghastly, he took great pleasure in taking something beautiful and breaking it until it mirrored his own tortured soul," Lazryn shared.

Taryn grimaced. "Your father…that's a horrible story to tell a child."

Lazryn walked past Taryn, staring at his reflection in the water's surface. "Do not fret, dearest Taryn, for the story does not end there. For on the day of their wedding, it is said that a man with swirling irises appeared in the young woman's chamber, making her a promise to never allow the king or his men to touch her."

Having known only one man with swirling eyes, the teen listened intently. "I'm sure he wanted something in exchange for her eternal safety. Do I even want to know what?" she asked.

The man flashed a weak smile. "All he asked in return was for her to bear him a single child."

"A child?" she gasped. "The man with the swirling eyes wanted to father a child with this woman?"

Lazryn glanced back over his shoulder. "As the story goes, the woman wed the ugly king. Afterwards, the king and his new bride celebrated with their subjects by hosting a spectacular feast. Before the party began to wane, the new husband led his bride to his chamber where he intended to deflower her. But once the door closed behind them, the man with the swirling irises appeared, stealing the King's voice. He used his peculiar gifts to lock the wicked man inside his own mind long enough to allow him to plant his own seed within the young woman's womb." Lazryn paused, glancing at the harp in his young friend's hands. "Before the mysterious man left, he laid an instrument in bed beside the woman. The King woke the next morning believing he had claimed his wife. So it came as no surprise when her belly began to distend and she gave birth to a child some nine months later."

Taryn's forehead creased. "I'm confused. The stranger left her a harp like this one, and promised that the king and his men could not harm her." She paused shaking her head. "Did the King just stop being wicked?" the girl questioned.

Lazryn's face twisted up with disdain. "The stranger kept his word and the King never laid a hand upon the woman, not ever."

"If he didn't harm her, why do I feel anger pulsing off you?" she asked.

Lifting his hand, covering his mouth, he shook his head and sighed forcefully. His body was stiff as anger and disgust swirled inside his chest.

Taryn held the harp out in front of her, staring at the instrument. She felt an overwhelming urge to pluck the golden strings. Unable to look away, she ran her fingertips across the thin wires. A beautiful sound filled the air. Closing her eyes, she listened to the soothing music. As soon as the air cleared and the sound was no more, she opened her eyes only to discover that she was drowning at the water's edge. A pair of hands gripped her shoulders and held her beneath the surface. As she fought to break free she screamed, filling the water above her with dozens of tiny bubbles, carrying away her last bit of breath. Sensing her life would soon be over, she closed her eyes in search of a moment's peace. As the calm washed over her, she was pulled from the water with immense force.

Water spewed from her mouth and nostrils as she was thrown to the ground, landing with a painful thud. Gasping for air while choking on the water, she watched as a large shadowy figure leaned over her.

"I may not be able to lay a hand upon your mother, but I may surely give you her share of suffering," the gruff voice hissed.

As he backed away, the sunlight exposed the man's face. His skin was pitted with six long scars running the length of each of his cheeks, and three across his forehead. He had a severely receded hairline, but the hair he did possess was jet black in color and pulled back into a long braid that hung several feet below his buttocks.

Taryn would have gasped at the sight of him, but she was too busy coughing, trying to expel the remaining water from her lungs.

"Take the boy to the dungeon and place him upon the rack. This time make certain the ropes do not snap," he ordered to one of the larger men that stood nearby, before heading toward a large stone castle.

Confused by what had just transpired and being referred to as a boy, Taryn willed an Imperium shield to surround her while gathering her wits, but the shield did not appear. She began crawling away, but was quickly scooped up by the large man and tossed over his shoulder. As the man walked, Taryn fought to break free of his grasp, but it was to no avail.

"Where am I? Why are you doing this?" she screamed, beating her fists against his back.

The large man chuckled. "You are at King Rutger's court, and he is quite displeased with your mother, youngling."

"My mother?" she mumbled.

A skinny man with long legs trailed behind them, patting Taryn on the head as they passed by a group of men carrying swords. "I do believe the boy was held beneath the water a tad too long this time." His words garnered hearty chuckles from the men.

After several more minutes walking, they came to a large wooden door. The skinny man opened it while the larger man stepped inside, making his way down a spiral staircase made of stone. There were wooden torches on either side lighting the passageway.

When they reached the bottom of the stairs, the men headed toward the center of the room where a torturous device set prominently displayed. The larger man slammed Taryn's petite frame against the wooden and stone rack, causing her to yelp from the pain. The skinny man quickly bound her wrists and ankles with rope. Once he had finished, he stepped back, appearing to admire his handiwork.

"There is no chance these ropes will break tonight," he snickered.

From the chamber's shadows, the hideous man from earlier stepped forth. "For your sake, I do hope you are right."

The skinny man shrank back against the wall. Trembling as the ugly man passed by.

In seeing his approach, a myriad of emotions rose frantically within her. For the first time in months, the frigid sensation of fear sat heavily within Taryn's chest. "Why? Why are you doing this?" she whimpered.

"Each day it is the same questions from you. Yet surely even someone of your tender age understands that no reason is needed," he replied in a soothing tone. He ran his fingers gently along Taryn's cheeks before a nefarious gleam filled his eyes. "Do it now," he ordered.

The large man tended to the wheel with wooden pegs at the top of the device and began turning it a full circle. Almost immediately, the ropes pulled taut, placing strain upon Taryn's frame. As he neared the full three-hundred and sixty degrees, immense pain shot through her body. Her joints were being drawn against, and the skin on her wrists and ankles began to burn from the friction of the ropes eating into her flesh.

Taryn held her breath, trying to keep from crying out in pain. As she did, King Rutger leaned his face over her own and stared down upon her.

"Again," he ordered.

Like before, the large man turned the device, making a full circle. The teen felt her bones starting to pull from their sockets.

Insurmountable pain coursed through every fabric of her being, and this time her cries flowed unabridged. Tears poured from her eyes, blurring the King's horrid face above her.

"That's it," he purred, stroking her cheeks vigorously. "Let me feast upon your screams and drink from your tears."

"Please," Taryn begged. "Please stop this."

King Rutger shook his head. "It is the burden of the son to pay for the sins of his mother." Bending over, the King licked Taryn's tears from her cheeks. "I want to hear you scream," he whispered as he motioned for the man to turn the wheel again.

The pain Taryn felt was unbearable, but she could not escape it. She could not use her gifts to put an end to her suffering, nor would her mind allow her to escape within its sanctuary.

֍Ꮆ֍Ꮆ

After several hours of being tortured, Taryn's broken and battered body was carried to yet another chamber. The large man knocked twice on a large wooden door before entering. Once inside, he dropped the teen onto the bed and then turned to leave.

Unable to move any part of her body, Taryn could only listen as the sound of an angry woman shouted at the man. The girl did not need to see what was happening to know someone was throwing metal objects in the direction of the door.

Fighting to stay conscious, Taryn stared up at the fabric draped overhead. If not for the sheer agony she felt in having every bone in her body currently broken, she may have appreciated the deep blue fabric with golden accents. Growing more certain by the second that the end was nearing, she closed her eyes and thought of Larkin. Images of his handsome face filled her with peace and love.

"In a life full of nothing but pain and sorrow, how is it you continue to find peace and love?" a familiar voice stated.

Opening her eyes, Taryn found Death standing over her. His swirling blue eyes were more vibrant than she had remembered. "Farren, am I going to die?" she whispered.

He shook his head. "Of course not, dear one. Though you are on the brink of death, you will never be mine to claim until peace finds a home within your heart."

Cold and confused, Taryn found herself without the energy to respond. She closed her eyes once more and stared into infinite darkness.

"My sweet, sweet boy," a woman whispered in Taryn's ear. She pressed her lips against the child's forehead. "One day I will find another, greater than the one who did this to us. I will make him pay. His suffering will be eternal. This, I promise you."

Taryn felt the bed shift beneath her as the woman left her side. A moment later, the air filled with the sound of music. She recognized it as the harp she and Lazryn had found earlier in the day.

As the music played, Taryn felt something strange happening inside her. Ever so slowly, she was beginning to heal.

I have my gifts back, she thought to herself. *King Rutger and his goons will be in for quite the surprise tomorrow.*

Giving in to exhaustion, Taryn fell fast asleep.

℠★℠★

The next morning Taryn woke to find herself able to move once more. In fact, she felt unbelievably amazing. Sitting up in the bed, she looked around the strange room. There was a small wooden table and two wooden chairs with thatched seats in one corner. Along a wall stood two wooden cupboards. Tossing back the covers, Taryn walked over and opened the first closet. Inside she found several articles of clothing. Their rough texture felt strange against her fingertips. As she held up a pair of the pants, she realized they belonged to a young child.

"These clothes are for a little boy," she mumbled, with the words of her torturers echoing in her head. "The men and the woman last night, they all referred to me as a boy." She paused, tossing the clothes back in the cupboard then moving to open the second closet. Opening the double doors, she gasped. "No. it's not possible." She paused again, this time grabbing the harp that sat upon one of the shelves. Looking it over thoroughly, her face wrinkled. "It's identical to the one I found yesterday in the creek."

With the instrument in hand, she headed toward the large wooden door. Only steps away, Taryn suddenly stopped when the door opened wide and in walked a beautiful woman. Taryn's jaw fell agape while taking in the woman's stunning features. She was utterly breathtaking with long golden hair, glimmering emerald eyes, porcelain skin and rosy lips.

"You're the young woman from the story," Taryn mused.

Bending down, she smiled warmly at the teen. "What have I told you about removing the harp from the cupboard?" she asked.

Taryn shook her head.

The woman reached for the instrument while placing a kiss atop Taryn's head. "Let us put this away for now, as you will hear it soon enough, my son."

"I do not understand," Taryn stated, trying to gain a better understanding.

Walking to the cupboard, the woman carefully placed the harp back inside. She secured both doors before walking back over to Taryn. "You must be famished," she smiled, while motioning toward the only window in the room.

Turning around, the teen watched as a tree branch full of crisp, juicy apples extended into the room. "You are an Ontogeny?"

"Yes, little one, I am." She picked an apple and handed it to the girl. "Go on, Maertas, take a bite."

Hesitantly, Taryn complied. The apple was exceptionally tasty, and was a welcomed sensation to her empty stomach. "My name is Maertas?"

The woman chuckled. "Of course it is, my precious. It is the name I bestowed upon you after you took your first breath of life."

Having taken another bite, Taryn chewed the tender meat of the fruit and swallowed it down. "Mother, what is your name?" she asked.

Taking a step back, the beautiful woman's brow furrowed. "You son, call me mother."

Taryn wiped the apple's sweet juices from her lips. "By what name does King Rutger call you, Mother?"

"My name is Calista, but you already know this," she replied.

Finishing her apple, Taryn stored both names to memory, as she had no idea how much longer she would remain in this strange, but telling vision.

৪৩৪৩৪৩

After spending much of the day alone with the woman playing hide-and-go-seek, picking flowers and snacking on various fruits and nuts, Taryn noticed a change in the beauty's behavior.

"What is it, Mother?" she questioned, as she played the role of son.

She dropped to her knees and tears began to pour from her eyes. "He will be coming for you soon, my sweet prince, and you will once more face the hell that was intended for me."

"Please do not cry. I will not permit him to harm another soul," Taryn insisted.

The woman shook her head, as her sobs grew louder. "Please forgive me, Son."

King Rutger appeared suddenly at the top of the nearby hill. "Bring me the boy, witch," he ordered.

Kneeling down beside the woman, Taryn kissed her cheek. "I will not allow him to use me to hurt you any further, this I promise."

Calista grabbed for her child, but the teen was already several steps away.

Taryn walked hurriedly toward the hideous man.

He chuckled, watching the boy approach. "What spirit you have, practically running to receive your punishment."

Inhaling deeply, Taryn held out her hand expecting an Imperium orb to appear. Her steps slowed, stunned when nothing happened.

Now bursting with laughter, the cruel king grabbed her wrist and jerked her towards him. For a brief moment, he studied the teen's arm. "Your mother is most impressive. I was certain that she would not be able to mend your bones so quickly after last night."

Calista is a Healer? she mused to herself.

King Rutger drug her back to the same river's edge from the evening before. Waiting for them was the large man and the skinny man who had helped the King torture her. Several feet away from them stood a handful of newcomers, all of which seemed highly curious, yet equally apprehensive.

Taryn was shocked senseless when the King wasted no time in tossing her into the water and holding her head beneath its surface. It was only after she nearly drowned did he bother to pull her limp body from the river. Through hazy eyes and waterlogged ears, she could barely make out the onlookers' who cheered.

After slapping her around for several minutes, she heard the King call out the order. "Take the boy to the rack," he said, his tone joyful and euphoric.

ಬುಂಬುಂ

Taryn woke the next morning to find the woman holding her hand with her head resting beside her on the bed. The harp lay at the foot of the bed. Her mind was full of intense memories of the beating the King and his friends had put on her, but it was something he had whispered in her ear that had her focus. *For reasons unknown to me and my men, I cannot, they cannot, lay a finger upon your mother. Though we cannot harm her, we may fracture both her heart and mind through breaking your bones and tearing your flesh night after night.*

ಬುಂಬುಂ

Day after day, week after week, month after month until it became year after year, Taryn suffered unimaginable torment at the hands of King Rutger and members of his court. She had come to consider it a good day when all of her limbs remained attached after one of their evening sessions. The cruel and twisted man found immense joy in drinking her tears each night.

Just when Taryn thought she could not handle another near drowning or follow up appointment on the King's rack, she closed her eyes, sucking in as much water as she could, hoping it would be for the final time. As her thoughts drifted in a single direction, focused on memories of Larkin, she began to hear a familiar voice calling out for her.

"Taryn, I command you to open your eyes at once. Do not force me to face your wolf, while bearing news of your demise," the man stated.

Her eyes opened wide, turning instantly from green to blue. Power emanated from her every pore, electrifying the air around them.

Cupping her cheek in one hand and stroking her hair with the other, Lazryn stared down upon her. Pain shone heavily within his tender green eyes. "You are safe now, Taryn. The King and his monsters can no longer harm you."

"You were there, too?" she asked.

He shrugged. "You were falling and I caught you. My fingertips brushed your temple and it was much like a movie playing in my mind's eye. I could see and hear everything that was taking place." Clearing his throat, he swiped away a rogue tear that fell from the corner of his eye. "I am truly sorry, Taryn, but I had to break the connection between us, for I could not bear to watch you suffer for another moment."

She smiled faintly. "It's okay, old man, I suspect the excitement of it all would have brought on a heart attack or something in someone as old as you."

Lazryn's face turned serious. "You jest in order to spare my feelings, my suffering, when it was you who lived through that boy's hell."

Taryn moved to her feet. "His name was Maertas and his mother was Calista. The harp," she said, her words catching in her throat. "The boy's father knew his son would be forced to bear his mother's beatings. She used the enchanted instrument each night to heal him, only to turn around and force him to suffer through it again the next day and the day after that. Over and over again, she made him face excruciating cruelty and humiliation." She paused, fighting the shivers that wracked her spine. As she did, the blue in her eyes intensified until they were practically glowing. "If she truly cared for her son, she would never have played that harp."

Watching the teen struggle with all that she had endured while trapped inside her vision, Lazryn cautiously stepped toward her. "As tragic as the child's life was, it is not your burden to shoulder, Taryn."

Her nostrils flared. "Don't you dare tell me what is or isn't mine to bear. His mother was there, and still she failed him daily."

"Loryn and I believed the story to be nothing more than dark folklore. I had no idea that truth lay within my father's words," he replied, snatching the instrument off the ground.

"Give me the harp," she demanded.

Defiantly, he shook his head. "This relic is surrounded by darkness, Taryn."

She held out her hand. "You have two options here, Laz. One, you can hand it over willingly or two, I can make you. Either way, I'm taking that harp home with me."

"The strings are stained with the boy's blood. Surely you know this," he pleaded.

Her jaw drew tight. "Yes, Lazryn, I know exactly what Maertas suffered through. I can still feel the agonizing pain from my bones being pulled from their sockets, and the copper taste of my blood filling my mouth." She paused, stepping to him. "But I also know that I was drawn to this place for a reason. Regardless of what you think, leaving this harp behind now, it would be reckless, not to mention stupid."

Extending the instrument to her, Lazryn sighed. "Very well then. For the time being, the instrument is yours."

Taryn grabbed hold of it firmly, locking her eyes with his. The moment Lazryn released his grip, the blue in her eyes faded, giving way to green. The electricity in the air disappeared almost instantly.

He looked at her curiously. "Are you aware when your eyes change color?"

She shrugged. "I guess so."

"What is it like?" he asked.

Glancing down at the ground, her cheeks turned a shade of pink. "Like normal, except not."

His brow arched. "Do you feel more powerful?"

Taryn shook her head. "My gifts remain the same, only my emotions change."

"Change...how?"

Shrugging, she walked over to the water's edge and looked down at her reflection. "Whatever I'm feeling, it becomes magnified by a thousand."

"Yet somehow you manage to remain in control. That is quite the feat, Taryn. I am most impressed," he lauded.

"I wouldn't be," she replied.

Tilting his head to one side, Lazryn's forehead wrinkled. "And why is that?"

Taryn licked her lips and took a deep breath. "Because you haven't seen the things I have. Larkin, Jonesy, Keiryn, Andyn, my dad...I've seen their deaths." She paused, turning to lock her gaze with his. "And I've seen yours, too."

He straightened where he stood. "A war has been festering amongst our kind for a millennium. If I am to die while fighting at your side, then so be it."

Closing her eyes, Taryn exhaled. Her emotions fought to escape, but she kept them locked securely away in her box. Looking him in the eye once more, her face was void of expression. "You are not destined to die fighting at my side, rather you will die by my hand, just like the others."

The color drained from his face. "Chrystian warned me you might say something like this."

"You spoke with Chrystian?" she questioned plainly.

"Yes. The last time you were with him, he sensed something changing within you. Something so deep that it threatened to fracture your very center. Then he witnessed your eyes transitioning colors.

He had hoped and prayed that it was simply an effect of you nearing your eighteenth birthday," Lazryn disclosed.

Taryn laughed. "You should tell him to pray that I never reach that particular milestone. My early demise may be the only thing that can save you...that can save any of you."

"Please, Taryn, do not say such things. For I know in my heart of hearts that you would never harm any of us."

Turning back to the water's edge, she smirked. "Oh yeah...how exactly do you know that to be true?"

His hands balled into fists while the veins in his neck began to bulge. "Just like your gut drew you here, Taryn, mine tells me that you would never hurt someone you love."

Opening her mouth to blast back a quick retort, Taryn found herself breathless as an image of a young boy with dark curly hair appeared next to her reflection in the water. His eyes immediately caught her attention.

"One blue and the other green," she mumbled, inching closer to the edge. "You're him, aren't you?"

The boy nodded and then pointed to the harp.

"Would you like to have it?" she offered.

He reached his hand out; taking hold of one side of the instrument while Taryn continued to hold onto the other. With his free hand, he held up a single finger.

"One?" she questioned.

Bowing his head, he ran his finger across the string furthest from him. The sound emanating from the single string caused the water to ripple outward in every direction.

A chill coursed up Taryn's spine, wracking her body with shivers. When her eyes focused back on the water, she immediately turned away, then slowly looked back again. There she found the image of the beautiful woman filling the space where her own reflection should have been.

Taryn glanced to the boy with wide eyes. "This is your mother."

The boy nodded, and then held up two fingers. Plucking the string next to the first, he smiled softly. The teen watched as the image of the beautiful woman faded away. As the woman disappeared, the air around Taryn filled with the sounds of a baby's cry. From below the water's surface rose a porcelain colored child with fiery red hair and enchanting green eyes.

Watching as the girl became enthralled taking in the sight of the innocent child, the boy held up three fingers this time. He struck the next string in line. The baby shape shifted into a young girl with hair the color of warm sunshine and intense green eyes.

"Who are you? Who was that baby?" Taryn questioned.

The girl tilted her head to the side and smiled shyly.

"Maertas, who are these children?" the teen asked.

He closed his eyes then motioned for her to do the same. With her lids pursed tightly against one another, she took a deep breath. Calm washed over her and she slowly opened her eyes.

The corners of her mouth curled when she found the earth coated with a moderate dusting of snowflakes. The large powdery flakes continued to fall around her.

Exhaling, the warmth of her breath turned white against the chill in the air. Peace poured over her in one continuous waterfall until she was brimming with euphoria.

Taryn chuckled and asked once more, "Who are these little girls, Maertas? Are they your siblings?"

The boy's smile softened and both of his eyes turned an incredible shade of blue. "Only when the fallen rise will there be hope for a new tomorrow." He paused, releasing his hold on the harp. "The answers which you seek may only be found by the tips of your fingers. Protect your wolf and he will fiercely guard what is yours without question." The blue in the boy's eyes turned to green as he began to fade beneath the water's surface.

"Please, Maertas, don't go. I need to know the name of your father," she pleaded as he sank further away. Taryn dropped the harp beside her and fell to her knees. She plunged her arm into the water grasping at the image of the boy. "Was his name Farren? Please, tell me."

He simply smiled and repeated, "The answers which you seek may only be found by the tips of your fingers."

Grabbing the teen by the waist, Lazryn lifted her into the air before planting her feet firmly upon the ground. "Please tell me that Chrystian was wrong, and that you are surely not losing your mind. Do you hear me, Taryn?"

The teen gently shook her head before glancing toward the water. "I'm not going crazy." She paused, swallowing hard. "Maertas had a message for me."

Lazryn's face softened. "You were summoned here by the boy?"

Taryn nodded her head as she knelt down beside the harp. With her eyes locked on the instrument, she stared at each of the strings. *What other secrets do you keep?* She thought to herself. Taking a deep breath, she grabbed hold of it, pulling it to her chest.

"I suppose there is no talking you out of bringing that relic back to Williams?" he questioned.

Taryn glanced up at him and shook her head. "Not a chance."

ଏ୪ଓଃଏ୪ଓଃ

Moving to the other side of the kitchen island, Theron wrapped his arms around his wife's waist. "Gracie, she isn't going to stand you and Ilya up." He paused, kissing the top of her head. "I think Keiryn was exaggerating when he said she was never coming back. Isn't that right, son?"

Shifting in his seat, Keiryn pressed two fingers against either side of his temples and rubbed. "Dad's right. Taryn and I rarely argue, let alone fight, so I'm just a little worried that I really upset her this time. That's all," he lied.

The ageless blonde shook her head and leaned against Theron. "I honestly don't understand why you and your sister would be fighting.

Especially about Nalani. Taryn seems to genuinely like the girl…it doesn't make sense."

"What doesn't make sense?" Taryn asked from just outside the doorway.

Spinning on his seat, Larkin's eyes fell heavily upon her petite frame. "I thought…you," he sighed, running his fingers through his hair.

Taryn appeared before him in a blink. "You seriously didn't think I would stay mad at Keiryn did you?"

He tilted his head and shrugged. "It was obvious you were upset when you left. Then you didn't come home."

She kissed Larkin on the lips before stepping back. "You worry too much." She winked, before sliding around him to where Keiryn sat. "I'm sorry if I said some things that may have upset you, brother. But I can assure you that I will try to spend more time with Nalani. I know how much she means to you."

Keiryn's brow arched as he stared at his sister. "So just like that, everything's better?"

"Son, is there something wrong?" Theron questioned with a curious look.

Taryn wrapped her arm around his shoulder and kissed his cheek. "Keiryn's fine. He's just bummed knowing that he will never best his baby sister."

Gracyn glanced between her husband and children, before her eyes paused on Larkin. The teen's tense broad shoulders and distant look spoke volumes. "Obviously something more happened between the three of you than what you're letting on." She stepped away from Theron, moving toward Larkin. "If you're trying to spare my feelings for any reason, I want you all to know that I am stronger than what I appear."

In a blur, Taryn moved to stand between her mother and Larkin. "Mom," she sighed, taking her mother's hands in her own. "I know you only want to help, but I promise this has nothing to do with you."

"You are my child, Taryn. And I'm always going to worry about you," she replied.

The girl motioned to Keiryn. "We're siblings, and all siblings fight at some point."

Gracyn took a deep breath. "Okay, darling daughter, I hear you. Message received."

Taryn smiled. "Since that pleasant conversation's been adjourned, I have a question."

"Do I even want to know?" her mother asked while rolling her eyes.

"Well, I was going to ask what time we were leaving to go prom dress shopping," the teen replied.

An electric smile curled on Gracyn's face. "You remembered."

"See, Gracie, I told you she wouldn't forget," Theron chuckled, winking in Taryn's direction.

Rising from his seat, Larkin shared a glance with Keiryn before walking over to the girl. "Taryn, before you leave, I'd like to speak with you."

"Sure," she replied.

The two teens headed upstairs. Once behind the closed door of her bedroom, Taryn sat on the edge of the bed while Larkin leaned with his back against the wall in front of her.

"So you're back and everything's better now?" he asked.

She stared at the floor for several seconds before a faint smile warmed her face. "I'm not sure everything's better, but at least now I know there's hope."

Larkin sighed loudly. "Hope is a definite improvement."

"I think so," she replied.

A moment of silence lingered between the pair before Larkin spoke again. "You were with Lazryn." He paused, running his fingers through his hair. "I'm glad you feel that you can go to him when you need to."

Rising to her feet, Taryn's eyes softened. "But you would prefer I came to you instead."

He shrugged his broad shoulders. "I want to be your everything, Taryn." He sighed. "I know that must sound ridiculous, but…but I do."

Moving toward him, the girl shook her head and gazed upon him adoringly. "You are my rock, my sanity. The calm within every storm that I have faced, and the sole keeper of my heart." She paused, clasping her hands behind his neck. "You, Larkin Taylor, you are my everything, and more."

The handsome teen wrapped his hands around her waist and leaned down. "I love you, Tare-Bear," he whispered before pressing his lips against hers.

೫৩೫৩

The car door slammed shut and Gracyn Knight released an audible growl as Ilya slipped the key into the ignition.

"When did prom dress shopping become an Olympic sport?" she asked.

Ilya smiled. "Prom definitely isn't what it used to be when we were teenagers. Between the prom-posals, the red carpet walk-ins and arriving in some fancy-smancy ride, a regular dress just doesn't cut it anymore."

Gracyn rolled her eyes. "That doesn't give those women and their daughters the right to act like that."

Listening to their exchange from the backseat, Taryn scooted forward. "Why don't we grab lunch and then we can hit a few more shops after?"

Tears filled her mother's eyes. "I wanted today to be perfect for all three of us, and it's turning out to be an absolute disaster."

Taryn placed her hand on Gracyn's shoulder. "Sure it would be nice if the stores weren't so crowded and people were a little more considerate of others. But spending time alone with you and Ilya is hardly a disaster. In fact, I would call today more of an adventure," the teen stated with a warm smile.

Gracyn placed her hand over Taryn's, giving it a gentle squeeze. "My sweet girl, you never cease to amaze me. Ilya has done an incredible job raising you."

Flashing a modest smile, Ilya shook her head. "The person she is has a lot to do with her genetics, and those came from you and Theron."

Sliding back into her seat, Taryn chuckled while fastening her seatbelt. "Okay, okay. Everyone is amazing. Can we go eat now?"

The two women shared a glance and chuckled before heading to the restaurant.

Pulling into the large parking lot, Ilya parked a few spaces down from the boutique's main entrance. "How strange. I was sure we stayed too long at the restaurant to have a chance at finding a parking place here, let alone a spot in the front row."

Opening the car door, Taryn shrugged. "Can't we just be thankful that we lucked out and scored a prime spot?"

"Well, I, for one, think this is a good sign. After all, my fortune cookie did say things are about to turn around," Gracyn smiled.

Taryn held the door open for both women, following in after them. Her eyes scanned the quiet space, noting only a handful of customers present. They all were smiling as they searched for their perfect dress.

Doing a complete three-sixty, Gracyn's face wrinkled with surprise. "Ilya, I thought you said this was the premiere dress shop here in Flagstaff. There's hardly another soul in the building."

"It is a bit odd," she admitted.

Taryn rolled her eyes as she scooted between the women. "It's probably slow in here because people over ate at lunch and don't want to deal with the dresses fitting tight due to having a bloated stomach."

Ilya slid her arm around Gracyn's, locking them at the elbow. "I think Taryn might be on to something," she stated, while arching a brow in the teen's direction as they passed by.

The trio took their time searching through the vast number of dresses. Taryn tried on several at both of her mothers' request. After six mermaid dresses and eight princess ball gowns she insisted that the women should try on a few dresses for themselves.

Gracyn placed one of the puffy gowns back onto its hanger. "You're not having any fun are you?" she asked.

Taryn wrinkled her nose. "I'm having fun, but some of those dresses...ugh," she replied with a cringe.

Her mother placed the dress back on the rack and smiled. "You're looking for something a bit more understated. Something that won't draw a lot of attention to you."

The teen nodded. "When I was on Mors, the brothers seemed to take joy in having me dress up in lavish gowns and wear their opulent jewels." She paused, glancing around the dress shop. "I guess I never realized it before, but being here, in a place like this...it takes me back."

"I suppose it doesn't help that you are the most famous Gaias, living or dead," her mother added.

Taryn sighed. "I would do almost anything to be just a girl that blended into the background."

Hearing her daughter's words struck a chord deep inside Gracyn's chest. She held back the tears that so desperately wanted to fall. "I tell you what, I'll go find Ilya and try on a few dresses. That will give you some time to look around without me hovering over your shoulder."

The teen hugged her mother. "Thank you."

ಬಂಧಬಂಧ

From across the store Taryn watched as her two mothers stood outside their dressing room doors, modeling a pair of more risqué evening gowns.

They look incredible, she thought.

Admiring them for a few minutes longer, an idea formed inside the teen's head, causing a wide smile to break across her face. She began aimlessly wondering the store while mentally plotting the details of her plan. When she had it all worked out, Taryn stopped, glancing back toward the pair of beautiful women. The sound of their laughter filled her heart with joy.

Focusing her attention back to the dresses, she looked to her left then to her right. Suddenly, her breath stilled and her eyes narrowed in on a simple, yet beautiful gown. Her feet carried her swiftly to where the dress hung. Running her fingers over the soft fabric, she exhaled while biting her bottom lip.

It's perfect, she thought to herself.

ꙮ

Heading up the long driveway, Gracyn and Ilya shared a quick glance after feeling a wave of power rushing over them.

"Why do I get the feeling that we're coming home to a party?" Ilya inquired.

Lifting her head from the seat, the teen sat up and stretched her arms out. "That would be my fault," she yawned.

"Why is that?" Gracyn asked.

Rubbing the sleep from her eyes, Taryn gave a tired grin. "Because I told Larkin we should invite everyone over for a cookout today." She paused, adjusting in her seat. "I knew if I mentioned it to either of you, you'd worry all day about what ten dishes you need to make for the dinner."

Gracyn chuckled. "I do believe our darling daughter is insinuating that we have a tendency to go overboard, Ilya."

The woman arched her brows. "Once we moved to Williams and started having guests over, I may or may not have began cooking enough to feed an army."

"Or two," Taryn added.

Ilya rolled her eyes theatrically. "She's right...an army or two." She paused as the vehicle came to a stop amongst the sea of cars. "Ibrym and his pack came, too?"

Opening the car door, Taryn stepped out of the SUV, listening to the energetic howls coming from the backyard. "It wouldn't exactly be a complete family get together if they weren't here with us."

"I still remember the first night Alderyc and some of the others showed up here," Ilya recalled, popping the hatch. She walked around, grabbing a bag with Taryn's shoes and jewelry while Gracyn carefully removed the garment bag containing the teen's dress. "At a time when most people were weary of you, they arrived with open minds."

Taryn grinned. "That's because they were always destined to be a part of our extended family."

"While you two discuss the California pack, I'm going to take this stunning gown inside," Gracyn stated. "It really is the perfect dress for you, Taryn."

"Thanks," the teen replied.

Ilya held out one of the smaller bags in Taryn's direction. When the teen reached for it, she paused before letting go. "What you did today was very sweet. You knew how much our little excursion meant to your mother, and you made sure the latter part of the day was perfect...but not too perfect."

Taryn nodded, moving the bag to her side. "Was I that transparent?" she asked.

"No, Sweetie, you played it perfectly leaving a few shoppers present in the boutique."

"I wanted to give her a happy memory...you know, to hopefully take the place of the darker ones," Taryn admitted.

Smiling with pride, Ilya closed the hatch and laced her arm with the teen's as they headed toward the front door. "I think it's safe to say you nailed it today. And that dress...you made us both so very happy with your selection."

"It's not a style I would normally go for, but there was something about it that told me it was the one," Taryn replied.

CHAPTER THIRTEEN

Taryn walked out the French doors and immediately spotted Larkin amongst the crowd. He flashed her a beautiful smile, then blew her a kiss as he continued tossing the football with some of their guests. She found Keiryn sitting next to their dad on a bench, watching Lucan and Gideon Skye play a round of horseshoes against Ibrym's father and uncle. He gave her a slight nod and then motioned toward the pool to where Nalani lounged about at the water's edge.

Walking in the girl's direction, Taryn greeted everyone along the way. Many pulled her into fierce hugs while others gave her quick pecks on the cheek. Finally making it to the pool, she took a seat next to the beautiful girl and dangled her feet into the cool water.

Nalani glanced up from staring at the rippling water and grinned. "If only you had a cellphone, I could have warned you about everyone being extra huggy today."

"Now what fun would that have been?" she retorted.

Glancing in Keiryn's direction, Nalani wrinkled her nose, her eyes now locked on Taryn. "I know something happened between the two of you. Something rather significant, I would guess. Whatever it was, is it better now?"

Taryn shrugged. "I'm not sure it's better, but it certainly isn't any worse."

Nalani lifted her legs from the pool, turning to face her friend. "He's a bit of a mess, and I want to help. But as much as I hate to admit it, I think you're the only one who can make things better for him this time."

"I know, and I'll try. But right now, I need to be present for our entire family and focus on them," she replied.

"Fair enough," Nalani smiled, looking past her friend. Spotting Kellan and Gerrick attempting to sneak up behind them, she shook her head as a warning.

Gerrick lunged forward first, followed by Kellan. "In you go, Kansas!" he shouted.

Anticipating the two boys' attempt to push her into the pool, Taryn discreetly spread her fingers, creating a long rope out of the water. Before they could lay a hand on her, the two teens were lassoed and pulled into the pool.

Surfacing, Gerrick slapped his hands against the water. "Come on, Kansas. Can't we get you at least once?" he moaned.

She shook her head. "You have to earn those stripes before you can wear them, brother," she teased.

Swimming to the nearby edge, Kellan pulled himself out of the water, splashing both girls as he exited. He glanced back at Gerrick who was still treading water and laughed. "I think that's as good as it's going to get with her."

༄ఎ౪ఎ౪౪

Sitting down in one of the lounge chairs, Taryn kicked her feet up on an opposing seat. She smiled fondly as her family lined up and filled their plates with a variety of food items. Andyn and Sydney, Alderyc and Ibrym's young female cousin, had their heads together as they filed through the line. Keiryn stood watch as his pack members went ahead of him and Nalani. The teen's eyes finally came to rest on her parents, Ilya and Maxym. The brilliant smiles that lit

~ 217 ~

their faces warmed her heart, as did their unabated laughter. Maxym's throaty chuckle reminded her of Larkin's laughter during simpler times.

"It would appear that your Larkin has slipped away from the festivities," Lazryn stated as he leaned over the back of her chair.

She moved her feet and motioned for him to join her. "He left with Ibrym and Alderyc about a half hour ago."

Taking a seat, he grinned wildly. "Do you know where they might be headed?"

"Toward Williams. Near the Desert Rose Cafe," she responded.

He chuckled. "Could you be a bit more specific?"

Taryn smiled. "I could if I wanted, but I think that would be borderline stalkerish."

"No," he teased with a childish grin.

Glancing back to the others, the teen sighed. "You told Larkin about what happened, didn't you?"

He nodded. "He trusts you without fail. But in this instance, I thought it would better serve us all if he knew what to expect the next time you pluck one of the harp's strings."

"Fair enough," she replied, leaning forward in her seat. Taryn looked to the far corner of the patio where Dedrick sat with Andyn and Sydney. "How are things going over at the Love's?"

"The twins fawn over the boy whenever they are home. In fact, they have began calling him bother," he shared.

"What about Hava? How's she taking the two of you staying with them?" Taryn asked.

"She is extremely welcoming." He paused, locking his gaze upon her lovely face. "But I suspect you knew she would be."

Shrugging, Taryn scanned the group again. "You saved her life, and Hava isn't the type of person to forget something like that. With your decision to spare her, you allowed her to have a full life. She married Beldyn and had the twins." Pausing, she looked to the tree line, following it as far as her eye could see. "You should make a plate before the guys go back for seconds."

He watched as Taryn settled back in her chair. Her furrowed brows gave him pause. "I am far too curious at present, to concern myself with food."

"Yeah. Why is that?" she asked.

Leaning back, he scanned the area, his gaze trailing behind hers. "Something has you distracted, and I want to know why."

Taryn stopped and leaned forward. "There's something strange in the air that I can't quite put my finger on."

"Is there reason for alarm?" he asked.

Shaking her head, Taryn rose from the chair. "Whatever it is, it doesn't seem to be a threat."

"Then perhaps we should join the others," Lazryn replied.

As the pair began to head toward the buffet, Taryn suddenly stopped and turned, staring at the pool. Her eyes fixated on the water as it started to churn. She stepped closer, scanning the tree line once more.

"Lazryn, are you seeing this?" she asked.

When there was no answer, she looked over her shoulder and gasped. *They're gone,* she thought.

Understanding she was no longer partaking in the group's reality, the teen turned her attention back toward the pool. The water had become violent as it splashed high into the air, and the sun's rays began to fade.

Her words held a distinct bite as she addressed the responsible party. "I should warn you, I am in no mood for riddles or games."

On the opposing side of the pool appeared a stranger cloaked in a shimmering dark cloth. The hood hung down, hiding a man's face while only his hands were partially visible. He lifted his arms and as he did, the water in the pool rose chest high on Taryn.

"Life is nothing more than a series of moves and counter-moves, thus the living shall always be part of the game," the stranger stated, his words both cold and hollow.

Taking a deep breath, Taryn took a step closer to the pool's edge. "If one does not have another to love, nor have another's love, I suppose life could be seen as such," she replied.

The wind picked up and howled as it blew through the nearby tree line.

"You, like the others before you, shall play my game. The only question is, will you be the King, the Queen, the rook, bishop, knight or simply a pawn," the man stated plainly. As he did, the churning water began to recede.

"So you want to play chess?" Taryn smirked, spying the watery chessboard and foot tall figurines hovering above the pool's surface.

"As you may have noticed, the first move has already been made," he stated with an icy chill hanging on his every word.

Taryn looked to the makeshift game board and for a brief moment, her eyes wondered back into reality. There she saw a strange, yet familiar man sitting amongst her family, dining on their food. Before she could utter a word, she was pulled back into the vision. Her chest began to heave as she narrowed her eyes on the cloaked man. "And you made the wrong move."

With a blink of her eyes, Taryn was once more walking behind Lazryn. "Everyone stop," she shouted as a bolt of lightning lit the sky. She rushed past the former Mortari to where Keiryn sat.

Sensing the heat rolling off his sister, he jumped to his feet. "What is it, Taryn?" he questioned.

The girl glanced toward where the Skye family sat. "Gideon, Lucan, I need for you to set up a perimeter around the house. No one crosses over, and nothing gets in. Understood?" she asked while glancing around at the others.

The men nodded, and without question they began doing as she ordered.

"What's going on, Taryn?" Theron asked.

"We're under attack," she replied.

Keiryn grabbed her wrist. "What can I do?"

"You need to focus on what lies beyond the tree line. Even if you sense familiarity within, you must not trust it. Even if it looks like me," she warned.

"And what about you?" he questioned.

Lifting her hands in the air, she created a barrier of white lightning just outside the Skye's perimeter. "Lazryn and I are going to Williams," she stated while motioning for her friend to open a gateway.

"Watch her back, Lazryn," Keiryn stated.

The man nodded and a second later, both he and Taryn disappeared within the gateway.

৪৩৫৩৪৩৫৩

Emerging in an alleyway, Taryn rushed to the street. She held her breath, scanning the area for any sign of Larkin. Picking up a faint hint of his gifts, she rushed toward him without concern for who might see.

In the area behind the school, she found Larkin and the others, not alone as she had hoped.

"Hello, Taryn," a familiar voice purred, glancing over his shoulder.

Her eyes fixated on Larkin and the two brothers as they were being detained on their knees with their arms held awkwardly behind their backs. They were Influenced into silence. Taryn stalked toward the man. "Tell your men to let them go, Dagrin, and I may let you live."

The handsome man smiled salaciously. "Come now, girl, everyone knows that you are too morally sound to follow through on such a threat."

His cronies laughed as they tightened their hold on the three men.

~ 221 ~

Appearing in a blur by the girl's side, Lazryn arched his brow while giving a taunting smirk. "Tell me, old friend, are you equally as confident that I will not end you?"

Dagrin widened his stance and stared smugly at the reformed Mortari. "I know you will try, Brother. But I am also confident in knowing that you shall fail." He paused, looking toward his captives, then back to the man and teen. "Two years ago you would have ripped their throats out alongside Chrystian and the others. Now, because of this girl with the pretty face and innocent eyes, you have become a stranger to all those who have known and cared for you."

"Do not pretend to possess knowledge of what may rest within my heart. Someone like you who has never truly loved or known real love, has no idea the price of what true betrayal and ultimate suffering can do to a man," Lazryn retorted.

Clapping his hands, Dagrin chuckled. "Keep repeating that sentiment, and one day you may actually believe it yourself."

When Lazryn stepped forward, Taryn placed her arm in front of him. "Do not let the uniformed ramblings of King Nothing crawl beneath your skin."

Dagrin's eyes narrowed on the teen. "Ah, do not be bitter, darling Taryn. You have no way of knowing how deep my gifts truly run."

Lazryn glanced between the man and the girl. The slight flare of the teen's nostrils told him there was truth somewhere in Dagrin's words. "What is he talking about, Taryn?"

"Should I tell him, or would you like the honor?" Dagrin taunted.

"Back at the house, the thing that had me distracted but not concerned, it was him. He was testing the boundaries to see how potent his little concoction was before going after Larkin," she stated coolly.

Dagrin clapped his hands together yet again with a pleased look upon his face. "Very good, Taryn."

Her friend looked to her with furrowed brows. "He used Larkin's blood, nails and fur?"

She nodded. "As we speak, there are no less than twenty Lessors surrounding my home and those that I love."

The men holding Larkin and the others howled victoriously into the air.

"Your men are a bit premature on their celebration, don't you think?" she asked.

With a smug smile, Dagrin shrugged as his eyes shifted from deep brown to a brilliant shade of green. "If only you could catch a glimpse of the strength backing us, you would not dismiss our confidence so easily."

Taryn tilted her head to one side while studying the man, then to the other. "Funny, I never thought green would be a good color for you. Surprisingly, it suits you."

His smile widened. "We all have secrets. Some more than others."

"That we do," she agreed.

"Life is but a game," Dagrin stated, rubbing his chin while glancing between the girl and her wolf.

Taryn's face turned stone cold. "You are correct. We are indeed playing a game. The only difference is, I am a queen and you are just a pawn." Her eyes turned a brilliant blue as she lifted her hand against the Lessor. Simultaneously, her Influence inundated those detaining Larkin, Ibrym and Alderyc, causing them to free the young men while one of her Imperium orbs crashed into Dagrin's chest. The power of her orb sent him flying through the air and landing nearly one hundred yards away. In a blink, she stood over him with a foot pressed against his chest.

Bending at the waist, Taryn hovered over Dagrin with one corner of her mouth drawn up. She cupped one of her ears, pretending to listen to something in the air. "Do you hear that?" she asked.

Stunned still by the immense power, he could only stare blankly ahead.

Although, she knew he could hear her every word, the teen bent down even closer and whispered, "All hail, King Nothing."

Her words hung in the air and the breeze swiftly carried them like a fallen leaf in the fall.

ᏸᏨᏨᏜᏸᏨᏨᏜ

Keiryn and the others stood anxiously awaiting the threat to make its move.

"What do you think is out there?" Gerrick asked his pack leader.

Nalani turned to Keiryn. "Do you know what it is?"

He drew his jaw tight and nodded slightly. "Between Taryn's wall of lightning and an overwhelming sense that Larkin's standing on the other side, I'm not sure."

Stepping closer, Maxym pressed for answers. "You think Larkin is out there?"

"Everything inside me says it is him. But it doesn't make any sense." He paused, looking to his friend's worried father. "Taryn would never leave Larkin in harm's way. Regardless of everything else, that will never change. So that piece of knowledge alone tells me everything I am feeling is wrong."

"But he's my only son, Keiryn," Maxym asserted.

Placing both his hands on the man's shoulders, Keiryn looked him in the eye. "And Taryn is my sister. I know above all else, she will protect Larkin and this family with her life."

After a silent moment passed, Maxym nodded. "You're right. Taryn would set the worlds on fire to protect my son."

Taking a step back, Keiryn heard a familiar voice whispering through the air. "Please tell me someone else can hear that too?"

Nalani listened closely to the breeze. "It's Taryn. She's saying all hail, King Nothing, but why?"

Before anyone had the chance to answer, a large gateway opened in the center of the backyard. Alderyc and Ibrym exited first, followed by three strange men. Next was Larkin and Lazryn, with Dagrin and Taryn trailing behind.

Several members of her family gasped at the sight.

~ 224 ~

Gastyn Wylder stepped closer. "Is this truly Dagrin, the first of the Lessors?"

Nodding her head, Taryn waved away her wall of lightning, allowing the remainder of Dagrin's followers to exit the tree line and make themselves visible. Each of the men and women walked like soldiers, with the exception of the blank looks on their faces and eyes.

Taryn stepped up on a nearby bench to address her family. "Today the threat against us became very real. Our enemies, my enemies will surge from the shadows in an attempt to unravel and destroy our community, our family." She paused, looking several of them in the eye. "So I make each of you this promise, I will not permit harm to come to any of you. In the end, if protecting you means destroying myself, it is a sacrifice I will make every time."

Without answering any questions, Taryn stepped down from the bench and nodded to Lazryn. He opened another gateway and she quickly stepped through.

⬥⬥⬥⬥⬥

"What is the meaning of this intrusion?" Coyan seethed, rising from his throne as the girl entered the castle uninvited.

Taryn's face was neutral, though the heat pulsing off her drew the attention of everyone present, including Chrystian.

Glancing briefly in his direction, she then scanned the room before turning her attention toward Coyan. "Don't worry, Coyan, I have no intention of staying long. I'm only here to drop off a few items that I want the Brothers C to hold onto for me."

Moving to stand beside her husband, Tedra whispered in Coyan's ear.

"Didn't anyone ever tell you, Tedra, that secrets don't make friends? I guess it doesn't matter, because we are never going to be friends," Taryn stated.

Straightening herself, Tedra glared at the girl. "I was merely telling my husband what an honor it is to have our castle blessed by you, the teen queen, yet again."

A smirk curled on Taryn's face. "What do you say that we drop the false pretense and call a spade a spade, huh, Tedra? I don't like you, and you don't like me. But, I will offer you some friendly advice anyway. You should try to find your way off of my radar."

The woman narrowed her eyes on the teen before she turned to her husband. After a few quiet words between them, Tedra moved to stand behind Coyan's throne.

Glancing between his wife and brothers, Coyan's gaze finally fell upon Taryn. "What is it you want us to keep for you?" he questioned, his words laced with disdain.

Taryn motioned to the others within the gateway. Soon a parade of prisoners led by Larkin and Ibrym appeared, filling the space around the brother's thrones. Lazryn and Alderyc were the last to emerge from the portal.

Chrystian rose to his feet. "What is the meaning of this?" he questioned.

Taryn stepped toward the three brothers until she was standing on the platform that held their thrones. "There was an attempt to harm my family today. As you are already aware, such an act does not sit well with me." She paused, motioning to Dagrin and the others. "These are the perpetrators, and I want you to hold them in your dungeon until I say otherwise."

Coyan glanced over the group, resting his eyes on Dagrin. "There's something different about you," he said, locking eyes with him.

Waving her hand, Dagrin suddenly looked to the floor. "He is different, but the how and why is of no concern to you. All you need to know is that as long as I am alive, they will be no trouble. I simply ask that you provide them with food and water."

Clad rose to his feet. "Why would we give this request consideration?"

Taryn chuckled while biting her lip and shaking her head. "First of all, Clad, this is not a request but an amendment to the original conditions of our agreement. Second, by complying without issue, it shows the Mortari are capable of evolving. Third, if you are capable of evolving as a people, then there is still hope for your souls."

Coyan waved his youngest brother to sit while looking to Chrystian. "Brother, is there anything you would like to say to your dear friend?"

The tallest brother rose from his seat and studied the girl's eyes curiously. "You have my word that Dagrin and his followers will not be harmed while in our keep." He paused. "I expect that we should plan for you to stop in periodically to check in on the prisoners."

She nodded.

Chrystian's gaze lingered on the girl a bit longer before he looked to her wolf. "Young Wolf, take your family and return home now. None of you belong here amongst our kind."

Tedra, Coyan and Clad shared a troublesome glance before they looked to their brother with wide eyes.

"Chrystian is correct. Leave now, and we will see that your captives are locked away," Coyan stated, the words choking him as he spoke.

Taryn briefly locked eyes with Chrystian before turning and walking toward the gateway. Larkin wrapped his hand around her waist as she neared, escorting her the final few steps.

Without looking back, she paused in her step. "One final thing, Coyan," she said.

He rolled his eyes and released a hefty sigh. "And what would that be, dearest Taryn?"

"If for any reason, I find Dagrin or one of his followers harmed or missing, I will hold you solely responsible," she warned. She then disappeared within the gateway.

৪০৫৪০৫

Upon their return home, Taryn and the others found their friends and family sitting, minus Keiryn, waiting in silence. The teen walked over to the deck, taking a seat next to Dedrick, Andyn and Sydney.

"It's a beautiful evening. So why aren't you guys in the pool or playing a mean game of kickball?" she inquired.

Andyn rose to his feet. "Sis, don't treat us like babies. Whatever you're going to say to everyone else, we can handle it, too."

A smile warmed her face as she gave a slight chuckle. "There's no point in talking about it, Andyn. What's done is done. From this moment on, we need to be diligent about what or who is in our surroundings. We need to listen to our internal voice. Don't discredit what your mind knows or better yet, what your heart is telling you."

Keiryn broke through the tree line, staring heatedly at his sister. Moving closer, he looked around at the many faces before focusing back on her. "So that's it? We're all just supposed to go about our lives like the past hour and a half didn't happen?"

"Yes, we need to continue living our lives. Otherwise, we've let them win." She paused, rising to her feet. "But at the same time, you never forget what happened here today."

"If that was supposed to be your motivational speech for the evening, it certainly fell flat," he retorted, his words holding more than a hint of irritation. He looked to Larkin, Lazryn, Ibrym and Alderyc, and once more back to his sister. "Most of us here don't even know what happen today, Taryn. You barked out a few orders, put up a shield of lightning around us and disappeared. When you returned, you had Dagrin and a few others, but then you let your shield down and in marched a small army." He sighed loudly. "What happened in Williams? How did Dagrin and his followers get so close without someone besides you noticing?" He paused again, this time shaking his head. "How did they get so close, and you didn't notice sooner?"

"Do you really want to know how they deceived me?" she bit.

Shaking his head, Keiryn motioned to the others. "If it affects the rest of us, we have the right to know."

Taryn's bottom jaw drew tight and a hint of flare could be seen in her nostrils. "The day Nelmaryc and his son were taken, Dagrin stole a tuft of Larkin's fur, as well as his claws and blood. Somehow, he identified a way to use those small bits of our friend to disguise himself and his new band of followers."

Keiryn's eyes widened briefly, before narrowing on her. "You will do anything to protect Larkin. Even if that means leaving the rest of us behind for slaughter."

"Would you have chosen any differently if it were you and Nalani?" she countered.

Stepping toe-to-toe with her, Keiryn shook his head. "You knew he was up to something…you said it yourself. That day in the woods, you should have destroyed Dagrin, then and there. If you had, none of us would have been in danger today. Not your precious Larkin. And not a single one of us."

Taryn pushed up against her brother, getting right in his face. "Tell me about all the lives you've taken, Keiryn. Tell me how it feels to have the weight of their souls, good or bad, weighing on your heart."

"Better them than us," he bit.

"Dagrin and his people are locked up inside the Mortari castle. I've placed my Influence heavily upon them. They are no longer a threat to anyone," she asserted.

"You killed a man to save me. Why can't you just do that again?" he questioned.

Taryn took a small step back. "Just because I can, doesn't mean that I should." She paused as the green in her eyes gave way to a stunning shade of blue, causing some present to gasp. "Don't ask of me, Brother, what I know you, yourself fear."

Larkin approached the siblings and stepped between them. "It's been quite the day for everyone here. Why don't we table this conversation for another time? Maybe when everyone's had a few to process it all."

Lacing her arm with Keiryn's, Nalani gave him a tug. "He's right. You and Taryn can talk this out later," she stated.

Keiryn wrinkled his nose, shooting his sister a glare. "You're right, Nals."

All eyes focused on the two siblings and their exchange.

Theron and Gracyn maneuvered through the crowd toward their children. As they approached, Keiryn and Nalani passed them. Theron reached his hand out, but his son shrugged him off.

"Not now, dad," the teen stated.

Gracyn moved ahead to Taryn. "Your eyes...they're so blue."

Moving to his sister, Andyn stared at her for a moment. "Is this permanent?" he asked.

Taryn smiled and blinked her eyes, restoring the green. "Lazryn believes it has something to do with me nearing my eighteenth birthday. Once the full strength of my gifts set in, they'll stay green again."

Andyn shrugged. "That's too bad, I sort of liked the blue better."

With the sun's light nearly gone, Taryn waved her hand, creating roaring fires in each of the three fire pits. Grabbing hold of Larkin's hand, she led him over toward the pool and took a seat in one of the lounge chairs.

ဆဂဆဂ

With the California pack gone, Taryn, Larkin and Lazryn joined members of the Skye and Love family near one of the fire pits.

Sitting next to Hava, Taryn leaned her head on the woman's shoulder. "Thanks for looking after Lazryn and Dedrick," she said.

"It's no bother to have them at the house. The girls both adore Dedrick, and you know how I feel about Lazryn," Hava assured her.

Taryn smiled warmly. "You should really let Lazryn take care of breakfast sometime."

Arching a brow in his direction, Hava questioned, "You can cook?"

Lazryn chuckled as he leaned forward in his chair. "I am knowledgeable around a kitchen. However, I do not think Taryn was speaking of my culinary skills. Instead, she was eluding to a little shop

~ 230 ~

that creates the most mouthwatering mini pastries on this or any other plane."

"They're almost too pretty to eat," Taryn added.

"Like that has ever stopped you before. Last time I think you had three," Larkin retorted.

She rolled her eyes at him. "Whatever. If I didn't eat mine all at once, I wouldn't get a second, let alone a third."

While everyone chuckled, Beldyn looked to one of the large windows, spying Dedrick and Andyn sitting on the couch watching a movie. He turned to the teen and shook his head gently. "I don't mean to pry, Taryn, but do you have knowledge of what happened to Dedrick before he came to Williams?"

"Why do you ask?" she questioned.

Beldyn shared a brief glance with his wife.

"Go ahead. Tell her," Hava assured him.

He took a deep breath and began. "When Lazryn left to go with you, the boy screamed in his sleep and wept while taking a bath. Hava and I, even the twins tried to console him. Yet nothing seemed to help."

Taryn gazed distantly at the fire. "He suffered terrible, terrible things before they found him at the castle."

"Did he share his experiences with you?" Beldyn asked.

She glanced back to the house, then shook her head. "No, I saw what happened to him when we touched."

"It was that day in the hallway, wasn't it?" Larkin questioned from nearby.

"Yes. Through his memories, I watched as Dagrin and his followers savagely murdered his entire family. Women, children...they didn't care. They even slaughtered the animals."

Lazryn pushed back in his seat. "What exactly did you see, Taryn?" he questioned.

"The light, it no longer affected them. Their eyes turned black as night, as if they had no soul," she answered.

"Did you see anything else?" her friend pressed.

She nodded as tears began to flow. "Draining them of their gifts, they took them to the brink of death. Then they ripped open their chests and devoured their still beating hearts," she whispered.

"That explains why he was so terrified when we found him in the castle," Larkin stated.

Taryn pushed to her feet, stepping closer to the fire while pressing a hand against her stomach. "It's not the only reason, Larkin," she admitted.

"What else did you see?" he asked.

"When the wolves discovered Dedrick amongst his family's remains, they were certain he had played a part in their massacre. So when the wolves presented him to Nodryck, they told him of their suspicions. Nodryck tortured and beat the boy every day since. Something he is quite skilled at," she shared.

Lucan and Gideon Skye began to whisper amongst themselves. A few moments later, they looked to Taryn.

"Dagrin's victims, do they become Necrowalker?" Gideon asked.

She shook her head. "What I felt in the vision was something entirely different than when they drank blood." She paused, glancing around the fire. "Dagrin's change is dramatic. He's evolved his practice from drinking blood to consuming beating hearts. He no longer has to fear walking in the sunlight. In fact, he doesn't fear at all."

"How did this happen?" Lucan questioned.

She shifted on the log she shared with Hava. "There is something profoundly different about him. Not just in his actions, but also in his thinking. He's always been cunning, but his greed makes him sloppy."

Beldyn looked to Lazryn. "What do you think happened to him that allowed him to evolve so quickly?" he asked.

"From the day that I met him, I knew Dagrin's soul was stained by darkness. Once he joined our ranks, his merciless and vile tactics quickly caught Coyan's eye. The eldest brother insisted that we bring him into the fold, and practically considered him a son," Lazryn shared.

"But something happened between them. Something that led to Dagrin becoming the first Lessor. Right?" Larkin asked.

Listening to the others talk, Taryn held her hand out just above the fire's flame. Vivid images of Dagrin began to flood her mind. No matter how offensive, she absorbed every detail in each frame, storing them away in her memory.

While explaining how both men were competitive by nature, Lazryn glanced to Taryn and recognized her distant gaze. Not wanting to interrupt what she was experiencing, he continued to share what he knew of the rift between the two men. "You see, being the eldest of the three brothers, Coyan automatically held the role of leader when the war began between us and the Elder Council. However, it was Chrystian's fierce and unyielding rage that initially grew our numbers, and allowed us to become what we have. He was devastated by the loss of his wife, and it was better to be with him than against him."

Withdrawing her hand from above the fire pit, Taryn spoke, "Dagrin appeared in your lives during a brief time of moderate calm. The period of time Chrystian's rage transitioned into intolerance."

Lazryn nodded. "That is correct. During his brother's change, Coyan grew bored and found Dagrin to be a suitable surrogate." He paused, giving a sigh with a slight roll of his eyes. "Temporarily blinded by his fondness of the man, Coyan chose to ignore the fact that his new found son was more ambitious than even he himself. Dagrin longed for masses to bow at his feet, and for all Mortari to call him king. After his change was complete, Chrystian observed this behavior in the newcomer and sat upon his throne, constantly laughing and taunting his elder brother. After nearly a decade, Coyan could no longer tolerate his brother's goading and decided to disprove him. He put together a series of games where members of our kind would face off in battle, or they would fight against a dozen humans at a single time. Of course it was more about the slaughter and how vile one could prove themselves to be that was the object of the games. As the games came to an end, Coyan was pleased that Dagrin still stood, and to also have proven his younger brother wrong. He was about to crown Dagrin his champion, when the man spoke up. Dagrin did not feel the games were a true test to his strength, so he challenged Coyan to a dual of fists and swords." Chuckling, he paused. "Coyan was a fierce and feared Mortari who wielded hefty gifts, however, he was a bit soft when it came to any real physicality. Chrystian sat quietly, watching as his elder brother stammered and stuttered about. As much as he enjoyed watching his brother spiral, he valued his family's reputation more. Chrystian rose from his throne and accepted Dagrin's challenge on behalf of the family."

Gideon and Lucan exchanged glances with Hava, Beldyn and the others who had gathered to listen to the tale.

"I take it this is not what is written in your history books," Lazryn stated.

Stepping closer to the fire, Gastyn shook his head. "You have first-hand knowledge of the situation, and yet there is nothing about this in our ancestral pages."

"Is anyone here truly surprised?" Taryn asked while walking over to Larkin and taking a seat on his lap. "The Elder Council wrote their own narrative for millenniums without contest. There's no way of ever truly knowing what is true in their version of our history versus what was written to suit their agenda."

Several heads nodded in agreement with the teen's statement.

"Lazryn, if you would, I think we would all like to hear the rest of the story, in your own words," Gastyn stated with a hint of marvel in his words.

The former Mortari nodded in response and continued. "Dagrin believed his brute strength would be more than enough to overpower any of the brothers, including Chrystian. So the pair squared off in a pit where the use of their gifts was not permitted. Chrystian, being his usual self, stood with barely an expression upon on his face while his opponent jumped about, working himself into a frenzy. When the horn sounded, Dagrin charged Chrystian and began landing fist after fist to his head and torso. After more than ten minutes of making no attempt to stop the assault or to throw a fist of his own, a staggering Chrystian regained his footing." Lazryn paused, leaning in nearer to those listening. "You see, Dagrin had thought that he had bested my childhood friend. He simply did not, or could not, comprehend what factors motivated Chrystian in war. For when the middle brother regained his footing, a wild and dark smile curled on the corners of his mouth. Chrystian spat out a mouthful of blood and howled into the air. Dagrin's stance instantly changed, and you could see the fear rushing into his eyes. He charged Chrystian once again, but found himself on the receiving end of a series of powerful blows. Chrystian struck him repetitively until the man could no longer see from his eyes or speak from his mouth. My dearest friend all but destroyed the would be usurper."

From his seat, Beldyn asked, "Are we to make the assumption that Dagrin drank blood due to this beating?"

"Yes and no," Lazryn answered while rising from his seat. "After that night, Coyan shunned his son and banished him from our home. Dagrin knew the only way to redeem himself in the eyes of his fellow Mortari was to challenge the brothers once more, and most importantly, to win the battle. Dagrin was not seen nor heard from for nearly a decade, when he abruptly returned. His eyes were now the color of blood, and he had a small following in tow. Once more, he made the challenge to the brothers. However, like the time before, Chrystian proved to be a formidable opponent. The fight began a bit more balanced this time, but once Chrystian was no longer interested in fighting, he finished Dagrin off with ease. Though Coyan now despised the man he formerly thought of as his son, he saw potential for the chaos and destruction Dagrin and his kind could inflict without endangering his own people."

Looking to Lazryn, Taryn shook her head and smiled. "The first time I saw him, Chrystian had returned to the castle looking disheveled. They exchanged blows rather than fighting with their gifts."

He nodded. "While there is no love loss between the duo, Chrystian is always willing to provide Dagrin with another opportunity to try defeating him in hand-to-hand combat."

While everyone discussed this new information, Andyn and Dedrick approached Taryn.

"Hey, sis. Do you think Dedrick and Lazryn could move back into the house with you?" Andyn asked.

Grabbing a hand of each boy in her own, Taryn smiled warmly. "I'm afraid that isn't a good idea right now. You see, there are forces at work all around us and I…I'd hate to see Dedrick or you get caught in the cross fire."

Andyn looked to the younger boy and shrugged. "Well, we tried," he said before wandering off to hang with his true pack members.

Lingering, Dedrick wrinkled his nose. "You're not mad at me anymore, are you?"

Taryn's eyes softened as she glanced back at Larkin, then leaned closer to the boy. "I know what you've suffered through, Dedrick, and I am truly sorry for adding to your pain. I should have handled your presence better."

He shrugged. "It's okay."

"No, really, it's not. Your family and friends were savagely murdered, and you were helpless to stop it. When you needed comfort and reassurance, I was more concerned with myself and trying to justify my own feelings." She paused, placing a hand on either of his shoulders. "Will you forgive me?"

The young boy smiled and wrapped his arms around her neck. "Of course, I will," he whispered. After a few lingering moments, he released his grip. "I need to find Andyn. I want to tell him that you and I are friends now."

Taryn smiled as she watched the boy run toward the large group of teens lingering around the deck.

Pulling her in close, Larkin nuzzled his nose against the side of his love's neck. "You made the kid's day." He paused, looking around at their family and all the smiling faces. "It's not going to stay like this, is it?"

She shook her head. "No, it's not."

"Whenever you're ready, I'd like to talk about what happened earlier," he whispered.

Rolling her eyes, Taryn released a hefty sigh.

"Don't get irritated. I'm not talking about what happened here or in Williams. I mean, what happened on Mors…with Chrystian," Larkin stated.

Turning just enough, Taryn pulled Larkin's mouth to hers, bestowing a tender kiss upon his mouth. "We could go right now. It's not like anyone is going to miss us."

He gave her a wild smile. "Ladies first."

৪৩৫৩৪৩৫৩

Atop the Superstitious Mountains, Taryn rested her head on Larkin's lap, while they stared up at the night sky.

"The view here is incredible," Larkin stated with awe hanging from his words.

Taryn smiled as she took in his handsome face. "I couldn't agree more."

Running the tips of his fingers down her cheek, Larkin exhaled. "So did you and your moms find a prom dress on your girl's day out?"

She gave a slight shrug. "Maybe."

Larkin arched his brows. "I saw the look on Ilya and Gracyn's faces. You definitely found a dress."

"This prom thing means a lot to my mom. She wants everything to be perfect." Taryn paused, sitting up. "I think it's her way of trying to steal back some of the time we missed together."

"I don't blame her. If I had the chance to reconnect with my mother, I would probably do the same," he replied.

She placed her hand over his heart. "Your mother lives on inside of you, Larkin. I feel her presence all around you and your father."

Tears welled in his eyes as he placed his hand over hers. "I know you were just a baby back then, but do you remember her at all?" he asked.

"I see brief flashes of her face. She had such a warm smile and a joyful laugh. Her heart overflowed with love for you and your dad," Taryn replied.

Larkin swiped away his tears. "My mom was an incredible woman, and an even more amazing mother. I know she is watching over us wearing one of her famous smiles. And I'm certain that she approves of Ilya and my dad's relationship. She wasn't the kind of woman who would want him to be alone just because she could no longer be here with him."

The girl nodded. "I believe she would want us all to be happy and to find peace while we're still alive."

Reaching up, Larkin ran his fingers through the length of Taryn's hair. "What does peace even look like for our kind? I can't help but wonder if we were to see it, would we be able to recognize it?" he replied.

Taryn tilted her head back, looking to the stars. "Peace is not having too look over your shoulder at every turn. It's being able to live without the constant worry of what rules we might have broken, or who is offended and what monster is awaiting us in the shadows."

Placing his thumb on her chin, Larkin gently pulled her gaze to his. "A lot of people believed that peace would come after what happened during the Trials last fall. They thought you could somehow make everything right again."

"I wish I could be what the people believe me to be, but I'm not. I am fallible. I suffer from visions that leave me questioning my own sanity and each day's reality" She paused, running her fingertips down his muscular arms. "I see good where others only see bad. I befriend the known evils and protect them no matter who opposes it."

Larkin's brows furrowed slightly. "You're talking about Chrystian, aren't you?"

She nodded.

"When we were on Mors, why did he address me specifically? And why would he make a point to say that none of us belonged with their kind?" he asked.

She rolled her eyes and sighed heavily. "You already know that I've been struggling with certain things."

Larkin nodded. "Like whether or not you will be the reason the others and me die?"

"Not so much the reason, more I see myself as your would be killer," she admitted.

He shook his head. "Well, I, for one, don't believe it. You would never harm any of us."

"Maybe not, but that doesn't change the things I've seen. My visions always hold some form of the truth, and that's part of the reason why Dagrin and his followers were able to get so close today," she admitted.

Larkin's eyes narrowed and a hint of confusion washed over his handsome face. "Are you trying to say that Dagrin, King of the Lessors, was somehow able to exploit your visions?" he asked.

"Not Dagrin," she responded.

"If not him, then who?" he asked

Taryn looked off into the distance, taking in the soft glow of lights surrounding the Phoenix area. "Today, before I identified what I was sensing, a cloaked man came to me in a vision. He told me that I would play his games like those before me."

"What does that even mean?" he questioned.

Biting her lip, Taryn sucked in a deep breath, holding the air idle in her lungs for several seconds before exhaling. "Lazryn told you about what happened when I strummed the harp."

He nodded.

"Did he also share with you the story his father told both he and Loryn as children?" she asked.

"Yes, he did. He also explained how you lived through the boy's hell while trapped inside the vision. One he somehow was able to access when he grabbed hold of you."

"Forget about me and the boy for a moment and concentrate only on the story. The man with the swirling eyes." She paused, giving her words time to sink in. "There is only one man I know of that possesses eyes like in the story."

Larkin gasped. "Farren? You think the man from the story is Death?"

She rose to her feet and shrugged. "Think about it. A man with swirling eyes who makes an impossible promise, and then gifts the woman a magic harp to heal their child." Taryn began stepping toward the edge when she suddenly froze. Something Farren had said to the boy during her vision spun in her mind. *Though you are on the brink of death, you will never be mine to claim until peace finds a home within your heart.*

Watching her, Larkin jumped to his feet. "What is it, Tare-Bear? Is it another vision?" he asked.

With wide eyes, she shook her head. "Right after I left my mental hell and returned to reality, I had assumed that his mother was using the harp as a means to keep him alive for her own selfish reasons." She paused, running her fingers through her hair. "What if I was wrong? What if the boy could not die, and she used the harp to relieve his suffering?"

"So if you're correct, Farren, one of the Immortals, had a child with a Gaias woman millenniums ago, and he permitted his son to be abused in place of the woman?" Larkin mused aloud.

"I know it doesn't sound like the Farren I have come to know, but this happened a very long time ago," she stated.

Larkin paced back and forth several times before pausing in his step. "Was he in love with her, or was he just going through a sick and twisted phase? And seriously, why would he want to have a child with someone like us?" he asked.

Taryn sighed. "I don't know. Maybe he wanted a child and this was the only way he could have one. The King's cruel behavior would guarantee that Farren would see the boy every night, and would be able to stay near him until he was healed by the harp's melody."

"But why? Why would he do that?" Larkin questioned.

The girl chewed her bottom lip while considering the possibilities. After a few minutes passed, the promise the boy's mother had made in her vision began echoing inside her head. *One day I will find another, greater than the one who did this to us. I will make him pay. His suffering will be eternal. This, I promise you.*

"The child's mother said she would make the one who did this to him pay. The pain during the vision was so horrific that I assumed she was talking about King Rutger...but what if she meant the boy's father?" Taryn shared.

Larkin moved toward her. "There's no way one of our kind could ever touch a true Immortal."

Shrugging, Taryn wrapped her arms around Larkin's neck. "I don't know. If one of them were to ever hurt you," she stated, her words breaking off.

He smiled. "I know, Tare-Bear. I know. I love you, too."

Resting her head on his chest, she took a deep breath. "He wanted me to know that I wasn't like them," she whispered.

Larkin crooked his head to look down at her. "That you're not like who?" he asked.

She pushed back slightly. "That I'm not like the Mortari. It's what Chrystian was trying to say."

A nervous chuckle escaped Larkin's throat. "You're serious?"

Nodding, Taryn took a full step back.

"Is it because of your visions?" he asked.

She closed her eyes and exhaled. Taking a moment to gather her thoughts, she looked to Larkin. "It's not just the visions. It's everything I feel inside of me. Everything I taste when I breathe. Everything I touch feels corrupted somehow…everything, with the exception of you."

Reaching down, Larkin took both her hands into his and lifted them to his lips where he placed a soft kiss upon each. "As much as I hate to admit it, Chrystian's right. You're not like the Mortari. You're not like the Elder Council either." He paused, staring into the depths of her shimmering green eyes. "You're unlike anything this or any other world has even seen, Taryn. And regardless of what you may believe, I know your heart is pure and your intentions good."

Her heart fluttered as she stared back at him. "And what about the things Keiryn said today? Do you think I made a mistake leaving Dagrin alive?" she asked.

A soft smile crept across his face. "Ending him sounds like the easy solution, but that doesn't mean it's the right solution." He paused, reaching up and tracing his fingers along her jawline. "It took you only a single blow to stop him."

She smiled back. "Why do I get the feeling there's a but?"

He moved his hands around her waist, pulling her in close and nuzzling the tip of his nose against hers. "Who am I to judge you for not taking a life? Besides, Dagrin and his followers are no longer a threat, and if I'm being completely honest, all I can think about right now is how much I want to kiss you."

Without another word, Larkin crushed his lips against hers. As they continued to kiss, brilliant shafts of lightning lit the sky overhead.

CHAPTER FOURTEEN

The next day during their lunch period, Taryn and Larkin sat at their group's table in the cafeteria. Neither teen could take their eyes off the other.

Sitting across from them, Andyn and Eben batted their eyes at one another before finally wrinkling their noses.

"Come on, sis. I'm trying to eat here," Andyn groaned.

Taryn smiled as her eyes remained focused on her great love.

Kellan rolled his eyes as he strolled past with his plate. "Seriously you two, have you already forgotten about what happened yesterday?" he asked.

Larkin tapped his left temple with his index finger. "Nope, got it all right here," he retorted, his eyes never leaving Taryn.

The twins, Bentley and Hadley, sighed in unison as they watched their friends with dreamy eyes.

"I think it's sweet how they can't take their eyes off one another," Hadley stated.

"With everything that's happened, I think it's a testament to the power of their love. Nothing and no one will ever come between them," Bentley added.

"Never," the girls stated in unison.

Grabbing his tray, Andyn rose from his seat. "I love ya, sis, but I can't take another second of your little love fest."

For the first time since they sat down, Taryn turned her gaze to her little brother. "Did Sydney tell you she's staying the weekend with us?"

The boy's cheeks flushed. "Um, no…she didn't mention it."

"She wanted to be here for prom. You know, to see the dresses and how the guys all clean up in their tuxedos," Taryn shared.

Andyn bit his bottom lip nervously. "Yeah, she likes all that girlie stuff."

"Yes she does, but she also likes you, baby brother," Taryn replied.

Larkin turned his head and grinned. "And we all know that you like her, too."

The boy's cheeks were absolutely glowing. Unable to find his voice for once, Andyn shyly ducked his head and headed off to scrape his tray while his table broke into laughter.

"That boy has it bad for Syd," Kellan chuckled.

Dagney elbowed Thorne, who had just high-fived Kellan. "I think it's rather sweet the way they are together. He is such a little gentleman when he's with her." She turned her gaze to Thorne and the other boys. "Some of you could take notes and learn a thing or two about how to treat a lady."

Thorne laughed, but was almost instantly quelled. He pointed toward the far set of doors leading outside. "Taryn, I think someone would like a word with you."

Taryn looked over Larkin's shoulder to where her older brother stood peering in the long rectangular window. "I don't think he slept much last night," she stated.

"Do you want company?" Larkin asked.

She shook her head. "No. I think some conversations are better left between siblings."

He gently reached out and took her hand in his. "If things get heated..."

"You know I can handle myself," she replied with a soft smile.

Reluctantly, Larkin released his hold on her and nodded. "I'll see you at home?"

Leaning forward, she gave him a peck on the lips. "We'll go for another run tonight. Just the two of us."

Larkin blinked and she was gone.

ജ౦ദ౦ദ౦ദ

Brother and sister raced across the open terrain until they neared Wahweap Bay.

"Nothing quite like a run to clear your head," Keiryn commented, while stretching his legs.

Taryn moved to the water's edge and knelt down, staring at her reflection. The image flickered between one of herself and one of Calista before settling fully on the woman. She watched as the beautiful woman stared up at her. Her eyes were haunting as they held a quiet rage that pleaded for release. Hearing Keiryn approach, Taryn ran her fingers over the calm surface, disrupting the image.

"If you're thirsty, we can head over to the marina and grab something to drink," he suggested.

Taryn nodded and the pair began walking. "Last night, things got a little heated between us."

He smirked. "A little?"

She paused her step. "Would you like it better if I said you were acting like a serious donkey?"

Arching a brow, he playfully bumped his shoulder into hers as they continued their journey. "I'm sorry. I should have handled the situation better, but in all fairness, you've said things recently that needed to be explained. When things went down with Dagrin and his followers yesterday...I thought I was going to lose my mind."

"I know. You are rather predictable," she replied.

"What's that supposed to mean?" he asked.

A smiled curled on one side of Taryn's mouth. "What if I were to tell you that I am playing a game of chess, and last night I was in need of a pawn?"

This time it was Keiryn who stopped in his tracks. "A pawn?" he questioned. "You do know we're both Knights, right?"

Taryn laced her arm with his and gave it a tug. "Of course I do, but I'm serious about the game, Keiryn," she warned.

"I'm not following you," he replied.

"Yesterday near the pool, I saw a man dressed in a cloak. He used the water to create a large chess board, and he told me that I would play his game like those before me," Taryn explained.

He shook his head. "It wasn't a vision?"

Taryn shrugged. "It was more of a shift in the planes. Like an alternate state of being. I was with you, but I was also with him…but he was also with you."

"Now I'm completely lost," he muttered.

"It's hard to explain, Keiryn, but I need for you to trust me. I also need you to know that I will always protect our entire family, no matter what," she stated.

"What I said last night…it was in the heat of the moment and," he replied before being cut off.

"And you had every right to be upset, minus my decision not to murder Dagrin," she stated firmly.

"How can you say that knowing, if given the chance, he would kill any of us without a second thought?" Keiryn countered.

She rolled her eyes and released a low growl. "He was no longer a threat. If I had taken his life, I would be no different than the Elder Council or the Mortari."

Keiryn's nostrils flared as he jerked his arm away from hers. "You act like he's an innocent, Taryn. Like all the lives he's destroyed don't even matter to you."

"So you think if I had killed him, it would somehow erase the wrong done to his victims? That it would end the hurt their families feel in their absence?" she bit.

With anger present on Keiryn's face, the water in the marina began to churn as dark clouds formed overhead. "I get that you don't want blood on your hands, Taryn, but at some point, you are going to have to decide...your purity or our survival."

Taryn's eyes fixated on her brother's face. "If you're angry, take it out on me, not on the people in this marina," she warned.

Glancing around at the menacing clouds and violent waters, Keiryn understood that he had unleashed his gifts without even knowing it. He quickly pulled back, restoring the calm. "I didn't realize what I was doing," he gasped.

She shook her head and sighed heavily. "You have to remain in control at all times, Keiryn. Especially now."

"I messed up," he admitted.

Taryn's face softened as she placed her hand on his shoulder. "Look, I hear you. I even understand your reasoning, but I cannot do what you're asking. I need to understand the reasons why Dagrin did what he did, and how he was able to turn the tables and use Larkin's gift against us."

"He's a bad man who has lived a very, very long time, Taryn. What else is there to know or understand about the situation?" he retorted.

She shook her head and took a deep breath. "Simply because a person does bad things, does not automatically mean that they are innately bad." She paused, her eyes pleading for his understanding. "Sometimes they're pushed beyond their emotional and mental limits and darkness consumes them. And then other times they are led down a dark path by others."

"It sounds like you're making excuses for everything that Lazryn and Chrystian have done," he snarked.

Taryn growled and punched her brother in the chest, causing him to stagger backwards. "Ugh. You are such a guy sometimes," she fumed.

"Ouch!" Keiryn winced. "I'm telling mom that you hit me we get back."

Her jaw dropped. "What are we, five?"

Keiryn bit his knuckle and turned away from her with his body shaking.

"Seriously, glass boy, I didn't hit you that hard. So dry your tears, we have a lot more to discuss and not much time," she said.

When he turned to face her again, his cheeks were bright pink and tears filled his eyes. "You should have seen your face," he laughed.

Taryn's brows furrowed. "Boys," she groaned while shaking her head.

After a few moments passed, Keiryn's laughter began to wane. "Come on, sis, I had you going there for a minute," he smiled.

"I'm sure Kellan and Gerrick would be proud of you if they were here," she stated, a hint of annoyance in her tone.

Seeing that his sister was not in a joking mood, Keiryn quelled the last bit of laughter and addressed the issues. "Look, I hear you and I get it. Lazryn was the Mortari's enforcer for centuries, and look at him now. He would defend any member of our community, and he has your back." He paused, rubbing one side of his neck. "It almost kills me to say it, but I'm glad he came to Williams. You need someone with the knowledge that he has on your side. And he is definitely on your side, Taryn."

"He was my sanity while I was on Mors. I'm not sure what I would have done if it weren't for both him and Farren," she confessed.

The air grew heavy with silence as Keiryn gazed softly at his sister.

"I know what you're thinking," she said.

He glanced to the waters of Lake Powell and then back to her. "So would it have made a difference if you knew then what you know now?" he asked.

"Of course it would have. I didn't take pleasure in seeing any of those people die, but I can't change what was. I can only learn from the past," she replied.

"You said you needed to know why Dagrin did the things that he's done. Do you have an idea what that answer may be, or did I misunderstand what I thought you were saying?" he questioned.

"No. You didn't misunderstand. In fact, I'm about ninety percent positive I know the who...at least I now know his face. I just don't understand the why," she admitted.

Keiryn sighed loudly and dropped shoulders. "Looking at you, I can see the wheels are working overtime. So I suppose you have a plan to find the answers to your burning questions?"

She nodded. "You're not going to like it, and neither is Larkin, but I believe it is the only way to gain the knowledge that we need."

His face turned sour. "You're going to strum that demon of a harp, aren't you?"

Taryn bit her bottom lip and shrugged.

୫୧୫୧

Sitting in the living room with Jonesy, Andyn, and Dedrick, Larkin ran his fingers through his hair and stared out the large windows.

"Dude, they'll be back when they're back," Andyn groaned while pushing Larkin's elbow away from his head.

Scooting to the edge of the couch, Larkin's shoulders hung heavy. "Keiryn wasn't exactly happy last night."

"A lot of us weren't," Jonesy added, garnering a stern look of warning from his friend.

Walking in from the dining room, Theron chuckled. "What do you think he could possibly do to her, Larkin? It's not like Keiryn is going to overpower his sister."

Standing, Larkin shook his head. "You know with Taryn it's all about her emotions. Keiryn knows how to push her buttons, and I'm afraid that he might set her off. What happened yesterday had an effect on her, even if she didn't let you see it," he divulged.

Dedrick looked to his new friends. "Seeing those monsters, it reminded me of what happened to my family." He paused, pulling his knees to his chest. "They are savages, and I wish Taryn would have killed them. Maybe then the nightmares would stop."

Sharing a glance with Theron, Larkin nodded and then walked over, taking a seat next to the boy. He placed his arm around Dedrick's shoulders and leaned in. "Taryn told some of us about what happened to you and your community. There are no words to describe the horrors that you have seen." He paused, looking the young boy in the eyes, giving him a comforting smile. "But you should know, Dagrin and the others, Taryn made it so they can't hurt you or anyone else anymore."

Shivers racked his body as he lowered his head. "I hope for all our sakes that you are not mistaken," he said meekly.

Andyn sensed the boy's fear and quickly joined in on the conversation. "Dedrick, Taryn's the best. There isn't anyone who could challenge her and win. If she says that bloodsucker and his goons aren't a threat, then they're not a threat," he reassured his friend.

The young boy lifted his chin and gave a faint smile. "You really think so?" he asked.

"Of course. Taryn saved me from my dad, and she promised that he would never hurt me again," Andyn answered.

Glancing to Larkin and then back to his friend, Dedrick shook his head. "You all have such faith in her."

Larkin nodded. "Taryn's earned our trust and our respect through her actions. We know her word is binding and that she will always have our backs."

"My family and I belonged to a nomadic community. We rarely set up camp in any one place for more than a few weeks at a time. When that man and his monsters attacked, we had not even fully unpacked," the boy explained.

Theron stepped in front of the fireplace. His warm gaze fell upon the boy. "I think I can speak for everyone when I say that we are glad you were spared. You are a welcomed addition to our Williams' family."

Larkin began to open his mouth to speak when he was overcome by an immense wave of power. "They're back," he said while rising to his feet and looking out the windows.

Brother and sister appeared in the backyard only moments later. Taryn punched Keiryn in the arm before wrapping her arm around his neck, causing him to lean at an awkward slant as they walked towards the house.

Unable to wait a second longer, Larkin rushed to the door.

Pulling away from her brother, Taryn wrapped her arms around Larkin's waist, placing her head on his chest. She inhaled deeply, taking in his scent. She pulled back just enough to steal a look into his soulful hazel colored eyes.

Tracing along her hairline, Larkin smiled. "Everything okay between you two?"

She nodded. "I need a quick shower then we can head out for our run."

Joining his father near the fireplace, Keiryn smirked. "It sort of sucks that when he's around the rest of us fade into the background."

Theron arched a brow. "As much as I dislike the thought of having lost my little girl before I realized she was mine, I'm glad he can put a smile on her face."

"I guess so," Keiryn replied.

Glancing at his son, Theron noticed several dark spots on the t-shirt he was wearing. "Did you hurt yourself while running with your sister?" he asked.

Looking down, Keiryn scratched at the dark red stains. "Yeah, I cut my hand while we were climbing up the side of one of the canyon walls. Taryn healed it so quickly that I didn't realize I had gotten any blood on my clothes," he offered.

✥✥✥

The following day, Taryn and Larkin skipped Gastyn's afternoon class to meet up with Keiryn in one of the caves on the south rim of the Grand Canyon.

They were nearly two hundred feet into the cave when they settled in and placed the lanterns they carried strategically about in order to light the space.

Looking to her brother, Taryn held out her hand.

"I see someone's in a hurry," he teased while removing the harp from his oversized duffle bag.

Larkin stepped between the two siblings. "Are you certain this is the only way?" he asked her.

Taryn nodded. "I know this isn't ideal. But we really don't have any other leads. Every day that we do not take action is another day this cloaked stranger has on us…on me."

"I don't get it. What makes you think this harp is going to tell us anything?" Larkin questioned.

Grabbing hold of the instrument, Taryn sighed. "The last time Chrystian and I were alone, he asked about the contents of the box you found in the garden on Hypatia. When I told him that there were only books, he became irritated, even flustered." She paused, kneeling on the ground. "I could be wrong, but I believe he had hoped I would find this harp."

Larkin knelt down beside her. "How would he even know that it existed?"

"I don't know. But my gut is telling me that this is what he was after," she remarked.

Moving to the other side of her, Keiryn knelt down. "I don't like this at all," he stated.

She cupped his cheek and smiled. "No worries, big brother. I have you and Larkin looking out for me."

Placing his hand between her shoulder blades, Larkin nodded. "Remember if anything goes wrong, we're both right here." He leaned in, kissing her temple.

Taryn took a deep breath and strummed the second string on the harp. As its sound filled the air, the girl stared ahead, watching as a bright light filled the tunnel in front of her. The glow barreled closer until it consumed her.

Larkin and Keiryn held firm as her tiny frame began to thrash about beneath their grip.

After several intense moments, Taryn's body suddenly turned limp and the boys guided her to the cave floor.

Keiryn removed the harp from her hands while Larkin swept the lose strands of hair from her face.

"This isn't fair. It should be my burden, not hers," Keiryn stated as he stared down at his sister.

Sighing as he settled in next to her, Larkin looked admiringly at his love. "I know. If I could trade places with her, I would in an instant." He paused, glancing over to his friend. "Think about how strong she is. Not just because of her gifts, but also mentally. She has seen and felt things that none of us dare to imagine on our best days."

Keiryn looked down and gently rubbed the palm of his hand. "All we can do is be here for her when she wakes up," he stated.

ഇൽ

Taryn's eyelids began to flutter about as light gave way to the dark. A faint orange glow pulsed as the weakened flames of a fire danced a final time.

"I was hoping you would wake," a woman's voice whispered in her ear.

The teen sat up and immediately her forehead began to throb. She winced as the right side of her ribcage joined in. "What's wrong with me?" she asked.

The woman placed a wet cloth on the back of the girl's neck. "One day, maybe you will listen and keep your distance from those horrid boys."

Pressing the palm of her hand against the center of her forehead, Taryn groaned. "Boys? What boys?"

"How hard did they strike you?" the woman asked while moving closer to the sputtering fire.

The teen scooted forward. Glancing around, she spotted stars in the sky above. "How long was I out?" she questioned.

Filling a small stone bowl with water, the woman lifted it to Taryn's mouth. "Longer than the last," she answered.

Pushing away the bowl, Taryn studied the woman. Her appearance was haggard. Dirty red hair. Dirty pale skin, but somehow she could still see the beauty hiding beneath it all.

Testing the situation, the teen spoke, "Mother, what is it that I have done to provoke the boys to harm me?"

A warm smile lit the woman's face. "The world we know has narrowed as our numbers have grown. We are not permitted to reveal our gifts to the humans, but each day is a battle to preserve what little land we have. When those boys see you, they see a threat to their own survival." The woman lifted the bowl once more to Taryn's lips. "Please drink, my love."

After drinking the water gone, Taryn laid back and closed her eyes.

ಬಂಬಂ

"It's been over an hour," Keiryn whispered.

Larkin gently stroked Taryn's cheek with the back of his knuckles. "There's no telling how long she'll be gone. Lazryn said the last time she was out, it tooks hours for her to wake."

Scooting over to his duffle bag, Keiryn pulled out a few bottles of water. "You thirsty?" he asked. When Larkin nodded, he tossed him one of the bottles and then rested his back against the cave wall.

"Yesterday while we were out, she said things were going to get worse."

Larkin sighed. "If anyone would know what's coming, it would be Taryn."

Jumping to his feet, Keiryn stared at his sister with furrowed brows. "Are you seeing this?" he asked.

"Seeing what?" Larkin questioned.

Keiryn's eyes widened. "Her hair, it's bright red and her skin is white as snow, all except her hands. Her hands are covered in blood."

"She looks normal to me," Larkin replied.

"I'm telling you, her hair is fiery red and she looks like a murderous porcelain doll from a horror flick," he insisted.

Larkin's forehead creased. "Maybe this is like the time you could hear Farren whispering in the wind. Your gifts are insanely powerful and the two of you are siblings. It could be that you're seeing some part of Taryn's vision," he reasoned.

Reaching down, Keiryn grabbed the lid to his water bottle and twisted the cap back into place. "I suppose so...but it is a bit unnerving seeing her like this."

Suddenly, Taryn sat up. Her eyes opened wide. Gasping for air, she grabbed hold of Larkin's forearm.

He cupped her cheek and looked into her eyes. "I've got you, Tare-Bear, but you need to slow down and inhale slowly." When he saw she was taking in air, he continued. "You're doing great, but now I need for you to breathe out."

Watching as she settled down, Keiryn realized exactly how deep the bond between his best friend and sister truly was. *She actually needs him,* he thought to himself.

A slight smile curled on Taryn's face. "I'm so happy to see you." She paused, looking over her shoulder in Keiryn's direction. "To see both of you."

"You good?" Larkin asked.

She nodded. "I want to strum the next string."

"Are you insane?" Keiryn snapped.

Taryn rolled her eyes. "Look, we need answers and I don't have any other ideas."

Larkin caressed her cheek, turning it towards him. "I think what Keiryn is trying to say is that maybe it's too soon. You could tell us about what you just experienced and then we can go from there."

She shook her head. "I can't." She paused pursing her lips while exhaling. "Don't you two get it? You already have a target on your back because of what you mean to me."

Keiryn turned, pounding the sides of his fists against the wall. "Dammit, Taryn, I saw your fiery red hair and the paleness of your skin." He paused. "And yes, I saw the blood on your hands."

She sat quietly as she stared at her brother.

Placing his back against the wall, Keiryn released a hefty sigh. "If I didn't know better, I would say you looked a lot like Adora James towards the end of that vision."

Taryn swallowed hard. "Keiryn, you need to go home."

"What?" he growled.

"I should have realized that you would be able to see some part of the vision." She paused, moving to her feet. "You know it's not safe, and I cannot permit you to stay."

"Taryn," he pleaded.

"I love you, brother, but you have to go," she insisted.

Keiryn bit his bottom lip and shook his head. "Let me guess, if I don't go willingly, you'll make me anyway."

Giving a slight shrug, Taryn stepped forward and hugged her brother.

"What if I wait outside the mouth of the cave?" he offered.

Gently, she shook her head. "I'm sorry, but you know why we can't risk it."

He pulled back. "Just promise me you'll stop after this. At least for today."

"I promise," she replied.

Keiryn looked to Larkin. "I'm counting on you, brother. Don't let anything happen to her."

"You have my word," Larkin assured him.

Leaning down, he kissed the top of Taryn's head. "I'll see you both when you get home. Okay?"

"Yeah," she agreed.

Keiryn gave Larkin a pleading glance as he headed out.

When she could no longer feel her brother's presence, Taryn joined Larkin near the harp.

"That couldn't have been easy," he stated.

She frowned. "No. It wasn't. But it's the only way to protect him."

"You don't need to justify your reasons to me. I only ask that you not push me away, too," Larkin replied.

"I won't as long as you don't ask me to stop," she stated.

Larkin sighed loudly. "As if I could."

Kneeling down, Taryn picked up the harp and quickly strummed the third string. As soon as its sound vibrated through the air, Taryn felt a deep chill settling into her bones. Blinking, she left the cave and appeared outside a familiar stone structure.

"I'm on Hypatia," she mused as the warmth of her breath visibly collided against the chill in the air.

A man bumped into her, catching her by surprise. "If you do not wish to freeze solid, I encourage you to keep moving."

Turning around, Taryn gasped. Behind her was a line as far as her eyes could see of women, children and men.

"Step forward," a gruff voice shouted, pulling Taryn from her gaze.

Doing as the man directed, Taryn moved to the bottom step in front of the Elder Council's castle.

"State your name, age and gifts," he ordered.

The cries of a child not far behind her drew her attention.

"Name, age and gifts," the man barked again.

"Wait a minute," Taryn said as she made her way back to the child.

The instant she left her spot, a man behind her stepped up and offered his information.

Taryn approached the woman holding the little girl. Both their eyes were dark and sunken. "Are you injured or ill?" she asked.

Tears pooled in the woman's eyes, freezing instantly. She winced at the pain, but did not cry out. "My husband died nearly a month ago and we haven't eaten in weeks."

Lifting her hands, Taryn placed them over the woman's eyes. Using her gift of Imperium, she released just enough warmth to thaw her tears. "Let's move you to the front of the line," she said.

The woman shook her head. "Silly girl. They are not going to permit someone like me and my daughter to enter the castle."

Taryn's eyes narrowed. "And why is that?"

Pulling the child close to her chest, the woman began to shake. "It will be two more years before my daughter's gifts set in, and I am but a simple Ontogeny."

So this is when the Elder Council begun separating people by their gifts, Taryn thought to herself.

"Next," the man yelled.

Glancing over her shoulder, Taryn noticed the man who had taken her place in line had been cast aside.

Suddenly her voice and will were no longer her own. Words left her mouth and her emotions swirled about with great ferocity. "This is not right," she shouted at the guard at the bottom of the steps.

"Name. Age. And gifts," he roared at the defiant teen.

"My name is Malayne Douth. I am two days' shy of my eighteenth birthday, and I am an Elemental and an Imperium," she roared back.

With a calloused look in his eyes, he smirked. "Denied."

"What do you mean denied?" she thundered.

The large man stepped forward, pushing her aside. "Next."

Her emotions erupted from deep within. "I will not be cast aside as though I my life does not have purpose. If you will not help these people, then I will."

Lifting both hands out directly in front of her, Malayne used her gift of Imperium to create a large tunnel to cover those waiting in line. Next she created fire-filled orbs and lined the top of the tunnel and the bottom of each side with the warm globes.

"What is the meaning of this?" the guard barked.

Malayne lowered her hands and stepped to the man. "They needed shelter while we work to find a solution." She paused, turning to face the tunnel. "If you are an Ontogeny, use your gifts to grow enough food to last two days."

The woman from earlier approached her with watery-tear filled eyes, as did others. "Bless you for your mercy and kindness," she sobbed as she allowed her daughter to hug the teen.

Looking into little girl's hypnotic green eyes, Taryn's mind began to spin. *It's not possible. She must be a distant relative or something... but the resemblance is uncanny,* she thought to herself.

With the commotion outside, the doors to the castle swung open and Taryn found herself placing the child back in the mother's arms before turning and marching up the stairs through the doors.

Several feet ahead of her walked a tall lanky man. "Follow me," he said, then gave a faint chuckle.

Understanding that she was being Influenced to do as he said, Taryn resigned herself to whatever was to come next.

He led her to a familiar chamber where it was standing room only. "Bow before your Elders," he directed.

Instantly, she did as he said. After several seconds passed, she felt his power over her subside and she was free to rise.

"Malayne Douth, you have interfered with Council affairs during a time of crisis. How do you plead?" a white haired man questioned from the other side of a long wooden table.

"I meant no disrespect. I merely intended to provide your followers with a chance to survive while a solution can be found," she answered.

"On whose behalf do you act?" the man asked.

Taryn found herself unable to speak, waiting for Malayne to reply. Emotions swirled inside the teen, but there was nothing she could do to lock them away.

"Well?" the voice questioned.

Inching forward, Taryn now had a voice. "My father was believed to have died on a great journey before I was born. And my mother's death came shortly before my twelfth birthday. So therefore, I am a ward of the Elder Council. My actions are a direct example of this great Council's compassion and care for the people without passage to leave this plane."

Whispers filled the room as the girl stood fast.

Smart girl, using their pride and ego against them, making it seem like the tunnel and orbs were somehow their idea, Taryn thought to herself.

After several moments passed, the tall lanky man from earlier walked past her and immediately she felt the need to follow. Under his Influence, she trailed behind as they left the room and walked down a series of hallways.

Along their way, she noticed several of her Gaias brethren in a large room with their hands bound with rondoring rope.

How curious, Taryn thought.

The tall man stopped abruptly and opened a large wooden door. "You shall wait in here," he stated.

Taryn walked through the door expecting to find a small cell, but gasped when it was anything but. The room was stunning, fit for a princess. A large bed was placed against one wall, draped in a golden blanket while several pieces of beautiful, hand-carved wood furniture finished off the room. Various gems decorated the arms of the chairs and tabletops.

"I do not understand," she whispered, though the words were Malayne's.

From the far corner of the room, a handsome man appeared. "This room is rather magnificent," he commented while motioning for her to take a seat.

She did as he said and asked, "Why was I brought here?"

He tilted his head and smiled as he, too, found a seat. "My dear girl, you have placed this Council in quite a predicament. You see, you have given the people outside hope."

"And that is bad?" she asked.

Leaning forward in his seat, he smiled softly. "You see, people without hope are far more pliable than those who dare to hope. They are resigned to their stations, as well as being more accepting of their fates."

"You do not wish for them to survive?" she questioned.

He arched his brow. "What I and the Elder Council desire is for our kind to survive. But in order for this to happen, we need to weed out the weak."

"What a horrid state of mind to think of them as less. Why not use the Healers to open the Adora Gateways to the other planes and allow them to spend their years there?" She suggested.

Settling back in his seat, he stared at the girl. "Do you understand that you are one of us?"

Folding her arms across her waist, she shook her head. "The guard outside said I was denied."

"Per our orders, he and the others are to turn away those who do not possess the full strength of their gifts. However, he was unaware of how truly special you are," he explained.

"Any number of the Imperiums and Elementals could have easily done what I did," she countered.

He shook his head. "It baffles me how you are unaware of your own strength. It would have taken at least five of our strongest Imperiums to create a tunnel similar to the one you created. And I assure you, not a single one of our kind could merge two competing gifts in the same manner as you did with the fire and the orbs."

"I do not know what to say," she replied.

"Do not speak, simply listen. There is another, who like you, wields immense power. He is the giver of this bitterness. The only way to stop the cold from claiming this beautiful plane is by ending his life," he stated.

She rose from her seat. "Does this man possess the ability to open the gateways?"

"It does not appear so," he replied.

"If the Elder Council would approve, we could abandon this plane and build elsewhere. No more lives would need be lost and the suffering would cease, and this man would die here alone," she reasoned.

"Impossible. My brothers will never abandon Hypatia or this castle," he barked.

"Then you and the other Council members sentence us all to death," she bit.

Standing, he moved closer to the teen. "What if I were to tell you there may be a way to spare the suffering of all. Would you be willing to do your part?"

Without hesitation, she replied, "Of course. We should all be willing to sacrifice for the greater good."

A smile blossomed on his face and a glint of darkness danced in his gaze. "Very well then, I shall not keep you waiting. On behalf of the Elder Council, I request that you make the journey to the blue bluffs to the north and challenge the man who is creating all this chaos."

Her eyes narrowed and her forehead creased. "I am not even of age."

His smile turned into more of a sneer. "My dear girl, you said earlier that you are a ward of the Council, did you not?"

He has you there, Taryn thought to herself.

Noting the look of defeat on her face, the man continued. "As our ward, we demand that you go to this man and issue a challenge. Should you be victorious, you will have a permanent home here in our castle.'

"And if I am not?" she asked.

His face turned void of all emotion. "Then the Council will make a statement about a brave girl who, while acting on behalf of the Council, lost her life to the frigid cold."

Taryn felt Malayne's emotions stirring, but also felt the presence of the tall man's Influence subduing her ability to act upon them.

"You shall leave at once and tell no one of this plan. You, and you alone, shall shoulder the burden of your actions." He paused, walking to her. He cupped her cheeks and placed a kiss upon the top of her head. "And Malayne, you should know, there is no hope for you on this journey."

His words struck a chord so deep in the girl, that even against the Influence she was able to find her words. "Keep my room ready and waiting for my return. We will see one another very soon."

ഇൽൽ

The journey to the blue bluffs was nearly a full two-day walk from the castle. As she neared, Taryn felt the cold fighting its way into her bones even more than before. In an attempt to further insulate herself against the frigid weather, she created a large tube with multiple layers of fire in between each. Not only did it prevent her from freezing to death, but it also cut through the snow and ice in front of her.

Taryn fought to drown out most of Malayne's thoughts as she walked, trying to make sense of what she had already witnessed. *The Elder Council had already collected the strongest Gaias across the plane. But why do that if they weren't intending to use them against this man, or while trying to flee to safety? Surely, their numbers could have overcome him. Another question, why were the Healers being held in that room with their wrists bound in rondoring rope? It really didn't seem that the Council was concerned or that they had a sense of urgency,* she thought to herself.

As she neared, she could see the outline of a person standing atop the bluffs with their arms held out shoulder level to their sides. Expecting a reaction due to her close proximity, Taryn prepared for the worst. Instead, she was able to continue walking without interference.

Now standing atop the bluff, she stared at the backside of the man. He had long golden hair and wore only a pair of pants. She approached, but he never moved. Not even a twitch of a muscle was visible.

"You there, why are you casting such suffering onto our people?" she asked.

The man remained silent.

She continued to move toward him, noting the strange texture of his skin. The bit of light cast down through the clouds caused it to shimmer.

He's covered in ice, Taryn thought as she stood directly behind him.

"Do you not speak?" she asked.

"I beg you," he mumbled.

Ducking beneath his outstretched arms, Taryn carefully maneuvered around to his front. His eyes were closed and the skin on his lips peeled off in thick layers. The man's brows and lashes were covered by a thick frost.

"You continue your assault even though you are causing yourself such pain," she gasped.

With his eyes still closed, he spoke once more. "I beg of you, please show mercy."

Placing her hands mere inches from his chest, she spread warmth around him. "I implore you to halt your assault," she begged while his eyelids began to flutter.

"I cannot," he said.

"You are sentencing thousands to death. Do you not care?" she questioned.

Tears began to streak down his cheeks. "My heart is heavy, and my burden unfair. But I cannot stop that which has begun. You must end this."

She shook her head. "Please, I do not understand. If you do not wish to harm others, why not simply stop?"

"I cannot, as my actions are no longer my own. But you, you are in a position to stop this. To stop me," he said.

Her brows furrowed. "Who did this to you?"

"The ones who seek power above all else," he answered.

"The Elder Council?" she mused.

He nodded. "I have witnessed the future, and a war is brewing. He shall not be satisfied until every Gaias and human cowers before him. And should they fail to cower, he shall see the demise of their very existence. Gaias will turn against Gaias." He paused, opening his eyes wide. "Our downfall has already begun. Everything will perish by Gaias hands."

Malayne swallowed hard. "Your eyes…they are green. And they are the mirror of my own," she gasped.

He stared at her with pleading eyes. "Sister, please, I beg of you. Take my life and end my suffering now."

"I cannot. How can I justify taking the life of someone who is not in control of their own will?" she countered.

"This is my will, my sacrifice for the good of our kind. You must rip out my heart and turn it to ash. Only then will a glimmer of hope remain," he whispered.

Tears filled her eyes. "I do not wish to harm you."

"You will be releasing me, sister, from what I have become. My heart will be at peace knowing our sacrifice creates a spark of hope for the future," he replied.

Staring at him through blurry eyes, she swiped at her tears. "Your eyes, they are turning blue," she whispered.

He smiled softly. "You must do it now before it is too late. For when my irises become blue permanently, there will be no stopping what I am."

"I cannot," she cried.

"You can and you must. My power is nearing its peak and when it does, this winter's frost will consume all that lives on this plane and any other. The sleep of our worlds will become permanent, and all hope shall perish," he replied, his tone tender and empathetic to her situation.

Tears fell like rain from her eyes as she placed her hand over his heart. "Please, forgive me," she said before encasing her hand with Imperium power.

As she began pressing her hand into his chest, Taryn found herself now seeing the events through the young man's eyes. The pain he felt was now her own, as was the overwhelming sadness teeming within Malayne's as she worked to snuff out his life.

"I forgive you, sister," the man whispered as he drew his final breath of life. Before the final light within him extinguished, he saw a small figure standing below in the snow covered meadow.

৩০৪৩৩০৪৩

Taryn's body twisted and seized several times beneath Larkin's grasp before her eyes opened. "That a girl, Taryn. Come back to reality," he whispered in her ear.

The tenderness in his voice calmed her racing heart. Though mentally, physically and emotionally spent from her most recent vision, Taryn managed to find a way to speak.

"I love you. Always and forever, Wolfy."

"I love you, too, Tare-Bear."

৩০৪৩৩০৪৩

The following evening, Taryn sat on the couch between Keiryn and Larkin, staring blankly at the empty fireplace. *Malayne was right, that young man's eyes looked exactly like hers. The color. The shape, even his long lashes and arched brows were identical to her own. He*

~ 266 ~

also wasn't surprised to see her. In fact, it was like he expected her to come. A sharp chill ran up her spine, pulling her from her thoughts.

She glanced around the room before standing to make her way to the windows, folding her arms around her waist. Scanning the tree line, she saw nothing out of the ordinary.

I swear I felt Malayne's presence, she thought to herself.

A subtle chill worked its way up her spine. When she exhaled, her breath lingered in the air like a fist sized patch of dense fog. Another chill struck, this time a cold burn spread into her shoulders. Again and again, the chills came until she looked toward the staircase. Standing on the bottom step was the young man from her vision of Malayne

Taryn glanced around the room. Larkin, Keiryn and Andyn continued to watch television while her mother and father sat with Ilya and Maxym at the dining room table working the puzzle she had given them.

Taking a deep breath, she started to cross the room. With each step she took, the young man took a step of his own up the stairs. By the time she made it to the bottom step, he was standing at the top, looking down at her. His eyes garnered her attention as they flickered between a brilliant green and a steel blue color.

He smiled as he stared down upon her. With a nod, he motioned for her to follow and began walking toward the bedrooms.

Glancing over her shoulder, the teen surveyed the room once more before heading up the stairs. When she made it to the top, she found the young man standing just outside her bedroom. She blinked once and he was gone.

Taryn cautiously approached the entrance to her room. When she looked inside, the young man stood in front of her dresser staring at the top drawer. Taking a deep breath, she entered.

"Why are you here?" she inquired.

He did not speak a word as he pressed his hand against the top dresser drawer.

Moving in closer, Taryn stared at the man. "You want me to open it?"

He nodded and stepped aside.

Arching her brows, Taryn let out a sigh. "I will if you want me to, but I need to warn you that this is where I keep my underwear."

The young man's eyes softened as he motioned for her to continue.

"Okay, but you can't say I didn't warn you," she stated.

Grabbing both nickel-plated knobs, Taryn gently slid the drawer open.

Without hesitation, he reached his hand inside and pulled out the book Taryn had stashed beneath the drawer's contents.

Her forehead creased. "You were after the book. Why?"

The man glanced in the direction of the bedroom door before sending a gust of air, forcing it shut.

Taryn watched him curiously as he turned and placed the book upon her bed. He then motioned for her to come closer. She complied without hesitation. Together, they looked down at the torn and tattered white cloth cover.

Reaching down, he lifted her right hand, holding it palm up inches from his face. He waved his free hand and the girl instantly felt a prick on her index finger.

She watched as a drop of blood pooled on her fingertip.

Once enough blood had gathered, he carefully guided her finger to the spine of the book. He nodded before releasing her hand. With wide eyes, he took a step back.

Taryn glanced between him and the book.

Seeing her obvious hesitation, the man made a swiping motion with his finger.

Taking a deep breath, Taryn stared at the dark smudges on the book's spine. *Is it possible all these stains are dried blood?* she thought as her stomach turned slightly. She glanced to him once more. Anticipation was clearly building behind his wide eyes.

"Here goes nothing," she said, swiping her bloodied finger over the other marks.

For a brief moment, it seemed as though the world stood still. The usual specks of dust floating in the air appeared motionless. Taryn walked over to the window, glancing outside. There she spied two birds in the air, but neither moved.

She turned, looking at the man. "What did we do?" she asked.

Pointing to the book, he spoke but a single word. "Open."

Walking back to the bed, she startled when looking at the book. Its cover was no longer tattered and torn. There were no visible signs of the blemishes or stains upon its spine.

The man nudged Taryn. "Open," he said again.

Unsure of what she would find within this strange book's pages, Taryn reached down and slowly lifted the cover. Unlike the times before, it lifted and immediately a bright white glow radiated from its pages, illuminating the entire room. Holding her breath, Taryn glanced to the man and then to the opened book. As the teen turned her head, her eyes locked on the sight before her. Trails of blinding light flooded the room, transporting the teen to a strange forest.

Glancing around trying to find the young man, Taryn began to walk to her right and then to the left. For as far as her eyes could see, there were trees covered in shimmering white bark that stood in perfectly spaced rows. The leaves were a gleaming silver, and dazzling glass spheres hung down much like an orange would.

"Hello?" she called out.

Taking a few steps back, the teen bumped into something. She turned to find the young man standing with a soft look upon his face.

"What is this place?" she asked.

He smiled warmly. "You, Taryn, are standing within the pages of the Book of Life."

Her eyes narrowed and her lip curled with confusion. "It's not possible to stand within a book's pages," she countered.

"Only a select group of beings may stand within the book's pages, Taryn. And only a handful of the select group may consume its knowledge," he replied.

Taryn's forehead creased. "Why only a select group, and how do you know who is able to consume from the book?"

"The Book of Life holds the history of nearly all our kind. If you are one of the chosen, you will be able to look into any of the hanging globes and watch the progression of that Gaias' life from beginning to end," he explained.

"Are you telling me that every Gaias that has ever lived is represented in this forest?" she questioned.

He shook his head. "There is a single tree that resides within this book that is out of reach, even to the great and powerful, Taryn Knight."

She pursed her lips and sighed loudly. "What makes the tree more special than the others?"

"The tree in question holds the knowledge of those who oversee our kind and their origins." He paused, reaching up and removing one of the globes and handing it to her. "That which you seek lies within the mind's eye. Clarity is to be had by those able to listen with their heart and feel with their head."

Taryn's jaw drew up tight. "Death once told me this very thing."

He flashed a faint smile. "Farren and I are familiars. You will soon understand the secrets that we hold, or you will unravel and bring about the undoing of all life."

The teen's nostrils flared. "The same as you nearly did all those millenniums ago?"

"My name does not permit me the luxury of choosing my own destiny. But you, Taryn with a Y, you have remained stagnate at the crossroads, leaning one direction, yet wavering toward the other for all of your life," he replied, his words cutting.

"I would rather die than allow myself to commit harm against those I love or the innocent," she bit.

"It is as Farren told you before, the sole determiner of one's fate is held within their own heart. I understood who I truly was, but I also accepted that my actions were carved in stone by another greater than myself. When Malayne appeared on the blue bluffs, I knew what must to be done, and I begged of her to end my life to allow hope to exist." He paused, taking a step back. "Hope is the tiny glimmer that shines through the darkest of times. But faith is knowing the light still exists, even when it is absent."

Taryn arched both brows and shook her head. "You and Farren definitely enjoy speaking in riddles."

With an ornery smirk, the man motioned for Taryn to place the globe against the center of her forehead.

"Okay. Let's see what secrets this little glass ball holds," she stated, pressing it against her flesh.

Her eyes rolled back in her head and her mind opened wide. She could see the boy's birth, and the sad look upon his father's weathered face. The man's green eyes filled with tears as he bundled the newborn. A few moments later, a second scream came from his mother and another child was born. This time it was a baby girl.

After both babies lay wrapped in animal fur, the woman looked to the man. "Husband, what shall they be called?" she asked.

With his strong frame, the man cradled the girl. "She shall be wise beyond her years, and her gifts more powerful than the mightiest will. We shall call her Malayne." Gently, he placed the baby girl in her mother's arms. He then turned and lifted the baby boy. "Our son, whose fate is already decided, shall be named Maertan. He will be strong and wield the power of the Elements against both friend and foe."

The woman shook her head frantically. "No. No. Not our son. Please Laertas, tell me you are mistaken and that is not our little boy's fate."

Hearing his father's name spoken aloud, Taryn dropped the globe.

"Malayne was right. You are her mirror image. But what she didn't realize in those brief moments before your death was that you were not only her brother, but also her twin." She paused, her chest heaving. "Your father, his face was older than in the pictures that I've seen…but his name was not Laertas Douth, it was Laertas Dominion."

Maertan leaned down, picking up the fallen globe. Lifting it over his head, it rose from his hand, reclaiming its place on the tree. "Why does learning this trouble you, Taryn?"

Fighting to control her breathing, she shook her head, running her hands over her face. "If Laertas is your father, that means he would have been more than two thousand years old at the time of your birth."

Taryn stared at the young man, waiting for him to say something. To say anything at all.

Suddenly shrill screams filled the air, returning her to her bedroom.

"Taryn, get down here," Theron shouted.

Still reeling from what she had learned only moments earlier, she worked to find her composure.

The door to her bedroom opened and in walked Larkin. "Hey, our parents finished the puzzle and now they're dying to know what it means," he said.

She nodded anxiously while running her hands through her hair. "Okay. We shouldn't keep them waiting."

Noting her rigid movements, Larkin tilted his head. "Are you okay, Tare-Bear?"

"Yeah. I think it's a bit of a residual affect from yesterday's vision," she fibbed, glancing to the bed. She stared long and hard at the empty space where the book had been only moments earlier.

"If you're ready, we should head downstairs. They're dying to know what the surprise is," Larkin stated.

"Sure. I just need a sec," Taryn replied, while walking over and opening her top drawer. Reaching in, she felt around until her fingers found the edge of the book beneath her undergarments.

"Okay, darling daughter of ours, we've managed to put together the puzzle you gave us, despite not having the box for reference. Now please enlighten us on what this big surprise is," Gracyn stated while glancing down at the three-foot by two-foot puzzle of the Eiffel Tower on the dining room table.

Pushing aside her earlier interaction with Maertan and the numerous questions that lingered, Taryn smiled fondly at both her mothers. "As the two most important women in my life, I wanted to say thank you, and I couldn't think of a better way than to send you and these two handsome men to Paris for a night out…tomorrow night to be exact. Your rooms are booked and dinner reservations made."

Ilya's eyes widened. "It's been decades since I last laid eyes upon the Eiffel Tower," she confessed.

Gracyn pulled her daughter into a fierce hug. "This is an incredibly thoughtful and kind gesture, Taryn." She paused, pulling back and sweeping a few loose strands of hair behind the girl's ears. "But I don't think we will have the time with prom taking place this Saturday, and everything else."

Taryn shook her head. "I have a dress, and my hair appointment is already scheduled. What could possibly prevent you from leaving for just a day?"

Stepping closer, Ilya glanced between Maxym and Theron and then to the girl. "I think what your mother is trying to say is that we don't have time for another shopping trip before leaving. Paris is not a place one simply visits without the proper attire. Especially for a night on the town," she explained.

"Wow, your lack of faith in me really hurts," Taryn teased while opening the French doors with a wave of her hand. "Do either of you really think that I would send you off on a date night with these two handsome men without having something spectacular to wear?" She turned, glancing toward the open doorway with a warm smile.

The others turned, watching as Lazryn walked in carrying two long garment bags. Dedrick trailed behind the man, carefully balancing two large boxes on his forearms.

"What is this, Taryn?" Gracyn asked.

"You will just have to be patient for a moment longer," she replied, while taking the boxes from the boy and placing them side by side on the table. Turning, Taryn motioned for Lazryn to step forward, giving he and Dedrick a wink. "Mom, yours is on the left. And Ilya, yours is the one on the right."

The two women looked at one another, their eyes lit with a child-like curiosity. Stepping forward, they nodded to one another and unzipped the bags in near unison.

Seeing the familiar dress hiding within, Gracyn's eyes filled with tears of happiness. "You attentive little angel," she cried.

"I watched as you and Ilya tried on dresses. I could tell when you put this one on that you loved everything about it," Taryn admitted.

Her mother pulled her into a fierce hug. "That was meant to be your special day and yet, you were scheming to give us our own day."

"I love you, Mom. I love both of you, and I wanted to give you a day away to relax and enjoy life," she replied, drawing Ilya into their hug.

After several moments passed, Ilya looked over to Lazryn. "And you," she said, breaking away from the others. "You helped her put this together."

"I only did as she asked," he acknowledged.

Ilya lunged at him, wrapping her arms around his neck. "Thank you," she whispered.

Theron joined his wife and daughter and kissed the top of Taryn's head. "Maxym and I are curious, you wouldn't happen to have a couple of penguin suits lying around anywhere, would you?"

The teen smiled. "They're hanging on the back of your closet doors."

"So when exactly does this excursion begin?" Maxym asked.

"At midnight tonight," Taryn answered. "Lazryn will return and open a gateway to take you to Paris. From there he'll see that you get checked in at your hotel, and then leave you to your day."

CHAPTER FIFTEEN

It was shortly past two in the morning when Larkin woke to a heavy pounding at the front door. Still half asleep, he made his way down the stairs toward the sound.

"I bet Keiryn locked himself out again," he groaned, as the knocking intensified.

Unlocking the deadbolt, Larkin opened the door. In a split second, he went from utterly exhausted to wide-awake. His razor-sharp werewolf claws unveiled themselves as a low growl resonated from deep within his throat.

"Chrystian," he bit with a heaving chest.

With a slight smile on his face, Chrystian nodded. "Hello, young wolf. I do not wish to disrupt your slumber, but it is imperative that I speak with Taryn at once."

"Why do you need to see her?" Larkin questioned.

With pursed lips and an arched brow, a hint of annoyance flashed across the man's face. "Will you wake the girl or not?" he questioned.

"There's no need to wake the girl. She's up," Taryn stated from down the hallway.

Larkin stood firmly in place between his love and the Mortari. "Whatever you have to say to her, you can say in front of me, too," he growled.

With his face flickering between annoyance with the wolf and delight in seeing the girl, he shook his head. "Very well, but the least you could do is invite me in."

Rolling her eyes, Taryn turned on her heel and headed toward the living room. "Let him in, Larkin," she called out from over her shoulder.

Settling into the lone chair, Taryn drew her knees to her chest as Larkin and Chrystian took opposing seats on the couch and love seat.

"What's on your mind, Chrystian?" Taryn asked, her head resting on the arm of the chair.

He glanced around the large room until his gaze landed upon her face. "It is only you and your wolf here tonight," he stated.

"Yep. My parents are on a quickie vacation, and Jonesy is staying over at the Taylor house with Andyn," she replied.

Scooting to the edge of his seat, Chrystian laced his fingers together and sighed. "I know you found the relic, Taryn. I am also aware that you have accessed its secrets…at least part of them."

Taryn noted the weight of his words as he spoke and found it quite curious. "And this bothers you, why?"

Adjusting in his seat, Larkin's hazel eyes rested heavily upon the Mortari. "He probably wants it for himself," the teen snapped.

Turning his head, Chrystian furrowed his brows. "Despite what you may believe me to be, young wolf, I am here to caution Taryn."

Lifting his hand, Larkin admired his monstrous claws while tapping them together. "And I would caution you in cautioning her."

Chrystian rose to his feet, and with a heated stare, he eyed the teen.

Shifting in the chair, Taryn once more rolled her eyes. "Do I need to send you both to separate corners of the room?" she sighed dramatically.

Before Chrystian could reclaim his seat, Keiryn rushed through the French doors, his chest heaving. "What's he doing here?" he growled.

"Not you, too," Taryn groaned as she rose to her feet. "Chrystian is not here to hurt me. He's simply trying to warn me about something, and you two Neanderthals are preventing him from doing so."

"But," Keiryn started to say, but stopped when Taryn lifted her hand.

"I'm going upstairs to change so Chrystian and I can go for a walk. If I have to come back down here for any reason before I am dressed, there will be three extra-large doghouses for each of you. Understood?" she growled.

Each nodded while exchanging heated glances with the other.

ഇൗൠഇൗൠ

In her room, Taryn slipped a hoodie on over her tank top and laced up her tennis shoes. As she finished tying her shoes, there was a faint knock at the door.

"I come in peace," Larkin stated from the other side.

"You're welcome to come in, but if you're going to try and talk me out of going, you'll be wasting your breath," she replied.

Opening the door, Larkin stood with his shoulders rounded and head hung low. "I was being a jerk, and I'm sorry."

Taryn sat down on the bed and patted the seat next to her. "Look, I get that you don't like or trust him. But Chrystian isn't here to hurt me, he's here to share something he knows."

Sitting down, Larkin shrugged. "I know, but I get so angry thinking about what he put you through while you were on Mors."

She took his hand in her own and laced her fingers with his. "Chrystian wasn't exactly himself during that time. There were several influencers coming at him from all directions." She paused, looking at him. "I'm not making excuses for him, but he loved Loryn almost as much as I love you. I was his hope of having her back, and

~ 278 ~

then that hope was ripped away. It also didn't help that Coyan was in his ear. He used Chrystian's affections for me against him."

"So does that mean if anything ever happened to me, you would be justified in going crazy and slaughtering hundreds, if not thousands?" he questioned.

"No. Because no one will ever be able to hurt you like that," she answered.

Larkin cupped her cheek with his free hand and leaned in, pressing his lips against hers. "I know how much you care about Chrystian. And I also know that it would destroy you if he ever did anything that would force you to harm him." He paused, kissing her temple. "All I'm asking is for you to be extra careful when you're around him."

She nodded. "I will be. I promise."

"Good. Now we'd better get downstairs before the peace treaty falls apart between him and Keiryn," Larkin grinned.

ಐಅಚಬಐಅಚಬ

Walking along the moonlit pathway, Taryn glanced up at Chrystian. His long hair and sharp features were stunning, making it hard for her to look away. "You know, I don't think I've ever noticed how truly handsome you are," she commented.

The tall man arched a brow in her direction. "Careful, child. What would your wolf think?" he teased.

She stopped, grabbing his forearm. "Seriously. There's something different about you lately. I mean, you've always been handsome, but now…now you're sort of beautiful."

Warmth filled his cheeks. "It must be from bathing in the blood of newborns," he replied.

Taryn's eyes narrowed and her nose wrinkled. "You are such a boy," she groaned while walking ahead.

Running to catch up with her, Chrystian sighed. "Please know that I do not bathe in blood."

~ 279 ~

She slowed her stride and stared at the ground. "Did you know that your kind murdered Larkin's mother in front of him when he was just a boy?"

He shook his head.

"Well, they did. I've already asked the world of him to accept Lazryn into our lives, knowing what he used to be." She paused, her frustration marring her normally beautiful green eyes. "So when I ask Larkin to accept my relationship with you, I'm asking too much."

Chrystian stared at her for a long moment as she strode further ahead. "I do not hear regret in your words. Nor even a pause to reconsider your friendship with me. Why?"

Turning on her heel, Taryn marched up to him and stared him in the eyes. "Because no matter how insane you make me feel, I love you, Chrystian." She paused, taking in his widening eyes. "Behind the dark façade you're constantly putting off, I know that you were once a kind, caring and selfless person. Even more so, I know that side of you is biding its time, waiting for the opportunity to present itself so you can reveal your truest self."

He swallowed hard as his jaw drew up tight. "You continue to believe you know what lies within my heart. But you could not be more wrong." He paused. "You claim to love me, yet you choose your wolf, time and time again."

She held her hand out, pushing him away. "Don't go there, Chrystian. You know exactly what I meant and how I feel about you. I consider you to be my family, even if your hard head and equally hardened heart refuses to accept it." She paused, turning and walking away. "As usual, we're way off topic. You came here to warn me about the harp. So tell me what it is you know."

He balled his fists and placed them behind his back as he moved swiftly to catch her. "The harp will answer all you seek, within the worlds you shall peek. Through glass spheres you shall learn, that all fires extinguished shall once more burn."

Taryn stopped abruptly. "Have you lost your mind, or is it that you've been a courier of death for far too long?" she snapped.

He watched as her eyes turned from green to blue. "Taryn, I am truly sorry for all you have endured. But alas, I have another message for you."

"Let's hear it then," she bit.

Taking a deep breath, he looked sorrowfully into her eyes. "Only when the fallen rise will there be hope for a new tomorrow."

Her eyes widened. "Where did you hear that, Chrystian?"

He shook his head. "Taryn, please understand."

"I don't want to understand. I want to know who told you this?" she demanded.

"Where my true heart lies, that is where I learned to speak those words. She said you were the only living being who would understand their meaning," he disclosed.

Taryn took a wide step back and stared at the man. "You've spoken to her?"

He moved closer, and she took step back. Placing his hands in the air, he pleaded, "Dearest Taryn, if you will allow me the opportunity, I will tell you what I know. At least that which I am allowed."

With her chest heaving, Taryn glared heatedly at her friend. "How long have you been in contact with Loryn?"

"During the Trials, a narrow door opened and she reached out to me through my dreams only days later." He paused. "The first few times I believed I had become tainted with madness. But soon, she provided me with proof of my sanity."

"Did she happen to mention how this doorway opened?" Taryn questioned.

Several silent moments passed as he stared at her speechless. He opened his mouth several times to speak, but the words would not come.

"Seriously, Chrystian. If you're playing games with me, I'm not in the mood," she warned.

"On all that I have ever held dear to my heart, I swear to you it is my desire to tell you all that I know," he replied.

Tilting her head to one side, she studied his body posture. It had become rigid. Appearing moderately painful. "Impossible. You cannot tell me that you swore a Blood Oath with a dead woman."

"When she comes to me, it is within my dreams, dreams dream. You see, only there are we safe from prying eyes, heeding ears and gaping jaws. It is within the sanctity of ones mind's eye that true secrets are stored. And it is only within this hidden sanctuary that I am permitted to speak freely of that which I know." Chrystian paused, looking to the teen. "Loryn told me of the box and where it could be found. She also shared with me its contents," he explained.

"Go on," Taryn nodded as she motioned for him to walk with her.

He joined her as she strode briskly through the woods. "The harp is more than a relic, Taryn. It is one piece of a two-part key."

Taryn picked up her pace, leaving barely a blur for Chrystian to follow. Minutes later, he found her standing at the water's edge of a nearby lake.

She stared across the gently rippling water with her jaw drawn tight and arms folded against her waist as he approached from behind. He took a lock of her hair and wrapped it around the tip of his index finger.

"Your reaction leads me to believe that you have already discovered the second part of the key," he whispered in her ear.

Closing her eyes, she leaned the back of her head against his chest. "When you sleep, what do you dream of?" she asked.

A quiet chuckle rose from his chest. "Silence. I dream of silence."

She opened her eyes and gazed across the water. "All the lives you have taken will never drown out the screams of your loved ones from that fateful night."

He wrapped his arms around her tenderly while one corner of his mouth curled upward. "We are quite the pair you and I, Taryn Knight.

Me being a monster in search of a soul. You being all that you are, but wanting nothing more than to be just a girl."

Taryn's body stiffened under his hold. "What makes you think I want to be just a girl?"

"Is that not what I heard you tell your teacher, Mr. Wylder, the day we met in the woods?" he asked.

She pushed his arms away and stepped to the side. "I never had that conversation with Gastyn, and we never met in the woods that day, Chrystian."

Gazing upon her with love in his eyes, he smiled. "I saw you then as I see you now. I see you for all that you are, and all that you have the potential to become where so many before you have failed." He paused, moving to cup her cheek in his hand. "It was not a lie, what I said to you. You may be in conflict with yourself, but your soul, it surely burns so bright that we can only gaze upon a glimpse of its true beauty." He paused again, his eyes soft, radiating with true admiration and love. "It pains me to know that peace is not yet yours. It pains me even further to know the part I must play. But rest assured, Taryn, they will soon come for you."

Placing her hand over his, she nodded. "I know, Chrystian. I know."

∞⊰∞⊱

A crystal goblet smashed against the far wall of Coyan's private chamber as he fell heavily into a plush chair. "Once more my younger brother betrays my confidence by seeking out that miserable girl," he growled.

Sitting opposite him in a chair of her own, Tedra leaned forward in her seat with a stony look upon her face. "It is as I have told you before, husband, Chrystian believes himself to be in love."

"He swore to wash his hands of her, and yet he is on that vile plane begging for her attention." He paused, glancing at his wife. "As we sit here, both my brothers pine away after a girl neither will ever have.

Clad is off painting another portrait of her that he will surely burn the moment it is complete, just like all the others before it." He paused again while rising to his feet. Walking over to the open balcony, he stared out across the land with narrowed eyes and heaving chest. "Love is nothing more than a cruel idea driven by those who possess a great need to be indulged and worshipped by another."

Moving swiftly to his side, Tedra draped her arm over his shoulder and purred, "I, for one, am grateful for the myth of love. For it was our shared torment that brought us together all those centuries ago, allowing our unbreakable union to form."

Coyan stood silent, staring coolly ahead.

Lifting her fingertip to his lips, Tedra traced their tender outline. "Soon, husband, the taste of jealousy and bitterness that you and I have long endured will be no more. Our enemies will cower before us, and nothing and no one shall remain to challenge our authority, nor our will."

He grabbed her wrist, turning it sharply to an unnatural position. "And let us pray, dear wife, that this time there will be no mistakes."

A wicked smile curled from the woman's mouth as the gleam in her eyes grew. Pulling her wrist free, she pushed up on the balls of her feet and kissed Coyan's cheek. "I promise you, husband, you will have your revenge. Soon we will watch the color fade from your brothers' cheeks as they witness the undoing, and ultimately the death, of their teen queen."

ജ്ഞ്ഞ

Taryn walked through the French doors and found her brother and Larkin pacing on opposite sides of the living room.

"You both look worried," she teased as she passed by on her way to the kitchen.

Both teens trailed after her.

"What did he want?" Keiryn questioned as he took a seat at the kitchen island.

The girl filled a glass with water and took a sip. Turning to face him, she smiled. "Chrystian wanted to talk."

Keiryn sighed heavily as he pounded his fist against the countertop. "Dammit, Taryn. That monster is one of the three original brothers…what is it going to take?" he bit.

Placing the glass on the counter calmly, Taryn stared at her brother. "You are entitled to your opinion, even if I believe you are wrong. But I am warning you, Keiryn, you need to find a way to put your emotions in check."

He rose from his seat and glanced between the two. "So now I'm in the wrong?" he questioned.

"Keiryn, I love you, but where I am concerned, you cannot be objective. You can't keep a clear head or be open-minded. You want to be my big brother, and for you that means you need to protect me from everyone else," she stated. When he opened his mouth to speak, she shook her head in warning. "You need to stop trying to control every situation and keep a close eye on your pack."

His jaw drew tight. "But…but…you know what he is," he growled.

Taryn smiled. "Do you recall when you and everyone else believed Jonesy was weak and I, alone, knew otherwise?"

He nodded.

"The situation now is no different with Chrystian. To you he may appear to be one way, but for me, I know what lies within his heart," she stated.

Larkin joined Taryn on the other side of the counter and slid his arm around her waist. "He was worried about you, and so was I."

"Yes, but you don't try to control me," she replied. Pressing up on her toes, she turned her head and kissed his lips. "School starts in an hour and a half. I'm going to go shower and get ready. If you guys are hungry, we should stop in and eat breakfast at the Desert Rose Café."

"Breakfast at the Rose sounds great," Larkin smiled.

Keiryn rolled his eyes. "You just want to eat pie for breakfast," he groaned.

Walking around the island, Taryn kissed her brother's cheek. "Yes, Keiryn, I want pie for breakfast. Do you have a problem with that?" she asked.

He shook his head and forced a smile. "Whatever little sister wants, little sister gets."

"Now you're catching on," she replied with a wink.

ဆလဆလ

Taryn turned off the water to the shower and reached for her towel. As she patted away the wetness on her skin, a massive chill coursed up her spine. Taking the towel, she wrapped it around her torso and stepped out from the shower walls. Scanning the space, her eyes finally came to rest on the large mirror mounted on the wall above the dual sinks. A thick layer of condensation covered the reflective glass. Using the palm of her hand, she swiped a long stripe through the moisture and leaned forward. Within the cleared area, she spied a small wooden table with two empty chairs on either side.

"Where's the chess board?" she asked, her tone neither hostile nor meek.

Silence lingered in the air for a few moments before a frosted, checkered board and coordinating figurines appeared atop the wooden surface.

"Is this more to your liking?" a familiar voice questioned.

Finding herself now dressed and sitting at the table across from the cloaked man, she shrugged. "Personally, I don't much care for games."

"And why is that, dearest one?" he asked.

"Oh, I don't know. Maybe it has something to do with being raised in the middle of nowhere, and being kept away from the world for the majority of my life. I guess that type of upbringing didn't afford me the luxury of learning to play well with others, or to appreciate multi-player games," she replied.

The cloaked man leaned forward in his seat, studying the board and its many pieces. "But alas, you shall play the game, just as those before you."

Taryn chuckled. "You're right about one thing. I will play your game. But unlike those before me, I will not lose."

"Say what you like, young Taryn. Your willfulness will make for great sport as I watch not only your imminent demise, but the demise of all those you hold dear," he replied.

Heat rose deep within the pit of the teen's stomach. Rising to her feet, she lunged across the table, grabbing the man's cloak.

In return, he seized both her wrists and pulled her in closer. The warmth from his breath caressed her cheeks as he spoke. "Foolish girl, you breathe only because I permit it to be so."

A smile slowly widened across Taryn's face. "Should I live in fear that you may decide to blink and wipe out my entire family?" she retorted.

Still gripping the teen, the man rose to his feet, pulling her even closer. He leaned his head down, pressing his lips against her ear and whispered, "Be cautious of the words that fall from your precious mouth, as they may be interpreted as an invitation to begin a new game of sorts."

Taryn jerked against his grip, freeing one of her arms. She swiped her hand across the board, knocking the figurines onto the floor. "Malevolence rolls off you in palpable waves, and your arrogance even more so." She paused, staring at the cloak where his eyes should be. "You lost one of your pawns, but it was expected." She paused again, raising her free hand to his cheek and gently pressing it against the silky material. "You're disappointed in me. Why?"

In a flash, the cloaked man released her wrist only to grab hold of her throat with a force she had never known in all of her life. He squeezed his fingers around her esophagus as he lifted her feet off the ground. "I know what it is you are doing, young Taryn, but you will not find what you are looking for. For I am the dark that plagues your heart, and the doubt that clouds your mind. I am the familiar taste that once rose from deep within the most guarded of places. You may have destroyed pieces of yourself, but some small fragments of those lost still remain hidden beneath your lovely exterior," he spat.

The teen grabbed his wrists with both hands, trying to leverage herself in some way, but it was to no avail. The more she fought, the more he tightened his grip. She soon found herself losing consciousness with a veil of darkness closing in around her. With a final attempt to free herself, Taryn reached out, grabbing the man's cloak. She pulled with all the strength she had left and the shimmering material broke free, surrounding her as she felt herself free falling into a pit of darkness.

ഇൽൽഇൽ

"Taryn, are you okay?" Larkin asked from the other side of the bathroom door. His words were weighted and his tone unsettled.

Hearing his voice jolted the girl from her vision. She startled, jumping back from her spot and dropping something from her hand onto the floor. Kneeling down, Taryn stared at the object with furrowed brows.

Larkin tried opening the door, but it was locked. "What's going on in there?" he asked, his words carrying a sense of urgency.

"Give me a second," she replied, her eyes still fixated on the small object. She moved closer and picked it up. Cupping it in the palm of her hand, she recognized it to be one of the figurines from the chessboard in her vision. Taryn quickly rose to her feet and placed the black knight inside the cup that held her toothbrush.

"Either you open this door now, or I'll break it down," Larkin warned.

Knowing he would not be put off any longer, Taryn hurried over and unlocked the door. When she turned the knob, Larkin rushed in, wrapping his arms around her.

"Whoa, Larkin. What's going on?" she asked, taken back by the waves of emotion rolling off him.

~ 288 ~

He pulled her in closer while carefully cradling the back of her neck and whispered, "For a moment, it felt like I was losing you."

Standing near the doorway, Keiryn stared at the pair. "You okay, Sis?"

Taryn pushed back from Larkin and glanced to her brother. "I'm good."

Keiryn's eyes never left hers as his face turned stony. "I'll be downstairs whenever you're ready to go."

Arching her brow, she stepped past Larkin, though he did not fully relinquish his hold on her. "Why are you angry?" she asked of her brother.

He rolled his eyes and sighed heavily. "I'm not angry, I'm just hungry. But I would prefer you to be dressed if he's going to hold you like that." Keiryn's eyes panned to the towel wrapped around her torso then back to her face. "You'll always be my little sister, Taryn."

She watched as Keiryn hung his head and moped toward the hallway. Once he was out of sight, she turned to Larkin. "What happened downstairs that made you come and check on me?" she asked.

Running one hand through his hair, he shrugged. "My eyes turned black, and it seemed it had something to do with you."

"But why? Why would you think that?" she pressed.

Sliding his arms around her waist, he pulled her close and gazed into her eyes. "One minute I was fine, and the next I felt like you were being pulled away from me." He paused, glancing toward the floor then back up to her. "The thought of losing you brings out the beast in me."

She smiled softly. "I'm not going anywhere."

He leaned down, pressing his lips against hers. After a few moments, he pulled back slightly. "I wouldn't let you, even if you tried," he smiled.

₧₧₧₧

Taryn sat in the corner of Gastyn's back classroom with a book in hand while her friends practiced using their gifts. Every once and a while a gust of wind would blow by, and she would look up briefly with a warm smile.

After nearly an hour had passed, Larkin took a seat next to her. "What are you doing, Tare-Bear?"

She lifted the book slightly with an arched brow. "When a person is holding a book in the manner of which I am doing, it usually is a good indication that said person is reading."

He kissed the top of her head and chuckled. "Except in this case, you haven't read a single word."

Taryn wrinkled her nose and shrugged. "Am I that obvious?" she asked.

"I don't think anyone else noticed. Even if they did, they wouldn't mention it." He paused, taking the book from her hands. Closing it, he laid it to the side. "That feeling I had this morning when you were upstairs, it was because you had another vision."

She nodded.

"You know you can tell me anything, Taryn. You don't have to handle it on your own," he stated.

"What would I say, and what could you do if I did tell you?" she asked.

"Anything you want. At the very least, I could listen. Maybe having a sounding board would do you good," he offered.

Taryn shook her head. "The visions I'm having now aren't the same as the visions I experienced before. This strange man possesses power like I've never known."

"Okay, so he's powerful. But he's not really there, right?" he questioned.

Leaning in closer, she looked him in the eye. "These aren't like the others. With him, I feel like I'm being taken to an alternate space and time. I also believe that if he really wanted to harm me, he could."

Her love's eyes narrowed and his nostrils flared. "Is that what I felt this morning, him trying to hurt you?"

"Yeah, it was," she admitted, glancing across the room to where the others were gathered watching Andyn animate several small stones. "He knows what I did during the Trials. He said that he was the worst parts of me, and that the things I thought I destroyed still exist."

"That doesn't make any sense," he replied.

Rising to her feet, Taryn shook her head gently and shrugged. "Whoever this man is, Larkin, he's dangerous. He has brought the winds of change upon us, and I feel a stirring deep within every fiber of my being."

Larkin jumped to his feet and wrapped his arms around her waist. "You're not alone, Taryn. Let us help you fight against whatever this is."

She glanced to the others for a long moment before looking back to Larkin. "I couldn't tell you, not even if I wanted. He's made everyone I care about part of his game."

ဆပ္ကုဆပ္ကု

Sitting on the edge of the pool with her feet dangling in the crisp water, Taryn stared at its placid surface. Leaning down, she walked her fingers just above it, creating a small chessboard.

"Studying up?" Keiryn asked as he sat down on the far side of her creation.

Taryn lifted her eyes to meet his and gave a faint shrug. "So does this mean you're no longer angry with me?"

"It wasn't like that," he stated.

Reaching down, Taryn picked the opposing king up from the board and studied it for a long moment before allowing it to lose its shape. As the water rolled from her hand back into the pool, Taryn looked to her brother. "I know, Keiryn. I'm also aware that you saw a glimpse of what happened between the cloaked devil and me." She she paused, allowing the chessboard and its pieces to disappear into

~ 291 ~

the water. "The window into your mind was opened wide enough for Larkin to sense what was happening. That's why his eyes turned dark and he rushed upstairs to check on me."

He shook his head. "When I saw that man with his hands around your throat, it felt real. Too real."

Taryn scooted closer to Keiryn and cocked her head. "Everything with this cloaked stranger is real. It's not a glimpse of what could be, or some manifestation inside my head. He poses a threat greater than any of the past Elder Councils or the Mortari." She paused, running two fingers along his brow line. "You and dad look so much alike, both so handsome. But his culinary skills are far superior."

He chuckled. "Like your cooking is any better."

"I wish I was more like Jayma, Hava and Ilya. They've all endured great loss, yet they only wish to comfort others," Taryn sighed.

Keiryn nudged his sister, then leaned his head against hers. "As much as I wish this wasn't your burden, I don't believe there is another living being that could wield the power you possess and not give into it." He paused, moving to kiss her temple. "Your heart is what sets you apart from the rest of us, and your intentions are rarely, if ever, selfish."

Pulling back, Taryn looked at her brother. "That's really sweet of you to say, but I'm not sure that you'll still feel that way after what I'm about to say."

He straightened his back and frowned. "What is it?"

Taryn took a deep breath and sighed. "Please understand that this is not what I want, but rather what I think best for all of us."

Keiryn looked at her, his jaw drawing up tight. "Just say whatever it is you're going to say."

She glanced to the water then back to him. "You and I need to keep our distance from one another, Keiryn. Not because I want to, but because this cloaked man will use our connection against us."

His eyes narrowed. "I may not be as strong as you, but my gifts are powerful. Besides, there are only a handful of people who know the real depth of my gifts." He paused, taking in the unwavering look in his sister's eyes. "We're stronger when we're together, Taryn. Don't let this monster convince you otherwise," he pleaded.

She shook her head. "Do you remember the first time I saw you at the Desert Rose?"

With a sullen look upon his face, he nodded.

"Do you remember the spark between us when we touched?" she asked.

He exhaled loudly. "Of course I do, Taryn."

"Then you know how deep our familial bond runs." She paused, cupping his cheek. "That man wanted you to see him choking me, Keiryn. He wanted to hurt you by hurting me. He knows you won't be able to purge that image from your mind, and that it will fester until you act out in response to it all."

Keiryn rose to his feet. "You give this figment of your imagination a lot of credit," he growled.

"And here you are, proving him right," she retorted.

His hands clinched into fists. "I can't leave you, Taryn. Not now."

She remained seated, staring downward as the water began to bubble in the pool. "Lazryn should be back soon with mom and dad. When they arrive, we will greet them and visit with them as if nothing has changed. After a few hours, you will pull them aside and tell them you've decided to move in with Nalani and her family on a more permanent basis. Then you will pack a bag and head over to the Skye's house."

"I won't agree to this, Taryn," he insisted.

Leaning down, she placed the tip of her left index finger atop the churning water's surface causing it to instantly calm. "Keiryn, this is not a request. You will comply one way or another, because I won't allow him to use you and our connection," she warned.

"So that's it, I don't have a say in the matter?" he questioned.

Pushing up from the pool's edge, Taryn moved to her feet and eyed her brother. "It will hurt me to take away your freewill, but if it's what has to be done to keep you safe...then so be it."

Keiryn leaned down, kissing Taryn's cheek. "I don't like this one bit, but I do love and trust you."

Her eyes softened. "I love you, too, big brother."

ᘓᑫᑊᘓᑫ

The two families, plus Lazryn sat around the dining room table enjoying a variety of pastries from a little bakery in Paris while Ilya and Gracyn gushed about their time away.

"The view from the Eiffel Tower was incredible. And our hotel...words cannot express how amazing it was. I am so glad Lazryn suggested it," Gracyn shared.

He smiled while giving a slight nod. "I am delighted to know that you approve, and that you all enjoyed your trip."

Maxym rubbed the palms of his hands together as he rose from his chair and then picked up his wine glass. "Well, I, for one, think we should start planning our next day trip." He leaned down, sharing a quick kiss with Ilya. "At times, it's easy to forget just how beautiful the rest of the world is, and all the culture it has to offer."

Theron, Ilya and Gracyn raised their glasses. "Here. Here," they said in nearly perfect unison.

"I'm glad you guys were able to get away, and that you had a good time," Taryn stated.

"We have you to thank for it, Taryn. It was really thoughtful for you to put this together for us," Theron replied.

The teen smiled as she glanced in Keiryn's direction then back to her parents. "I don't mean to cut the night short, but I'm rather tired. I think I'll head off to bed."

"Of course, sweetie. We'll see you in the morning," Gracyn replied.

Taryn rose from her seat and Larkin quickly followed. "I'm glad you guys enjoyed your trip. And thanks again for the pastries," he stated while snatching one final goody from the box.

Before they were out of sight, Taryn glanced over her shoulder, locking eyes with Keiryn. He gave a slight nod, letting her know he was not going to back out of their arrangement.

CHAPTER SIXTEEN

"I'm glad it's Friday," Kellan moaned from the other side of the lunchroom table.

The twins squealed as they looked up from their fashion magazine.

Bentley proudly held up an image from within its pages of a famous actress, flashing it around the table. "Tammy Rowan is wearing our dress," she shrieked.

Taking the magazine from her hands, Dagney scanned over the glossy image. The young woman wore a deep rose-colored mermaid gown with a jeweled bodice. "Are you wearing matching dresses?" she asked.

The two sisters looked at each other and instantly laughed. "Absolutely not," Hadley protested. "My dress is powder blue."

"And mine is mint colored," Bentley added.

Dagney looked at the image once more then handed the magazine back. "You both will look killer at prom tomorrow," she stated.

"You're going to look amazing in the deep purple number you bought," Hadley smiled.

"Thanks. It's not always easy finding a dress to match my auburn hair and pale skin without looking washed out or even worse, a holiday center piece." She paused, furrowing her brows at the twins. "I just realized that we have no idea what Taryn's wearing."

When the three girls looked in her direction, Taryn forced a smile and shrugged. "It's long, grey and white…sort of."

The girls stared at her for a long moment before turning their heads and sharing a look.

"You're such a tomboy," Bentley chuckled.

Hadley nodded with a sincere smile. "I'm just happy that she's coming this year. I'm sure you will look beautiful, Taryn."

Larkin placed his hand on the small of Taryn's back. "We don't have to go if you don't want to," he whispered.

"But I have a dress," she replied.

He shrugged. "I'm just saying that if you don't want to go, I'm good with it."

Smiling, she placed one hand on the back of his neck and guided his lips to hers. "And that is reason one-thousand-nine-hundred-ninety-nine why I love you."

ಬಃಀಬಃ

The following day, Taryn sat on the edge of her bed staring into the tall mirror that leaned against the wall. Her hair was swept up with soft curls in an elegant updo, with a few tendrils left to frame her face. Her nails were manicured, and her makeup was clean and classic.

Her mother peeked her head into her bedroom, drawing her attention. "Are you ready for the dress?" she asked.

Taryn turned, observing the sparkle in her mother's eyes and the brilliant smile she wore. "Give me thirty minutes and then you and Ilya can help me with the dress."

"Of course," her mother replied with a widening smile. She stared at her daughter for a few moments longer before shutting the door and leaving Taryn to herself once more.

Rising off the bed, she went to the dresser. Opening the top drawer, she reached in and pulled out the old book.

"Surely thirty minutes is long enough to learn something more," she said aloud as she returned to the bed.

Using her gift of Imperium, Taryn made a small blade and sliced her left index finger. She turned the book on its side, running her bloodied finger over the spine. Placing the book onto the bed, she took a deep breath and pulled open the cover.

In an instant, she found herself standing within the strange but beautiful forest, just like the time before. The teen began walking through the rows of trees. The further she walked, the more she was in awe of this well-kept secret of their kind. Several minutes passed before she spotted a faint glow in the distance amongst the shimmering white and silver trees.

Realizing her time for exploration was nearing its end, she ran like a breeze towards the golden glow. As she neared, she suddenly stilled and her breath caught in her throat. Before her stood a stunning tree with golden bark, diamond leaves, and sapphire colored globes.

Taryn slowly stepped closer until she finally stood beneath its branches. Reaching up, she placed her hand on one of the globes and immediately felt the presence of others. She spun around, finding Maertan watching her from under a nearby tree.

"What are you doing here?" she asked.

He tilted his head slowly from one side to the other before a soft smile warmed his face. "So eager for answers when one does not yet know the questions."

"Perfect. More riddles," she sighed loudly.

Maertan moved toward the golden tree. "The fruit upon this tree is not the same as the others, Taryn. For if you decide to steal a glimpse within, it may lend shape to the course of your very destiny."

Her brows furrowed. "When a Gaias dies, are they automatically enrolled in Speaking in Riddles 101?"

"It is not my intention to cause confusion, but to merely encourage a deeper state of understanding," he explained, while kneeling down and collecting a clear globe from the forest floor. Lifting it toward her, he nodded for her to take it. "It is best if you start from the base of this particular tree and work your way up. Only then will you have reference for understanding."

Taryn's eyes panned to the ground and narrowed on the numerous globes that rested underfoot. *How did I not see these before?* she thought to herself.

"This tree is temptation, and may only be sought by the one it represents. It is meant to lure and ensnare your gaze. And as such, it blinds you to its fallen fruit in hopes that you will ignore the past and accept a future of its bidding."

The girl rolled her eyes and snatched the globe from his hand. "Why can't you talk like normal people and just say that you want me to start with this one?"

Maertan's smile faded and he rose to his feet, taking a wide step back from the teen.

Glancing down at the sphere, Taryn immediately found herself watching a series of dark events from the moment she learned of Nelmaryc's Trial, all the way to the moment when she freed herself from the icy prison her wicked emotions had trapped her within, stopping her fiery inferno from claiming all living things.

With the events of that time lingering fresh in her memory, Taryn tore her gaze from the globe and stared at Maertan. Without a word she tossed it aside and picked up another from the ground.

She immediately opened her mind's eye to the memories stored within. This time she watched the death of the Mortari who had stolen Keiryn's gifts. The sensation of him locking onto her power as she withdrew her dead brother's gifts bit deep inside her heart.

With a heaving chest, Taryn smashed the globe against the base of the tree. "Watching myself claim the life of another in order to save my brother isn't exactly a clip I enjoy seeing on my highlight reel,

Maertan. I did what was needed to save Keiryn's life, and I won't apologize for it. But it doesn't make me any less guilty of the offense," she bit.

The young man gazed upon the girl softly. "Your heart, as pure and well-intentioned as it may be, misleads you. Your mind, for as wise and clear as it may be, it too, misleads you."

Taryn's nostrils flared and lightning flashed overhead. "Who do you think you are to presume to know what lies within me?"

His eyes never left her face as he gave a slight nod. "Only when your soul walks amongst the dead, will peace find its way into your heart and mind." He paused, disappearing only to reappear behind her. Leaning down, he whispered in her ear, "Your soul burns brighter than those before you. You are the willful, the mighty, the conqueror, the threat and the sacrifice forged into one unsuspecting vessel."

Taryn's eyes widened. "The sacrifice?" she questioned.

Maertan reached around, grabbing Taryn's hand. "Only you may decide what that means," he stated before fading away.

She looked down at her hand and found a single jasmine flower. When she glanced up, she was back in her bedroom, still cradling the lovely bloom.

"Knock, knock," her mother said as she and Ilya entered Taryn's room with her dress and accessories in hand. "We hope you don't mind, but neither of us could wait another minute."

Taking a deep breath, Taryn smiled. "As usual, you both have perfect timing."

Ilya set the box on the bed and studied the teen's hair. "You look so grown up with your hair fixed like this." She paused, glancing down at the teen's hands. "Where did you get this," she asked, taking the flower from Taryn.

Before the girl could answer, Gracyn spoke up. "Why would you even ask such a question, Ilya, knowing that our girl is also an Ontogeny?"

Ilya chuckled. "I know. That was a bit ridiculous on my part."

Taryn's heart warmed watching them work together as a team on her behalf. Neither trying to take the lead, but both simply trying to make her happy and share in the evening's festivity.

"Would you mind placing the flower in my hair?" she asked, looking to Ilya.

The woman smiled warmly. "Of course, sweetheart."

ঙেୠঙେ

Pacing in front of the living room windows dressed in his tuxedo, Larkin paused, glancing towards the staircase. He ran his hands through his hair, taking a deep breath and then continued pacing.

Theron patted Maxym on the shoulder as the man watched his son with amusement. "You would think that they were getting married, as anxious as your boy is."

Maxym chuckled. "He hasn't seen her since breakfast. And it's killing him that she's upstairs and can't see her until Ilya and Gracyn give him the okay."

"Well let's see if we can help nudge things along." Theron paused, walking to the bottom of the staircase. "Come on ladies. We have an eager young man down here who wants to see his date."

After a few moments, the men heard Taryn's bedroom door open and hurried footsteps heading their way. When the two women came into sight, they were beaming from ear-to-ear.

"Is the masterpiece finished?" Theron teased, as Gracyn and Ilya descended the stairs.

The women held hands as they neared the bottom steps.

"Brace yourself, Theron. Your little girl is about to melt your heart," Ilya smiled.

"I'll consider myself warned," he replied.

Gracyn walked over to Larkin, placing her hand on his forearm. "It's time," she said.

He nodded and turned, knocking his knuckles against the large window in an attempt to gain Keiryn, Nalani, Lazryn, Andyn and

~ 301 ~

Dedrick's attention as they lounged about in the backyard. Lazryn waved as the group began making their way toward the French doors.

Larkin stood near the bottom of the stairs, while their parents flanked the sides. A few feet behind him, the remainder of the group stood staggered.

Taking a deep breath, Taryn stood in front of the mirror calming the whirlwind of emotions that swirled within her. *You stupid, crazy, beautiful dress…why do you elicit such strong emotions from me?* she thought to herself.

With a final glance over, she walked toward the open doorway and into the hall. Her heart beat frantically, knowing it would take only a few more steps before she was visible to Larkin. Pausing, she closed her eyes and cleared her mind of all non-prom related thoughts.

Once settled, she held her breath and stepped forward. Immediately, she could hear gasps coming from below. They only grew louder as she came fully into sight.

At the bottom of the stairs on her left stood Ilya and Maxym, while her parents were to the right. As much as it warmed her heart to see them all so happy, it was Larkin who truly caught her eye. He stood tall in his classic black tuxedo, white button down shirt and silver-grey vest and tie. Her heart paused as she took in the view.

Larkin gazed toward the top of the stairs, shaking his head in awe at Taryn's beautiful glow. As she took the first step down, his breath caught in his chest. It wasn't until she stood directly in front of him that he could breathe again.

"You look beautiful, Taryn," he gushed.

A hint of pink flooded her cheeks. "And the dress?"

"The dress is amazing, but you…you're always breathtaking," he replied, kissing her cheek.

The others stood quietly, watching the pair share a tender moment. Nalani gaped at the simple elegance of her friend's dress. It was a strapless, two toned, floor length ball gown with a dropped chapel train. The bodice was white with lace and jeweled detailing, while the skirt portion was silvery-grey in color with white embroidered flowers flowing at key points from the waist down. On her hands, she wore dainty, fingerless, white laced gloves to complete the look.

"Your sister looks stunning, and that dress…it's just, wow. She looks so elegant, and yet edgy somehow," she whispered to Keiryn.

He glanced to Nalani and smiled proudly. "She is stunning."

After several quiet moments passed, Gracyn spoke up. "If you two would like to make your way toward the fireplace, we have your corsage and boutonniere setting on the mantle."

Larkin took Taryn by the hand, leading her past the others and to the fireplace. He reached up, selecting the corsage. Carefully he slipped it over her wrist.

"Smile," Gracyn shouted as she snapped several photographs.

Taryn grabbed the boutonniere, pausing at times while pinning it to Larkin's jacket so her mother could capture the moments on film. Once finished, she turned, looking to her family with a soft smile.

"I'd like to take a few photos with our parents, if someone wouldn't mind," she stated.

Andyn rushed to Gracyn with his hands out. "I'll take the pictures," he offered.

The woman handed him the camera and joined her daughter in front of the mantel.

ဆဝ၆၃ဆဝ၆၃

Their friends and family arrived, moving the group onto the back deck where additional photographs were taken. Taryn posed between Bency and Dagney, with the twins on either side of them, when she suddenly stilled. Her warm smile faded as she glanced to Lazryn.

The former Mortari rushed to her. "This is your night, Taryn. If you wish for me to tell him to leave, I will."

Theron arched a brow and stepped forward. "Tell who, what?" he asked.

"No. I should tell him," Taryn replied as she headed towards the woods.

"Who's here?" Theron asked, his tone firm.

Taryn paused in her step. "It's Chrystian. He's waiting in the tree line."

Her father's brow furrowed. "If he's that close, why am I not sensing him?"

She sighed loudly. "Because he's holding in his gifts. He knows none of you want him here, and he's trying to be respectful."

"Was he respectful when his kind murdered my wife?" Maxym growled.

"Look, you guys go on and keep the fun going. I'll be back in a few minutes," she replied.

Larkin gently grabbed her hand. "Taryn, it should be me who goes and talks to him."

Glancing back over her shoulder, she arched her brows.

"Will you let me do this for you…and for us?" he asked.

She nodded and watched as he headed toward the trees. After a few moments, he disappeared from view.

Blocking out the others around her, Taryn focused on the tempo of both Larkin and Chrystian's hearts. Chrystian's beat slow and steady while Larkin's thumped furiously inside his chest.

After several long, intense moments passed, Larkin emerged from the tree line.

Laying eyes upon his son, Maxym sighed with immense relief.

Thank you, Chrystian, Taryn thought to herself as her face flickered between joy and sadness.

Pausing, Larkin locked eyes with Taryn and smiled lovingly. He glanced over his shoulder and stared back at the trees. A second later, Chrystian came into view, carrying a large satchel over one shoulder.

Taryn's eyes lit. "Larkin, what's going on?" she questioned.

He slid his arm around her waist and gently kissed her forehead. "Chrystian, he means something to you. I may not understand it or like it, but I trust you and you trust him."

Her jaw fell slightly agape as her green eyes shimmered, looking adoringly at her love. "Thank you for always being so wonderful to me."

Groans of disapproval began to surface amongst the group as everyone made a wide berth for the Mortari brother.

Taryn pursed her lips as her shoulders fell.

Before she could utter a word, Larkin spoke up. "If this man's presence bothers you, please feel free to wait inside or to leave."

Lazryn's eyes widened as he looked to the teen. "Larkin?" he questioned.

Shaking his head, he looked to the man he called friend. "I know what you're thinking, but no one has Influenced me. This is Taryn's home, and it is her night. Anyone who wants to cause problems will have to answer to me," he warned.

"Son, he's a monster," Maxym growled.

Larkin turned to his father. "Dad, please. Go inside if it bothers you."

Keiryn stepped up with his pack standing firmly behind him. "Your dad has a point, Larkin. He is a monster," he frowned.

Ibrym and Alderyc shared a look as they stood silent with their pack brothers and sisters who were present for the night's events.

Sensing the depth of disapproval lingering in the air, Chrystian paused in his step. "It was not my intentions to cause any disruptions of tonight's festivities. I merely intended to leave a few gifts for Taryn."

Gracyn stepped forward, placing her hand on Taryn's shoulder. "I trust you and Larkin know what you are doing?"

"He won't hurt anyone here," Taryn replied.

"That's debatable," Keiryn snapped. "He's like a super stalker, creeping around in the forest watching you, Taryn."

"And you're like a donkey's butt, always forgetting that I can hold my own," she retorted.

A smirk grew on Chrystian's face. "You most certainly can," he lauded.

"You think this is funny?" Keiryn growled. "You show up here and disrupt our family time, and you dare to stand there acting innocent?"

Chrystian's eyes locked on the teen. "Dearest Taryn, I believe it is time for you to send this one away."

She rolled her eyes. "Keiryn, if you can't handle him being here, then you should go inside." She paused, looking to Chrystian. "And you, you aren't allowed to provoke anyone, understood?"

Chrystian glanced between the siblings then nodded. "Forgive me, Taryn. This night is yours."

The girl gave him a stern look before turning to her brother. "Keiryn, are you finished?" she asked.

He gave a slight tilt of his head in response before stepping back with his pack.

Seeing both had backed down, at least for the moment, Taryn's face softened and a soft smile formed on her face.

Larkin stepped back, glancing to the Mortari. "Okay, Chrystian, you're up."

He nodded once again and stepped closer to the girl. Glancing around, he took in the numerous unhappy and untrusting faces surrounding him. A taunting smile curled momentarily from his lips before softening into a tender look. "This dress suits you well, Taryn. Far better than any garment we dressed you in. It is a simple, yet beautiful dress for a complex girl." He paused, moving closer while examining the flower in her hair. "Loryn would approve," he said while gently touching the flower's soft petals.

"Her last act upon the earthly planes was to sacrifice herself to spare you from the pain. She loved you immensely, Chrystian. And that flame will never extinguish," Taryn replied.

Chrystian pulled his gaze from hers and reached into his satchel. "I want this night to be truly exceptional for you, as there has never been, nor will there ever be, a star that shines as bright as yours."

The twins sighed dreamily while listening to him speak. Both watched eagerly as his attentive eyes drank in their dear friend.

"He's so hot," Bentley whispered.

"The bad boy with a tender heart and a smooth tongue," Hadley added.

Kellan and Gerrick shot them looks of disgust. "He's Mortari. He steals other people's gifts," Gerrick growled.

Jayma stepped up between the two couples. "The girls are right. He is a handsome devil, easy on the eyes and ears."

The boys groaned in unison until Larkin shot them a look of warning.

Chrystian pulled a thin box from beneath the cloth, glancing toward Larkin. "Young wolf, if you would be so willing," he said while placing the satchel down. He looked to the young man and motioned for him to near.

Larkin stepped forward, his brows furrowed.

The man lifted the box between the young couple and opened the lid.

"Chrystian, it's too much," Taryn said, taking in the beautiful teardrop diamond necklace and matching earrings.

"Always so graceful," he replied.

"These are real?" Larkin asked.

He nodded, looking to the girl. "This is my gift to you, Taryn. It would please me very much if you were to wear them on this special occasion." Extending his arms, he held the boxed jewels out to Larkin. "Wolf, this would be an appropriate time for you to place the necklace around her lovely neck."

Larkin looked to Taryn. "Is that what you want?"

She glanced to the Mortari and smiled with an arched brow. "I will gladly wear your gifts, Chrystian. But I must say, I am impressed at how they match my dress perfectly. It's as if you knew what I was wearing before anyone else did."

He swallowed hard and lifted his chin. "It is no secret that I look in on you from time to time. I may have witnessed you finding this very special dress."

"Why don't you just admit it, you're a full blown creeper who stalks my baby sister," Keiryn growled.

Taryn glanced to her brother then back to Chrystian. "He's become quite the over protective brother here as of late," she sighed.

"It would seem that he has grown even more aggressive in his cares over the past twenty-four hours," Chrystian noted, with his eyes locked on the young man. His stare lingered for a moment longer until he turned his focus back to Taryn. "Wolf, if you would do the honor."

Larkin pursed his lips, hiding a hint of a smile. Taking the earrings from the box, he handed her one at a time, watching as she slipped them into place on each ear. Next, he removed the necklace from the box. Moving to stand behind her, he draped the beautiful necklace around her neck, securing the clasp.

Feeling the weight of the stone against her flesh, Taryn placed her hands over it and smiled softly. "Thank you, Chrystian. It's beautiful."

"These trinkets pale in comparison to you, my dear Taryn." He paused, glancing to Gracyn. "You, mother of Taryn, are also a vision of loveliness."

Theron stepped up, placing his arm around his wife's waist. "For having the reputation of merciless killer, you certainly possess a mouthful of pretty words."

Arching his brow, Chrystian gave a slight shrug. "You see me as a threat, so I will take it as a compliment."

"Chrystian, we're getting a bit off topic," Larkin stated, nodding his head in Taryn's direction.

An amused grin curled from his mouth. "Ah, yes, our dear Taryn." He paused, turning back to the satchel and lifting it off the ground.

Flipping the top back, he reached inside and carefully slid the bag down past the framed canvas.

Taryn's jaw dropped as she took in the painted image of herself in the gown she was currently wearing. "Um, I don't know what to say, Chrystian."

With tears welling in her eyes, Gracyn stepped closer. "You look like an angel, Taryn," she wept.

"Why…why would you do this?" Taryn questioned.

Chrystian grinned. "I am only the courier of this gift, Taryn. It was Clad who painted your image."

She stepped closer, running her fingers just above the canvas. "Why would he paint me?"

"During your time on Mors, Taryn, you caused a stirring within some of the inhabitants. You returned life to a soulless vessel, and inspired a deep longing for something more." He paused, glancing between Keiryn, Gracyn, Andyn, Julius and Jonesy before turning his focus back to the girl. "The blood pumping through your veins will be the sole determiner of all fate."

Suddenly, Keiryn stepped forward. "Is that a threat?" he growled.

Chrystian arched his brow and stared at the young man. "You are not yourself today. Perhaps you could use a timeout to clear your mind."

"Maybe it's you who needs a timeout before I break your neck," Keiryn growled.

The Mortari locked his eyes on him. "You should take heed of the wolf's earlier warning, young one. For if you were in your right mind, you would know this is not a battle you will win."

Keiryn's blue eyes narrowed. "You stand there in all of your monstrous glory thinking you are better than us. Thinking that we cannot see through this ruse that Taryn chooses to drink down. Interfere in our business, and I will see you dead."

Having heard enough of their testosterone filled banter, Taryn turned and stared firmly at her brother. "Stop it now, Keiryn." She paused, moving toward him, her eyes locking with his. Within she noted a strange darkness looming. "Where have you been? Who have you seen?" she demanded.

His jaw drew up tight and the veins on his neck bulged. "Why ask? It's not as if you care. You sent me away," he seethed.

Taryn stood directly in front of him, watching as he continued to become more agitated by the second. Looking down, she saw his hands clenched into fists, but his right was slightly bulkier than the left. "What's in your hand, Keiryn?" she asked.

He shook his head. "You always side with the monsters. First the black dog, then your pet Lazryn, and now one of the original brothers. He is nothing more than a murderer without conscience," he spat, venom dripping from his words.

"What is in your hand, Keiryn?" she asked again.

"You're a traitor to our kind, Taryn. You've lost your way, and now there's no redeeming your soul," he stated.

Reaching down, Taryn grabbed his wrist. "Either you show me what you have, or I will make you show me," she warned.

When he failed to respond, she forced her Influence upon him, causing him to release his fist. As she stared at the familiar chess piece in his hand, her eyes turned from green to blue. She swiped it from his palm and glanced around the yard before her eyes panned upward toward her bedroom window. There, she spotted the cloaked man staring down at her.

"Keiryn, where did you get this?" she asked.

He rubbed his temple. "I don't know. Maybe from the kitchen counter," he gasped, doubling over at the waist.

Taryn balled her hand, crushing the knight figurine as swirling clouds formed overhead. Kneeling beside her brother, she glared daggers in the direction of the dark man.

"Help him, Taryn," Nalani yelled from the other side of Keiryn. Tears marred the beautiful girl's face as she pleaded for his sister to heal him.

Taryn reached down, placing one hand over Keiryn's heart, instantly relieving his pain. She rose to her feet, her eyes never leaving the cloaked man. "A fate worse than death awaits you for what you have done," she whispered, her words carrying through the air as lighting struck overhead.

"Keiryn's going to be fine now, Taryn. But you need to take a deep breath and calm yourself," Larkin whispered in her ear.

Hearing his voice pulled her from the edge at which she stood. "A war is coming, and we need to be ready," she replied, lacing her fingers with his.

Approaching with caution, Chrystian looked at his friend. "The evil that plagues us will not stop until it has either claimed you for its cause, or destroyed you to seek the next in line," he warned.

She pulled back her shoulders and stiffened her jaw. "Thank you for the gifts, Chrystian. But it is time for you to return home now. Please, give my thanks to Clad for the beautiful painting," she stated, her tone neither cool nor warm.

He nodded and backed away, taking in the numerous faces before disappearing like a blur with his satchel.

80C380C3

Larkin stood behind Taryn, arms wrapped around her waist while resting his chin on her shoulder. The pair stood near a door, watching their friends dancing in the center of the gym. "I'm sorry tonight didn't turn out better," he whispered.

Leaning her head against his, she sighed. "I look at them and think about my mom, dad and Keiryn…what life would be like for all of you if I hadn't ever been born."

He pulled her closer. "Don't ever talk like that, Taryn. You being here, being alive…it's everything to all of us. If not for you, we would still be at the mercy of the Elder Council and living in fear of the Mortari."

"At least you had some semblance of order and knew where you stood." She paused, shaking her head. "I know it's silly to think about what could have been when there is no changing the past. But it feels like everything is working against me. Like I shouldn't know happiness, and I shouldn't have you."

"Now you're just talking crazy," he sighed.

"Tonight should have been simple, but it wasn't. The harder I fight and the more I learn about past Gaias, I feel like the universe is working against me," she admitted.

He slid his hands around her waist until he was standing in front of her. "So what are you going to do about it, Taryn? Are you going to lay down and let it have its way, or are you going to fight?" he asked.

A stern look formed on her face. "I'm going to fight whatever this is until my dying breath. Even then, I'm not sure I will be able to stop fighting."

Cupping her cheeks in his hands, Larkin smiled. "And there's the girl we all know and love. Don't ever forget who you are and what you mean to so many of us. There isn't anything or anyone you cannot defeat when you put your mind and your heart to it."

"You're so good to me. I mean, you invited Chrystian to come to the house when you could have just as easily sent him away," she stated.

"Me and Chrystian, we have something in common. You. He told me how he wanted tonight to be special for you, and that he had brought gifts. I figured since he seems to make you happy more often than not, who am I to stand between your friendship," he explained.

Taryn chuckled. "I can just imagine how that conversation started."

"I'll tell you about that later, but right now I would love to dance with my date," he stated, holding out his hand.

She shrugged and smiled. "Whatever Wolfy wants, Wolfy gets."

CHAPTER SEVENTEEN

Three weeks after prom and only a few days before their high school graduation, things around Williams and in the Gaias world remained quiet. After the incident with Keiryn on prom night, Taryn had fully expected to have more unpleasant encounters with the cloaked man.

Every once and a while she would pick up a scent of a stranger's gifts as they passed through Williams, though she never sensed any stopped, not even to fill up their cars.

Relaxing on the couch, she lay with her head resting on Larkin's lap as they binge watched a television series.

"How many seasons does this have?" she asked.

"Four," Larkin answered.

"That's two seasons and three more episodes to go," Maxym groaned as he joined them. "I thought we were going to go on a run today, Son?"

"I'm sorry, Dad. Taryn and I started watching this last night and it's strangely addicting," he admitted.

Taryn sat up, stretching her arms. "You should go for a run with your dad. We can watch the rest of this later," she suggested.

"Are you sure?" he asked.

"Of course. It'll give me time to go hang out with Ilya for some girl time," she replied.

He looked to his father. "Well, it looks like we're going for a run."

∞⋘∞⋘

Freshly showered for her visit with Ilya, Taryn stepped onto the back deck, focusing on sensing Larkin. She could tell that he and his father were already more than fifty miles away to her south. *Boys,* she thought to herself with a smile.

She bent down to tie her shoelace when a sharp pain struck deep inside her chest. A second later she glanced up, watching as a gateway opened.

Emerging from within, Lazryn's face wore a pained expression. He glanced around, before looking to the girl. "Where is Larkin?"

"On a run with Maxym, why?" she asked, rising to her feet.

"Call him home, Taryn. The north California pack requires your presence right away," he answered.

Another sharp pain stabbed into her stomach. "Someone's being tortured," she grimaced.

"Call Larkin home," he pressed.

"There's no time. We need to get to our friends right now. I feel there are lives hanging in the balance, and every second is crucial," she replied.

He shook his head. "It is not wise for you to go without your wolf. You will need him to pull you from the edge that you so often walk," he warned.

Her eyes narrowed. "Open the gateway now," she ordered.

"Not without Larkin," he insisted.

"Open the gateway, Lazryn. This is no longer a request," she warned.

His jaw drew tight. "Once you are through the portal, I will locate Larkin and we will join you there. I beg of you, Taryn, do not act with haste."

"I can only promise that I will do whatever is necessary to save the ones I love. And every second we stand here, their light dims a little more," she replied.

Raising his hand, he created a gateway. In the blink of an eye, Taryn rushed in, disappearing from his sight.

ഇൻ രാ

On the other side, Taryn rushed out, finding Ibrym pacing with his brother amongst their entire community outside the family home.

He rushed towards her and grabbed her by the hand. "We need your help, Taryn, and we need it now." Leading her to the doorway, he grimaced as agonizing screams pierced the air. "It doesn't look good. Not for any of them. Brannyn, Brysyn and..."

Feeling the pain radiating from the injured, Taryn cut him off. "And Sydney."

In an instant, she was at the little girl's bedside. Her eyes widened, taking in the numerous cuts and bruises covering the child's petite frame. Taryn held her breath briefly, feeling Death's presence lingering nearby. Though he did not show himself, she made her intentions clear.

"Go away, Farren. Your services are not needed here," she growled.

When his scent began to weaken, Taryn knelt at the little girl's side, placing one hand on the girl's head and the other over her heart. As Taryn forced her gift of Healing into the child, images of the violent attack that had left Sydney in this condition flooded her mind. Flashbacks of Andalyn's suffering at the hands of her father and Karvyn surfaced, causing the teen to lose focus briefly. Once the little girl was no longer in peril, Taryn pulled the wicked memories of the attack from her mind.

Turning to Ibrym and the others, she drew her jaw tight. "She's going to be fine. I've removed all traces of what happened from her memory. I don't think it would be good for her to see everyone so worked up and emotional. She won't wake up until tomorrow, so that gives them a chance to process what happened and put on a brave face for her," she explained.

"Thank you, Taryn. Thank you," the girl's mother wept as she pushed past the teen to sit beside her daughter.

Ibrym briefly studied Taryn's face before motioning for her to follow him. "The twins got it worse than Syd. I'm fairly certain that every bone in their bodies are shattered," he disclosed.

Without a word, she followed him down the narrow hallway to the family room. Once inside, she worked quickly to relieve the brothers' suffering and to Heal their injuries. And like with the young girl, Taryn removed the memories of the event from their minds.

As she began to rise to her feet, Brannyn reached up, grabbing her wrist. "I feel your power running through my veins," he whispered.

She cupped his cheek and smiled. "You, Sydney and your brother will all be okay."

His brows furrowed. "We were taken...I don't remember anything else."

"Some memories are better off forgotten, my friend," she whispered, before leaning over and placing a kiss on his forehead.

Larkin walked up behind her and placed his hand on her shoulder. "Ibrym and the others would like to speak with you," he stated.

She nodded, rising to her feet. "You guys get some rest and I will see you later."

Sleepily, the twins nodded.

ᏠᏦᏣᏠᏦᏣ

Ibrym stood in front of his pack, discussing the day's terrible events. "One of the men who was seen entering the gateway came through here a few weeks back. Did anyone talk to him or learn his name?" he asked.

"His name is Laramyn, and he lives on the Dartous plane," Taryn announced, her tone void of all emotion.

The pack leader's eyes narrowed. "Dartous is one of the richest planes inhabited by our kind. Did one of the twins tell you this, Taryn?" he questioned.

"No one has to tell me that which I have already seen." She paused, watching as an image of Syndey's torture displayed itself fully inside her mind. "Lazryn will open a gateway and a small group will be allowed to enter. Once there, no one speaks, except for me. Is this understood?"

Lazryn stepped up. "I do not believe this wise, Taryn. You need perspective about the situation. The two brothers and the girl are fully recovered, thanks to you."

A faint smile flickered upon her face. "No one speaks except for me," she stated once more.

The man sent Larkin a pleading look. "Will you not speak to her and attempt to alter this course?"

Feeling heat rolling off her in waves, Larkin knew his words would fall on deaf ears. The only thing he could do is stand by her side and pray he could convince her to rein in her emotions, if need be. "No one else speaks. Lazryn, open the gateway," he stated, his eyes focused on Taryn.

Shaking his head in protest, Lazryn opened the portal. "Stay close to her, Larkin. It would bring me great pain if she were to lose herself today."

Taryn's face remained neutral as she noted his concern. She watched as Ibrym and Alderyc each chose five members of their community to join them. Once their selections were complete, she headed toward the portal.

The group emerged near the center of the large village. Taryn barely glanced around before lifting one hand toward the sky. Dark clouds muted the sun's rays as the wind began to howl.

Residents of Dartous poured onto the brick streets, surrounding Taryn and the others.

"Bring Laramyn and his associates to me, now," she demanded, taking in the numerous rotund faces.

Larkin stepped closer, placing his hand on the small of her back.

A middle-aged man with pale blond hair and grey eyes stepped forward. "I am Chief Counsel Member Laramyn," he replied smugly.

With a smile curled on her face, Taryn lowered her hand and locked eyes with the man. "You and a few of your associates paid a visit to my friends in California today, leaving them gravely injured."

He crossed his arms and smirked boldly. "What proof of these accusations do you hold?"

"During the Trials I made a promise to those who sought their freedom and who wanted peace. Today, you made a considerable mistake by challenging that promise," she stated, her words lacking emotion as she glanced around at the many faces.

"You have no proof of such actions." He paused, glancing back over his shoulder at the members of his community. "However, it would not matter if we did or did not commit these acts. Every Gaias knows that you will not harm a living soul."

His defiant words spurred laughter amongst his people, having no effect on the girl.

After a few moments passed, the smile on Taryn's face widened, causing chills to wash over the crowd as she replied. "I am afraid you have been deceived by the very one who seeks your destruction. Did he promise you immunity from my wrath if you carried the burden of his dirty work?"

"No one promised us anything, because we did not do the things you are accusing us of," he countered.

In a blur, Taryn appeared in front of the man and placed her thumbs over his eyes. She unleashed the horrific memories she had taken from the twins and Sydney, pushing them into his mind.

His body began to twitch until he fell backwards onto the ground.

She stood over him, watching as their suffering became his own.

"It was him and the other council members. The rest of us had nothing to do with it," one woman pleaded.

Taryn's gaze darkened as she focused in on the auburn haired woman. "How dare you claim innocence when you heard their cries and did nothing to help. There are hundreds of you, and nine of them. Yet somehow, you all decided collectively to turn a blind eye to such immoral savagery." She paused, pulling the suffering from Laramyn. "This community prides itself in its bountiful harvest and ample supplies, but you do nothing to ease the suffering and hunger of your less fortunate fellow Gaias."

"They would have killed us if we went against them," a man reasoned.

"And what did you think I would do for allowing three innocent lives to be treated as if they did not matter," she countered, positioning her palm upward.

The clouds overhead began to rotate as countless bolts of lightning rained down, striking their fields and orchards without mercy.

She looked to Lazryn. "Send their livestock to the other planes that are in need."

Noting her restraint, he nodded and did as she asked.

Rising to his feet, Laramyn steadied himself by leaning on a nearby man. "Foolish girl, we will simply regrow all that you have destroyed."

"Only a Phoenix shall rise from the ashes. So I must ask, are you a Phoenix?" Taryn questioned.

Larkin's eyes narrowed on his love, he could feel the smoldering beneath her flesh as the flames died down.

"Of course I am not a Phoenix," Laramyn growled.

"As punishment for all those who were capable of taking action, but chose otherwise, I hereby sentence you to learn the true meaning of hunger. You will consume nothing but water for twenty-one days. Only then will you be permitted to regrow your crops and feast upon your bounty once more. Until this time, your fields will be nothing more than ash," she announced.

"You would starve our children to punish us," a woman shouted.

"Unlike the vast majority of you, I do not harm children, nor the innocent. They will be able to consume whatever they desire from the community storage barns while you look on." She paused, glancing around. "You will all survive this, though it won't always be comfortable. Perhaps when it is over, you will have more compassion for your fellow Gaias."

"The other communities will not permit this," Laramyn challenged.

"Too bad not a single one has a say in this. But I will offer a few words of warning. Do not attack those I promised to protect, and you will never have to see me again," she replied.

She motioned to Lazryn who immediately opened an Adora Gateway. The others filed through with Taryn trailing casually behind, casting her Influence upon the guilty.

ଓଓଔଓ

From inside the living room, Larkin stared out one of the large windows, watching Taryn as she sat poolside. "I don't know how I feel about what she did," he confessed.

Seated on the far end of the couch, Lazryn glanced over his shoulder at the girl. "It may seem harsh, her sentence, but it is far less severe than what she is capable of. For the malice they perpetuated upon the twins and the girl, I do believe she showed incredible restraint today."

Running his hands through his hair, Larkin sighed. "She pulled their memories of the attack deep inside herself. I worry about what that's going to do to her."

"One may only speculate as to her reasons for doing so, but I believe she did not want her friends to relive any part of their nightmare," Lazryn offered.

~ 320 ~

Larkin knocked on the window, attempting to gain her attention. When she continued to stare at the water, he headed toward the French doors. "I think you're right about that, but I'm betting there's something more to it."

When the doors opened, Taryn glanced up.

"I know you wanted to be alone, but there's something I need to understand," he stated, grabbing a chair and pulling it close to hers.

She shrugged. "And what's that?"

"I know you, Taryn, and I know that you wouldn't want Sydney, Brannyn or Brysyn to suffer." He paused, leaning in closer. "But something tells me that is not the only reason you removed their memories."

Taryn leaned back, resting her arms at her side. "When I saw Sydney lying there broken, all I could think about was Andalyn. She was so small and helpless, yet she suffered so terribly during her short life."

Placing his hand on her knee, he gave it a gentle squeeze. "What happened to her was terrible. But today you saved Syd and the twins. That's where your focus needs to be. Not on the past or something you can't change."

Her jaw drew up tight. "I was right here, Larkin, and I did nothing to save her." She paused, rising from her seat. "Everything inside of me was screaming that something was off, and I still failed to save her."

"You cannot carry the weight of the world on your shoulders. None of us can." He paused, jumping to his feet and moving closer to her. "The guilt of her death doesn't rest on you, Taryn."

Her face soured. "Guilt no longer resides within me. But whatever this is I'm feeling...I welcome it."

Larkin locked his eyes with hers, taking in the internal chaos churning inside. For several long moments, he remained quiet until finally shaking his head. "I get it. Holding onto the memories of their suffering helps you to accept what you did today," he stated, his words barely above a whisper.

"What they did to Sydney and the twins was beyond savage. Yet nearly all of them stood by watching with smiles on their faces as our friends were beaten, burned, whipped, and bled within a millimeter of their lives." She paused, turning away from him. As she did, the water in the pool swelled. "I wanted them all dead for what they did to our friends."

He glanced over at the churning wall of water rising from the pool. "Did you not see each one of the faces at Ibrym's today? They all wanted the guilty parties dead, too. And do you want to know why?" he questioned, grabbing hold of her wrists. "It's because someone they loved and cared for was nearly murdered and then dropped off on their doorsteps as some sick and twisted gift."

Taryn turned away, looking toward the woods. "A split second is all it would take for me to end a person's life. One irrational thought. One moment of losing control." She paused, taking a deep breath. As she inhaled, the trees began to pop and crack as their tops bowed over, nearly touching the ground. "Do you understand how simple it would be for me to wipe out their entire community? To erase them from existence?" She paused again, turning to face him. "I can never allow myself to cross that line. Lines can become blurred and then there are no boundaries."

"That's so cool, Taryn," Andyn shouted as he came around the corner of the house with Dedrick by his side.

The boy with dark curls and green eyes peaked around the wall of churning water and shrugged nervously. "Yeah. Cool," he repeated.

Taryn's eyes briefly flickered between green and blue before returning to their normal emerald green color. The trees immediately sprang upright while the water from the pool fell back into its well with a large splash, soaking both boys.

Andyn looked at Taryn, then to Dedrick. A moment later, he burst with deep-hearted laughter, wrapping his arm around his friend's neck. "My sister is the best, man," he grinned.

A faint smile appeared on Taryn's face. "He sounds more like Kellan every day." She paused, the glint of happiness disappearing. "I'm not sure how to tell him about Sydney. He's going to want to see her right away."

"Will she be awake?" Larkin asked.

"Before we left, I made sure she wouldn't wake up until tomorrow morning. I'm hoping everyone will settle down by then. I didn't want her hit with a wrecking ball of emotions," she explained.

From the other side of the pool, Andyn waved. "Are you guys up for a swim?"

"What are you going to do?" Larkin whispered.

Taryn glanced to Andyn then back to Larkin with a twinkle in her eye. "The only thing we can do right now. Go for a swim," she replied with a tender smile.

Taking Larkin's hand, Taryn tilted her head, and the couple took a few long steps and jumped into the pool. Andyn's laughter once more filled the air, followed by the sound of more water splashing.

ഇരുഗ്ഇരുഗ്

Standing off to the side, Theron watched as the graduates posed in their caps and gowns while their friends filled in around them. He shrugged his shoulders, sending his daughter another pleading look.

"Mom, did you get the picture?" Taryn asked, glancing around at her friends.

The beautiful blond woman fumbled with her camera until the image appeared on the small viewing screen. Her shoulders dropped. "Kellan was making a face, and Thorne's eyes were closed," she sighed, her disappointment obvious to all.

"I wouldn't be making faces if I wasn't standing next to Gerrick," Kellan explained.

Walking toward them on the sidewalk, Gastyn waved his arms. "Now I would normally insist you not do what I am about to suggest, but this is for the sake of staying on schedule. Taryn, would you please assist your mother in capturing a proper photograph?" he stated.

She glanced over her shoulders. "Are you guys okay with that?"

"If it means those of us who already graduated can go find a seat, then count me in," Dalen replied with a smile. "No offense, Mrs. Knight."

"None taken," she replied with a soft smile.

"Okay guys, I'll make it quick," Taryn announced.

She pulsed her Influence onto her friends. Almost instantly, they all fell into place. Their eyes looked straight ahead, while warm smiles curled on their faces. In a matter of seconds, the chaos that had once reigned went silent, and Gracyn began snapping dozens of photos.

After a few minutes, Taryn cocked her head with arched brows. "Are we good now?" she asked.

Gracyn's cheeks turned rosy pink as she lowered the camera. "Of course. I think I'll have enough," she replied.

Taryn withdrew her Influence from her friends. "Are you guys cool if my mom takes a few candid shots?"

Kellan looked around the group with arched brows, then to Taryn. "Sure. We're in."

Gracyn and the other parents snapped several more photographs before Gastyn insisted the current graduates needed to fall in line.

Taryn and Larkin held hands as they walked down the sidewalk toward their places.

"The kid really stepped up with Sydney," Larkin stated, while glancing over his shoulder at the young couple.

She shrugged. "After I explained to him that Syd was targeted in an attack, the first question he asked me was if I had taken away her memories."

He unlaced their fingers and slid his hand around her waist. "Because of what he and Andalyn went through?"

Taryn nodded. "It took him back to that dark period of time in his life. I lessened his memories…I didn't remove them all."

"He looks like he's in a good place now," Larkin shared.

"We talked about what happened to Karvyn and Ardyn. I reminded him that neither one was alive. So they could never hurt him again," she stated, leaning her head into him as she took her place in line.

Larkin repositioned himself to stand in front of her. He cupped her cheeks and smiled. "Andyn's a lucky guy to have you looking out for him." He paused, straightening her tilted cap. "In less than an hour, we will be free to do as we please. To go wherever you want, Tare-Bear."

She grinned. "But first we have to survive our graduation party."

Larkin shrugged. "As long as I get to steal you away for a little while, I'll be happy."

"I'm yours forever," she replied.

"Mr. Taylor, please fall into line," Gastyn said with a stern voice as he headed in their direction.

"I'll see you in a few," he smiled, kissing her on the cheek before hurrying back to his place in line.

Gastyn flashed a playful smile as he passed by the girl on his way to corral a few of the other students.

ဆဝ‍ဃ‍ဆဝ‍ဃ

After listening to the school choir sing and the principal and valedictorian both give their speeches, the graduates rose from their seats. In an orderly fashion, the seniors made their way to the stage.

Taryn stared at the many friendly faces in the crowd smiling up at her and the others. It warmed her heart to see Lazryn sitting between Hava Love and her mother.

When her name was called, Taryn walked across the stage. Cheers erupted. A blush warmed her cheeks as she reached out to accept her diploma and shake the principal's hand.

As she paused, giving her mother time to take a picture, she sensed a change in the air.

"Hello, dear one," a familiar voice stated.

Her eyes immediately darted to the man whose hand she was holding. "Farren, why are you here?" she asked.

His swirling eyes softened. "You know what cause permits me to be visible to you."

The teen's jaw drew tight. "If you've come to claim someone I care about, it's not going to happen," she warned.

A slight smile crept across his face. "You are fierce as always, my child."

Taryn's eyes locked on his. "Speaking of children. Was it you who fathered a child by the name of Maertas?"

"So it is true, you have indeed found the Harp of Life," he stated, his tone void of emotion.

Her brows furrowed. "Is Maertas your son?"

"He was a purposeful selection, created to do what we as Immortals cannot," Farren disclosed.

Taryn shook her head. "What's that supposed to mean, Deadman?"

Death drew her in closer, his breath caressing her cheek as he whispered. "Calista was a mighty beauty whose internal strength hid far beneath her ethereal glow. Her mother's jealousy did not come naturally. It only surfaced after the seed was planted."

"Farren knows he is not welcome to join our game. His interference will cost you dearly, just as it cost the brother and sister from Kansas their lives," an angry, but familiar voice warned.

Taryn pulled back, finding herself face to hood with the cloaked man. She jerked her hand, but could not break free of his hold.

"I'm not afraid of you," she replied sharply.

"Perhaps not, dearest Taryn. However, I never said you should fear only me," he laughed.

Taryn glanced over her shoulder to her friends and family. Each rose from their seats holding out a chess piece in front of them.

"Who shall it be, Taryn? Who shall be the first piece to fall from the board?" He paused, disappearing only to reappear seconds later between her two mothers. "The little girl and the twin brothers came extremely close to owning the honor. But perhaps it is best reserved for one, or both of these lovely ladies."

As the teen started to respond, she found herself shaking the high school principal's hand once more. At that precise moment, her mother snapped a picture of her.

Taryn forced a smile and hurried off the stage.

․ℂℎℎℂ․

Lounging poolside, Taryn and the other girls soaked up the sun's rays as the adults prepared a massive feast to celebrate the many graduates.

"What are you and Larkin going to do now that you've completed high school?" Bency asked.

She shrugged. "I was thinking about setting a schedule and visiting all of the planes each month."

Nalani propped herself up on her elbows, giving Taryn a questioning look. "Seriously, Kansas, you just graduated. You should be making plans to go explore the world instead of worrying about making a schedule to babysit a bunch of ingrates."

Rolling onto her back, Taryn looked up at the clear sky. "You act like I attended school faithfully every day. I barely showed, and when I did, my mind was anywhere but there."

"You don't owe anyone an explanation, Taryn," Dagney stated, repositioning herself on her towel. "Whatever you and Larkin choose to do, just make sure you schedule some alone time for the two of you."

"Isn't there anything you want to do?" Bency asked.

"You know, there is something," she replied, hopping up from her towel and heading toward the house.

"Um, I didn't mean this exact moment," Bency called out.

Nalani and the twins chuckled as the others returned to their tanning.

ꕥ

"Are you certain you want to do this today?" Lazryn asked.

Taryn nodded.

Larkin glanced between the two. "Taryn, we can do this another time. Besides, Ilya would want to come too," he stated.

"No one else needs to know where we're going. There's something I need to see for myself, and the less people who know, the better," she replied.

With a heavy sigh, Lazryn lifted his hand. "For the lady, one Adora Gateway to Galatia, Kansas," he stated, giving a slight bow.

"Don't pout, Laz. It really doesn't suit you," she replied, stepping toward the opening.

Larkin moved to her side, taking her hand in his. "Care to provide a hint as to what you're looking for?"

"Sure, when I figure it out for myself you'll be the first person I tell," she sighed.

The two men shared a cautious glance before Taryn disappeared into the doorway.

ꕥ

Stepping out on the other side, Taryn found herself standing near the salvage yard. Running her fingers along the old wooden fence, memories from her childhood came rushing back.

Noting the smile flickering on his love's face, Larkin stepped directly in front of her. "Of all the days we could have come here, you choose today. Why?"

Taryn took a deep breath. "Today during graduation when I was accepting my diploma, Farren came to me."

The teen's brows arched. "Farren?"

She nodded as Lazryn stepped closer.

"Did he say who he was there to collect?" Lazryn inquired.

"No…and he wasn't the only one to pay me a visit," she stated.

Larkin stepped closer. "Seriously, Taryn, you're just now telling us about it?" he admonished.

She rolled her eyes. "Look, he was angry that Farren showed himself to me. He made a few threats and…well, that's why we're here."

Drawing his jaw tight with his nostrils flaring, Larkin released a hefty sigh. "If I didn't love you the way that I do…ugh," he growled.

"You're going to have to get over it. What's done is done. I can't change the past," she replied, pushing past him.

Larkin looked to the former Mortari. "She's maddening," he sighed.

Smiling, Lazryn patted him on the shoulder. "The good ones usually are."

Rolling his eyes, Larkin turned, trailing after them.

As they walked through the quiet little town, Taryn said nothing. One-by-one people emerged from their homes, loading up their families into their vehicles and driving south.

"Where are they all headed?" Larkin asked.

Keeping her course, Taryn pointed southeast. "There's a mom and pop burger and ice cream stand about twenty-five miles from here. This will be easier if they're all gone," she stated.

"What exactly will be easier?" he asked.

"I need access to the home I shared with Ilya. There may be something there that I couldn't see before. Something that might help to answer at least some of my questions," Taryn explained.

Larkin placed his hand on the small of her back as they pressed forward.

Arriving at Taryn's childhood home, the trio lingered outside the front door briefly before entering.

"Wow. This place is so small. How did Ilya ever expect to keep you and your gifts contained in here?" Larkin asked.

"It was wise of her to bring Taryn to Galatia," Lazryn stated. "The nearest interstate is miles away, and there isn't much else to bring outsiders here unless they are farmers. With the unpredictable Kansas weather, it made the perfect hiding place for her."

As Taryn listened to her friend explain, she found his voice fading and another taking its place.

"The task is complete, Brother," Thantos stated.

"The girl's father, sibling, and cousin are no longer in harm's way. Her uncle retains his memories, but I have hidden them from those who may try to gain access. He is the keeper of our secrets, at great sacrifice to himself," Farren replied.

"And you are certain he will not fail us?" Thantos questioned.

"Her blood runs through his veins. Though he may not be as gifted as she, he does possess a certain quality and place within their society that will keep them safe until she awakens," Farren responded.

Silence lingered in the air for several moments.

"Brother," Thantos whispered. "This girl, are you certain she is the one?"

"I have watched her while still inside her mother's womb. This child is the one he has longed for. Her gifts and heightened emotions are the ultimate weapon against all living creatures. Should he claim her, nothing will survive," Death replied.

Only able to hear the conversation and not see either of the men, Taryn listened intently, waiting for the brief silence to pass.

"What makes this child so different from the others?" Thantos asked.

"Before taking her first breath, this child willingly gave her heart to another. They are forever bound to one another. He to her, and she to him," Farren stated.

Taryn's eyes opened wide as she returned to Larkin and Lazryn's conversation.

"Well, do you know, Taryn?" Larkin questioned.

Walking between the two, she headed toward the short hallway. "Do I know what?" she asked.

"Where the marks on the baseboards came from," he stated.

Taryn paused in her step, kneeling onto the wood floor. She ran her fingers across the old trim. "I never noticed them before," she replied.

He knelt beside her. "While we were in the living room, they just sort of appeared."

"Farren marked the house with them before Ilya and I moved in. I think they were meant to help keep us hidden," she stated.

Lazryn eyed the teen. "How is it you are so certain?"

Rising to her feet, Taryn glanced at her friend. "Well, since I just listened to a conversation between him and one of his half-brothers, I would say that's how."

"You had a vision?" Larkin asked.

She shook her head. "No. I couldn't see anything, but I heard enough."

With the guys looking on, their eyes laden with questions, Taryn took a deep breath and headed into her former bedroom.

As she entered, thousands of unpleasant memories came rushing back to the forefront of her mind. Her mouth tasted of bitterness.

"Taryn?" Larkin questioned, sensing the change in her mood.

She held her hand up, waving him back. "Please. I need a few moments to myself."

He stood in the doorway, his hand against the wooden frame, staring at her. His heartache mirrored her own, knowing she had been here, hidden away from him for so long.

"Sure, Tare-Bear. I'll go wait in the kitchen with Lazryn until you're ready to talk.

The moment his eyes left her, the teen fell to her knees. Her chest tightened, feeling as though she could not breathe. Her head spun, recalling all the lonely nights she had cried herself to sleep in this very room. Allowing the raw emotion to flow through her, Taryn lay on the floor and stared blankly at the ceiling.

꿍ൠ꿍ൠ

Coyan stood before a select group made up of more than one hundred of the Mortari's finest Elementals. "The time has come my faithful ones, for us to rise up and reclaim what is rightfully ours. For far too long we have remained idle, biding our time for the perfect opportunity to strike at the heart of our enemy." He paused, looking to where his wife and Nodryck stood with wide smiles upon their faces, and nodded in acknowledgement. "I make this solemn vow that within two days' time, Taryn Knight and her family will no longer be a thorn in our side. We will once more rule the planes and take what we want. Do what it is we want. And yes, my children, we will murder as we want."

Cheers erupted from the crowd. After a few moments passed, Coyan motioned for them to quiet down.

"Now I am certain that most of you are curious as to how we go about ending the girl who cannot be defeated." He paused, watching as several heads began to bob. "We incite her rage by going after her family. She will be frenzied with emotion. And when she comes seeking revenge, we will inundate her with thousands of lightning bolts, guaranteed to drain even the most stubborn of Gaias."

More cheers filled the air as he looked to his wife once more.

Tedra stepped closer to the crowd, silencing them instantly. "Bring out the beast," she shouted.

A few moments later, the large double doors opened wide, displaying the menacing monster that waited to unleash his own form of vengeance.

Gasps filled the air while numerous Mortari pointed their hands at the beast standing before them.

Tedra looked to Nodryck and grinned. "Do not tell me that you are unable to recognize the man beneath the monster."

Nodryck moved closer to get a better look. After a few seconds, the beast's eyes met his. A slow smile bloomed across his face. "The teen queen is going to be beside herself when she lays her eyes upon her creation."

"I may have had a slight hand in his final transformation. However, we will give her sole recognition. It will only fuel her impending downward spiral," Tedra replied.

"And what of your brother-in-laws?" he inquired.

The dangerously beautiful woman smiled wildly. "Clad will comply, as he has no other choice. But Chrystian on the other hand, I will be eager to see where his cards fall when all is said and done."

ଽଔଔଔ

Taryn walked into the kitchen, joining Larkin and Lazryn at the small round wooden table.

"Did you find what you were looking for?" Lazryn asked.

She shook her head. "No. I don't think so."

"Are you ready to head back to Williams? You know your mother was probably devastated when she realized we left without saying anything," Larkin stated.

Taryn knew he was right about Gracyn and Ilya both, but she wasn't ready to leave without finding what it was that called to her.

Suddenly the teen rose from her chair. She walked over to the sliding glass doors and stared at the house next door.

Larkin stepped up behind her. "What is it?"

"Can't you feel that?" she asked, placing her hands flat against the glass.

He shook his head and glanced back at the table toward Lazryn.

"Words cannot express how disgusted I am by the part that I played in their demise," the man stated, hanging his head low.

"It wasn't by your free will, Lazryn. You were Influenced, and had no other choice but to take the boy and girl to Coyan," Taryn replied.

Lazryn leaned back in his seat. "It makes me no less guilty. I should have left their company long ago, but I held onto the hope that Chrystian would someday join me." He paused, looking at the girl. "Did you feel that?"

In a blur, Taryn opened the sliding glass door and disappeared through it.

"What's going on?" Larkin questioned.

Lazryn waved the teen to go outside as he trailed close behind. "There is someone in the house next door."

"I don't feel the presence of anyone except for you and Taryn," Larkin stated, his eyes widening.

In a flash, both men rushed to find Taryn.

Inside the house next door, the girl stood at the foot of a twin-sized bed. A heartbreaking song played from the freshly wound music box sitting atop a nearby dresser.

"What is it, Taryn?" Larkin asked.

She turned around and within her hand she held a black pawn figurine. "We need to go home, now," she stated, her tone dripping with urgency.

Inside the pink and purple bedroom, Lazryn opened a gateway to Williams.

Taryn placed the chess piece in her pants pocket, glancing between the two men before rushing through the portal.

CHAPTER EIGHTEEN

Taryn's eyes widened as she stepped through the gateway, taking in the scene unfolding around her. Wind swirled violently around her while numerous power orbs flew through the air in both directions. Andyn's dragon, Iggy, circled overhead, breathing fire in the direction of an unseen threat.

Hearing the terrified screams of her loved ones sparked life into a part of Taryn that she believed no longer existed. Their cries brought to the surface the pain and anguish of all those she had witnessed murdered during her time with the Mortari. Sydney, Brysyn and Brannyn's torture played fresh in her mind. Her eyes turned the color of a golden fire as she focused in on those most frightened. In an instant, she was standing in front of Andyn, taking in his wide eyes and newly resurfaced pain.

"You said he was dead, Taryn. You promised," he screamed.

Sensing a powerful orb heading in her direction, Taryn turned, holding her hand out, stopping it in the air.

From behind Andyn, Dedrick's eyes widened watching the girl in action.

Within the tree line, a bestial howl thundered above the chaos.

"Ardyn Mitchell. How's this possible?" she growled, turning the orb to dust.

"He's here for the kid. Take Andyn and run," Kellan yelled in her direction.

The girl turned her focus back to Andyn. "I promised you he would never hurt you again, little brother. And I intend to keep that promise."

Having lobbed another massive orb in the monster's direction, Gastyn grabbed hold of Taryn. "This creature is not the same as the man you once faced. He is the very essence of evil."

Maxym limped over to where they stood. "Whatever he's become, he doesn't seem to feel pain, and his orbs are covered with thousands of pins that burrow deep beneath the surface of your skin." He grimaced while grabbing hold of his thigh. "He's managed to land a blow on at least half of us. I'm not sure how much more we can take."

Scanning the open space, Taryn watched as her friends began to fall one-by-one, struck by the beast's current onslaught of orbs. Andalyn's pained cries flooded her ears, and images of the horrific torture the little girl and her brother had experienced at the hands of this monster and Karvyn rushed back, sending her crashing onto her knees. The overwhelming fear Sydney had felt during her attack rose like acid in her throat.

Taking their suffering into her heart, Taryn made it her own. Her eyes flickered between colors until they turned a shimmering blood red. She rose to her feet and screamed, "No more."

Jumping out from the shadows, the man-beast roared deeply with laughter. His eyes were black as night as he rushed towards Andyn.

In a blur, Taryn moved to stop him. As she did, a powerful orb slammed into her petite frame. It was unlike anything she had ever felt before, and it sent her flying through the air until she crashed into a nearby tree.

The sky turned dark as night as lightning crackled furiously overhead. Regaining her footing, Taryn cracked her neck from side to side. With a snarl on her face, she rushed back in. "Chrystian," she thundered.

Nearing the man as he stood behind the beast, the fire in Taryn's veins weakened. She watched as Chrystian pulled one hand back while pushing Ardyn to the ground with the other. The girl's eyes widened.

Within his hand, Chrystian held the still beating heart of the beast.

Lazryn and Larkin looked on protectively as Taryn stepped closer to the intense Mortari.

"I was going to," she began, but the remainder of her words caught in her throat.

Chrystian stretched his fingers on the hand holding the heart. Instantly, the bloody organ caught fire, turning to ash. With an arched brow, he blew the remaining ashes from his hand.

Taryn glanced down at the lifeless body resting at her feet and then back to him. "Why? Why did you stop me?" she asked.

"He was never your monster to slay." Chrystian paused, stepping over the dead man's deformed arm and cupping her cheek. "You are the light within the darkness. The hope within my heart." He paused again, kissing her forehead. "In this moment, it is your loved ones that require your care."

She grabbed his wrist. "What about you? Coyan's going to be furious that you interfered."

"I will handle my brother and his wretched wife," he assured her.

Taryn's nostrils flared. "I swear, if they do anything to you."

Sweeping her hair back from her face, he smiled tenderly. "Our paths were always destined to intertwine. Tonight will not be the last you see of me." He paused, pulling her into a fierce hug. "I love you, sweet Taryn. But now it is time for me to face the consequences of my decisions, and for you and my brother-in-law to Heal your wounded." He pressed his lips against her ear and whispered, "You must play the harp and open yourself to the understanding of your true destiny."

Taryn pulled back, her eyes locked on his. For a brief moment, she felt the immensity of his love engulfing her. "Chrystian?"

"Heal your family and strum the melody," he replied, before disappearing like a blur.

Having been watching from nearby while checking on his friends and family, Larkin's heart ached seeing the torment dancing between his love and her friend.

Lazryn knelt opposing Larkin on the other side of Kalil who was writhing in pain. He placed one hand over the man's heart while resting the other firmly against the ground. Drawing life from the earth, he pushed it into the injured man. "His love for her ascends far beyond what our eyes are able to see. He would do anything to protect her, and I fear it may cost my friend his life," Lazryn stated as he glanced between the boy and his girl.

"I may not like him, but I am grateful that he intervened," Larkin sighed, before turning his attention to Lucan who lay wounded nearby.

Taryn turned, looking at the numerous injured scattered about the backyard. She lifted her hands, holding them shoulder height and closed her eyes. Listening to their rapid heartbeats, she spread her gift of Healing over them all. Within seconds, calm returned to each of the injured and their wounds were no more.

Rising to his feet, Keiryn rubbed his temples. After a few moments, he looked to his sister. "I don't understand what happened."

Taryn appeared at his side in a blur and whispered. "You were the greatest threat, so he removed you from the equation."

"But he never struck me. Not even once," Keiryn mumbled.

She turned, locking eyes with him. "I'm not talking about Ardyn."

His spine straightened. "It was him, the cloaked man from your visions."

Taryn nodded.

"He's not going to stop is he?" Keiryn questioned.

"No. I'm afraid not," she replied.

Standing inside the secret cave hidden within the walls of the Grand Canyon, Lazryn stood with furrowed brows. "Are you certain this is what you want to do, Taryn?"

Looking down at the harp, she shrugged. "Need trumps want, so I'm doing this with or without your blessing."

Larkin placed his hand on her shoulder. "Take it easy, Tare-Bear. You know grandpa is going to help, but he's trying to look out for you."

Lazryn barely arched a brow at the teen's jab at his age.

"I know. I'm sorry, Lazryn," she sighed.

"Your thoughts are with Chrystian, as are mine. He made a conscious decision to intervene, and it may cost him dearly. But it is as I had said before, my remaining allies within their ranks will notify me if Coyan or the others decide to act against him," he reassured her.

Taryn lifted the harp, studying the strings. "He didn't have to do what he did."

"Ardyn was no longer a man, but still his death at your hands would have weighed heavily upon your young shoulders," Lazryn reasoned.

She lowered the instrument and stared at her friend. "And what do you think will happen if they harm Chrystian? Do you think I will shoulder that burden any less?"

Larkin stepped in front of her. "That's not what he's saying, Taryn, and you know it. You're still on edge from whatever it was you overheard back in Galatia. I can feel the emotions churning inside you even though you've said nothing about it."

Leaning into him, Taryn took a deep breath recalling Farren's words. *Before taking her first breath, this child willingly gave her heart to another. They are forever bound to one another. He to her and she to him.*

"Everything is blurring together, and nothing makes sense. One vision tells this story while another shows something else." She paused, taking a deep breath and straightening herself. She glanced between the two. "He is one step ahead, and he's winning."

Lazryn stared at her in silence.

"Please go and keep watch over our friends," she stated.

The man nodded. "I will return every quarter hour to check in on you."

"It means a lot knowing you will be there watching over them," Larkin stated.

"You keep your eyes on our girl here, and I will take care of the others," Lazryn replied before disappearing into the open portal.

Larkin looked to Taryn. "Are you ready?"

Nodding, she knelt onto the ground with the harp in hand. Expecting to fall when the vision took over, she positioned herself carefully.

"Larkin."

"Yeah?" he replied.

"Regardless of whatever happens when I play this harp, I want you to know that I love you with all my heart," she stated.

Before settling in behind her, he kissed her cheek. "I love you, too."

Having no idea of how to play a harp, Taryn closed her eyes and fumbled her fingertips over the strings. The string's pitch pierced the air, sending chills up and down Taryn's spine. Her fingers began to find their own way, strumming the chords in a curious manner, filling the hidden space with a beautiful sound.

Taryn's body began to sway as her mind drifted further into the sound. Her feet began to float until she found herself standing in a dark tunnel.

"Hello," she called out. When no one answered, she took a step forward.

After several seconds passed, flickers of light began to appear in the distance. As she stood watching, they moved closer to her, growing larger as they neared. Her eyes narrowed, seeing the outline of various faces within each flicker of light.

"What do you want from me?" she asked.

No sooner had the words left her mouth, Taryn found herself engulfed in their glow. The light so blinding that she had to lift her forearm to shield her eyes.

When the light faded, the girl slowly lowered her arm while scanning the area. There she spied a small room with four simple straw walls and a thatched roof. The furnishings were meager. Along one of the walls was a mound of freshly placed dirt. The horrendous smell caused her to gag.

As she walked to the doorway, a young boy with pale, blonde hair rushed inside. He ran to one of the corners and collapsed as tears streamed down his cheeks.

Taryn approached the small child, his emotions washing over her like a tidal wave. She reached out her hand to comfort him, but he could not feel her touch.

"You boy, come here," a young woman's voice called from the doorway.

"Please do not beat me," he cried, covering his head.

Stepping back, Taryn watched as a blonde girl who appeared no more than eighteen stepped closer.

Wrinkling her nose as the stench permeated her sinus cavity, the woman stood over the boy. "Why did you take the apple from the market place?" she asked.

Still cowering with his head covered, the boy trembled with fear. "I have no food of my own," he answered.

"What of your mother and father?" she questioned.

He shook his head. "I have no father, and my mother died last week."

Kneeling down, the woman tilted her head from side to side. She reached her hand down and stroked the boy's pale locks. "Is that your mother over there?" she stated, pointing to the fresh mound of dirt.

The boy looked up at her with tears flooding his intense green eyes. "I did not know what else to do, and I have no one to help me."

Assisting him to sit, the woman caressed his cheek. "For someone so tiny and frail, you are also brave, Colyn."

His eyes widened. "Do you know me?"

She smiled, pulling a juicy red apple from a small leather satchel. "We are all brothers and sisters in this life."

The boy's gaze fell upon the tender fruit. "May I, please?"

She nodded, placing the apple firmly in his hand.

Colyn quickly devoured the fruit then wiped his mouth with his dirty sleeve.

"Are you still hungry?" she asked.

The boy nodded.

From within her bag, she pulled out another juicy red apple and handed it to the boy.

As with the first, he devoured the second piece of fruit. Leaning his back against the wall, he stared at the pile of dirt. "I have no one," he whispered.

The woman smiled wildly. "That is untrue. Now you have me, and I will make all your dreams come true."

Colyn looked up at the woman. "Will you be my mother?"

She shook her head. "I have a family who has dreamt of having a little boy just like you."

The child's brows furrowed. "A family?"

"If that is what you want, it shall be yours," she replied.

He glanced to his mother's grave, his eyes laden with sadness.

"She would want this for you, Colyn. You will have all the things she could dream for you. All you need do is accompany me on a seven-day journey to your new home," the woman explained.

"But what will we eat?" he asked.

The beautiful blonde held her hand palm down just above the ground. Within seconds a small vine broke through the crusty soil.

The leaves on the plant grew and blossoms appeared. After less than a minute, a ripe watermelon sat at the boy's feet.

With his jaw agape, the boy backed into the wall. His eyes wide with fear. "You, you're a witch."

"I am no witch, Colyn. But like you, I am Gaias born," she replied, creating a thin blade with her Imperium power and slicing the watermelon in half.

"No. I am nothing but a lowly beggar. I have no powers inside of me," he responded.

She shook her head. "My sweet boy, that is simply untrue. You see, those men from the marketplace intended to cut off your hands as punishment for your attempted thievery. But it was your gift of Influence that spurred their change of heart."

"But I did not do anything," the boy stated.

"You are only seven years of age. Yet when you placed your hands upon those grown men, they had no other choice than to follow your will," she shared.

Colyn held up his hands, eyeing them carefully. "The power comes from my hands?" he asked.

"The power comes from a place deep within you. It requires a pathway to leave your body, and for all Gaias, that is through our hands and fingertips," she disclosed.

"Was my mother a Gaias?" Colyn questioned.

"She was an Animator. But these are bits of information I could share with you along our journey to meet your new family. Should you decide that is what you want," she purred.

The boy's brilliant green eyes mirrored her emerald ones as he nodded.

"Then let us be off," she smiled.

Something about the beautiful woman struck Taryn as odd. *What is her name?* she wondered silently.

Taryn watched as the woman rose to her feet and extended the boy her hand. Colyn eagerly accepted and the pair began walking. Pausing in the doorway, the boy glanced over his shoulder to the mound of dirt and smiled tenderly.

With the small room to herself, the teen walked over to the mound of dirt and knelt down. "Something's not right here. It makes me wonder what happened to you?" she stated aloud.

After a few moments, she rose to her feet. When she turned around, a half-rotted corpse of a woman stood before her. Without any time to react, Taryn found herself being gripped on her wrists by the living dead woman.

"You will know my fate," the dead woman whispered.

Suddenly, Taryn could see a vision of the woman tucking Colyn beneath a thin blanket. She sang the boy to sleep before leaving their hut. The woman crept past a few houses until she came to a large willowy tree not far in the distance.

From the darkness a familiar young woman with blonde hair and green eyes appeared. Without a word, Colyn's mother fell victim to the woman's Influence.

With hollow eyes, she led the woman back to the shack she shared with her son. Once inside, the blonde woman grinned wickedly. Placing her hand over the mother's chest, she began stealing her gifts until the woman's heart beat no more and her skin turned pale grey.

Taryn blinked and found herself standing on a sandy beach as two people splashed about in the waters in front of her. As the pair approached, she noted the long, thin white garment each wore. Both had hair kissed by the sun and emerald green eyes.

"Please, Ardet, the Elder Council?" one girl questioned the other.

Ardet splashed her. "They would be fools not to consider you, Elanya."

Bile rose in the back of Taryn's throat. *Elanya Delrayn*, she groaned to herself.

"Think about it. If you could find a way to use your gifts to tie those who are Afflicted to the Elder Council's desires, you would be a legend amongst our kind," Ardet gushed.

Elanya laughed. "And how do you purpose I accomplish such a feat?"

With a mischievous smile on her face, Ardet grabbed Elanya by the hand. She led her past Taryn to where the rest of their clothes waited. "Sit with me," Ardet said, patting the sand beside her.

"I need to return home before my mother begins to worry," Elanya stated while taking a seat.

Reaching into a cloth sack, Ardet pulled out a small book and held it in front of her friend.

"What is it?" Elanya asked.

Ardet smiled. "A gift from someone who understands the particular nature of your gifts."

Taking it from her hands, Elanya opened the book and began skimming through it. After only a few pages, she set the book in her lap and turned to her friend. "Did you read this?" she asked.

"No. It is a gift for you, not me. Besides, I do not possess half your strength," she replied.

Elanya sat silent.

"Why not take a few days to study the book's contents. Then if you feel confident, I will speak to my contact with the Elder Council on your behalf," Ardet offered.

The girl nodded. "Yes. A few days would be nice."

Patting her friend on the knee, Ardet rose to her feet. "I had better get home before I am missed."

Elanya smiled faintly giving another nod.

"Do not linger here long, my friend. A girl all by herself near dusk makes an easy target for the Mortari," Ardet stated before covering her mouth with her hands. She watched as a familiar sadness washed over her friends face. "My apologies, Elanya. I did not intend to stir memories of your father's death."

The girl shrugged. "It was an honest mistake."

"I am truly sorry," she replied, before taking her leave.

With her friend gone, Elanya sighed and opened the book once more. This time she consumed every word upon its pages.

The sound of nearby screams pulled the girl from her studies. Jumping to her feet, Elanya slipped her dress over her still damp undercoat. She tucked the book inside the top of her dress and quietly crept in the direction of the screams.

Curiously, Taryn followed behind her.

Nearing an open field, Elanya spied two men draining her friend of her gifts. Ducking behind a nearby bush, she held her breath, drawing her gifts in close.

After several moments passed, she felt the absence of the awful men. Rising to her feet, Elanya ran to her friend. Seeing Ardet's lifeless body laying before her caused a stirring within her.

"What is going on here?" a strange man called out from atop a nearby hill.

"My friend, she's been murdered by the Mortari," she cried.

In a flash, the two men appeared by her side. "Most likely the pair we have been tracking," one commented.

Elanya pulled Ardet's head into her lap. Caressing her cold cheeks, tears flowed from the girl's eyes. "You should have done more. If you had, my friend would still be alive," she sobbed.

"While we are truly sorry for your loss, we simply cannot cover every inch of land on every known plane," the other explained.

Anger rushed through her veins, waking her need for vengeance. "You who are Afflicted should serve the Council and put down our enemies," she growled.

"You are obviously distraught, child. Perhaps we should accompany you home," one of the men suggested.

Watching their exchange, Taryn noticed Elanya's eyes flickering from green to red and back again.

Her father died at the hands of the Mortari and now her friend. It's no wonder she hated the Afflicted. She blamed them for their deaths, Taryn thought to herself.

The scene surrounding Taryn shifted, and the girl found herself standing in the midst of a pale blue fog.

"I know you're there. I can feel your presence," the teen stated.

"As I feel yours," a woman's voice whispered back.

Taking a step forward, Taryn made a slight sweeping motion with her hand, pushing the fog back several feet. "I played the harp and have witnessed a number of events from the past. But I still don't understand what any of it has to do with me."

The fog lowered and a woman wearing a sparkling white gown appeared.

"Calista," Taryn stated, her tone lacking any hint of surprise.

With a sly grin, the stunning woman moved nearer to the teen. "You know who I am, but do you know who you are?"

The teen sucked in a deep breath and smirked. "Why do all the dead people insist on speaking in riddles," she sighed.

Calista disappeared only to reappear behind the girl. "Do you know who you are?" she asked again, while tracing her hand over the teen's honey colored tresses.

"My name is Taryn Knight, and I come from Williams, Arizona on the Earthly plane," she stated.

The woman smiled softly. "I did not ask for your given name, as it does not define who you truly are."

Taryn shook her head slightly. "I don't understand what it is you're asking."

Moving to face the girl directly, the stunning woman reached out, placing her hand over the teen's heart. "You carry a fire inside that no other before you could survive. It is because of this; I know exactly who you are."

Remaining silent for a moment, Taryn stared at the woman. "You believe that I am the one who will be the undoing of Maertas's father."

Withdrawing her hand from the girl's heart, Calista took a step back. "I do."

"And what happens should I fail?" Taryn questioned.

"My darling, the blood that courses through your veins combined with your overwhelming sense of right versus wrong will not permit you to fail," Calista stated.

"But if I did, there would surely be a consequence," she replied.

The woman waved her hand in the air, stirring the nearby fog into an image of the harp. The teen watched as a new string formed at the rear of the instrument. "Your story would be claimed by the harp, and we would wait for the next great hope of our kind."

"Is that what each of the individuals were that I saw within the harp…they represent the past great hopes of Gaias kind?" Taryn asked.

"Yes, each represented a form of hope. But upon the grand stage of all the planes, only you wield all that is necessary to be victorious. Only you may determine your fate," Calista stated.

Taryn stood still, searching the woman's eyes.

"You are weary of the words I speak. But I assure you, Taryn, when the times comes, you will see clearly beyond the depths of your emotions," the stunning woman offered.

Taryn opened her mouth to speak but was immediately silenced as her eyesight faded. A white light appeared to her before giving way to numerous images from her past visions.

First several flashes from Maertas' childhood appeared. The horrific drownings, beatings and stretching he had endured replayed through her mind.

Next came Adora James. Taryn watched the numerous beatings the boys inflicted upon the girl as others looked on with wild smiles. A young woman in the background caught Taryn's eye. Before she could catch a good look at her, the images disappeared.

Malayne Douth's troubled images quickly filled the void. Taryn once more saw the mother and her young daughter that Malayne had spared. She also followed her on the journey to stop the ice age that was sure to consume Hypatia. As Malayne unknowingly snuffed out her brother's life, Taryn could not help looking back to the snow-covered valley. There she spotted the young girl, no longer accompanied by her mother, watching from afar.

Next came images of Colyn Danbrym sitting on the dirt floor of the small shack he and his mother had called home. She felt the sting from his tears as he buried his mother. When the strange woman appeared, she caught Taryn's eye. The teen stared at the young woman, sensing something familiar within her.

The images faded, giving way to Elanya Delrayn's life. Something about her friend Ardet struck Taryn as odd. When the teen watched the girl's face, she saw what appeared to be a flicker of change. One face that strongly resembled others she had seen before.

Before Taryn could give it any further thought, several windows opened in her mind, inundating all of her senses.

Images of a young man with dark curly hair and piercing green eyes appeared, highlighting what the teen could only assume was a progression of his life. Her mind tried keeping up with the numerous images, but there were too many. In one vision he was marrying a blonde woman, while in the next a red head. After taking in nearly three dozen similar images, they switched to that of a little blonde girl.

Taryn watched as the girl grew older, but was stunned when she noticed the girl following the curly haired man. Anger and jealousy rolled off the young girl in palpable waves.

Why is she so angry? Taryn thought to herself.

Seconds later the images disappeared, leaving the girl more confused than before.

"You know who they are, Taryn. Deep down inside your veins you know who you are," Calista whispered in her ear.

"Who are they to me?" the teen questioned.

As the last word fell from her lips, a series of images pulsed through her mind. Images of Maertan, her Uncle Julius, her mother, Ilya, Lazryn, Loryn, Jonesy, Ardyn, Karvyn, Andyn, Andalyn, Tedra,

Dagrin and several more that she did not recognize. Her pulse quickened as she tried to make sense of it all.

With the slideshow slowing, two final images appeared to her. One of a man with dark curly hair and another of a man with blue swirling irises.

Laertas Dominion and the man I saw in my backyard that first day when the cloaked stranger appeared, she mused.

Another image appeared. The man with the swirling irises held a baby boy within his arms. His smile was unnerving, sending chills coursing through Taryn's body.

Suddenly she heard familiar voices.

"She must wake now," Lazryn stated with great urgency.

"We don't know what will happen if we attempt to pull her from this vision," Larkin warned.

Lazryn growled into the air. "What do you think will happen should she wake to discover Chrystian has been executed, and we did not at least make an effort?"

Still on her knees, Taryn pulled her hands away from the harp's strings. "They're going to destroy Chrystian for stopping Ardyn," she stated while steadying herself.

Larkin placed his hands on her shoulders, easing her weariness. "One of Laz's allies reported that Chrystian is being tried for acts of treason against the Mortari, and for being a sympathizer to you."

Her heart rate increased and her eyes turned a glistening shade of blue. "Take me to Mors," she demanded.

"They are pulling witnesses in from all of the planes to speak against you," Lazryn warned.

Taryn rose to her feet. "Take me to Mors."

"Have you considered this may be exactly what they want?" Larkin insisted.

Glancing over her shoulder, Taryn's face lit with warning. "I'm going to save him with or without your support. You are the keeper of my heart, Larkin Taylor, so you above all should understand why this is not up for discussion."

Taking a deep breath, the young man nodded. "Just promise me you won't allow your emotions to lead."

She shrugged. "I'll try my best not to."

Lazryn opened a gateway and watched as Taryn and Larkin entered. Once they were through to the other side, he opened a second portal to Taryn's home.

CHAPTER NINETEEN

Perched atop a steep mountain, Larkin stared down at the ever-growing crowd in the valley below. "What are you planning to do?" he asked.

"I'm going to save Chrystian," she replied, her eyes returning to their normal shade of green. "Are you with me?"

Taking a deep breath, Larkin nodded. "I'd walk through fire for you."

A faint smile curled from her mouth before she motioned for him to follow. In a blur, Taryn ran toward her friend with Larkin following close behind.

Stopping a few yards in front of Chrystian, the girl looked him over as he lay on the ground. His ankles were shackled to a nearby boulder and his wrists bound with rondoring rope. He also sported two black eyes and gashes all over his body.

Sitting upon his throne between his wife and youngest brother, Coyan chuckled. "Ah, dearest Taryn, you never disappoint. I knew you would come for my brother."

A chilling smile curled on her face. "Who says I'm only here for Chrystian?"

Coyan's face soured. "He does not wear your symbol of protection. Therefore, we are permitted to handle my brother as we deem appropriate."

"If you truly believe that matters to me, then you are a bigger fool than I believed you to be," she retorted while closing the distance between herself and Chrystian. Dropping to her knees, she cupped his cheeks, forcing her gift of Healing deep within her injured friend.

Larkin stood back, watching her comfort the man. As he did, a gateway opened behind him and the entire Williams community exited it.

"What are you doing here?" Larkin asked as they gathered around him.

"Lazryn said Taryn needed us, so we came," Keiryn replied.

"Even though it's for Chrystian?" Larkin questioned.

Keiryn nodded. "For whatever reason, he's important to her, and that's good enough for me."

Larkin's face wrinkled. "Since when?"

He shrugged. "He intervened to spare my sister from killing a monster because he understood what it would do to her."

Lazryn joined Larkin and Keiryn. "I fear that he may have only postponed the inevitable. After today, nothing will ever be the same for any of us…especially Taryn."

"What makes you so sure?" Larkin questioned.

"Taryn will be forced to fight the Mortari to protect Chrystian. In the process, they will lose their lives and the girl we know will cease to exist," he reasoned.

Shaking his head, Keiryn exhaled loudly. "She can use her Influence against them."

"If she casts out her gifts, the weaker of their kind will latch onto her power. The temptation will be too much, and they will begin to draw from her, sealing their fate," Lazryn explained.

With clenched fists, Larkin glared at Coyan. "I won't let them do this to her."

"That is noble of you, but there is no other course of action for her to take. Their blood will forever mar her hands, and in turn, leave a stain upon her heart," Lazryn replied, his words heavy.

ଽଔଽଔ

With his wounds healed, Chrystian steadied himself as he looked around at the massive crowd that had gathered. When his eyes fell upon Taryn's face, he smiled softly. "For more than a thousand years, I have behaved in such a manner that should deny me the goodness of a friend such as you."

Shaking her head, Taryn caressed his cheek. "You were heartbroken over the loss of Loryn. Her sacrifice spared you from being her executioner, but it blinded you with sadness and despair. And while I understand, you know that I could never agree with your choices."

"Yet you choose to be here with me during my final moments," Chrystian replied.

"Enough," Coyan growled as he rose from his throne.

Tedra joined her husband. "Regardless of your opinion of my husband and his followers, Chrystian was agreeable to this course of punishment."

Taryn turned to her friend with furrowed brows. "Is this true?"

"I am afraid so. I knew my actions would have consequences, but to prevent you from taking a life I would do it a thousand times over," Chrystian revealed.

"You know that I won't allow this to happen," she replied, glaring at Tedra.

Reaching up, Chrystian ran his fingers down her cheek. "You look so much like my Loryn, and possess her feisty spirit as well."

Taryn's forehead creased. "You did this so you could be with her again."

"I did this for you, Taryn. For I know the truth of who you are, and the immensity of power that courses through your veins," he whispered.

Her eyes narrowed on the man.

"Step away from the prisoner," Coyan ordered.

With her eyes still fixated on Chrystian, she watched as he motioned for her to step back.

"I won't let this happen," she swore.

"Did you play the harp?" he questioned.

Taryn nodded.

"Then you know what it is you must do," he replied.

She backed away slowly. "But I don't. I couldn't decipher what it showed me."

"The answers are only a heartbeat away," he stated.

Larkin wrapped her in his arms and walked her back to their group.

"For a man that is being sentenced to death, he doesn't seem too concerned," Keiryn stated.

"I need a couple of minutes to myself to sort some things out." Taryn paused, looking to Lazryn. "Will you distract Coyan and Tedra for me, please?"

"I will do what I can," he replied with a nod.

"Keep Chrystian alive, and I'll be back shortly," she stated.

Larkin grabbed her hand. "I should go with you."

She shook her head. "No. This is something I need to do alone."

"I want to help," he replied.

Taryn looked at him softly. "I love you, Larkin. But this is something only I can sort out."

He kissed her temple before releasing his hold. Together, the men watched as she disappeared like a blur.

Keiryn looked to the men. "What can I do to help?"

Larkin and Lazryn shared a glance before turning their eyes toward Taryn's brother.

"When the time is right, I need for you to punch me as hard as you can," Lazryn whispered.

A smile curled on Keiryn's face. "Seriously?"

The man nodded. "Your sister requested more time, and this is the only way I know to gain Coyan's attention."

Coyan began to walk in Chrystian's direction, prompting Lazryn to turn his back to Keiryn. "If not for you being Taryn's sibling, I would end you here and now," he growled.

"You think you can take me?" Keiryn thundered back.

Coyan arched a brow in their direction.

Lazryn turned to face the boy and chuckled darkly. "I have more than a millennium's worth of knowledge and power over you. There is no way for you to beat me."

"We'll see about that, old man," Keiryn shouted as he drew his fist back. Channeling all of his might into his swing, the teen connected with Lazryn's jaw, sending the man soaring through the air.

Landing on his feet, Lazryn wagged his index finger at Taryn's brother. "You should not have done that, boy."

Rushing him in a blur, Lazryn struck a blow to Keiryn's chest. The pair continued their exchange as Coyan looked on with joy teeming in his eyes.

ဆဏ္ဍဏ

Standing along the cliff near the Mortari's castle, Taryn gazed out across the churning water. Her head and heart were at odds as she replayed the numerous images shown to her through the harp.

Images of Loryn, Ardet, her uncle Julius, her mother, Ilya, Maertan, and Ardyn appeared more often than the others.

"What is it they all have in common?" she thought aloud. "Loryn and Maertan both willingly sacrificed themselves. Julius was the keeper of secrets, while my mother was a distraction. Ilya hid my existence, but Ardyn...I don't understand his purpose."

As Taryn tried to put the pieces together, an elderly woman with long white hair and sparkling emerald eyes appeared by her side. The teen's eyes narrowed on her weathered face.

"Do I know you?" Taryn asked.

The woman smiled softly. "You ask what it is they have in common, when the real question is not what, but who."

Turning to face her directly, Taryn shook her head. "Okay, so who do they have in common?"

"My dear girl, you already know," the woman replied.

Taryn's jaw drew tight. "If that were true, then I wouldn't ask the question."

Reaching out, the woman took Taryn's hands into her own. Turning them palm side up, she locked eyes with the girl. "All the answers that you seek are inside you."

Pulling away, Taryn bit her bottom lip. "They plan to kill my friend if I don't figure this out. And while the thought of wiping out an entire group of beings makes me physically ill, I won't allow them to harm him." She paused, taking a deep breath. "So could you please stop with the riddles and help me?"

The woman nodded, placing her hands over the teen's eyes. "Remember, Taryn, only you can decide your destiny."

With the woman's final words, a series of bright lights filled the teen's vision. For several long moments Taryn watched various scenes from the past playout in her mind. A vision of Loryn paused in her head. Taryn took in how the beautiful young woman stood tall with tears streaking down her cheeks. Following her gaze, the teen noted thatched roofs burning in the background as Chrystian stalked closer.

Loryn's salty tears pooled in the back of Taryn's throat, choking the girl as she took in the immense bloodlust shining bright in Chrystian's eyes. As he reached out for Loryn's throat, Taryn suddenly felt a sharp pain in her chest. Opening her eyes, she looked out over the water below. Her brows creased, noting the strange calm across its surface.

"I still don't understand," she whispered.

A swift breeze swirled around her, stirring a sweet fragrance in the air. Looking down, Taryn watched as hundreds of jasmine flowers bloomed around her. She reached out, grabbing one as it kicked up into the air. Lifting it to her nose, she inhaled its sweet scent.

৪০০৪৩০০৪৩

Battered and bruised, Keiryn and Lazryn continued to land blow after blow on one another.

Having grown bored of watching them, Coyan looked to Tedra and nodded.

The woman lifted her hands and instantly the pair stilled. "Enough of this nonsense," she shouted.

Gracyn stepped to where her son and Lazryn stood like statues. "Remove your Influence from them now," she demanded.

A wicked smile curled on Tedra's face. "Mother of Taryn, you would be wise to remember that you are a guest on our plane. At any time should we feel threatened, we would be more than justified in taking action to quell the concern."

Staring daggers at the vile woman, Gracyn's nostrils flared.

Taryn suddenly appeared in front of her mother, edging the woman back. Holding her hand out in Keiryn and Lazryn's direction, she freed them from Tedra's Influence.

"Ah, you have returned just in time to witness Chrystian answer for his crimes against the Mortari," the woman taunted.

Taryn's expression turned frosty as she locked eyes with Coyan's wife. "We shall see who answers for their crimes," Taryn retorted. After a few moments passed, she helped her brother to his feet.

Watching Taryn approach their group, Larkin noted a distinct change within her in comparison to earlier. "You okay?" he asked, noting the chill surrounding her.

Taryn nodded, while taking her place next to him. Her eyes scanned the numerous groups huddling uncomfortably in the large valley.

"Who are all these people?" Kellan asked.

"They are representatives from each community amongst the various planes," Lazryn replied.

Kellan shrugged. "If this is about Chrystian, then why are they here?"

Silence lingered within the group as all eyes turned to Taryn.

"They are to serve as witnesses to what Coyan believes will be his ascension," she replied quietly.

Theron shook his head. "He's already king of the Mortari...and he knows he cannot defeat you."

Smiling at her father, Taryn shrugged. "We all have dreams, and this is his."

"Well he's in for a bit of a surprise if he thinks he could ever best you, Kansas," Gerrick stated, hyping up their group.

Andyn approached Taryn with Dedrick following close behind. "I'm sorry I blamed you for Ardyn. Seeing him...it made me remember."

Taryn drew the boy into a fierce hug and whispered in his ear, "No matter what happens today, I want you and Dedrick to stay close to Keiryn. Understood?"

Pulling back, Andyn briefly locked eyes with her. "Sure...we'll stay close to him."

"Good," she replied, tousling his hair with her fingers.

The boy sighed with furrowed brows. "Whatever you have planned, be careful, sis."

"No worries, little brother," she replied, turning her attention to Coyan, Clad and Tedra.

Leaning in, Larkin pressed his lips against her ear. "What are you going to do, Taryn?"

She glanced to him briefly before fixing her eyes upon the dark trio. "I'm going to do whatever is needed to end this once and for all," she whispered back.

"This isn't who you are," he stated, his tone laden with worry.

Turning, she cupped his cheek. "I love you. I always have, and I always will. Nothing will ever change what you mean to me."

He placed his hand over hers, sliding it to his lips. Kissing it softly, he stared into the depths of her emerald eyes. "I love you, too, but I don't want to lose you."

She smiled tenderly. "Larkin Taylor, you could never lose me, even if you tried."

Watching the exchange between the girl and her wolf, Coyan's nostrils flared. "That insolent child will not be smiling when we inundate her with hundreds of lightning shafts."

One corner of Tedra's mouth curled as she arched a brow in her husband's direction. "We will be rid of her and your vile brother," she purred.

Tilting his head to one side, the dark man stared at his wife. "After all this time, his choice still stirs bitterness within you."

Tedra placed an index finger over his lips. "Tell me husband, has his perpetual state of suffering over the past thousand years not brought you both joy and elation?"

He smiled darkly, turning his eyes to his younger brother. "Tonight the charade comes to an end. Chrystian will pay for his past, and Taryn will know what it is like to fall from favor."

A dangerous gleam shone in Tedra's eyes as she glanced between Chrystian and the girl.

"Clad," Coyan stated, grabbing his youngest brother's attention.

Looking to his oldest brother, Clad swallowed hard. "Yes?"

"It is time," he announced.

Bowing his head briefly, Clad stepped back and motioned to a small crowd gathered on the opposite side of the large boulder.

Moving swiftly, the crowd stood before the trio. And just as quickly, they moved out, leaving a member of their group.

"Nodryck," Taryn growled, staring at the man as the groups erupted in chaos.

Tedra waved her hand, silencing the masses with her Influence. Stepping aside, she nodded. "Husband.

Coyan nodded in return while a devilish smile curled on his face. "It would appear that the vast majority of you were not expecting to see the former head of the Elder Council standing with the Mortari." He paused, looking around the open space at the various faces. "To demonstrate how both sides have evolved, we thought it best to allow our dear friend, Nodryck, to chair today's proceedings." Coyan paused again, this time locking eyes with Taryn. "He will serve as both judge and jury. And in the event it is deemed necessary, he will also be the executioner."

With her hands balled into fists, Taryn stepped forward. "Judge carefully, Nodryck, for you, too, shall one day be judged."

His black eyes narrowed on the girl as he held out his hand, creating a whip from imperium power. Flicking his wrist, he caused the ends to bite into Chrystian's flesh.

Grimacing from the pain, Chrystian shook his head. Laughter soon filled the air as he looked to the man. "Taryn was spot on when she said you hit like a child whose gifts have yet to set in."

Nodryck's jaw drew up tight and his nostrils flared. "You dare mock me?" he bit.

"We dare," Chrystian retorted, sending Taryn a sly wink.

The dark haired man turned to Coyan with an arched brow. After the man nodded to him, Nodryck turned, facing Taryn and her family with a deadly grin. "This prisoner has time and time again turned his back on his blood in favor of the enemy child known as Taryn Knight. His most recent actions resulted in the destruction of the prized beast, formally known as Ardyn Mitchell." The man's eyes pierced through the William's group, falling heavily upon Andyn.

The young boy stared back at him with flared nostrils.

"Your prized beast was sentenced to death by the former Elder Council, headed by Odyn. I find it curious that he managed to find his way into the Mortari's possession," Taryn stated.

A woman with white hair and porcelain skin stepped forward from the Mortari's group. "That would be my doing," she laughed.

"Ah, you do remember my faithful servant and Seer Rishyn. Don't you, Taryn?" Nodryck taunted.

"The white witch is of no concern to me. Her gifts were weak…inadequate at best," Taryn retorted.

The woman's face lit with anger. "I still managed to get inside your head."

"Care to give it another go?" Taryn taunted.

"Enough," Coyan thundered. His fierce gaze drawing the pale woman back in line.

"No. It's not enough," Taryn roared back. "You and your legion of fools have ruined countless lives. You have chipped away and corrupted the purity of principles that govern all Gaias kind."

Suddenly, lightning rained down, saturating the short distance between the two groups.

Taryn's eyes widened as the hair on her neck stood on end as the cloaked man appeared behind her.

He waved his hand once over, creating a large chessboard from the earth in front of the teen. Moss covered game pieces with precise detailing moved about the board until finding a square to call their home.

"Your passion is unrivaled, even when compared to those who played the game before you. You, child, are truly a fierce individual, and now my all-time favorite opponent," he whispered in her ear.

Taryn stared for several long moments at the board before her. Tilting her head from one side to the next, she began to see flickers of faces appearing upon the various pieces. Larkin was the king, and she the queen. Keiryn and her father were both knights, while Gastyn and Lazryn served as bishops. The rooks consisted of her mother and Julius while several other members of her immediate family and friends filled the position of pawns. She scanned the opposing side of the board. The teen's forehead creased as her eyes glanced over the numerous pawns. However, one of her opponent's expendable pieces drew her gaze even more than the others. *Chrystian?* she puzzled.

"We both know it is Coyan's intentions to see his brother's execution play out on this grand stage. The only uncertainty is your response to his desires," the cloaked man jeered.

Glancing over her shoulder, Taryn rolled her eyes. "Please. Anyone who has crossed my path knows the depths of how far I will go to protect those I care for, and Chrystian is no exception."

"Ah yes, the simple truths of Taryn. A teen who will fiercely advocate for all that she believes in, while simultaneously walking the edge of conflicted morality," he chuckled.

His words rang like fire billowing in her ears. "Chrystian will not be harmed today," she growled.

The man reached around, waving his hand in front of her face, stirring a compelling vision within her mind. "You have but two choices, my child. You may stand by and watch as your beloved friend dies by a rain of lightning." He paused, allowing the haunting vision to fester inside her head. Tears streaked down Taryn's cheeks as she watched dozens of lightning bolts strike Chrystian, draining him of his final breath of life. "Or the alternative. You intervene, claiming the life of every last Mortari on the plane. Including those who have grown sympathetic to their plight in protest of your gifts."

Images of fire raged in her head as the scent of copper grew in her sinuses. Everywhere she looked, death surrounded her. Lifeless bodies smoldered before turning to ash while blood rained down from the sky. Her irises turned black as night as the sight consumed every ounce of her being.

"What say you, dearest Taryn? Do you permit your precious Chrystian to pay for his crimes, or do you destroy all living things to protect a monster?" the man whispered before fading away.

With wide eyes and her pulse beating rapidly, Taryn stared at Coyan and his wife.

Seeing the wild look growing in the girl's eyes, the eldest of the Brothers C held his hand out in Chrystian's direction. "Fall back now, Taryn, or I will end his life this very instant," the eldest brother roared.

Trembling with emotion, Taryn took a step back into Larkin's waiting arms.

"What is it?" he asked, feeling the weight of her struggles swirling within his own self.

"I cannot contain that which rises within me. The voices of my guiding light will no longer be silenced, no more will they subside," she rambled.

Spinning her around, Larkin looked into her eyes. He gasped at what he saw. A storm churned within her unlike anything he had ever seen before, and a familiar face revealed itself. "But you destroyed her. Your rage is supposed to be gone," he gasped.

She shook her head gently. "She was merely silenced for a brief period of time. I can no longer run from what I am, Larkin. My destiny led me here, and the worlds as we know them will never be the same."

"This isn't you, Taryn. Don't let your emotions define you. You are nothing like these monsters. When I think of what is good, I see you. I know your heart, and I know who you are," he pleaded.

Reaching up, she caressed his cheek. "Always and forever, you will be my heart. I will never cease to exist as long as you draw breath." She paused, tears welling in her eyes. "I love you, Larkin Taylor. Not even the bonds of death are strong enough to change that."

"No, Taryn. Please. Please don't do whatever it is you're thinking," he begged.

"Only when the fallen rise will there be hope for a new tomorrow. Today, the fallen must rise," she whispered.

Tears rolled from the well of his eyes, streaking down his cheek. "I love you no matter what happens. It changes nothing between you and I."

Watching the pair's exchange, Coyan looked to Tedra.

"The teen queen is brimming with emotion." She paused motioning for the Mortari's strongest Elementals to fall into formation. "We must act now."

Coyan nodded to Nodryck, prompting him to speak up.

Giving a slight bow, the former leader of the Elder Council stepped up with a thunderous voice. "As the presiding judge and jury over this prisoner, I hereby condemn him to death."

The light breeze that swept through the valley noticeably changed course.

"This moment doesn't have to define you," Larkin whispered as he took a step back from his love.

With a final tender glance to the keeper of her heart, Taryn turned to face Coyan and the others.

Falling back with his family and friends, Larkin looked to Keiryn and Lazryn. Heartbreak shone heavily within his eyes.

"What is she going to do?" Keiryn questioned.

Larkin shook his head with a slight shrug. "The only thing she can...she's going to end it."

Taking a step forward, Taryn locked stares with Coyan. "If you are so intent on taking a life today, then take mine."

Gasps filled the air as Keiryn and Larkin both tried to rush to her, but found themselves impeded by one of Taryn's protective shields.

A smile curled on Coyan's face. "You would give your life in place of my brother's?" he questioned.

Taryn looked to Chrystian. The pair shared a series of tender glances before she replied, "I will, but on one condition."

Rolling her eyes, Tedra growled. "And what would that be?"

"Once it is done, everyone is to be returned to their homes untouched," the teen replied.

"No," Clad shouted as he stepped forward. "Sweet Taryn, please...please, I beg of you. Do not agree to this. Allow my brother to accept the consequences of his actions."

Raising his hand, Coyan forced his Influence upon his youngest brother in an attempt to hush him. "Quiet, you fool," he bit.

Tears fell from Clad's eyes as he struggled against Coyan's gift. "I will not be silenced this time," he muttered.

Watching, Taryn noticed the slightest of movement in Tedra's right pinky finger.

Instantly the youngest brother's eyes hollowed and his body stilled.

That's a bit curious, Taryn thought to herself.

With Clad silenced, Coyan turned his attention back to Taryn. "Your request sounds most agreeable, providing you make no attempt to change your mind on the matter."

"No," Larkin shouted from behind her shield of protection as he beat against the invisible wall.

Taryn looked to Chrystian with the greatest of care in her eyes. "You have my word," she stated.

"You cannot trust them," Lazryn shouted.

Taking a deep breath, Taryn walked to where Chrystian stood.

"Why are you doing this?" he whispered as she worked to remove the rondoring rope from his wrists.

She shrugged. "It's the only reasonable course of action I can take."

Lifting his hands, he wedged a loose tendril of hair between his fingers and swept it behind her ear.

"Hold still," she sighed.

"This choice comes at a price. Are you certain you are prepared to pay?" he questioned.

Unwinding the loosened rope, Taryn looked the man in the eyes. "If you're asking if I'm ready to leave Larkin behind, the answer is no."

"Then why offer yourself in my place?" he pressed.

"Because someone told me I had only two choices, but neither one of those outcomes are acceptable to me," she answered.

Chrystian grabbed her hands, pulling them close to his heart. "Everyone believes it is your gifts that make you special, but I say it is your unyielding love for all life that makes you unique." Leaning down, he kissed the top of her head. "Your sacrifice will not be in vain."

Taryn looked up at him with tears in her eyes. "Promise me you will look after the old man and my family."

"Of course," he nodded.

Wrapping her arms around his neck, she hugged him fiercely. "Prove me right, and show them why you are worth saving."

"Whatever you want, dearest one," he replied.

Taking a deep breath, Taryn released him and stepped back.

"When you see Loryn, tell her that I love her, please," he whispered.

Sweeping the tears from her eyes, Taryn nodded. She looked to Larkin and mouthed the words, "I love you."

Tears poured from his eyes as he struck his fists against the wall.

"Are you ready to die?" Nodryck asked darkly.

With her eyes firmly locked with Larkin's, she nodded.

Nodryck motioned for the Elementals to raise their hands. In seconds, hundreds of lightning bolts lit the sky overhead.

Taryn sent one last tearful smile to her love before looking toward the sky. She lifted her hands and lightning began to rain down on the very spot in which she stood.

Larkin and the others beat violently against the wall, their screams of horror and protest sounded like a soothing song to Coyan's ears.

When the lightning stopped, smoke and debris filled the air and the scent of Taryn's presence was absent.

Larkin pushed through the diminishing shield and ran toward where she had stood.

"Stop, Larkin. You do not know what you will find," Lazryn shouted to his friend. He started to follow the teen, when Chrystian held out his hand.

"The boy must view her remains with his own eyes," Chrystian warned.

Reaching the spot where she had stood, Larkin dropped to his knees. He searched blindly, hoping to find and cradle her body. But when the dust settled all that remained was a single coral colored rose.

"What is the meaning of this?" Coyan demanded, pushing Nodryck out of his way.

"She is gone. She is truly gone" Clad gasped, his face tormented between a happy and sad smile.

Larkin stared at the gleaming rose, cupping the precious flower within his hands. "She's gone. She's really gone," he cried out.

"What form of trickery is this, Brother?" Coyan thundered, his heated gaze biting into Chrystian's flesh as he looked around for any hint of the girl's presence. "You and she planned this. You opened a gateway and freed her before she could be destroyed."

"Taryn stood bravely and accepted her fate. But you, eldest brother, are, as always, paranoid without cause," Chrystian bit back.

With a heaving chest, Coyan turned to his wife. "No one leaves here today until I am certain the girl is dead," he seethed.

Nodding, Tedra raised her hands, spreading her Influence across the land. Those who had attempted to flee found themselves unable to continue. Turning around, they rejoined their perspective families.

"Perhaps Taryn followed in Loryn's footsteps when faced with the prospect of death," Clad stated with a heavy heart.

Tedra curled her fingers into the air and Clad instantly grabbed at his throat and began stumbling about. "Do not speak of that cowardly woman in my presence," she growled.

Having heard the woman's disgust for his sister, Lazryn approached. "I did not realize you were familiar with my sister."

Tedra's eyes turned blood red as she looked to the man. A sinister laugh rose deep from within her slender frame.

In a blur, Coyan appeared at his wife's side. "What is it?" he asked.

Releasing her hold on Clad's throat, she smiled darkly. "Tonight we make Mors run red with the blood of our enemies."

CHAPTER TWENTY

Opening her eyes, Taryn found herself standing in a veil of absolute darkness.

"The Void...great," she mused aloud.

"Hello, Taryn," a familiar voice whispered.

The teen took a deep breath and replied, "Loryn."

"Do you have a message for me?" the woman asked eagerly.

With a heavy sigh, Taryn shook her head. "He said he loves you."

"Chrystian was always the romantic," Loryn gushed.

Growing quickly annoyed, Taryn growled. "Just because I'm dead now, doesn't mean we're going to be best friends. I literally just died leaving Larkin, whom I love more than anything, standing on Mors with your lunatic in-laws."

Loryn chuckled. "You still do not understand. We will never be just friends, Taryn."

Lightning crackled overhead, illuminating the area around them. Lurking within the darkness, Taryn spied several familiar faces.

"You haunted me in life with no reason, and now you think you're going to haunt me in death, too?" the teen seethed.

The still air began to swirl about while the intensity of the lightning strikes increased.

"Unleash what you hold inside, and I promise you will see Larkin very soon," Loryn stated.

"Don't you dare threaten him," Taryn warned as the ground beneath their feet trembled.

Loryn grinned wildly. "You will see your precious Larkin very soon, this I promise."

Taryn's eyes began to glow a radiant shade of sapphire blue. "Remove his name from your mouth, or I swear I will make you suffer for all eternity."

An incredible bolt of lightning pierced the darkness, striking inches away from Taryn's feet, sending her soaring through the air.

Landing on what felt like a feather, Taryn's eyelids fluttered, displaying her emerald colored irises. Her jaw dropped open as she took in the shimmering tree branches overhead.

"How did I get here?" she mused, while rising to her feet. She glanced in multiple directions until she spied a familiar face. "Maertan, how did I end up here?"

The young man walked toward her. "How could you not?" he retorted with a warm smile.

She shook her head. "I don't understand. I died and went to the Void. How is it that I'm here now?"

"You gave your life to save the lives of many," he answered.

She looked to the ground. "I couldn't allow them to kill Chrystian."

"You did far more than save one man's life, Taryn, though you are too modest to say so." He paused, motioning for her to walk with him. "The life you surrendered on this day was your debt to pay."

She gave a slight chuckle.

"You find your death funny?" he questioned.

Taryn shrugged. "Not exactly. I guess I assumed in death that all the riddles...well, they wouldn't seem so much like riddles anymore."

Maertan grinned as he continued to stride ahead. "Do you remember the last tree you visited while here?"

She nodded. "It was beautiful."

"It was yours," he replied.

Taryn took a deep breath. "Is it possible to check in on those I left behind?"

Halting in his step, Maertan turned and looked at her with a furrowed brow. "After all that you have witnessed, it is curious how you are still so unaware."

"Unaware of what?" she asked.

"Unaware of who you are," a deep voice answered from behind them.

Spinning around on her heel, Taryn stared at the familiar muscular man wearing brown leather pants and an old-fashioned loose fitting white shirt. "Laertas Dominion?"

He nodded.

"Maertan and Malayne are your children," she stated.

"Yes. They are two of my children," he smiled proudly.

Taryn shook her head. "Exactly how many children do you have?"

"Several," he answered, his face changing slightly.

Taking a step back, Taryn eyed him closely. "How did you do that?" she asked.

Suddenly a boy appeared by her side. "We have always been able to alter our appearance," he stated.

The teen's eyes grew wide. "Maertas?"

"My son has worn many faces during his lifetime with as many names to match," a woman answered.

"Calista," Taryn gasped, staring at the beautiful woman.

She smiled warmly at the girl. "In death you are free from the bonds that once restrained you. How is it possible that even now, you still do not know who you are?"

Taryn looked around as even more familiar faces appeared. Adora James, Colyn Danbrym, Elanya Delrayn, and many more she did not recognize.

"This is ridiculous. It makes no sense," she stated, taking in the various shades of blonde hair and green-eyed individuals circling her.

The old woman she had seen on Mors approached her. "What do you see?"

Taryn stared into the woman's eyes. After a few moments, she shook her head. "There are fires burning in the background. Screams piercing the air. Anger, heartbreak, bitterness, jealousy, disdain, hate and betrayal…it's everywhere."

"What does your heart tell you?" the woman asked.

"Hope survives always, where there was love. No amount of anger or jealousy can defeat it," she exhaled.

The woman stroked Taryn's cheek. "You are my mirror when I was your age."

Suddenly images of a small child running through a flower filled meadow flashed through Taryn's mind. Tears welled in the teen's eyes. "It can't be. He said you died that night."

She nodded. "Yes, my father was led to believe that I was murdered. For if he would have known the truth, we all would have perished at the devil woman's hands."

"How did you survive?" Taryn asked.

"Not all who pretend to be evil are truly so. The same as not all who pretend to be good are truly as they seem," the old woman answered.

"He deserves to know the truth," Taryn stated.

"Will you be the one to tell him? Not only of my part, but the entire story from beginning to end?" she asked.

Taryn shrugged. "I'm certain with time, I'll figure out how to do that trick with the mirrors like Loryn."

Her words garnered chuckles from those around.

"Do you still not understand who and what you are?" the woman questioned.

Taryn stepped back, bumping into Maertan. "I'm sorry."

"You have no reason for sorrow, Taryn Knight," he replied.

Suddenly, Loryn appeared next to the old woman. She gazed softly at the teen before glancing around those who surrounded the girl. "We have been gentle thus far, sweet Taryn. But alas, we are out of time."

"It's not as though time is an issue anymore. I'm dead, remember?" Taryn replied.

Calista spoke up. "I see it now. It is not the girl's fault that she remains unaware of what she truly is. Death and Thantos placed a lock within her mind to keep her identity hidden from the others, and to keep the depths of her powers from breaking free."

"For the fallen to rise, she must remember," Adora stated urgently.

"Remember what?" Taryn demanded.

All eyes fell heavy upon the girl.

"Within you sleeps a giant. If that giant does not wake soon, your precious Larkin and all that you have fought so gallantly to save, shall perish," Calista warned.

Taryn's nostrils flared. "Then stop with the damned riddles and visions and just tell me whatever it is I need to know. Because I promise you, if anything happens to Larkin, not even death will prevent me from unleashing a fury unlike anything you have ever seen before."

"And so the giant stirs," Elanya marveled.

A few feet from the circle, Farren and Thantos appeared.

"The path which you seek is not a simple one. For the fallen to rise, you must face all that is or has ever been. The pain will be excruciating, likened to the sensation of a thousand deaths," Thantos stated plainly.

Taryn's jaw drew tight. "If Larkin dies while you're wasting time, it will be you who experiences a thousand deaths. I promise you, I will not leave the Void until my thirst for revenge is satiated."

Fixating his eyes on the teen, Thantos moved closer. "You would dare to challenge me?"

"Call me crazy, but I'm not exactly fearful of a half-naked Immortal dressed in a cloth covered in golden leaves," she replied.

He leaned in, staring eye-to-eye with the girl. "Then enlighten me. Tell me what it is you do fear?"

Her face softened as she thought about the one thing that truly terrified her. "I am afraid of a broken heart."

"But you gave your heart away before you were born," Thantos challenged.

"Larkin is the keeper of my heart. And should he be harmed in any way, I fear I will lose myself in a pit of angry darkness," she whispered.

Silence lingered for several moments, before Farren spoke. "There, Brother, are you satisfied that she is the one?"

Straightening himself, Thantos looked to his brother and nodded. "It is undeniable she is the child we have sought for so long."

Farren disappeared only to reappear beside the girl. "My dearest friend, your suffering will be great, and for this I am truly sorry. For only within the pain, may you find your truest self."

Looking up at her friend, Taryn shook her head gently with furrowed brows. "I'm not afraid."

"Lack of fear will not vacate your suffering," he replied.

Taryn smiled. "Do your worst, Deadman."

With a nod from Farren, the others took several steps back, leaving the teen to stand alone.

Death looked at her softly. "To find yourself, you must first possess the clarity of understanding. And to understand you must bear the weight of knowledge." As he spoke, the orbs from the trees began to fall. The sound of breaking glass filled the air, and the silver colored vapor held within each began to circle above the teen. "At first the pain will seem bearable, but as more orbs break and the knowledge within saturates, you will feel the weight of all past deeds, good or bad, right or wrong. They will build upon your shoulders until you can no longer stand. The onslaught will continue to compound until you are consumed in the lifetimes of all those before you. You will share in the taste of their victories, as well as the bitterness of their defeat. You will know their pain while you beg for tenderness, and choke on the knowledge of their intentions." He paused, looking up at the ever-growing cloud above the teen. "Should you survive this task, you shall know all that lives within the hearts of men and women alike."

"Survive?" Taryn questioned.

"A single caveat accompanies this task. At any point should you beg for death, I must come and set your soul free. It will be the final page in your most unique story," he answered.

She shook her head. "But I'm already dead."

Death smiled. "One must die for the other to rise."

Rolling her eyes at his final riddle, Taryn took a deep breath and stood tall. She trembled with anticipation as the monstrous cloud of silver vapor lowered around her.

Suddenly a question that had long bothered her reared its head. "Wait. I want to know who fathered Maertas."

Before her question could be answered, the first wave of knowledge pressed against her petite frame. She gasped, feeling the heaviness that it held within.

"Be strong, our precious Taryn," Calista whispered.

৪০৩৪৩

What seemed like hours passed as tears streamed from the eyes of those keeping vigil around the girl. They watched as her body twisted and contorted. The depths of her suffering conveyed through every muscle spasm and earth-shattering scream as she fought to possess the ultimate knowledge of her true identity.

"Knowing her strength does not lessen the pain in my soul in watching her suffer so. She was an innocent, just as my dear Maertas was once upon a time," Calista wept.

Loryn placed a comforting arm around the beautiful woman's shoulders. "She fought gallantly in life, as I know she will in death. We must stay strong for her...all of us."

Moving from his position, Death began to circle Taryn where she lay.

"Do not touch her," the old woman warned.

Pausing in his step, he stared at the girl briefly. "She has crossed over into the final threshold. In mere moments, her truths shall be revealed and her destiny will be hers to claim."

The others gathered around as her convulsions slowly began to subside.

Suddenly, Taryn's spine arched for a final time. Her emerald green eyes opened wide, displaying the truth within before giving way to a spectacular sapphire blue.

"Go, dear child of ours, and claim your destiny. Right the wrongs and restore peace once more," the old woman whispered.

An immense fire grew beneath the girl, turning her body to ash.

ಬಂಛಬಂಛ

From beneath the waters of Havasu Falls with the moonlight shining down, Taryn rose bare and reborn. Gazing downward at her reflection, she marveled at the brilliant intensity shining within her swirling blue irises.

"I am coming for you," she whispered with a wicked smile into the cool night air.

CHAPTER TWENTY-ONE

Sitting upon their thrones, Coyan and Tedra stared at the group from Williams who sat only yards away, their wrists bound with rondoring rope, and their mouths silenced by Influence.

"Only when the final scouts return may you have your fun, dearest wife," Coyan growled.

"After all that we have done together, you choose now to show concern." She paused, her lip curling on one side. "You reek of fear over a girl that no longer breathes."

Leaning over the arm of his throne, Coyan glanced at Larkin. "The fire I witnessed within her eyes was real. Should she not have perished at the hand of our select group, there will be hell to pay upon her return. Which shall only be multiplied if we harm her family."

"I am not now, nor have I ever been, afraid of that child. Her gifts were an anomaly. She is nothing special," Tedra bit.

"Then certainly there is no harm in waiting while our scouts scour the planes in search of her and any remaining Gaias," Coyan sighed.

Rising from her seat, Tedra glanced down at her husband. "I have used my gifts to search the planes for any lingering sign of the girl. But it would appear that she followed in the footsteps of your precious

Loryn, and returned herself to the earth in the form of a coral colored rose."

"And how did she know such a feat was possible?" Coyan challenged.

Feigning a smile, Tedra leaned down and kissed her husband's cheek. "She possessed the gift of sight beyond her own mind. Spending time with your brother and her new best friend, Lazryn, would make it more than plausible for her to know what happened that night."

"But what if," he began to argue.

"Dearest husband, I grow tired of your worry. Even if Lazryn or Chrystian were fast enough to open a doorway for her to slip through, she would be locked there, unable to return to Mors. Her gifts do not include opening Adora gateways," Tedra growled.

Coyan waved his hand. "On with it then, woman. Claim the lives of those who will appease you so that this day may end."

A dark smile curled on the woman's face. "As you wish, husband."

Tedra motioned to a group of guards. "Bring the following men forward. Lazryn the defector, and Chrystian the traitor."

The guards pulled the two men from the group and walked them to opposing spots before Coyan and Tedra.

"What is your wish, my dearest Queen?" the guard holding Lazryn asked.

Tedra smiled. "I wish to hear them beg for mercy."

"Never," Lazryn seethed, regaining his ability to speak.

Shrugging, Tedra reclaimed her seat. "You will scream for me just as your sister screamed all those many years ago."

"We will never give you that which you desire," Chrystian spat.

Glancing at the numerous faces in the massive gathering, Tedra laughed. "These good people are all dying, but perhaps speeding up the process will give you pause to reconsider. You either give me that which I want, or I shall make all of them scream until you have a change of heart. That is, providing either of you still have one now that your precious Taryn is dead."

"Careful, Tedra, your jealousy is showing," Chrystian jeered.

She turned to her husband, arching an angry brow. "Are you going to permit him to speak to me in such a way?"

Rolling his eyes, Coyan raised his index finger to his throat making a cutting motioning. "The next foul word from his mouth, slice both their throats."

Tedra looked to the men who knelt opposite of one another. "Not so feisty now, are we?"

Before either man could offer a retort, a portal opened up between them. A guard rushed out and bowed at Coyan and Tedra's feet.

"We have found the girl. She was in her home when we made a second sweep," he stated.

Larkin and the others perked up, trying to hear the exchange.

"Impossible, I scanned the planes myself," Tedra bit.

The guard knelt on one knee. "I am only but a humble servant."

"If it is her, then bring her forward," Coyan snapped, giving a sideways glance to his wife.

The guard rose to his feet and ran back to the gateway. He stepped inside and moments later he and three other guards appeared, escorting Taryn. From her elbows to her wrists, she was bound with a thick layer of rondoring rope.

Larkin and the others rose to their feet. Tears welled in his eyes. "Taryn's alive."

Tedra's eyes widened, taking in the impossible sight. The intensity shining within the girl's emerald eyes did not escape her attention. "What form of trickery is this?" she demanded.

The guards closed the gateway and stepped aside.

"What? Are you not happy to see me, Tedra?" Taryn asked.

Her jaw drew up tight and her nostrils flared. "Oh no, dear girl. I am glad you arrived when you did so you may witness the deaths of your two closest friends."

Taryn turned around, looking to Larkin and her family. "During my time away today, I gleaned a bit of insight."

Tedra's lip curled. "By all means, please do enlighten us."

Looking over her shoulder, Taryn smiled. "All things begin and end with family. But this shouldn't surprise you, as I'm sure you are more than aware of this fact."

Stepping forward, the woman's eyes lit with rage.

Taryn turned, winking at Larkin and the others before returning to stand only feet from Tedra and Coyan. "Now that you and I are on the same page, I politely request that your guards remove their knives from the throats of my family."

The guard holding the knife to Chrystian's throat lowered his weapon.

"Wise choice," the teen acknowledged.

"You are bound by rondoring rope. You have no power here," Tedra hissed.

Taryn took another step closer. "Are you prepared to test your theory?"

Tedra looked to the guard holding his knife against Lazryn's throat. "One nod from me and your dear friend dies."

Looking at the woman, Taryn sighed softly. "I will only ask one more time. Please remove the knife from my grandfather's throat."

With wide eyes, Tedra stared at the teen for several moments before stumbling backwards. "No. It is impossible. The child died that night."

"A wise person once told me that not all who pretend to be evil are truly so. The same as not all who pretend to be good are truly as they seem." Taryn paused, glancing to Lazryn before returning her eyes to the woman. "Do you care to guess who spoke these words?"

"My Influence permitted no other course of action," Tedra retorted.

Shaking her head, Taryn glanced to Coyan. "But you see, that is your error. It was not you who Influenced Clad that night, it was Coyan."

"No. I planned everything so carefully," Tedra replied.

"Hatred and jealousy got in your way. You left Coyan to Influence Clad. And as Clad demonstrated earlier today, he is not as susceptible to your husband's Influence as you believe," Taryn explained.

Heat began to roll off Tedra in palpable waves.

Taryn turned to the guard still holding Lazryn. "You really should free my grandfather."

Rolling his eyes, Lazryn exhaled. "I am not certain now is the appropriate time to make jokes about one's age."

"Taryn does not jest in this matter, my friend. Though she was kind enough to leave off the part about you being her great, great, great grandfather," Chrystian chuckled.

Emerging from the crowd of Mortari, Clad stared at the teen while placing his hand over his mouth. After several moments, he gasped, "You are the grandchild of Lily?"

Taryn smiled and looked back to Lazryn. "This man who holds you, shares in our bloodline as well. But he possesses a dark heart and will never change." Pausing, Taryn turned to Tedra and winked. A rumbling came from the ground and suddenly green tendrils thrusted upward from the earth, snatching the man holding Lazryn. In the blink of an eye, the man disappeared beneath the soil and a beautiful bouquet of flowers formed above his remains. The teen arched a brow in Lazryn's direction. "Perhaps that was a bit too theatrical."

Still dumbfounded by what both Taryn and Chrystian had said, Lazryn remained silent, rubbing the back of his neck.

Coyan rose from his seat. "Who is responsible for this?" he thundered.

Moving behind her throne, Tedra pointed to Taryn.

"She is incapable of such an act. Her wrists are bound and her gifts rendered useless," he reasoned.

Lifting her hands, Taryn stared at Coyan as the rondoring rope snaked its way from her wrists, falling to the ground.

"It is impossible. Your gifts cannot pass through your hands as they were bound by rondoring rope," he gasped.

"My gifts flow freely from sheer will. You could wrap me from head to toe, and will never stop the flow," she replied.

Coyan looked to Tedra. "Do something," he ordered.

The woman looked away from her husband.

"For all these years, you have played her fool. Blinded by the jealousy that lives in your heart for your own flesh and blood."

"You do not know what it is you speak of," he growled, his mind reeling from what he had witnessed.

"Oh, but don't I?" the teen questioned, backing away.

"Lily is dead, and you and my brother are both delusional fools," he retorted.

Ignoring him, Taryn walked over to Lazryn and knelt down. "Are you okay?"

With tear filled eyes and trembling lips, he pulled the girl into a fierce hug. After several moments passed, he rose to his feet, bringing her with him. "Though I have no words, my heart tells me you speak the truth."

Joining them, Chrystian slid his arms around both their shoulders. "I think she possesses Loryn's great love and fierceness."

"That she does," Lazryn agreed, taking a moment to stare into her eyes. "How can this be?"

She smiled. "We have much to discuss, but first I need to say hello to the rest of our family."

Rushing over to the others, Taryn looked around at the many faces. The rondoring ropes fell from their wrists while Tedra's Influence lifted from all those affected.

Larkin pulled her into his arms and showered her with kisses. Her mother and father joined in their embrace, as did several other members of their community.

After several moments passed, Taryn stepped back from the group. "I know you all have a lot of questions, and I promise to answer them as soon as I can. But right now, there are a few things I need to take care of."

Gracyn grabbed her daughter by the wrist. "Please wait." The teen paused. "You said that Lazryn is your grandfather?"

"He is yours as well," Taryn confirmed.

"But how?" the woman questioned.

Sucking in a deep breath, Taryn bit her lip and looked around the valley. "It's quite an involved story."

"Please do share, Taryn. As I believe it is time for all Gaias to know the truth about what happened that night," Chrystian stated.

Taryn nodded in agreement and made her way to the large boulder. Climbing on top, she prepared to address all who were present. Sensing an Adora gateway opening, she quickly closed the portal while glancing over her shoulder at Tedra and Coyan. "I believe it is important that everyone hear the story. Don't you?" she questioned.

Tedra's nostrils flared.

Chrystian created several helix orbs in order to project Taryn for the entire crowd to watch and listen.

"Once upon a time there was a powerful child who was abandoned by her father. She and her mother were left to fend for themselves during a time when men ruled the world mercilessly. Each year, as the girl grew older, her gifts increased exponentially. Her mother died when she was only twelve. Angry and alone, the girl decided to seek out her father. A few years after her journey began, she found him. Though his face had changed ever so slightly. He was married to a stunning redhead at the time, and they had a child. She watched them day in and day out for nearly a month. Jealousy festered within her until it soon consumed her every breath. But one day the girl went to spy on her father and his new family, and she discovered he had left them as well. Determined to locate her father once more, the girl began yet another search. Of course, she found him and he had a new family with a slightly altered version of his face. Deciding to confront her father, the girl marched up to him and told him who she was." Taryn paused, glancing to Tedra with pity in her eyes. "Instead of opening his arms to his flesh and blood, he shoved her away. She lashed out with her gifts. But nothing she did had any effect on him. In fact, he told her to go away and to never bother him again."

"That's horrible. I know exactly what it feels like to not be wanted by your father," Andyn stated.

Taryn gazed softly upon the boy before returning to her tale. "The girl soon turned into a young woman. Her gifts flourished into something beyond that of a common Gaias. Realizing her own strength, she devised a plan to make the man pay, even though he would never know what she had done. Years later she returned to the town where the redheaded woman and her child lived and befriended the girl. Sensing a familiar power within the young girl, she taught her how to use and manipulate those gifts. Driven by jealousy and hate, the first daughter stalked her father and all of his many children, and even some of his grandchildren."

"How long did this continue?" Gastyn questioned.

"For the duration of the man's life," Taryn replied.

"How many children did he father?" a woman in the distance shouted.

"Before his death, the man had contributed genes to more than seven dozen children."

Gasps filled the air.

"Keep in mind, his first child murdered nearly three-fourths of those children before their sixth birthdays. Those she did not kill, she used in other ways. Manipulating them to do her bidding by pretending to be someone other than who she truly was. Like her father, she was a master at altering her appearance, and her Influence was unrivaled until more recently. But it is her most recent act of horror that ignited the flames that have brought us to this moment."

Taryn paused, looking to Chrystian and Lazryn. "You see, her father finally found peace while living in a small farming community. There, he had two children, a boy and a girl. The boy was older and he loved him very much, but then his wife told him she was expecting second child. When his daughter was born, a light grew within the man's soul. Love blossomed deep inside him. After a few years of truly enjoying being a father, the man died peacefully in his sleep."

She paused again, casting a glare in Tedra's direction. "The first daughter had watched as the previous events unfolded. Riddled with hate and jealousy, she intended to make both of the children pay dearly for having been bestowed their father's favoritism. She watched them every day for years. She encouraged the town elders to shun them and their mother. And when a new family settled in, she watched as love blossomed between this family's middle son and her father's favorite daughter. She tried to come between them by seducing the young man, but he turned her down no matter what face she wore. Not even her Influence could challenge their love. So after a few years, she befriended the eldest of the three boys. He, himself, was no stranger to hate and jealousy. For his middle brother had the favor of all who knew them. He was a gifted Healer, and their parent's constantly sang his praise."

Taryn stared darkly at Coyan. "Having already put in place an unknowing member of her bloodline within the Elder Council, the original daughter, along with the eldest of the three brothers, convinced the council member to help them with their plan. One night the Elder Council sent an army to assassinate a specific community of Healers. There the legend of the Mortari began. Three brothers and their closest friend survived the attack while they watched all of their loved ones die. With immense heartbreak consuming the friend and the middle brother, the eldest shared with them the knowledge of how to steal the gifts of others to prolong their lives. He assured them it was a necessary evil to keep the Elder Council from eradicating their kind. With bloodlust in their eyes over the loss of their wives and the friend's young daughter, they agreed."

"Lily Girl," Lazryn gasped.

Taryn's eyes met his. "Your sweet Lily lived that night because Clad could not reconcile murdering a child. He, too, was fond of her. In the heat of battle, he snatched her up and ran to a nearby village where he paid a family to take her far away and to never speak of his involvement. That family kept their word. And in the years that followed, Clad would detour your hunts to keep her out of harm's way."

Lazryn fell to his knees. Sobbing, he pounded his fists against the earth. After several moments, he looked up at Taryn. "Tedra is my half-sister," he seethed.

She nodded. "She is."

"And she set this all into motion?" he growled.

Taryn shook her head. "She was not alone."

Chrystian helped his friend to his feet. "The witch will not go unpunished. I promise you this."

"But what of the children you speak of. Would we be familiar with what they may have accomplished on behalf of his first child?" a man questioned from a group off to her right.

Taryn's eyes focused solely on Lazryn as she called out the names of the most well-known. "Adora James. Malayne Douth. Colyn Danbrym. Elanya Delrayn."

Gastyn shook his head. "This does not make sense."

"It does if your father was cursed to live until he found peace," Taryn replied.

"It is impossible for our kind to live beyond a half-century unless they are Mortari. But even they have only existed for a little more than a millennium," he reasoned.

"Once lived a beautiful young woman named Calista. She was given to King Rutgar to be his bride. A man with swirling blue eyes, much like those of Death's appeared, promising to protect her as long as she bore him a child. She did, and in return she experienced hell on earth. Everyday her child was tortured beyond the limits of life that we know. He could not die. So each night she put him to bed and played the Harp of Life to heal his wounds," Taryn explained.

"That was the story my father used to tell Loryn and I," Lazryn exhaled.

"It was not a story, but it was his life. Laertas Dominion's true identity was Maertas, the child carried by Calista, and fathered by someone beyond this and every other world," Taryn replied.

"Who would want their child to suffer so?" Gracyn wept.

"Someone who resented the station given to them by their father. Someone who grew bored watching over the planes and their inhabitants," Taryn stated.

"You cannot prove any of this to be true," Tedra spat.

Taryn jumped down from the boulder and faced the woman. "It's over. Your reign of evil ends here."

"I have someone even more powerful than you in my corner. He will not permit you to harm me," she proclaimed.

A chuckle escaped Taryn's chest. "Oh, I have no intentions of being the one to cause you harm. But I will not stand in their way," Taryn replied, pointing to Lazryn and Chrystian.

"You cannot do this," Tedra thundered.

"No. You shouldn't have given in so easily to your emotions," Taryn roared back, causing lightning to crackle overhead. "But you willingly allowed yourself to be used as an evil pawn for all these years."

Preparing to fight, Coyan lifted his hands. "Brothers and sisters rise up and strike down this demon of a girl."

Before a single Mortari could respond, the earth trembled. Multiple tendrils appeared, pulling several of their members beneath the soil. Flowers instantly bloomed over their graves.

"More theatrics," Chrystian grinned.

A Mortari that stood nearby stared at Taryn. "Why did you spare me?" she asked, confusion present on her face.

Turning to the woman, Taryn's face turned void of emotion. "Because you do not possess evil within your heart. But should you, or any of your remaining brethren choose to continue living as Mortari, the flowers will be on your grave before you hit the ground. Understood?" Taryn warned.

The woman nodded and stumbled as she backed away.

A smile curled on Taryn's face as she moved in a blur to where Chrystian held Coyan and Lazryn held Tedra. "Before she pays with her life, I have a question for her," Taryn stated, watching as the woman struggled in her half-brother's grip. "On your headstone, do you want it to read Tedra or Ardet?"

"I should have killed your precious brother and father when I had the chance," Tedra seethed.

Leaning in, Taryn whispered in the woman's ear.

Enraged by the teen's words, Tedra screamed into the air. "No. He promised it would be me. It can only be me."

Appearing suddenly next to Larkin, Taryn wrapped her arms around him as Lazryn and Chrystian began dismembering the evil couple.

"All this death. Are you certain there isn't another way?" Larkin questioned.

"Should they be permitted to live, the evil in their souls will only continue to fester. It will spread like cancer when we least expect it, and I cannot allow for that to happen," she replied.

He swallowed hard. "But what about it leaving a mark upon your soul?"

Taryn smiled softly. "I've made peace with that part of me. She is in a place where she can no longer be affected by what I am now."

"And what exactly are you?" Larkin questioned as he looked into her green eyes.

"It depends on what the night brings," she replied, glancing to where a fire now raged.

"Is that Coyan and Tedra?" he asked.

Taryn nodded. "This is the only way for there to be peace amongst the planes.

Larkin kissed her on top of her head. "After all these years, how is it they could finally best Coyan and Tedra?"

With arched brows, Taryn raised her hand. "Guilty."

"I don't get it," he replied.

"Maybe not, but you soon will," Taryn shrugged.

"What's that supposed to mean?"

Taryn shook her head and sighed. "I am at peace with knowing who and what I am. I hope when the sun rises tomorrow, I am still standing and you will choose to be with me."

Larkin's eyes grew wide. "What are you talking about, Taryn?"

She stood silent, staring at him.

He ran his hands over his hair. "Why won't you just tell me what's going on here?"

She bit her bottom lip and shrugged. "I can't explain it, but I can show you. Before tonight is over, you will bear witness to what, and who, I truly am."

Taking a deep breath, Larkin threw his hands in the air. "Okay, then let me ask you this. Whoever, whatever it is you are now, does that person still want to be with me?"

"Always and forever," she answered.

"Then what's the problem?" he questioned.

She shrugged, leaning into him.

"Sorry to interrupt love birds, but we have a lot of people who are confused, scared and hungry that would like to go home if that's allowed," Keiryn announced.

Pushing back from Larkin, Taryn shook her head. "No. They must witness what is yet to come so that they may tell their children and their childrens' children."

"Then I suggest we get things moving along," he replied.

With a brief glance at Larkin, Taryn turned and marched back toward the boulder. Passing several members of her family along the way, her eyes focused straight ahead.

"Taryn, what is it?" Lazryn asked as he followed behind her.

Standing on top of the large rock, Taryn looked down at him. "Are you ready to meet your grandfather?"

"My grandfather?" he questioned.

Ignoring his question, Taryn looked the crowd over.

"Will this require helix orbs?" Lazryn questioned.

Approaching on his left, Chrystian chuckled, wrapping his arm around his neck. "It is time to get to know the other side of your granddaughter, my friend. Let us take a few steps back and allow her the space needed to fulfill her grand destiny."

Looking at his longtime friend, Lazryn arched a brow. "Do you know what she is up to?" he questioned.

"Of course. Loryn has told me all that she is permitted to," he replied.

Lazryn stopped in his tracks. "But my sister is dead."

"Yes, but even in death, she remains incredible," Chrystian answered.

"Whatever this is, do we know how it ends?" Lazryn asked cautiously.

With a wild smile, Chrystian looked to Taryn. "The ending is Taryn's to write. Only she possesses knowledge of how the final act ends."

Lazryn's forehead creased.

"Do not fret, grandpa, for your granddaughter is full of surprises," Chrystian chuckled.

CHAPTER TWENTY-TWO

Taryn stood upon the boulder, a look of fierce peacefulness on her face.

Gracyn approached the rock. "What are you doing up there?"

Suddenly a dozen helix orbs filled the sky.

"The story I was telling earlier, it's not quite finished." Taryn announced.

Her mother's face wrinkled with confusion.

"For your own safety. You need to step back with the others," her daughter warned.

Theron wrapped his arms around his wife's waist and walked her back to stand with the rest of their group.

Once more, Taryn prepared to tell the story. She formed a massive chessboard from the earth and provided the appropriate pieces as she spoke. "Many of you were forced here today to witness Chrystian's execution, or what someone had hoped would be my undoing."

The crowd quieted, listening closely as the girl spoke.

"Tedra, whose birth name was Ardet, was being used as a pawn by the one who began this entire nightmare. Unlike most of the pieces on this individual's chessboard, she was never capable of being anything other than what she was. Her heart was as black as night from the moment she was born. This made the heartless woman ripe for the game maker. When her father failed to complete the task he was created for, she quickly filled the void by being molded into the very thing he needed to set the pieces upon the board once more. Whenever a plan failed to go as he had hoped, he would simply create a new piece." Taryn paused, looking to Hava Love. "The demon known as Karvyn was actually the child of Coyan and Ardet. They threw her away and allowed the unknown man to raise her. She corrupted everything she touched, and she took pride and found joy in the destruction left in her wake. But when I came along and removed her from his board, he was eager to switch up his pieces once more. However, he did not fully grasp who and what I am, because I had powerful allies in my corner. They began preparing for this before I ever took my first breath."

"Do these powerful allies have a name?" Chrystian inquired, while looking around at the numerous Gaias.

Taryn nodded. "Indeed they do. The first being Farren, also known to many as Death. The second being Thantos, keeper and protector of the Void. Some of you may not realize, but they are half-brothers."

Gasps filled the air as her words traveled throughout the large group.

In her silence, Andyn and Dedrick, moved closer to Keiryn.

Taryn looked to her younger brother with great care shining in her eyes and smiled. He nodded in return.

"When I was a toddler, the fish that my parents had purchased for my brother and I died. Keiryn and I snuck down to play with him and there he was, floating lifeless at the top of the water. I reached my finger up, touching his side, and he instantly sprang back to life. His name is Ralph and he still lives today." She paused, looking about the crowd. "I know many of you are wondering why this part of the story matters, because so many of you already believe me to be a freak. But here's the thing, that night my parents decided they had no other choice but to split our family in two to protect us all. Me with my mother, and Keiryn with my dad. But there was another person in play here. You see, my Uncle Julius and my mother were very close, half siblings who shared a father. Nodryck was the nephew of Julius' mother, so he was no relation to us. He just assumed that our families were great friends. He also believed my mother and my uncle to be secret lovers, which of course could not have been further from the truth. Julius and his mother knew how awful and cruel that side of their family could be, so they kept all their other relationships hidden. Being his usual mean-spirited self, Nodryck sought to make my mother and Julius suffer anyway."

Taryn paused for a brief moment before continuing. "While we were on the run, he had his lackeys track my mother down. She hid me behind a dumpster and led them away, which allowed her to be captured. During the same time, the Mortari were investigating my father. But as the Mortari often did, they were multi-tasking that day. Not only were they spying on and losing my father, but they murdered my second mother's friends at a shelter house as they picnicked. At the same time, my two powerful friends were also hard at work. Farren spoke to Ilya, leading her to me. He then saw to it that my mother's mind was not accessible to the Elder Council, or any other curious beings, while Thantos locked my father and brother's memories away and relocated them to Williams."

Taryn glanced tenderly in Julius' direction. "I'm afraid my Uncle Julius had it far worse than the rest of us. He had to feign my Cousin Jonesy's death, give him away and permit his son's mind to be locked up while his own remained fully intact, but absolutely impenetrable. He had to watch as my mother was treated despicably by his cousin. Even Larkin and his parents were not spared from the shakeup, sending them back to Williams with no memory of my family."

Taryn paused again, this time glancing toward the night sky and taking a deep breath. "So you see, each time there was a shake up around me, this game maker was forced to mix up his board. This was the first mistake of many," she stated with a pleased look upon her face.

"After my time on Mors, it became more difficult for my allies to hide the truth about who I was. So many things were in play, but they did all they could to protect my family, and in turn save me from myself. You see, my emotions were directly linked to my gifts. If I was happy, it was sunny. If I was sad, it rained. And Heaven forbid I become angry, as I could set the worlds on fire or cast them into an ice age." She paused, looking to Larkin. "The game maker figured this out about me, so he placed triggers all around, hoping that I would lose control. That was the point of the Trials last fall. I was supposed to lose myself and destroy everything." Taryn paused again, holding her hands over her heart as she gazed upon Larkin. "But once again, the game maker underestimated the power of true love. Larkin pulled me back from the edge, thwarting his plans."

"What is different about today?" Chrystian prodded with a goofy grin.

Taryn shook her head and chuckled. "He tried to use a monster that felt no pain against my family. The plan was to rile me and have me take its life, casting a mark upon my mortal soul. However, my good friend, and distant uncle, spared me from the task."

Chrystian took a theatrical bow, causing the teen to smile widely.

"Which brings us to what happened earlier today…it was real. I died and went to the Void. I spent time with my ancestors and learned a lot about myself while there."

Absolute silence filled the air as Taryn looked to Larkin.

"The game maker insisted I had but two choices. I could either stand by and watch Chrystian die, or I could intervene and unleash hell upon all of Mors. Unable to find the upside in either scenario, I chose to create my own option. Something that I felt was the better choice because I wasn't prepared to live in a world without Chrystian, nor was I prepared to carry the burden of knowing I had blood on my hands. Even if it was Mortari," she disclosed.

Andyn stepped forward. "Did Farren return you to us?"

"Sort of," she replied, shuffling the pieces about on the board. "In the end, it was the other part of my family that guided me back to you. Family that I would have never realized I had if the game maker hadn't insisted on giving me ultimatums and provoking the giant that slumbered within me."

"You're losing us, Taryn. What family, and what giant?" Keiryn questioned.

She looked to her brother. "The day I nearly died, you heard a man whispering in the wind."

Keiryn nodded.

Panning her eyes to Ilya, Taryn looked softly upon the woman. "And the voice that guided you to me and spoke to you on occasion while we lived in Galatia, that, too, was Farren. You could hear him because his blood runs through your veins."

Lazryn stepped forward, shaking his head in protest. "No, Taryn. Tell me you are wrong. Death cannot be my grandfather."

She smiled softly. "He is not, but he is your blood. You see, it was his other half-brother who reached out to Calista and made the bargain."

"What you are saying is that Immortal blood runs through our veins." Lazryn paused, rubbing the back of his neck. "Why would a superior being do such a thing and create all this chaos?"

Taryn's gaze fell heavy upon a particular member of their community. "Why don't you ask him yourself," she replied, staring at the young child.

Following her gaze to Dedrick, Lazryn shook his head. "Have you gone mad, Taryn?"

"Let's ask Dedrick, or perhaps he would be more inclined to answer if we called him by his proper name. What say you, Diederick, do you care to enlighten the masses?" Taryn stated smugly.

Lifting his palm in her direction, Lazryn shook his head as tears streamed down his cheeks. "I will not permit you to inflict harm upon this child."

Silence grew heavy in the air as the teen stared tenderly at Lazryn.

"Taryn speaks the truth, Brother. Loryn warned me the devil would be found underfoot," Chrystian offered.

"So says the monster who claims he speaks to his dead wife," Lazryn growled.

"The confusion you feel right now, it's because Diederick is fighting to hold onto you. He knows his secret is out, and that his time as the ruler of men is nearing its conclusion," Taryn explained.

Lazryn struck himself on the side of the head with an open palm several times. "He is just a boy," he wept.

"No, Lazryn. He is a coward who hides behind the façade of a child," Taryn insisted.

Dedrick suddenly charged forward, and as he did, his appearance flickered between several images before taking his true form.

Taryn held her position as the grown man with dark hair and swirling blue irises approached.

"You are a formidable opponent, Taryn, but you will not win this game. However, I am curious as to what gave me away," he stated.

The teen chuckled as she stood poised. "Your second to the last mistake was believing Chrystian could ever be your pawn, when clearly, he has always been my knight."

The swirling within Diederick's eyes began to churn violently as the lightning crackled overhead. "Foolish girl, I will deal with my brothers when I am finished destroying you and your family."

"And threatening my family is your final mistake," Taryn thundered, creating a shield around her loved ones and all the other spectators.

Diederick released a mighty howl as he began to increase in size. "You may not cower before a boy, but you will certainly cower before a god."

Suddenly a dozen other average sized beings appeared behind the ruler of men.

Taryn taunted the man. "Are you afraid that you are incapable of defeating a teenaged girl on your own?"

He waved the other Immortals back. "At least my allies care to show when summoned."

With a wink, Taryn's smile increased as Farren appeared to her left and Thantos to her right. "My allies are here as spectators only. They plan on enjoying the show."

"Big words for such a tiny girl. Your gifts may leave these simple Gaias in awe, but I am an Immortal. You shall bow at my feet or break beneath my power," he thundered.

Farren addressed his brother. "For far too long you have gone without having to answer to our father. In your boredom, you have shuffled the lives of those you were charged to protect, and left nothing but chaos and mayhem in your wake."

With his arms outstretched, Diederick stared at Death. "Please do tell us of how this puny girl won your favor, Brother. I am certain it shall be an exhilarating tale. Though I am most certain father will not approve of your backing one of these Lessor beings."

"Before the next tomorrow, you shall beg for her to show you favor," Thantos roared.

Diederick frowned. "And of course, father's least favorite could not help but tie himself to this teen."

Hopping down from the boulder, Taryn walked over to the fire. Moving her hands in a strange pattern, the fire responded by rising upward, piercing the sky.

"In case this is meant to serve as a tryout of sorts, I regret to inform you that we already have a keeper of the flame," he laughed, garnering hearty chuckles from those standing at his back.

Taryn arched her brows. "That's rich coming from the same guy who spent months trying to provoke me into setting the worlds on fire." She paused, giving a slight shrug. "Seems to me if your keeper of the flame was all that, then you would not have needed me. The same goes for your keeper of the frost."

From behind her shield of protection, Chrystian watched with great anticipation. "You tell him as it is, Taryn," he shouted.

Lazryn looked to his friend. "Loryn foretold you this would happen?"

"The outcome of their faceoff is yet undetermined. However, your sister believes that Taryn possesses a great secret, that if revealed, will bolster her ability to triumph in this battle, and beyond," Chrystian shared.

Without warning, Diederick rushed Taryn, landing a backhanded blow. His hand being nearly as wide as she was tall, sent her flying into the air.

Reaching her hands out, Taryn formed two chains with clawed hooks on the ends from Imperium power. Casting them downward, she adhered them to the ground below and slowed her momentum.

Landing on her feet, she looked at the giant and grinned. "Is that the best you've got," she taunted.

Looking toward the teen's friends and family who stood nearby, the Immortal grinned darkly. He turned back to face the teen. "I can see your judgement, Taryn. You truly believe these Lessor beings have value, regardless of how useless their existence proves to be."

"What, did daddy not love you enough so you have to take it out on them?" she questioned, motioning to the crowd.

Diederick's eyes filled with anger. "Do not speak of things of which you know nothing."

Taryn shrugged with a hint of arrogance. "You're right, it wasn't because daddy didn't love you enough. It's because he didn't love you more. He put you in charge of all living beings, yet you hold resentment and jealousy towards Farren and Thantos for being charged with caring for the dying and the dead."

"Shut up, you stupid girl," Diederick thundered.

"No. Your father chose them because he knew you would only cause torment to those who passed. You wreak havoc on the living, but death is the longest, most permanent state of being," she roared back. Deiderick took another swipe at the girl, but she disappeared before he could make contact.

Appearing at the mouth of the valley, Taryn wagged her finger. "I'm not done yet. You have treated both the Gaias and Human races as puppets. Wars have waged because of the lies you told and the hate you have spread. You have used us all for your personal entertainment." She paused as lightning crackled overhead. "It all ends today."

Deiderick's jaw drew tight. "How dare you speak to your master in such a way."

With her hands balled into fists, Taryn stared daggers at him. "If this is the course you choose, I will see that you are the master of nothing."

After staring at the teen briefly, Deiderick began to chuckle. The sound of his laughter grew until it became thunderous. "This insolent gifted mortal child actually believes she can best me." He paused, turning toward the massive crowd of Gaias. "Such an egregious offense cannot go unpunished. Fortunately for me and my brethren, I have nearly a million of you to make examples of."

Panic set in with the crowd, and chaos ensued.

Deiderick held his hands out in front of his chest, then balled them into fists. Instantly, the ground began to shake and the sound of the earth cracking rippled through the air.

Turning to the lone teen standing in the distance, he released a hair-raising chuckle. "You believe yourself special, when you are clearly nothing when compared to me. All your will and might cannot save your wretched kind from its fate." He paused, unclenching his fist and releasing the land from his grasp. "You see, Taryn, I never needed your gifts. You simply made the game more interesting."

Watching as the masses fought to run up the steep terrain, Taryn took a deep breath and closed her eyes.

Deiderick stared at her with amusement. "Foolish girl, you may call upon the dead, but they shall not rise. They may haunt the living, but they may never live again."

Blocking his words from her mind, Taryn searched deep inside herself. Sensational waves of panic and fear washed over her, rolling off her fellow Gaias when they realized they had nowhere to run.

"You pretend to not hear me, yet I suspect if I were to threaten your precious Larkin, you would acknowledge my words," he called out.

When the girl still did not respond, Deiderick motioned to the two Immortals standing to his right.

Rushing toward Taryn, the duo began to circle her, forming a vortex that ensnared the teen.

With her hair whipping violently around her face, Taryn's eyes opened wide and she peered through the swirling wind.

A victorious gleam grew inside Deiderick's eyes. "The moment you stole away for yourself has cost you and your friends dearly." Pausing, he turned to where her family stood. He blew against the shield she had created causing it to shatter.

Their screams pierced the air. While attempting to flee, they soon found themselves unable to move.

"Your kind sickens me. Scattering about at the first sign of conflict. You are the truly weak." Deiderick paused. He walked over, reaching down and plucking Larkin from the crowd. With a dark smile, he placed the teen upon the boulder. "I know what this boy means to you, Taryn. But does he?"

She began to take a step forward, when Deiderick wagged his finger.

"Tsk, tsk. I would not do that if I were you. You see the winds my brothers encased you within, they are razor sharp and will cut the flesh from your bones should you try to go anywhere," he warned.

Taryn glared at the man. "You asked if Larkin knew what he meant to me. But isn't that a question better answered by him?"

Arching his brow in her direction, a smirk grew from one side of Deiderick's mouth. "What does it matter whose lips the words fall from unless this is your feeble attempt to stall the inevitable."

The teen stood silent as she gazed tenderly upon Larkin's still frame. After several moments passed, she finally spoke up. "You say you know what he means to me, but I sincerely doubt that you do. For me, Larkin is my everything. The air that I breathe. A quiet place where I can rest my head when I grow weary. When I look into his eyes, I see endless, beautiful possibilities. He is the unknowing keeper of all my secrets and..."

Cutting her off mid-sentence, Deiderick smiled. "And he is the keeper of your heart. Isn't that right, Taryn?"

She nodded her head. "Yes. Larkin is the keeper of my heart."

"And what do you think would happen should your heart become broken?" he taunted while tapping Larkin on top of the head.

Taryn knelt down on one knee within the swirling cage and bowed her head, ignoring the man.

Locked inside his motionless body, Larkin's mind raced, taking in every detail of Deiderick and Taryn's interaction. *His intentions are obvious. No matter what happens here, he plans to murder us all. But why is he still trying to provoke Taryn? Why does he want her to be the one to destroy us? He's certainly more powerful than any other being, so why does he need her to do his dirty work for him?* Suddenly all the pieces fell into place and Larkin discovered a profound understanding of the situation. *Deiderick's not allowed to harm us directly. His father won't allow it. That's why he's so desperate for Taryn to lose control. And that's why he's taunting her with me.*

Desperate to warn her, Larkin began to fight Deiderick's Influence. Pushing outward against the walls inside his own mind, he started to feel a flicker of freedom in his left pinky. As the sensation crept throughout his entire body, he screamed as loud as he could. The deep sound echoed inside him until suddenly his voice pierced through to the night air.

Deiderick looked at the young man with wide eyes. "This cannot be. No one can escape my Influence."

"While you've been busy taunting Taryn, I've discovered something about you, Deiderick," Larkin stated with great authority.

The Immortal's nostrils flared as he bared his teeth and growled at the young man.

Looking to Taryn, Larkin shouted, "Deiderick cannot inflict harm upon us. His father won't allow it." He paused, jumping down from the boulder and rushing to his family. "He has no power over any of you. Break out of the box he's trapped your mind in and free yourselves."

After several seconds passed, Theron began to move and then Maxym. The others quickly followed suit until their entire group broke free from Deiderick's grasp.

Larkin looked to where the northern California pack stood with their family. "Quickly, everyone. Help Ibrym and his pack, and then work to free the others," he directed.

Turning around, expecting to face the giant, Larkin startled, finding himself standing toe-to-toe with Dagrin.

With a smug look upon his face, the king of the Lessors pushed up against the teen. "It seems you were not expecting to see me again, house-wolf."

Holding his ground, Larkin stared into the man's eyes. "I'm not afraid of you, Dagrin. But you should be very afraid of me."

A hearty laugh rose from deep with Dagrin. "Your venom no longer holds power over me. And your precious Taryn is unable to come to your rescue. So you see, it is you who should fear me."

Deiderick looked down the length of the valley at the girl who remained kneeling on one knee. "You should rise, Taryn, and watch the demise of your little wolf. My creation will destroy him within minutes, if not seconds."

The evil Immortal and his followers all laughed, taunting the girl as she remained still.

Dagrin drew back his fist and landed the first blow upside Larkin's jaw, causing the young man to stagger backwards.

"Come now, boy. That was barely a tap. You had better toughen up quickly if you want this fight to last more than a minute or two," the Lessor taunted.

Finding his footing, Larkin steadied himself. As the man neared, he reached out, striking him several times in the head with closed fists.

Dagrin stumbled about, momentarily dazed, before regaining his composure. Putting up his fists, he and Larkin began exchanging blows. One after another, they took headshots and blows to the torso. After several moments passed, Dagrin began to wobble.

Seeing his champion in distress, Deiderick decided it best to intervene. "Hit him again, and I will instruct my brothers to tighten the vortex that surrounds the girl."

Distracted by the man's words, Larkin looked to Taryn. Seeing the threat menacing all around her, he started to move toward her when he was suddenly blindsided by a boot to the head.

Unleashing a hellish assault, the Lessor howled into the air with joy. Blood began to run down Larkin's forehead and cheeks while he struggled to remain standing.

After several more strikes, Larkin fell onto his knees.

"No," Maxym shouted as he rushed down the mountainside toward his son. Making it only a few steps, he slowed.

With one hand holding onto the back of Larkin's head and the other drawn in the air, Dagrin readied to deal the young man a final blow. Clenching his fist tight, he began to feel a strange sensation creeping up the back of his neck.

"What is happening?" Dagrin questioned, looking to Deiderick.

The Immortal shook his head. "It does not matter. Finish him," he ordered.

The entire crowd of Gaias began to sound off as they felt it too.

Aware of what was happening, Farren and Thantos urged the crowd higher upon the mountainside.

Dagrin returned his attention to the young man only to discover his wounds had begun to Heal. The gash on Larkin's forehead was no longer visible, and the blood that had marred his face only seconds before evaporated right before his eyes. "I do not understand," he mumbled.

Rising to his feet, Larkin pushed the man away. "It's coming for her."

"What is coming?" Dagrin questioned.

Larkin's breath caught in his throat as lightning began to illuminate the sky directly over Taryn. "I have to reach her," he gasped. With all his heart's desire, he wanted to protect his love, but his feet carried him to the base of the mountainside to where his father and other members of their community stood watching.

Thunder sounded overhead, shaking the earth beneath their feet as the lightning's intensity strengthened.

Lifting her chin, Taryn's eyes opened. Slowly, she began to rise to her feet. "Where I have sought peace, you have waged war. When I provided opportunity for change, you brought discord and corruption." Standing tall, she gazed upon the masses before turning her eyes to Deiderick. "Your blood flows through so many of our veins, yet you care nothing for us."

Drawing his jaw up tight, Deiderick's face shone with absolute disgust. "Maertas was to be the only one. He was to be my escape from a life full of servitude."

"You saw a means to an end for what you perceived to be an injustice carried out by your father for assigning you to watch over all living things," Taryn replied.

"It is easy for you to judge me, but you have no idea the hell I have endured as the keeper of the living," Deiderick retorted.

Taryn's face remained neutral while her eyes teemed with emotion and her tone carried a chill. "Even now I feel the hate pouring out from your every fiber."

"What does it truly matter, Taryn? You already know that I cannot directly harm another because of the chains my father shackled me in. My allies and I will retreat into the other realm while you and these insects continue about your daily lives," Deiderick growled.

"It matters because you are incapable of change. If you were permitted to return to the other realm, you would once again grow bored and continue to play your games at the expense of the living," she replied.

The Immortal arched his brows with a hint of a smile. "You are not wrong in believing that I would once more grow bored. But you see, I have gleaned great knowledge through this loss. And when your end comes, perhaps I will find another beautiful Gaias to bare my child, and this time there will be no mistakes."

Taryn closed her eyes, recalling every ounce of suffering Maertas experienced over his lifetime, and the pain his mother had felt. "I cannot permit you to return to the other realm only to wage war upon our kind once more," she exhaled,

Deiderick laughed. "You still believe that you are somehow more powerful than me. I am here to tell you otherwise."

The cloud-to-cloud lightning began to intensify even more over Taryn and the two Immortals who stood watching over her.

Opening her eyes, Taryn displayed the glowing blue hue of her irises.

Larkin looked on eagerly as others gasped at the sight. Even in the distance, it was easy to see how her stunning eyes swirled about.

"Everything begins and ends with family, Deiderick. Ours is no exception. While you were busy playing your games and ruining the lives of many a good people, another was keeping watch over me. He chose not to interfere when Farren and Thantos devised their plan to keep me hidden from you and the others. Instead, he checked in on me from time to time to verify for himself that I did not carry your poor traits or contempt for the living," the teen disclosed.

"Lies," Deiderick spat. "My father has not stepped foot outside the gates in more than seven millenniums. Now you are trying to infer that he has somehow played a hand in your upbringing."

"He has never interfered until today. You forced his hand, and he has made his wishes known to me," Taryn stated, her words laden with warning.

Deiderick shook his head defiantly. "I am not afraid of you, child. I shall leave this awful plane and return to my home where I will once more plot the destruction of all living things."

With those final words spoken, the hair rose on the back of Taryn's neck. A second later, two massive lightning bolts shot down from the sky striking the two Immortals guarding her. The vortex disappeared, and Taryn rushed toward Deiderick with lightning following her every step.

Larkin and the others watched with bated breath as the great power chased her down. For every Gaias understood that lightning equaled certain death for their kind.

Taryn jumped onto the giant boulder as lightning struck at her heels. Using the rock as a springboard of sorts, she leapt into the air heading toward Deiderick. As she neared, a massive lightning bolt shot from the sky. Taryn reached her hand out, grabbing the pure energy and plunged it deep inside Deiderick's chest. The mighty Immortal fell upon his back as the lightning drained him of all his powers and returned him to average size.

Landing skillfully on the balls of her feet, Taryn stared down at the once powerful being.

Rushing toward her, Larkin stopped just shy of touching her. "Are you hurt?" he asked.

Smiling softly, she shook her head. "No, Larkin. I'm not injured."

"But the lightning…you grabbed it? And you plunged it into his chest?" he questioned with furrowed brows.

"Yes. I did both of those things," she replied.

He shook his head. "How? How did you do it?"

"Because of what and who I am," she answered.

Taking a deep breath, he ran his hands through his hair anxiously. "I don't get it, Taryn. You are still Taryn, right?"

She nodded. "I'm just a bit different compared to the girl I was twelve hours ago."

Before Larkin could ask another question, one of Deiderick's allies with glowing red eyes stepped closer. "Is he dead?" the man inquired.

"He lives, though he is no longer the same." She paused, stepping back to address the massive crowd. "Today you have all served as witness to a new beginning. The tyranny that this Immortal has inflicted upon your kind for far too long has finally come to an end."

Larkin's brows furrowed. "What do you mean, Taryn, when you say your kind?"

Her vibrant blue irises swirled like a gentle ocean as she gazed upon him. Lightning fell from the sky and she reached out, taking it into the palm of her hand. After holding onto it for several moments, Taryn forced the pure energy back into the atmosphere.

"I've always had Immortal blood flowing through my veins. But now it is the only blood," she confessed.

Tears welled in Larkin's eyes. "Are you telling me that you're an Immortal now?"

"I have always been two beings living in conflict within a single entity. When I died earlier today, that changed everything. I am no longer just Taryn Knight, I am the Lightning's Fury," she answered.

Gracyn moved closer to her daughter with Theron trailing directly behind her. "No, Taryn. This isn't fair. We just got you back. I just got you back," she sobbed.

"I am sorry, but this is what and who I am now. And it will never change," Taryn replied.

Keiryn joined their parents as he stared cautiously at his sister. "You need to finish your business here, Taryn. These people need to return to their homes. It's been an emotional and exhausting day to say the least."

She nodded in agreement, and then looked to Chrystian and Lazryn. "Would you both mind seeing to it that everyone is returned to their home planes safely?"

Placing his hand on her shoulder, Farren announced, "We must take our leave now as well."

Taryn turned toward Larkin. Confusion reigned heavily upon his face as he stared at her.

"Only Immortals may enter the other realm, Taryn," Thantos reminded.

"Yes. I know," she replied curtly.

Sucking in a deep breath, Larkin forced a hint of a smile to curl on his face. "Go on, Taryn. It's okay. I'll see you soon."

"Always and forever," she replied, before disappearing with the rest of the Immortals and Dagrin in tow.

An obnoxious laugh from the crowd that was left had everyone turning in the direction of Nodryck. Tears streamed from his eyes as the laughter poured out uncontrollably.

With barely a flicker of movement, Chrystian looked at the man with a cold gleam in his eyes.

Nodryck's laughter subsided abruptly, and fear shone heavily on his face as black vines curled out of the ground, snaring around his ankles.

Gasps filled the air as the vile man was pulled below the ground. A black, bleeding rose bush sprang up where he had stood.

Turning to face Lazryn, Chrystian gave his friend a wink. "I never really liked theatrics, but that was most pleasant."

€Ω€Ω

Maxym looked out the large window to where Larkin sat on the far edge of the deck. "It's been nearly six months, and he still goes outside every day and stares at that path, waiting for her walk through the tree line."

"She's surprised us all before. There's no reason this time should be any different," Theron replied hopeful.

Overhearing the men's conversation, Gracyn and Ilya sipped their coffee in the kitchen doorway.

"I miss her so much," Gracyn stated, fighting to stave off the tears welling in her eyes.

Ilya leaned in, giving her friend a slight nudge. "We all do. Things haven't been nearly as lively...well, since she left."

"You mean since she was stolen from us," Gracyn sighed with bitterness.

Sensing the need to change the subject, Ilya glanced back at the clock inside the kitchen. "Lazryn and Chrystian should be back any moment, and the others are scheduled to arrive in a few hours. I think it best if we get started on the pumpkin pies."

Gracyn gave a long look to where her husband stood with their best friend gazing out the window. "This would have been my first Thanksgiving with my family back in tact." She paused, looking to the woman. "She will come back, right?"

Ilya smiled softly. "Anything is possible where Taryn is concerned."

ಐೞೞೞೞ

The sound of quiet chatter filled the house as the Williams group dined on their Thanksgiving feast.

Keiryn sat opposite from Larkin, watching as his friend absentmindedly ran his fork over his potatoes while giving the occasional glance to the empty chair to his right. At the table in the far corner of the room, he observed his mother feigning yet another smile while listening to Beldyn tell a story. Pushing back from the table, he rose to his feet. "I can't take this anymore."

Theron looked to his son. "Please, Keiryn, not today."

"If not today, then when? When do we finally discuss what happened on Mors?" he demanded.

Moving to his feet, Larkin stared at his friend for a long moment before glancing around the room. "You all act like Taryn's gone, but the truth is, she's never been more present in our lives." He paused, moving toward the oversized windows. "You think I go outside because I'm waiting for her, but the thing is, she is in every breath we take, in every breeze that blows. She lives in the grass, the trees and the flowers. Taryn may not be here in body, but she most certainly is in spirit."

Chrystian rose from his seat. "Larkin speaks the truth. I have lived more than a thousand years, and I promise you the planes have never known such peace and prosperity until Taryn's sacrifice. Her presence has never been more potent than it is now."

Slamming her silverware onto her plate, Gracyn fought back her tears. "Please, stop."

"My apologies. I did not intend to upset you," Chrystian replied.

Everyone settled back into their seats and returned to their meal when the hair on the back of their necks began to stand on end.

"Hello," a familiar voice stated near the foot of the stairs.

Larkin turned, taking in the vision of loveliness standing across the room. There stood his love, with long flowing honey blond hair, swirling blue eyes and a warm smile. "Taryn," he whispered as tears welled in his eyes.

"I'm sorry I couldn't make it here any sooner. But I was hoping you might still have room for one more at your table," she stated, looking in the direction of the empty chair.

He nodded his head eagerly. "Yeah, of course. There's always a place here for you."

Taryn looked around the room at all the stunned faces. "The food smells divine," she offered, trying to ease the shock.

Moving to her side, Larkin escorted her to the empty seat next to his. "Would you like me to fix you a plate?" he asked.

"Sure," she replied.

Gracyn rose from her seat. "No, please let me."

Taryn smiled softly at her mother. "That would be nice."

ഔൠൠ

Having finished their meal, Taryn and Larkin went for a walk in the woods while the others cleaned up from the celebration.

"How have you been?" he asked, breaking the silence lingering between them.

She shrugged. "Okay, I guess."

He chuckled. "You're an Immortal, and you say you're just okay?"

"It's not what you'd expect it to be. I mean, we don't lounge about on pillows made of clouds all day. We have a tremendous amount of discord from the very top all the way to the absolute bottom...well, at least we used to," she shared.

Larkin arched a brow in her direction. "Used to?"

Pausing in her step, Taryn reached out, grabbing hold of his hand. "Please know that I never wanted to stay away for so long."

"Then why did you?" he asked.

"Because it is what was required of me, to stay until every matter was resolved," she replied.

With her hand firmly in his, Larkin began walking the path once again. "I'm sure it's all very involved."

She sighed. "Actually, it's not that involved at all. We settle our disputes, no matter how large or small, by battling one another."

Larkin stepped in front of her, halting their walk. "Are you okay? Did they hurt you?" he questioned while looking her over.

Shaking her head, Taryn chuckled. "I'm fine. I mean, I really didn't have to do much after what happened on Mors." She paused, taking a deep breath. "It seems that all Immortals fear lightning even more than Gaias do."

A proud smile curled on his face. "So what does that mean exactly? Where does that leave you in their world?"

Taryn's cheeks warmed. "I sit to the right of Deiderick's father."

"Why would you be embarrassed by this?" he asked.

She threw her hands up. "I don't know. It's just odd to think I'm eighteen years old and I have beings who have lived since the dawn of time bowing when I walk past."

Taking a step back, Larkin bowed. "Do they do something like this?" he asked with a grin.

Placing her hand beneath his chin, she looked him in the eyes. "Don't you ever bow to anyone, Larkin Taylor. Especially not to me."

Noting the seriousness in her eyes, he immediately straightened himself. "I'm sorry, Taryn. I didn't mean to offend you."

She took a deep breath and motioned for him to follow. "You could never offend me. But it isn't appropriate for you to bow to anyone."

"Okay. You do know I was just playing around, right?" he asked, sliding his arm around her waist.

"I know. But promise me you will never do it again," she replied.

"Sure. Whatever you say," he agreed.

They walked in silence for nearly a mile before Larkin spoke again.

"How long are you here for?" he asked.

She shrugged. "I have certain responsibilities, but I could be here on most days."

"Is that what you want, to be here with us...with me?" he questioned.

Taryn looked up at him, noting the fear shining within his hazel eyes. "You know what I want. Always and forever."

Pausing in his step, Larkin released a hefty sigh. "Immortals never grow old and they never die, Taryn, but the rest of us will. Are you prepared to watch as your loved ones grow old and die? As I grow old and die?"

"Death holds no power over me. I know with absolute certainty that there is life after death. And I will never be apart from the ones I love, because there is no realm I cannot enter." She paused, tears filling her eyes. "No realm that we cannot enter."

"What exactly do you mean by we?" he questioned.

Suddenly a hint of panic shone within her eyes. "Please don't hate me."

"I could never, Taryn," he stated with a look of confusion upon his face.

She looked to him with waves of emotions swirling in her eyes. "Hear me out and we will see if you still feel the same."

"I promise you there is nothing you could ever say that would change how I feel about you," he swore.

Tears fell from her eyes and rolled down her cheeks. "You are not just the keeper of my heart, Larkin. You are my heart."

His brows furrowed. "How is that a bad thing?"

"I gave you my heart before I was born, and that bound us together in all ways. I am an Immortal, and as an extension of me, you too, are now an Immortal," she disclosed.

Larkin's eyes narrowed, then widened, then narrowed again, before he stumbled backward into a nearby tree. He ran his hands over his hair numerous times as he shook his head. Crouching down, he began to mumble to himself.

"I'm so sorry, Larkin. At the time, I didn't know what the repercussions would be for doing such a thing. I just remember hearing your heart beating on the outside of my mother's womb and thinking I never wanted to be without you," she confessed.

From his crouching position, he looked up at her. "You remember that?"

She nodded. "Ever since I became the Lightning's Fury, I remember everything."

He rose to his feet and stepped closer to her. "Give me your hand."

Surprised by his request, she furrowed her brows. "What?"

"Give me your hand, Taryn," he demanded.

Complying, she extended it toward him.

He stepped closer, pressing his chest against her palm. "Can you feel that?" he asked, placing his hands over hers. "You didn't just give me your heart, Taryn, I gave you mine."

Staring into his eyes, Taryn watched as they changed from hazel to blue. "Does this mean what I think it does?" she gasped.

"I thought you knew what lived in the heart of men?" he grinned.

Taryn swiped the tears from her eyes. "Your heart is no longer that of a man."

With a quiet chuckle, Larkin pulled her into his arms and crushed his lips against hers.

ೞ〰ೞ〰

From the back deck of their home, Chrystian, Lazryn and several others watched as thousands of flowers bloomed, covering their entire yard and beyond.

"I guess this means they're still together," Maxym grinned, pulling Ilya in close.

Theron slipped his arms around Gracyn's waist, resting his chin on her shoulder. "It looks like our little girl is happy."

With tears flooding her eyes, she nodded. "That's all I ever wanted."

Keiryn joined Chrystian and Lazryn on the edge of the deck, placing an arm around each of their shoulders. "I guess I should have listened to my favorite uncle and best grandfather when you said everything would turn out as it was meant to be," he grinned.

"Having someone on the other side does come in handy from time to time," Chrystian replied while pretending to have something in his eye.

"Are those tears that I see, Chrystian?" Lazryn teased.

The tall man rolled his eyes, feigning annoyance. "Knowing her has been a true privilege, and it has made us all better men for it."

ೞ〰ೞ〰

On Christmas Eve, both the Williams and North California community met on the south rim of the Grand Canyon.

~ 414 ~

While the two groups exchanged greetings, Ibrym looked to Keiryn. "What are Taryn and Larkin up to?" he asked.

He shrugged, while walking to the edge with his friend. "There's no telling with those two."

"The permanent gateways between all the planes has everyone talking. Families who have been separated for centuries are now able to come together," Ibrym shared.

Alderyc joined in the conversation. "It's incredible how they're using their newfound powers to better the lives of everyone...even the humans."

Taryn and Larkin suddenly appeared next to Keiryn, causing him to jump.

"Come on, guys. I've asked you to stop doing that," he grinned, pulling his sister into a fierce hug.

"Taryn, are we doing what I think we're doing?" Andyn questioned from the top of the Jeep where he sat with Sydney.

With an ornery grin, she shook her head.

He pumped his fists into the air. "Yes!"

"What are you up to?" Gracyn asked while leaning in to give her daughter a hug.

"You'll just have to be patient for a few more minutes," Taryn answered.

"Hello, granddaughter," Lazryn greeted her with a hug.

Chrystian nudged the girl with his shoulder. "I hear rumblings that the Void is no longer shrouded in darkness."

"It has actually turned into a bit of an oasis for those passing through," she replied.

Leaning down, Chrystian kissed the top of her head. "As someone who loves your aunt Loryn very much, I thank you."

"It was my pleasure," she grinned.

"So, darling daughter, do you plan on enlightening us on why we're all here?" Theron asked.

Taryn glanced around the group. "Oh, I just thought everyone might enjoy a little bit of canyon jumping before Santa comes."

"Canyon jumping?" Ibrym questioned with an arched brow.

Andyn grabbed the pack leader's hand. "Stick with me and I'll show you how it's done."

After a brief tutorial, the night sky lit with a stunning display of lightning.

The joyful sound of laughter and howls of excitement pierced the air for hours.

ঽഗঽഗ

As the night's fun came to an end, Taryn and Larkin hugged their friends and family goodbye and headed toward the edge.

Keiryn and the others watched as the pair leapt with ease across the canyon as bolts of lightning arced in each of their hands.

"Kansas is one badass chick," Gerrick sighed with great admiration.

"That she is, brother. That she is," Kellan agreed.

EPILOGUE

The Eros Plane, December 3, 2037

Standing atop the cliff, Chrystian smiled tenderly as he listened to the sound of soft steps approaching. "Hello, Taryn."

"Uncle," she replied.

Taking a deep breath, he steadied himself. "I see Larkin stayed behind at the cabin."

Stepping up beside him, she leaned her head on his shoulder. "I thought it best. This way it gives us time to reminisce about the peculiar start of our friendship."

He wrapped his arm around her and kissed the top of her head. "The first time I laid eyes upon you, I wanted you dead."

"I know," she whispered.

"Why? Why would I ever want to harm someone as good as you?" he questioned.

Taryn shook her head and sighed. "The night that you and your family were attacked by the Elder Council, you had been Influenced to react a certain way when you saw Loryn. She did far more than spare you from killing her. She saved your eternal soul."

Stunned by her words, Chrystian backed away. "What exactly do you mean?"

"Dagrin was never meant to be King of the Lessors. You were. Tedra, Ardet or whatever you want to call her, intended for you to kill Loryn by way of consuming her blood. Dagrin was the alternate when things did not go as planned with you," she disclosed.

Disgust flickered in his eyes. "I may not have been the monster she wanted, but I was a monster nonetheless."

"If they had not attacked your family, you would never have done the things you did. And we would never have met," she insisted.

He grinned. "Is that your way of saying the glass is half full, even when it is clearly half empty?"

She shook her head and sighed.

"These past two decades living in Williams with your family and friends has put my heart at ease. I am no longer the monster I once was, and it all started with you," he confessed.

Wrapping both arms around his waist, Taryn snuggled her head against his chest. "Out of all of the planes, this is my second favorite view. Not only is it beautiful to look at, but it is the place you let your guard down and really gave me a glimpse of the man inside."

"Many years ago when you faced Deiderick, you said that I could not have been his pawn because I was your knight...did you mean that?" he asked.

Taryn looked up at him with love shining brightly in her blue eyes. "With every move Deiderick made, he brought you closer to me. Each time he thought you would be my undoing, you were my protector. Thus, making you my knight."

Chrystian kissed the girl's head once more. "Promise me you will look after Lazryn and Clad in my absence."

"I promise to make sure they both stay out of trouble. Though with Clad being on his honeymoon, that may prove to be easier said than done," she replied.

He smiled. "He and his wife make a handsome couple."

"Yes, they do. I thought their ceremony was simple, but beautiful," Taryn agreed.

"I never thought I'd live to see the day when my younger brother would willingly settle down," he stated.

"That makes two of us," she confessed.

A few silent moments lingered between them before he looked out over the water. With tears flooding his eyes, he took a deep breath. "For the first time in a long while, I am afraid, Taryn."

She took his hands in her own. "There's no need to be. I'm here for you, Chrystian. And when you emerge on the other side, Loryn, Larkin and I will be waiting for you."

Pulling away from her, he straightened his jacket and ran his fingers through his hair. "It is time."

Tears pooled in Taryn's eyes as she watched over her dear friend. "All you have to do is let go, Chrystian, and peace will find you."

He flashed her a final smile before looking into the sunset. The light in his eyes faded and a single tear rolled down his cheek. With his final breath, he whispered, "I'm coming, Loryn."

In the blink of an eye, her friend was no longer there. In his wake, he left behind a stunning white orchid.

Swiping away her tears, Taryn turned to the tree line and looked at Larkin.

"His presence will certainly be missed in Williams," he stated upon approach.

She nodded. "It was time for him to be reunited with Loryn."

Stopping a few feet away, Larkin sighed. "I guess it's a good thing that Lazryn is moving in with Keiryn and Nalani. Their newborn twins should keep grandpa preoccupied for a while." He paused, reaching into the inside pocket of his tuxedo. "I know you promised Chrystian that we'd be there when he arrived on the other side. But you see, I promised him that we would give him and Loryn time away from prying eyes."

"If Chrystian and Loryn wanted time to themselves, all he had to do was ask," she replied.

"He did, but he asked me instead," Larkin divulged.

"Why?" she questioned.

"Because he didn't want you to worry. And also because he couldn't think of a better spot for me to do this." Larkin paused, dropping onto one knee. He held a small box out in front of Taryn and lifted the lid. Inside set a beautiful emerald cut diamond ring. "Taryn Knight, will you do me the honor of becoming my wife and allowing me to love you for all eternity?"

Taryn's breath caught in her throat as she gazed down at Larkin. Happy tears flooded her eyes as she began to nod her head. "Yes."

Larkin removed the ring from the box and slid it over her left ring finger. "I love you, Tare-Bear."

"I love you, too, Wolfy," she replied.

Pulling her into a fierce embrace, he stared into her eyes. "Always and forever."

"Forever and always," she replied, before pressing her lips tenderly against his.

###

Thank you for reading.

ABOUT THE AUTHORS

Karin Reeve and Jolie Marvin, are two fun-loving, mid-west girls who share a passion for writing and who believe no one is ever too old to follow their dreams. A chance meeting a few years back quickly blossomed into a lasting friendship and the eventual creation of the epic young adult fantasy series, The Oath Saga. The duo has a tremendous talent for weaving intricate stories with complex characters and vivid imagery. Taking this journey together was rewarding, challenging, and unbelievably amazing.

To find out more about Karin's upcoming solo projects and announcements, please visit her website, www.karinreeve.com and Facebook author page at www.facebook.com/karinreeveauthor/ .

To find out more about Jolie's upcoming solo projects and announcements, please visit her Facebook author page at www.facebook.com/joliemarvinauthor .

Made in the USA
Lexington, KY
30 October 2016